P9-DEJ-201

A TIME FOR PATRIOTS

A TIME FOR PATRIOTS

DALE BROWN

WM

WILLIAM MORROW

An Imprint of HarperCollins*Publishers*

This book is a work of fiction. References to real people, events, establishments, organizations, or locales are intended only to provide a sense of authenticity, and are used fictitiously. All other characters, and all incidents and dialogue, are drawn from the author's imagination and are not to be construed as real.

A TIME FOR PATRIOTS. Copyright © 2011 by Air Battle Force, Inc. All rights reserved. Printed in the United States of America. No part of this book may be used or reproduced in any manner whatsoever without written permission except in the case of brief quotations embodied in critical articles and reviews. For information address HarperCollins Publishers, 10 East 53rd Street, New York, NY 10022.

HarperCollins books may be purchased for educational, business, or sales promotional use. For information please write: Special Markets Department, HarperCollins Publishers, 10 East 53rd Street, New York, NY 10022.

FIRST EDITION

Library of Congress Cataloging-in-Publication Data has been applied for.

ISBN 978-0-06-198999-5

11 12 13 14 15 OV/QGF 10 9 8 7 6 5 4 3 2 1

This novel is dedicated to the volunteers: the ones who support their communities and fellow citizens in thousands of different ways with no thought of remuneration. It is the ultimate gift to society: the gift of selfless service.

CAST OF CHARACTERS

PATRICK McLANAHAN, Lieutenant-General (retired), U.S. Air Force, and Mission Pilot, Civil Air Patrol (CAP)

ROB SPARA, CAP Lieutenant Colonel, Battle Mountain CAP Squadron Commander

DAVID BELLVILLE, CAP Captain, Squadron Vice Commander, Commander of Cadets, and Ground Team Leader

MICHAEL P. FITZGERALD, Ground Team Deputy Leader

BRADLEY JAMES McLANAHAN, Cadet Captain, CAP

RON SPIVEY, Cadet First Lieutenant, Ground Team Member

RALPH MARKHAM, Cadet Technical Sergeant, Ground Team Member

LEO SLOTNICK, CAP Mission Scanner

JOHN DE CARTERET, CAP Mission Observer

KENNETH PHOENIX, President of the United States

ANN PAGE, Vice President of the United States

JOCELYN CAFFERY, Attorney General of the United States

JUSTIN FULLER, Director of the Federal Bureau of Investigation

Special Agent Philip Chastain, FBI

Special Agent Cassandra Renaldo, Department of Homeland Security

Agent Randolph Savoy, FBI, Cybernetic Infantry Device (CID) Pilot

Lieutenant Colonel Jason Richter, U.S. Army, CID Engineer and Pilot

Charlie Turlock, CID Engineer and Pilot

Wayne Macomber, Tin Man Commando

Brigadier-General Kurt "Buzz" Givens, Base Commander, Joint Air Base Battle Mountain

Darrow Horton, Former Attorney General of the United States

Timothy Dobson, Central Intelligence Agency

Judah Andorsen, Nevada Rancher

Reverend Jeremiah Paulson, Leader of the Knights of the True Republic

WEAPONS AND ACRONYMS

AGL—Above Ground Level

AN/UWQ-1—Avenger optionally manned mobile air defense unit

ARCHER—Airborne Real-time Cueing Hyperspectral Enhanced Reconnaissance—aerial imaging system used by the Civil Air Patrol that assists visual searches

ATC—Air Traffic Control

Avenger—mobile optionally manned air defense vehicle, carrying both Stinger surface-to-air heat-seeking missiles and a 20-millimeter Gatling gun

BAM—aviation identifier for Battle Mountain

C-57 Skytrain—advanced blended-wing transport plane

Cessna P210 Centurion—single-engine pressurized light airplane

CFI—Certified Flight Instructor

C-Four-I—Command, Control, Communications, Computers, and Intelligence

CID—Cybernetic Infantry Device, a large manned robot

DF—Direction Finding, following a radio beacon to its source

Dimenhydrinate—over-the-counter drug to relieve airsickness

ELT—Emergency Locator Transmitter, a radio beacon that activates after a crash to help locate an aircraft

ETA—Estimated Time of Arrival

EWO—Electronic Warfare Officer

FAA—Federal Aviation Administration

GA—General Aviation, dealing mostly with aircraft below twelve thousand pounds gross weight

GED—General Education Diploma

G-loads—Gravity forces, a measurement of how many times over or under the force of gravity is being exerted on a body

GPS—Global Positioning System, satellite navigation

Hazmat—hazardous materials

HRT—Hostage Rescue Team

IC—Incident Commander

IFR—Instrument Flight Rules

IMSAFE—Illness, Medicines, Stress, Alcohol, Fatigue, Emotion— a checklist to judge whether a crewmember is fit to fly

I-O—Input-Output

L-Per—a device used to home in on a radio beacon

Medevac—medical evacuation

MRE—Meals Ready to Eat

MSL—Mean Sea Level, the elevation above sea level

NextGen—Next Generation, a GPS-based air traffic control system

NORDO—No Radio, an aircraft that has lost its ability to communicate

NTSB—National Transportation Safety Board, a government agency that investigates accidents involving aircraft, cars, trains, etc.

OSI—Office of Special Investigations, the Air Force's investigation agency

OTM—Other Than Mexicans, illegal aliens from countries other than Mexico

PDA—Personal Data Assistant

PETN—Pentaerythritol Tetranitrate, a powerful high explosive

PIREPS—Pilot Reports, weather and flight condition reports given by pilots

PT—Physical Training

PTSD—Post-Traumatic Stress Disorder

R&D—Research and Development

RDX—Research Department Explosive (cyclotrimethylenetrinitramine), a powerful high explosive

RPG—Rocket-Propelled Grenade

RQ-15 Sparrowhawk—unmanned reconnaissance aircraft

RTB—Return to Base

SAREX—Search and Rescue Exercise

Scopolamine—an antiairsickness drug

SIGMET—Significant Meteorological, a report of possibly hazardous weather conditions

SQTR—Specialty Qualification Training Record

Technicals—homemade attack vehicles

UAV—Unmanned Aerial Vehicle

VFR—Visual Flight Rules

VoIP—Voice over Internet Protocol, a way of using the Internet for voice communications

Wilco—"will comply"

WMIRS—Web-based Mission Information Reporting System, the Civil Air Patrol's computerized reporting system

XS-19A Midnight—single-stage-to-orbit spaceplane

Zulu—Greenwich mean time, used as a universal time reference

REAL-WORLD NEWS
EXCERPTS

EXTREMISTS TO GOVS: RESIGN OR BE REMOVED:
FBI Warns Letters Could Provoke Violence—Devlin Barrett, Associated Press—April 2, 2010—WASHINGTON—The FBI is
warning police across the country that an anti-government group's
call to remove governors from office could provoke violence.

The group called the Guardians of the Free Republics wants to
"restore America" by peacefully dismantling parts of the government, according to its Web site. It sent letters to governors demanding they leave office or be removed . . .

As of Wednesday, more than 30 governors had received letters
saying if they don't leave office within three days they will be removed, according to an internal intelligence note by the FBI and
the Department of Homeland Security. The note was obtained by
The Associated Press . . .

. . . The FBI associated the letter with "sovereign citizens," most
of whom believe they are free from all duties of a U.S. citizen, like
paying taxes or needing a government license to drive. A small
number of these people are armed and resort to violence, according
to the intelligence report.

Last weekend, the FBI conducted raids on suspected members of a Christian militia in the Midwest that was allegedly planning to kill police officers. In the past year, federal agents have seen an increase in "chatter" from an array of domestic extremist groups, which can include radical self-styled militias, white separatists or extreme civil libertarians and sovereign citizens.

THE PEOPLE BEHIND THE SEARCH: Update on Nebraska Plane Crash—Krystle Kacner, KDLT, Sioux Falls, South Dakota—November 27, 2010—Earlier this week, the Civil Air Patrol found a missing single engine plane that took off from Chamberlain, headed for Omaha.

The plane that crashed Sunday night was found in northeastern Nebraska, and resulted in the death of the two people on board. But before the aircraft was found, a lot of people put in a lot of work.

"At first it was a little nerve wracking, because it was my first mission, but then as I came here and started doing everything we were supposed to, it wasn't really thinking, it was just doing," said Cadet Chief Master Sergeant Elizabeth Foy.

Cadet Chief Master Sergeant Elizabeth Foy got the call early in the morning, right before she headed off to school at O'Gorman High School.

But, once she arrived at the Sioux Falls Civil Air Patrol headquarters, all her training started to kick in.

"It's more of you need to get it done faster, there's no goofing off . . . As part of the ground team, it was making sure we were looking at all times outside the window making sure all the leaders stayed on track," said Foy.

. . . "Yes I'm a sophomore in High School but I can make a difference, so that's really the greatest part for me," said Foy . . .

ANOTHER SAVE FOR NEVADA WING!—gocivilair
patrol.com—December 11, 2010—Congratulations are due to all
who participated in mission 10M0964A, resulting in the location of
a lost hunter in Lincoln county. N9459M, piloted by Rick Parker
and crewed by Clyde Cooper and Bill Petersen, spotted the 83 year
old man and talked in a Sheriff's ground team. The man was air-
lifted by helicopter to medical facilities.

Eleven total personnel and two aircraft were involved in the
search. AFRCC [Air Force Rescue Coordination Center] has officially awarded Nevada Wing its second find and save for this fiscal
year.

A TIME FOR PATRIOTS

PROLOGUE

This is the porcelain clay of humankind.

—JOHN DRYDEN

ELKO, NEVADA

SUMMER 2013

"Severe thunderstorm activity along your route of flight," the Federal Aviation Administration Flight Service Station weather briefer began. "Convective SIGMET Seven Charlie for Nevada, Idaho, California, and Utah, heavy-to-severe thunderstorms in a one-hundred-mile-long band fifty miles southeast of Battle Mountain, Nevada, moving from two-two-zero at fifteen knots, tops above flight-level three-niner-zero, with heavy rain, hail, and damaging winds with gusts over fifty knots."

Cripes, the young pilot thought, it was one of the worst weather observations he had ever heard. Frank Post was a software engineer from Silicon Valley, an honor graduate of Stanford University, and a fairly new instrument-rated private pilot, with a bit less than two hundred hours of flying time, most in his used single-engine Cessna C-182R Skylane. He looked at his wife sitting beside him, still wearing that impatient expression he had been forced to put up with for the past day and a half.

"Where are the thunderstorms now?" Frank asked on the phone. His wife, Kara, rolled her eyes and looked at her watch for the umpteenth time that afternoon. Kara had been in real estate, but the real estate market had all but dried up in California in the current economic meltdown, so she did part-time fill-in work for other agents, mostly doing escrow paperwork and staging and showing homes. She never liked the idea of owning something as complex and extravagant as an airplane, and only agreed to go on this weeklong cross-country trip because she was assured of being able to see her parents in Kansas as well as Frank's folks in Nevada.

"The northern edge of the band of thunderstorms is about fifty miles south of Battle Mountain," the briefer repeated.

Frank's face brightened, and he made a sausage-shaped drawing on the sectional chart he had on the desk in the flight planning room to indicate where the storm was, then drew an arrow representing the storm's direction of movement. Kara looked at the circle and looked relieved as well. "So from Elko I can outrun the storms," he said, "and if the controller tells me the weather is getting close, I can deviate farther north around them."

"Do you have weather-avoidance or -detection equipment?"

"No," Frank replied.

"How about NextGen?"

"No," he repeated. NextGen, or Next Generation, was the new air traffic control system that used datalinks aboard an aircraft to broadcast its GPS satellite-derived position, ground speed, course, and altitude to air traffic control, rather than using ground-based radar. NextGen was designed to increase air traffic control coverage and efficiency and eliminate radar blind spots in higher terrain, but it was expensive and not required to be on small general aviation aircraft for several years.

"Radar coverage is spotty in that general area," the briefer said. "Unless you're up pretty high or right on the airway, you may be in and out of radar coverage." Left unsaid was the fact that air traffic control radars were designed to track aircraft, not weather—although newer digital systems were better than the old analog ones, weather avoidance was not a major part of a controller's skills.

"I'll plan on being on the airway, and I have oxygen just in case I need to go higher." Kara scowled at that comment. She hated wearing the little rubbery oxygen masks because they dried her nose and throat and made her claustrophobic.

"Roger," the briefer said. He continued his briefing with terminal weather conditions and forecasts. Although their destination on this trip was Sparks, Nevada, where they planned to visit the in-laws, the planned overnight stop was Carson City because they had very inexpensive fuel there at the self-serve pump, almost two dollars per gallon less than Reno. The forecast was for cooler temperatures behind the front, but skies would be clear and winds were out of the west, right down the east–west runway at Carson—perfect. The briefer then read winds-aloft forecasts, which were not much better than the radar summary—strong south-to-southwesterly winds ahead of the front, switching to westerly winds behind the front, with light-to-moderate turbulence forecast above twelve thousand feet. He concluded his briefing with, "Anything else I can help you with today?"

"I'd like to go ahead and file," Frank said. Kara smiled, silently clapped her hands, then turned to her son, Jeremy, and told him to start packing up his drawing pads and colored pencils, which he had scattered all over the flight-planning-room floor.

The briefer was silent for a long moment, obviously not expecting the guy to launch into such mean-looking weather. But it was not his job to tell a pilot to fly or not to fly, just to give him all the information he requests. "Stand by and I'll call up the flight-plan page . . . Okay, I have IFR, Cessna Two-Eight-Three-Four Lima, a Charlie-One-Eighty-Two slant Golf, departing at twenty hundred Zulu, route of flight Battle Mountain, Lovelock, Carson City direct at ten thousand feet. Go ahead with the rest."

"Two-point-five hours en route, no remarks, five hours' fuel on board, alternate is Reno International," Frank replied. He gave his name, his San Carlos, California, address, his cell-phone number, three souls on board, and his aircraft's colors of white with blue stripes.

"Your flight plan is on file," the briefer said after entering all the information into his computer and waiting for an "ACCEPTED" message from the FAA's computer servers. "PIREPS are strongly encouraged on one-two-two-point-zero. Have a safe . . . and very *careful* flight, sir." The briefer was trying everything he could to get this pilot to cancel this trip short of just telling him, "Wise up, jerk, and keep your stupid ass on the ground."

"Thank you," Frank said, and hung up the phone. He turned to Kara. "There's a line of thunderstorms south of our route of flight," he told her as he quickly packed up his charts and flight plan, "but I think we can outrun it because it's moving pretty slow. If it moves up quicker, we can fly farther north around it, and if we can't, we'll turn around and land back here at Elko."

"No, we're *not*," Kara said adamantly. "I've had enough of this little cow town. Two days stuck here because of thunderstorms— I've had enough."

"I think it's a cute little town."

"All we've seen of it is the McDonald's down the street," she said.

"The hotel was nice, the people are nice, and the casino has a bowling alley and movie theater."

"I'm not taking my son into any of those casinos—I don't care if they offered free ice cream and movies for life." She turned to her son. "Jeremy, I asked you to please pick up your stuff. We're going . . . *finally*."

"I have to go *cagada*," the boy said, using the Spanish word for *crap,* and he hopped up and dashed off.

"Again?" his mother commented. "I hope you're not coming down with something."

"I'll start untying the plane and do a preflight," Frank said. "Be careful going outside on the ramp."

Jeremy was gone for more than fifteen minutes. "What took you so long?" his mother asked. "Are you runny again?" The boy nodded, embarrassed. "I think that last sundae at McDonald's was not a good idea. Maybe you should wear the you-know-what this time."

"I am *not* wearing a diaper," Jeremy said. "I'm ten."

"It's an adult diaper," Kara said. "If you wear it, you don't have to pee in the bag thing, and if you have an accident, it'll be easier to clean up."

"I am *not* wearing a diaper," Jeremy insisted.

Frank came back into the flight planning room and looked at the pencils and drawing pads still on the floor. "What's going on? Why aren't you guys ready?"

"Jeremy spent a while in the bathroom."

"Are you loosey-goosey again, buddy?" Frank asked.

"Daaad . . . !"

"Well, you should put on the personal hygienic undergarment, then, buddy," his father said with a smile.

"You mean the *diaper,* Dad! I'm not wearing a diaper!"

"The astronauts wear them, and you want to be a Space Defense Force astronaut, right?"

"When I have to do a four-hour space walk, then I'll wear it," Jeremy said.

"All right, all right," Kara said with growing impatience. "If you make a skid mark in your pants, let's hope your grandparents don't see it. Pick up your stuff and let's go."

6

It took another few minutes for Jeremy to collect his stuff. While he waited, Frank took his iPhone out of his pocket and punched up an app that downloaded NexRad radar images. He immediately saw the line of thunderstorms that had been forecast, and noted they were farther north than anticipated.

"How's it look?" Kara asked.

"Mean and nasty—we'll definitely have to deviate around them to the north," her husband replied. He was suddenly very anxious to get going, so he skipped his intended bathroom visit. "C'mon, guys, we need to go," he urged his family. Soon they were on their way to the plane, the boy's hands filled with stray colored pencils.

Outside they were greeted with brilliant sunshine, a welcome change to the past two days of booming thunderstorms and swirling winds. Frank noted that the wind was from the southwest and breezy on occasion, which would mean a slight crosswind takeoff, but nothing he couldn't handle. In minutes, he started the Cessna 182 Skylane's engine, received his IFR clearance and taxi clearance from Elko Ground Control, and was soon on his way, splashing through a few large puddles, taxiing a little bit faster than he normally did in order to get airborne as quickly as possible.

There was no one else in the pattern or on the taxiways. Frank did a hurried run-up check of the magnetos, then hustled through the rest of the checklist. "Everyone ready to go?" he asked over the intercom.

"Ready, Dad!" Jeremy replied enthusiastically.

"I'm ready," Kara replied, turning and checking to be sure her son's seat belt was tight.

"Here we go." He pressed the microphone button: "Elko Tower, Cessna Two-Eight-Three-Four Lima, number one, runway two-three, ready to go," he radioed.

"Cessna Two-Eight-Three-Four Lima, Elko Tower, runway two-three, cleared for takeoff."

"Three-Four Lima, cleared for takeoff, runway two-three."

Frank taxied onto Runway 23, and instead of locking the brakes, running the engine up to full power, and then releasing the brakes, he kept on rolling, then applied full power as he turned onto the runway centerline. The engine smoothly roared to full power, and the four-seat Cessna responded as spritely as ever, accelerating quickly . . .

. . . except there was a sharp banging sound on the left side of the plane, from the direction of the left main gear tire, getting louder and louder as he accelerated. "What the . . . something's wrong," Frank muttered, and he jerked the throttle lever to idle.

"What's wrong?" Kara asked, the concern evident in her voice. "What's going on, Frank?"

"Why are we stopping, Dad?" Jeremy asked.

"Sterile cockpit, guys, remember—no talking until level-off except for an emergency," Frank said. He pressed the mike button: "Elko Tower, Three-Four Lima is aborting the takeoff, possible flat tire."

"Roger, Three-Four Lima," the tower controller said. "Cancel takeoff clearance, turn right at the next taxiway, and contact Ground."

"Three-Four Lima, wilco."

"Hey, Dad?"

"I said no talking, Jeremy."

"But, Dad . . . ?"

"This better be important, Jeremy!"

"I think it's your seat belt, Dad. Something's hanging out of the plane." The pilot looked out his left side window, and sure enough, there it was: in his haste to depart, he forgot to fasten his seat belt, and the buckle end had started banging on the side of the plane. How in hell could he miss that?

"Thank you, buddy," Frank said in a low, contrite monotone. "Good call." He taxied off the runway, contacted Ground Control, and received a clearance back to takeoff position. In the run-up area, he pulled power to idle, pulled the parking-brake handle, had Kara hold the toe brakes on her set of rudder pedals just in case— her husband was usually admonishing her to keep her feet *off* the pedals, and now he wanted her feet *on* them—unlatched the door, and pushed it open. With the propeller turning, it required a lot more strength than he thought to open it, and the noise was a lot louder than he expected.

"Hopefully I'll never do *that* again," Frank said after he had everything retrieved and reconnected. He took a moment to catch his breath—he noticed his heart pumping rapidly just from the excitement of being in all that noise and windblast. "I'm sure the guys in the tower got a big laugh out of that." He made sure he fastened his seat belt this time, then looked around at everyone else's belts. "Okay, everyone ready to go?"

"Dad, I need to use the bathroom," Jeremy said.

"What?" Frank thundered, then immediately felt bad for shouting. "But you just went!"

"I just gotta go, Dad."

"If we go back, will we miss those thunderstorms?" Kara asked. "Will we have to spend *another* night here?"

"We might."

"Then we'll have to skip seeing my parents in Reno," Kara said cross-cockpit. "We can't stay in Reno—we have to go straight home from Carson City. Jeremy can't miss any school, and I have no more vacation days off left on the books."

Frank didn't reply to her, but instead asked, "Is it number one or number two?"

"Number one," the boy said, but if the father had turned back to look at his son, he would've noticed the little anxious expression that meant that number two might be stirring as well.

"Then you'll have to do it in the piddle pack," Frank said. "We're leaving. Hold it as long as you can."

"Okay, Dad," Jeremy responded meekly. Frank called Elko Tower, received another takeoff clearance, and in moments they were rolling down the runway again. This time there was no banging or anything else gone wrong, and they were airborne.

The skies were bright and sunny until thirty minutes into the flight, but soon Frank saw it—a dark white, gray, and brown mass of clouds on the horizon. He could see the northern edge of the squall line, but it was far to the *right* of course, not to the left as he had hoped. The thunderheads were towering skyward, and as he flew closer he swore he could see them rolling up even higher, driven by enough heat and raw energy to light up a city.

"Salt Lake Center, Cessna Two-Eight-Three-Four Lima."

"Three-Four Lima, Salt Lake Center, go ahead."

"I'd like to deviate twenty degrees north for weather."

"Deviation right approved, report when direct Winnemucca again."

"Three-Four Lima, wilco."

"Why are we turning?" Kara asked.

"To get as far away from those buildups as we can," Frank said. "If we start turning now, we won't be as far off course when we pass them, and we won't have to make as big turns. It's a fairly slow-moving system—we should miss it easily."

"Three-Four Lima, Salt Lake Center . . . uh, verify that you do not have weather-avoidance or -detection equipment?" the air traffic control controller radioed.

"That's affirmative, Three-Four Lima does not have weather equipment," Frank admitted. Several times this summer, which seemed to be particularly thunderstorm-active in the West, he wished he had spent the extra money on the portable navigation unit that also downloaded weather and NexRad radar images via XM satellite radio. But it wasn't required equipment, he rarely flew in bad weather or at night, it was a lot more money than the unit he had purchased, and the monthly subscription costs were astronomical—the wife was already pissed about how much all the airplane stuff cost already.

"Roger," the controller responded. "On your new heading off

the airway, I'm going to need you higher to stay in radar coverage. Cessna Two-Eight-Three-Four Lima, climb and maintain one-two thousand."

"Leaving one-zero thousand, climbing to one-two thousand, Three-Four Lima," Frank responded. He pushed in the mixture and propeller controls, fed in power, and started a shallow climb.

"Do we have to go on oxygen now?" Kara asked.

"Only if you feel you need to," Frank replied. "Go ahead and get the masks out." The portable oxygen bottle and the three masks were in a canvas bag behind the pilot's seat, so it was easy to open it up and get the masks out. Kara swabbed the inside of each mask with an alcohol pad, making sure to wipe hers twice—she always thought it was a veritable germ breeding ground.

As soon as they passed eleven thousand feet, the turbulence began. They felt an occasional light bump at ten thousand, but now it was a consistent light chop with an occasional moderate bump, and the higher they climbed, the worse it got.

"Three-Four Lima, Salt Lake Center, how's your ride?" the controller asked as they leveled off at twelve thousand feet.

"Light, occasional moderate turbulence," Frank reported. "When can I go back down to ten thousand?"

"Not until after Battle Mountain, sir," the controller replied.

"Can I get VFR on top at ten-five?" "VFR on top" was an option for pilots on an IFR flight plan to fly at VFR altitudes—even-numbered altitudes plus five hundred feet flying westbound—if they were clear of clouds.

"Negative, Three-Four Lima, that's below my minimum vectoring altitude in your present area," the controller responded. "You'll have to wait until you get into Battle Mountain Approach's airspace. Maintain one-two thousand."

"Maintain one-two thousand, wilco, Three-Four Lima," Frank replied. His only other option to fly at a lower altitude out of the turbulence was to cancel his IFR flight plan, but he didn't feel comfortable with that until he was around those thunderstorms—

the mountain ranges in this area were pretty high, and if he lost contact with the ground, he'd be in a world of danger.

"Dad, I don't feel so good," Jeremy said. His wife immediately found an airsick bag, opened it, and gave it to her son. The turbulence was gradually increasing in intensity—it was now getting close to continuous moderate turbulence with an occasional jolt that made their bodies strain against their shoulder harnesses.

"Can we get out of this turbulence?" Kara asked.

"Not for another twenty minutes or so."

"Twenty minutes?"

" 'Fraid so." He looked out his left window and was surprised to see how close he was to the thunderheads—probably less than twenty miles now, the minimum recommended spacing. The turbulence was undoubtedly being caused by the spillover from the tops of the thunderstorm anvil pounding at them from above—the spillover could toss hail and ice as far as twenty miles or more from the center of the storm. "Those thunderstorms are moving a lot faster than forecast." He looked at his GPS navigation device— sure enough, they were fighting a fifty-knot crosswind. The storm was catching up to them.

For a moment Frank thought about turning back toward Elko. But that would really screw up their schedule. And if they had to spend more than one night in Elko—the forecast for tomorrow had the thunderstorms moving back in and staying for days—he could get reprimanded for missing that much work. He could take an airline flight from Elko to Oakland, but that meant more money wasted, and *then* he would have to take the airlines *back* to Elko to get his plane. Turning around was an option, but not a very good one.

"Three-Four Lima, Salt Lake, are you still VMC?" the controller asked.

"Affirmative, Three-Four Lima," Frank responded. "We're getting a little bit of rain."

"How's your ride?"

"Light, occasional moderate," Frank lied. It was more like continuous moderate, with more frequent bumps hard enough to make the top of his headset hit the headliner.

"The closest cell is at your ten o'clock, fifteen miles," the controller said. "You may need to turn southeast to avoid it."

"Roger," Frank replied. "Can you vector me around the cells? Can you keep me away from the cells?"

"Three-Four Lima, turn left heading one-seven-zero, vector for weather, maintain one-two thousand, clear to deviate as necessary to stay VMC if possible."

"Heading one-seven-zero, Three-Four Lima." Now they were paralleling the storm, actually flying away from their destination. If the controller was making a strong suggestion to the pilot to turn back toward Elko, this was it. But the storm seemed to know it. Now that they were on a clear avoidance track, the storm seemed to awaken, transforming into the snarling ugly beast it really was and turning to pursue. But the storm had one more trick up its sleeve first.

Frank was relieved to actually see breaks in the cloud wall and decided to steer right for them. "I can see blue skies on the other side," he said. "We can get through this." He tried to aim right for those breaks, but it seemed as if he was almost flying sideways. The severe turbulence was more persistent now. He heard a *BEEP BEEP BEEP!* and saw a yellow flashing light—the turbulence had caused the autopilot to disconnect. He grabbed the control yoke tighter and fought to maintain control. He knew enough to let the plane wander in altitude a bit and not try to fight the up- and downdrafts.

"Three-Four Lima, turn left heading one-five-zero, vectors for weather, cleared in the block one-two thousand to one-four thousand," the controller radioed. Frank realized with shock that he was flying almost *north* in his vain attempt to fly through the break in the storm, but now he could see nothing but a mass of dark gray. The turbulence had eased up a bit, but now the plane was being pelted by heavy rain and gravel-size hailstones. He had no idea what his altitude was—it took every ounce of concentration to steer to the heading and keep the wings relatively level.

The storm had sucked him in with fleeting glimpses of clear skies, and now its jaws were closing *fast*. "Salt Lake, Three-Four Lima, this is not good," Frank said. "I need to get out of this."

"Say again, Three-Four Lima?"

"Dad?"

"Not now, Jeremy."

"Three-Four Lima, Battle Mountain Joint Air Base is at your six o'clock, fifty-five miles, turn right heading one-six-zero."

"Dad?"

"Jeremy, what is it?"

"Ice on the pitot tube!" Frank looked and found the pitot tube and the leading edges of both wings covered in ice. It was July, and Elko had to be ninety degrees when they left . . . how could there be *ice*? Frank turned on the pitot heat, then started a right turn . . .

. . . and then a gust of wind and turbulence lifted the left wing up so suddenly and so severely that they rolled completely inverted. Frank heard someone scream . . . and realized it might have been *himself*. He fought to roll wings-level again, but the artificial horizon was tumbling uncontrollably and the turn-and bank indicator seemed frozen in a full-scale right turn. The nose shot skyward— or it might have been earthward, he couldn't tell for sure. Pulling and turning the yoke in any direction didn't seem to do a thing.

"Dad?" Jeremy asked.

"Not now, Jeremy."

"But, Dad, your heading indicator, your turn-and-bank . . . look at your—"

"I said not now, Jeremy, I'm trying to fly." Suddenly more light seemed to come in through the windscreen. The pilot realized that a thin film of ice was obscuring the view outside, but he could see!

They were out of the thunderstorm! "Okay, okay, I got it," Frank said on intercom. "We made it. We . . ."

And just then he realized that the ground was rushing up to meet them—they were in a nearly vertical spinning dive heading straight for the ground. The pilot centered the controls and shoved in the left rudder, managed to somehow stop the spin, pulled back on the power, and raised the nose almost to level . . . just before the plane smashed into the ground.

"Cessna Two-Eight-Three-Four Lima, radar contact lost, how do you hear Salt Lake Center?" the controller radioed. He waited a few moments, feeling his skin turn cold, his throat turn dry, and little hairs stand up on the back of his neck. "Three-Four Lima, how do you hear Salt Lake Center?" His supervisor was already standing beside him. "Shit, Bill," he said, "I think I lost him."

"Salt Lake Center, United Twelve-Seventeen."

"United Twelve-Seventeen, Salt Lake Center, go ahead."

"We're picking up an ELT beacon on two-four-three-point-zero," the airline pilot radioed.

The controller felt his lower lip start to tremble. That UHF frequency was the international emergency channel on which an airplane's ELT, or emergency locator transmitter, broadcast—and ELTs automatically activated after a crash. A hand touched his shoulder—it was his replacement, come to relieve him so he could get away from the console, pull himself together, and start his grim report. "Copy, Twelve-Seventeen, thank you," he said.

"I'll get on the horn to the Air Force," the supervisor said.

"No, I'll do it," the controller said. He threw off his headset, kicked himself out of the chair, picked up the phone between his seat and the assistant controller, and hit a red button marked *AFRCC*. He took a deep breath and waited for the direct line to activate.

"Rescue Coordination Center, Sergeant Goris," came the reply from the duty controller at the Air Force Rescue Coordination Center at Tyndall Air Force Base in Florida, which directed all air and sea rescue missions in the United States. "Ready to copy, Salt Lake Center."

"This is Adams, Salt Lake Center. Lost radar contact with a Cessna 182, five-five miles north-northwest of Battle Mountain, Nevada, in an area of heavy thunderstorms. Airliner at flight level three-five-zero reports picking up a VHF ELT overhead that vicinity."

"We're on it, Salt Lake," the voice on the other end of the line said. The controller could hear an alarm sounding in the background. "Colors, fuel on board, pilot's name, and souls on board?"

The controller picked up the flight-plan strip from its holder. "White with blue stripes, five hours, three . . . three souls on board," he read, his voice catching when he read the grim number off the flight's data strip.

"Roger, Salt Lake," the voice said. "When do you estimate the weather will move out of the area?"

"It's moving pretty fast and it's not very big, just long," the controller said. "About an hour."

"Thanks, Mr. Adams," the voice said. "I'm sorry. Tyndall is clear."

WAREHOUSE COMPLEX OUTSIDE LINCOLN
MUNICIPAL AIRPORT, CALIFORNIA

THAT SAME TIME

"Okay, guys, this is it," the Federal Bureau of Investigation special agent in charge, Gary Hardison, said. He was surrounded by two plainclothes agents, a team of four FBI Special Weapons and Tactics officers, and a squad of eight federal Alcohol, Tobacco, and Firearms agents, all in full body armor and tactical helmets and carrying submachine guns. "It's the culmination of eighteen months of undercover work to get close to this gang. It all happens in about an hour."

Hardison stepped over to a large presentation board with overhead satellite photographs of the objective and a hand-drawn diagram of their ingress plan. "Here's the hangar where they want to make the exchange, in the middle of the first row nearest to the taxiway. Be on the lookout for planes and pilots on the airport, but the weather has been stormy, so the airport manager believes there won't be any pilots on the airport. To be sure, he's deactivated everyone's gate access cards except ours so they won't be able to get onto the airport until we're done. We've verified that the other hangars are occupied, the identities of the owners have been checked, and the airport manager has deactivated their gate cards so they won't be able to get in.

"The objective hangar has a single plane, a King Air 350 twin-engine plane that the suspects want to use to transport the materials. We've had a Predator unmanned aircraft overhead all evening, watching for any signs that the gang tries to put anyone up on the roof—if they do, we'll be alerted, and we'll call it off if we can't take the shooter down. I'll be watching the UAV's video feed from here.

"Riley will go through the electric gate, which will be under observation by the gang," Hardison continued. "Stricker will follow in the sedan. They'll drive through, let the guards check them, the sedan, and the truck, then drive up to the hangar—I expect they'll have at least one perp with you in the truck and sedan and at least one perp staying back at the gate. Once they're cleared in and drive to the hangar, they'll go in first with the cash, and then they'll lead the smugglers out to the truck to let them test the materials. Once they approve the materials and we don't get any warning beeps, you'll take down the guys outside the hangar, and then we'll signal the SWAT and ATF teams to fly in to clear the hangar."

Hardison motioned to a lone uniformed officer. "Captain Derek Coulter from the Yuba County Sheriff's Department is in charge of the SWAT team," the FBI special agent went on. "After we take down the guys outside the hangar and the choppers are en route, he and his men will move in to close the airport and block the runway, taxiways, and exits. They'll be out of sight here in the warehouse complex until the takedown. Captain?"

"We have six vehicles involved in blocking the runways and taxiways, with two deputies in each vehicle," Coulter said. "Two will be near the hangar where the operation will take place, blocking the north end of the runway and the main taxiway. We'll be monitoring the tactical freq, so if you need any help or if the situation changes, we'll be standing by. We also have a chopper standing by at the fire department helipad, just a couple minutes away. My guys have worked with the FBI on numerous occasions. Good luck."

"Thanks, Derek," Hardison said. "To continue: The SWAT helicopters will touch down on the taxiway outside the hangar, which hopefully will be the first indication to those inside the hangar that something's up. The hangar door should be closed; there's a single walk-through door on the left side of the hangar door. The hangar has a twenty-foot-high roof with a lot of beams overhead, so, everyone, be sure to clear upward as well as around. It's fairly cluttered in there with rolling tool chests, lights, jacks, and the like, so Hess, Scott, Edwards, and Caffery, be extra careful.

"The hangar has a bathroom in the southeast corner and a second-story studio apartment in the northeast corner—those are the important areas to cover," Hardison went on. "The bathroom has no windows—Harris and Vasquez, you'll have to make your way around the plane to cover the can. Be careful for air hoses and other trip machines on the floor, and the roof of the bathroom has a flat surface that they use to store shit, so cover that too. The apartment has a single window overlooking the hangar but no window on the door, so Carter and Meredith, you should be able to get up the stairs while McGinty and Cromwell cover the window from below.

"Hartman and Benz, you guys got the King Air 350. Entry door on the plane's left side, and small opening window on the right and left sides of the cockpit that's big enough to poke the muzzle of a gun out, so be on the lookout. There's an emergency exit on the plane's right side, but you should have lots of time to notice it if they try to pop it out to fire on you. Stay sharp. Once the hangar is clear, we'll bring in forensics and hazmat and start scrubbing the place down."

Hardison fielded questions, got an update on the weather and the status of the sheriff's department personnel, did a time hack with everyone, then dismissed the teams to do their own briefings and check their weapons and equipment. At the prearranged time, the teams headed to their cars, and the operation was under way. Four Bell Jet Ranger helicopters were parked in the large loading area between two long rows of vacant warehouses, and the SWAT guys started to board.

Riley drove the windowless panel van to the proper airport entrance gate, followed by Stricker in a small sedan. Inside the gate, a lone car sat under a tree at an airport car-rental parking lot. When the FBI agent flashed his lights, a man with sunglasses, a plaid shirt with a white T-shirt underneath, and what looked like cowboy boots got out of the car inside the gate. He did not appear to be carrying a weapon, but the FBI agent knew a clever gunman could conceal a half-dozen weapons with that simple attire.

The man walked toward the gate until he recognized Stricker in the sedan, then nodded back to his car. It started up—Riley didn't even see the other man in the car, which reminded him to stay sharp around these guys. The car drove toward the gate until the sensors in the pavement activated and started opening the gate, then backed up, turned around, and stopped just a few feet away. The van and sedan pulled in through the gate, and they waited until the gate began to close.

As soon as it did, the man in the plaid shirt got into the van on the passenger side and quickly checked the cargo area. At the same moment a second unseen man got into the passenger side of the sedan and ordered Stricker to open the trunk. When he did, yet another unseen man appeared, checked the trunk, flashed a thumbs-up, and disappeared.

"You guys are good—they came out of nowhere," Riley remarked.

"Let's go," the first man said, ignoring the comment. "Speed limit is ten miles an hour."

They drove past the self-serve aviation fueling station, across the transient parking ramp, and northward down an automobile access road along a row of hangars. No other cars or airplanes were in sight. They drove almost all the way down the row to the second-to-last hangar and stopped. The driver of the lead car pulled out a walkie-talkie and spoke, and a few minutes later a man came out of the hangar, carrying a suitcase.

"Right on time, Riley," the man from inside the hangar said. "I like that."

"Being late is a sign of disrespect, and it's bad business, Sullivan," Riley said. He nodded at the suitcase. "Is that all of it?"

"Half," the man named Sullivan said.

Riley narrowed his eyes. "What is this shit, Sullivan? We didn't agree to a split."

"I want to check the packages outside first," Sullivan said. He reached into his jacket and pulled out a small device that resembled a large garage-door opener. "If they pass, your friend there gets the cash. We'll bring the van inside the hangar to check the packages with the larger device, and if they check out, you can leave with the rest."

Riley hesitated, then shook his head. "Bring your larger device out here."

"It'll attract too much attention," the man said. He nodded to the second undercover agent and tossed the suitcase to him. "Check it." Stricker took the suitcase to his car and opened it. Inside were dozens of stacks of bills, mostly hundreds. He flipped through several stacks to be sure they weren't padded with counterfeit currency, then quickly counted the stacks. Each stack was $10,000, for a total of about $150,000.

Stricker closed the suitcase and emerged from his car. "Half the total. One fifty K."

"Now, that's worth a peek, isn't it?" Sullivan asked with a smile.

"That's all you get for one fifty is a peek," Riley said. "If you want to bring the van inside the hangar, it'll cost you another one fifty. Larry will take the cash while you test the packages."

Sullivan nodded at the second undercover agent. "You trust him with your three hundred thousand dollars?"

"Stricker knows his life won't be worth spit if he screws me," Riley said. "Let's get on with it."

Now it was Sullivan's turn to hesitate, but he nodded. "Let's do it." He walked toward the van and opened the sliding side door. Inside were four large steel cylinders, about three feet high and twelve inches in diameter. He nodded. "The real deals, not homemade containers."

"I'm not crazy enough to drive around with amateur-built containers," Riley said. "Do you know how to operate it?"

"No, but my guy Carl does," Sullivan said. He spoke into a walkie-talkie, and a few minutes later a man emerged from the hangar. He had trouble walking, his hair was thin and missing in several spots, and one eye looked clouded over. He took the detector from Sullivan's hand and examined the casks. "Carl was a pilot for the Department of Energy for fifteen years," Sullivan went on. "He flew that shit all over the United States in every kind of plane. One accident, and they fire him without benefits. Three years later, he finds out he's got leukemia."

The man named Carl turned the device on, waited for it to initialize, then looked at the display. "No leaks."

"Every agency has got radiation detectors nowadays," the undercover agent said. "I'm not driving around waiting to get popped by some local yokel."

Carl examined the first cask, then punched commands into a small keypad on the side of the large steel container. A motor opened a thick steel shutter, revealing a tiny window on the side of the cask, and Carl held the detector up to the open window.

"Shouldn't he stand away from that window?" Riley said.

"Carl knows a few more doses won't kill him any quicker," Sullivan said. "Carl?"

"Beta particles and gamma radiation . . . fairly high levels," Carl said. He closed the window.

"That's the iridium-192," Riley said. "The stuff's half-life is pretty short, but you said that was okay." Sullivan nodded but kept on looking at Carl as he worked.

Carl checked another cask. "Gamma radiation only. Very high levels."

"Cobalt-60," Riley said.

Carl checked the third cask. "Neutrons, protons, beta particles, and gamma rays. Plutonium-239." Lastly, he checked the fourth.

"Alpha particles, beta particles, and uranium. Neptunium." He closed the window, stumbled back to Sullivan, and gave him his detector back. "The tester inside will give us the exact amounts and levels, sir."

"Thank you, Carl," Sullivan said, clasping him on the shoulder as he walked by. "Get ready, okay?"

"Yes, sir."

"Neptunium-237, as ordered," Riley said. "The rest of the cash, and you can take 'em inside your hangar. My man Stricker will count all the cash, drive out to our rendezvous point, and I'll stay until you accept the packages."

"Done," Sullivan said. He radioed again, and another man brought out a second suitcase. Stricker counted all the bills, carefully this time, nodded in agreement, and drove off. Sullivan radioed for the hangar door to be opened.

When the inspection shutter on the first radioactive waste container had opened, the radiation dosimeter on board the Predator unmanned aircraft orbiting overhead detected the released radiation and transmitted an alarm to the command center in the warehouse complex near the airport. "The first cask was unsealed," Hardison said to his assistant. "Spin 'em up." The assistant went outside and signaled to the strike-team leader to prepare for takeoff, and the helicopter pilots began starting engines.

At that moment a Yuba County Sheriff's Department cruiser turned into the entrance to the warehouse complex that concealed the four helicopters. The assistant looked at his watch, wondering what the deputy wanted. The cruiser parked about thirty yards away from the front row of helicopters, and a man in a suit, tie, and sunglasses emerged, taking his identification badge out and slipping it into his top jacket pocket with the seven-pointed sheriff's star visible. The assistant hadn't met the sheriff, but he thought he recognized him.

The newcomer gave the pilots a thumbs-up as he approached the assistant special agent in charge. "Sheriff Adamson?" the assistant asked.

"No," the man said, and he withdrew an automatic pistol from under his jacket and shot the assistant in the chest three times. Immediately he withdrew a small device from his jacket, pressed a button, then walked inside the warehouse. Two seconds later, a three-hundred-pound homemade explosive device in the backseat of the police cruiser detonated. The first row of helicopters disappeared in a ball of fire and engulfed the second row, and in a fraction of a second all four choppers were destroyed and twelve SWAT officers perished.

The man trotted to the door to the office that was being used as the command post and dropped to one knee just as Hardison dashed out, weapon drawn, rushing to see what caused the horrific explosion outside. His bulletproof vest saved him, but the force of the three bullets hitting his chest dropped him. The man calmly looked down at the agent and shot him in the head twice, then turned and headed out.

The hangar door was almost open enough to drive the van inside when Riley noticed a Yuba County Sheriff's Department SWAT armored Suburban roar down the taxiway toward them. Shit, he thought, they're *early*! Where in hell are the helicopters? The vehicle screeched to a halt in front of the hangar, and two officers in black battle-dress uniforms and Kevlar helmets dashed out and a third emerged from the back of the vehicle, *carrying the two suitcases of money*!

"Hey!" Riley shouted, holding up his hands in surrender. "What the hell is . . . ?" At that moment he heard the explosion and the sounds of screeching and ripping metal from the direction of the warehouse complex, and he realized that the operation was blown—even before the driver of the Suburban pulled a pistol from his holster, aimed, and fired three rounds into the FBI agent's face.

"Report," the man named Sullivan said.

"The SWAT teams were eliminated, sir," the driver said. "The sheriff's department vehicles were placed to block ingress to the airport as much as possible, and the Bravo and Charlie strike teams are reporting to their postmission rally points. No casualties."

"Very well," Sullivan said. "Excellent work. Help the Alpha team get the casks on board the plane and secured, then report to your rally points."

"Yes, *sir*." The three men trotted inside the hangar, where the radioactive waste casks were already being unloaded by a forklift. Sullivan followed them inside, where he met up with Carl, who was looking over a sectional aviation chart. Sullivan noticed Carl's pale, sweaty skin and trembling hand as he took a sip of water. "Are you okay, Carl?" he asked.

"I'll be fine, sir," Carl replied. "I took the last of the meds a few minutes ago—that'll last me for several hours. Long enough."

Sullivan nodded and clasped Carl on the shoulder again. "You're a true patriot, Carl," he said. "A real hero."

"Thank you, sir," Carl replied. He tapped the sectional chart. "I'll be in constant radar contact in the valley at any altitude—no way to avoid that," he said. "But once I get over the Sierra, they'll lose me. I'll ridge-hop to the south, change courses, stay away from population centers, and make my way to the airstrip to off-load the three casks and refuel."

"Very well," Sullivan said. "You've planned this operation well."

"It was my honor and pleasure, sir," Carl said, "as will be the last phase. The strike teams all performed brilliantly."

"They did, thanks to your inspiration."

"Thank you, sir." Carl stood at attention and saluted. "It has been an honor to serve you, sir," he said.

Sullivan returned his salute. "Not me, Carl—we serve the True

Republic," he said. He embraced the pilot, and he could feel the trembling throughout Carl's thin body. The doctors had given him less than six months before the leukemia would consume him; the cataracts would blind him well before that. "Job well done, soldier. Carry on."

"For the True Republic, sir," Carl said, and he folded up his charts and headed for the King Air.

Long before the first FBI agents and police units arrived at the airport, the King Air was loaded up and airborne, heading east at low altitude. The men at the airport scattered via cars, motorcycles, and even boats, escaping to secure safe houses throughout the area to wait for nightfall and stay on the lookout for any sign of pursuit.

ONE

*I hear many condemn these men because they were so
few. When were the good and brave ever in a
majority?*

— Henry David Thoreau

Battle Mountain, Nevada

That same time

The recent thunderstorms had turned the yard—if you could call
their little patch of dirt, grass, and rocks a yard—into a brown
crumbly paste, like soggy half-baked green-colored brownies. The
unpaved streets were in a little better shape, having been com-
pacted by automobile and construction traffic, but it was still a wet,
sloppy mess that sunshine hadn't yet been able to ameliorate.

This could have been war-torn Iraq or Afghanistan, or some remote Chinese village . . . instead, it was a relatively new subdivision
in the community of Battle Mountain, in north-central Nevada.

Battle Mountain began life as a small railroad depot and mining camp in post–Civil War north-central Nevada, nothing more

than a small collection of warehouses, shops, saloons, and brothels. Although it became the seat of Lander County, the community never got around to becoming an incorporated town, city, or even a village. Even when the interstate highway was built nearby and the U.S. Army set up a B-17 bomber crew training base outside of town, the community never really grew far from its mining-camp, bump-in-the-road past.

And that's pretty much what Bradley James McLanahan thought of Battle Mountain: yet another bump in *his* road.

Just one month away from his eighteenth birthday, tallish like his deceased mother but husky and blue-eyed like his father, Brad—no one used his full first name except his dad unless they were looking for trouble—had had his share of moves and terrible postings, like all Air Force brats. Although he didn't think so, he actually had it pretty good compared to the kids of some other officers, because he had moved just a few times in the eighteen years his father, retired Air Force Lieutenant-General Patrick McLanahan, had been in the service. But to his thinking, Battle Mountain was his penalty for having fewer moves and bad postings.

Brad had been cooped up most of the morning playing computer games and waiting for the hellish thunderstorms to blow through, and now that the rains had stopped and the sun was coming out, he wanted to get the heck *out*. He found his dad in his tiny bedroom/office. "Dad, can I borrow the car?" he asked from the doorway.

"Depends," his father replied without turning. Patrick was seemingly staring out the window of his bedroom, one hand hovering in midair, his fingers moving as if he were typing on a keyboard. Brad knew—but wasn't allowed to tell anyone—that his father didn't need a screen because computer images were broadcast to tiny monitors built into special lenses of his eyes so the computer images appeared as big as if on a twenty-seven-inch high-def screen; he typed on a "virtual" keyboard that he could call up as well. His dad had been the guinea pig for many such high-tech gadgets in his years in the Air Force. "Kitchen?"

"Clean, dishwasher unloaded."

"Bathroom?"

"Sunday is my usual day to do the bathroom. Okay if I do it tomorrow?"

"Okay. Bedroom?"

"Picked up, bed made."

"Living room?"

"Presentable."

His father looked at him, trying to discern exactly what that meant. "Maybe we should check."

"Okay." He watched his dad's blue eyes dart back and forth as he made mouse-pointer movements by simply looking at log-off commands on his virtual screen. He followed his dad down the narrow hallway. Patrick peeked into Brad's bedroom across the hall, checked, nodded approval, then proceeded past the hall closet with the stacked washer and dryer, the kitchen/dining area, and finally into the living room. The McLanahans lived in a double-wide trailer, about half the size of their last residence in Henderson, Nevada, near Las Vegas, but large and almost ostentatious compared to many of their neighbors'.

Patrick scowled at a stack of magazines and junk mail in a pile on the coffee table. "That stuff needs to be sorted, recycled, or put away," he said.

"It's Gia's stuff, Dad," Brad said. His dad nodded solemnly. Gia Cazzotto was his dad's girlfriend—or former girlfriend, or wacko, or alkie, he didn't know which. She had been medically retired from the Air Force after ejecting from an EB-1C Vampire bomber that had been attacked by Russian fighters over the Arabian Sea last year.

After recovering from her injuries, Gia was sent to Washington to face charges for her actions just prior to the shoot-down. She was charged with causing injuries and damage to a peaceful vessel and its crew in international waters, inciting an international incident, disobeying orders, and dereliction of duty. Patrick went with her to lend support and to testify on her behalf, but was barred from doing so because he faced his own charges. She was found guilty in a court-martial and sentenced to three years in prison, reduction in rank to second lieutenant—she had been a full colonel, in command of a high-tech bomber unit in Southern California—and a less-than-honorable discharge. Her sentence was commuted by President Kenneth Phoenix hours after he assumed office, but the less-than-honorable discharge remained.

Gia was never the same person after that, Brad remembered. She was angry, quick-tempered, restless, and quiet. The charges against his father were dismissed by the president, which only seemed to make her angrier. The president could have completely pardoned her, but he didn't, saying that in good conscience he couldn't overturn a jury verdict, even if he believed what she did was in the best interests of the United States of America. That made her even angrier.

When his father accepted this job in Battle Mountain, she accompanied them for a while, helping to set up the trailer and watch over Brad while his father worked, but she was definitely no fun to be around like she was in Henderson. She started drinking: good stuff at first, top-quality Napa Valley Cabernet Sauvignons—Brad always got a little taste—then when the money ran low and she lost her job, it was whatever was cheapest. Soon after, she started disappearing, first for a couple days, then a couple weeks at a time. Who knew if she'd ever be back?

"Sorry. Don't worry about it," Patrick said, straightening his shoulders. He nodded toward the desk with the drawer with all the keys in it. "If it needs gas, you know what to do. Watch the speed limits. And no driving on the interstate. Got some cash?"

"Yes."

Patrick nodded. Damn, he thought, his son was grown up, almost his own guy. What in hell would living in this trailer feel like without him? "Call if anything happens."

"I know, I know, I will," Brad said. "Thanks." Like all of his friends, Brad got his learner's permit at exactly age fifteen and a half on the dot because a car meant real freedom in an isolated place like Battle Mountain—the nearest town of any size was Elko, more than seventy miles away and accessible only by the interstate, unless you really liked serious off-roading. The cops knew that, and they liked to ticket kids who drove at night or used the interstate highway, which was not allowed for drivers with only learner's permits.

The phone was ringing as Brad dashed out the door—no one he wanted to talk to right now used the home phone, so the quicker he could get away, the better. He had made it to the car and was just opening the driver's door when he heard the front door to the trailer open and his dad shouted, "Brad!"

"Gotta go, Dad," he shouted, not stopping. Sheesh, he thought, who calls the home number for him on a Saturday afternoon? All his friends used his cell number. "I'm meeting Ron and he needs—"

"Squadron recall," Patrick said. "Actual. Everyone. Seventy-two hours."

They did. All thoughts of freedom disappeared as he dashed back into the house. Hanging out with his friends, driving, playing computer games . . . all good, but they were all pretty lame compared to *this*.

Patrick and Brad raced back into the trailer, and within moments reemerged from their bedrooms dressed in completely different clothes. Patrick wore a sage-green flight suit and black leather flying boots. The black leather nameplate above his left pocket had a set of Civil Air Patrol wings, his name, the letters *CAP* in one lower corner and his Civil Air Patrol rank, *COL*, on the other (even though Patrick retired from the Air Force as a lieutenant-general, the highest rank he could attain in Civil Air Patrol without earning advancement points was colonel), along with Civil Air Patrol and Nevada Wing patches. Brad wore a camouflaged battle-dress uniform with blue-and-white cloth name tapes with *MCLANAHAN* on one side and *CIVIL AIR PATROL* on the other, along with a green camouflage cap, an orange safety vest, and black leather combat boots. Both carried backpacks with extra gear; Brad carried a smaller pack on his web belt. "Ready to go, big guy?" Patrick asked.

"Ready." Like the costumed heroes Batman and Robin heading to the Batmobile, the two raced to Patrick's four-door Jeep Wrangler and drove off.

The roads in the trailer subdivision were muddy from the recent thunderstorms, but the Wrangler handled them with ease. The subdivision was a temporary trailer housing settlement built during the expansion of the air base located nearby—at least it was *meant* to be temporary, until the sudden and dramatic downturn in the economy and the new president's response to the crisis made the trailers permanent. The roads were still unpaved, and now half of the trailers were empty.

It took about five minutes to get back on paved surfaces, and then another ten minutes before reaching the outer perimeter of the airfield. The perimeter was a simple sign and chain-link fence, designed more to keep tumbleweeds and coyotes out, and an unmanned guard gate. But Patrick and Brad both knew that their identities were already being remotely determined and recorded, and their movements carefully tracked by the air base's high-tech security sensors. Joint Air Base Battle Mountain didn't look much different from the surrounding high desert, but at this place, looks were deceiving.

What was now Joint Air Base Battle Mountain had a colorful past, most of which the public was unaware of, or at best indifferent to. It started life as Tuscarora Army Air Corps Field in 1942 to train bomber and pursuit crews for service in World War II. After the war, the airfield was turned over to Lander County, and some of the government land south of the field sold to mining companies. A few businesses and an air museum tried to make a go of it at the isolated airfield, but there simply wasn't that much business in remote north-central Nevada, and the airfield seemed to languish.

But the underground elevators, buildings, rail lines, power distributors, and ventilation systems that popped up around the airfield were never meant for miners: the U.S. government secretly constructed a vast underground cave network beneath Tuscarora Army Air Corps Base. The facility was designed to be a government reconstitution command center, a base far from population centers to which the heads of the U.S. government and military would escape and ride out a Soviet or Chinese nuclear-missile attack. After the attack was over, the officials at Battle Mountain would broadcast instructions to the survivors and begin rescue and regeneration efforts for the people of the western United States.

The facility was the ultimate in 1950s technology: it made its own power, air, and water; it was built to withstand anything but a direct hit with a one-megaton nuclear warhead; it even boasted an underground hangar with elevators that would take aircraft as large as a B-52 bomber belowground to safety. The base was so isolated that most miners and ranchers never realized the facility existed.

But when the Cold War ended, Battle Mountain was shuttered . . . until it was reactivated in the early twenty-first century by General Patrick McLanahan as the headquarters for a new high-tech aerial attack unit called the Air Battle Force. The Air Battle Force contained some of the most secret and amazing air-combat machines ever built: two-hundred-ton bombers with the radar cross section of a flea; bombers fitted with lasers that could shoot down ballistic missiles and satellites in low Earth orbit; even multiple flights of unmanned bombers that could fly supersonic combat missions halfway around the world. Still, the little community and its mysterious underground base went almost completely unnoticed by the rest of the world . . .

. . . until the American Holocaust, when the United States was attacked by waves of Russian bombers launching hypersonic nuclear-tipped missiles. Almost the entire fleet of American long-range bombers and more than half of America's intercontinental-ballistic-missile arsenal was wiped out in a matter of hours. But Battle Mountain's little fleet of high-tech bombers, led by Patrick McLanahan, survived and formed the spearhead of the American counterattack that destroyed most of Russia's ground-launched intercontinental nuclear missiles and restored a tenuous sort of parity in nuclear forces between the two nations.

Battle Mountain emerged from the horrific tragedy of the American Holocaust to become the center of American air-breathing strategic combat operations. All of America's surviving heavy bombers, intelligence-gathering planes, and airborne command posts were relocated to Battle Mountain, and a fleet of long-range unmanned combat aircraft began to grow there. The base even became a staging area for America's fleet of manned and unmanned spaceplanes—aircraft that could take off and land like conventional aircraft but boost themselves into low Earth orbit.

Even during the deep global economic recession that began in 2008, Battle Mountain grew, although the community around it barely noticed. Because of its isolation and dirt-low cost of living, many bases around the world were closed and relocated to Battle Mountain. Soon Battle Mountain Air Reserve Base became JAB (Joint Air Base) Battle Mountain, hosting air units from all the military services, the Air Reserve Forces, the Central Intelligence Agency, and even the Space Defense Force.

But then the economic crash of December 2012 happened, and everything changed.

Newly elected president Kenneth Phoenix, politically exhausted from a bruising and divisive election that saw yet another president being chosen in effect by the U.S. Supreme Court, ordered a series of massive tax cuts as well as cuts in all government services. Such government cuts had not been seen since the Thomas Thorn administration: entire cabinet-level departments, such as education, commerce, transportation, energy, and veterans affairs, were consolidated with other departments or closed outright; all entitlement-program outlays were cut in half or defunded completely; American military units and even entire bases around the world disappeared virtually overnight. Despite howls of protest from both the political left and right, Congress had no choice but to agree to the severe austerity measures.

Joint Air Base Battle Mountain was not spared. Every aircraft at the once-bustling base was in "hangar queen" status—available only for spare parts—reassigned to other bases, or mothballed. Most planes placed in "flyable storage" were not even properly mothballed, but just hoisted up on jacks and shrink-wrapped in place to protect them against sun and sandstorms. Construction at the base was halted, seemingly with nails half pounded, concrete footers half poured, and streets abruptly turning into dirt roads or littered with construction equipment that appeared to be just dropped or turned off and abandoned. There seemed to be no one on the base at all except for security patrols, and most of the visible ones were unmanned robotic vehicles responding to security breaches discovered by remote electronic sensors.

Patrick and Brad drove past the partially completed headquarters building of the Space Defense Force. They had passed just a handful of persons and vehicles since entering the base. "Man, this place looks . . . freakin' lonely, Dad," Brad said. "Aren't they ever going to finish those buildings?"

"There's no money in the budget right now," Patrick said. He nodded toward several trailers set up nearby. "Those will do for now." If the Space Defense Force survived the economic downturn, he silently added. President Phoenix was a big supporter, but like every other government program, it had been cut by at least 50 percent.

"Battle Mountain's town flower: the trailer," Brad said, reciting the oft-repeated joke.

The flight line was built up much more than the rest of the base because of all the flying activity before the 2012 crash, but now it appeared just as vacant as the rest of the base. Each large hangar had just one or two planes parked there—the rest were either in the hangars being cannibalized or on the south parking ramp encased in shrink-wrap. The most active flying units on the base were the RQ-4 Global Hawk reconnaissance planes, which had transferred here from Beale Air Force Base in Marysville, California; and the three surviving Air Force E-4B National Airborne Operations Center airborne command post planes, which along with the Navy's Mercury sea-launched ballistic-missile airborne command posts resumed around-the-clock operations after the American Holocaust.

Patrick drove to the older western side of the flight line, parked in front of a large cube-shaped hangar, and he and Brad retrieved their gear and headed inside. The hangar was shared with several nonmilitary organizations, everyone from the Lander County Sheriff's Department to the Nevada Department of Wildlife, so there was an assortment of fixed- and rotary-wing aircraft parked inside. They found two men at a large table inside the hangar, looking over topographic charts. One was wearing an Air Force–style green Nomex flight suit, similar to Patrick's; the other was wearing a camouflaged battle-dress utility uniform with an orange vest over the jacket. They looked up when Patrick and Brad came over to them.

"The McLanahans: first to arrive, as usual," the man in the flight suit, Civil Air Patrol Lieutenant Colonel Rob Spara, said. Spara was a retired Army Kiowa Scout helicopter pilot and commanded an Army helicopter training squadron before retiring; he held a variety of helicopter-related jobs now, doing everything from flying skiers to fresh powder on mountaintops, to air ambulance, to maintenance and repair. He shook hands with Patrick, then handed him a clipboard with a sign-in roster. "You're the first pilot to arrive, sir." Even though rank in the squadron was rarely observed, everyone called Patrick "General" or "sir." "Feel like flying the 182 today?"

"Absolutely," Patrick said immediately. He completed the sign-in, then had Brad sign in.

"Good," the other man, CAP Captain David Bellville, said. Bellville was the vice commander of the squadron and the commander of cadets, a ten-year veteran of the Civil Air Patrol, a twenty-two-year veteran of the U.S. Air Force, and a physician's assistant. "I'll be your flight release officer. I'll enter you into the ICU and give your crew a face-to-face when you're done preflighting." The ICU, or incident commander utility, was the computerized data-input system for the Civil Air Patrol, which did away with a lot of the paperwork required by the Air Force.

"I'd like to fly as scanner, sir," Brad said.

"You know you're not old enough, Brad," Spara said.

"But I finished all the training, and—"

"And you know how I feel about father and son flying together: if there was an accident, it would be an even greater tragedy," Spara interrupted.

"Then can I be on the DF on the ground team, sir?"

Spara had turned back to his incident planning and looked a little peeved at the question. "The initial mass briefing will be in thirty minutes, Brad."

"I can start inspecting the L-Per." Spara looked as if he hadn't heard him. "I'm here early, and I did navigation on the last exercise. I can—"

"Brad, we're trying to work here," Spara said. He paused, then nodded. "We'll put you on DF. Go start preflighting it. Briefing in thirty." He gave Patrick a short glance, and Patrick nodded and followed Brad to the equipment room.

As Brad unlocked the door, Patrick said, "I know you're anxious, big guy, but you shouldn't badger the squadron commander like that. He'll give out everyone's assignment in the mass briefing. He doesn't have time to address each individual in the unit."

"He gave out *your* assignment," Brad said.

"I think that was a courtesy, Brad," Patrick said. "I didn't ask him if I could fly as mission pilot."

"Courtesy because you're a retired general?"

"Probably." Patrick detected a slightly angry expression. "What?"

"Nothing."

"Spill it." Still silent. "You still don't like that I joined the Civil Air Patrol, do you?" Patrick asked. Brad glared at him. "I told you, I didn't do it just to keep an eye on you."

"Then why?"

"Because I'm a flier, and I was Air Force, and when we got sent to Battle Mountain and you transferred to this squadron from the Henderson squadron, I thought it would be fun, and it is. Plus, I give back to the community by volunteering."

"It was my hobby, not yours."

"So I can't have the same hobby as you?"

"It's not just that you're a general, it's because you're a flier," Brad said. "The CO looks down his nose at cadets and ground ops."

"That's not true," Patrick said. "He's a pilot, but he's also retired Army—he's been supporting ground troops his whole career. But that's not what's eating you either, is it?" Silence. "Wish I wasn't part of Civil Air Patrol? Get used to it—I'm not going to quit unless work really picks up, which seems unlikely for a while." Still silent. Patrick scowled, then asked directly, "What's eating you, Brad?"

Brad looked up, then around, then took a deep breath and said, "Nothing."

"C'mon, Brad, what's up?"

"It's nothing, Dad," Brad said. He retrieved the L-Per direction-finding device and turned. "I gotta go."

"Okay," Patrick said dejectedly. It wasn't the first time they'd tried to have this conversation, he thought, and it ended the same way every time.

Brad finished checking the direction-finding device, then brought it and his equipment over near the four-wheel-drive van to get ready for inspection and boarding. More squadron members had arrived, and he had time to visit with his friends and watch the local news for any information while they waited for the mass briefing. There weren't that many members yet in the hangar—folks who lived in Battle Mountain usually escaped on weekends, to Elko, Jackpot, Reno, Lake Tahoe, Salt Lake City, or to remote desert campsites scattered throughout the area. If they were available, more would show up later for follow-on or backup missions.

Ron Spivey was a bit younger than Brad and was going to be a senior in high school, like Brad. "Hey, Ron," Brad greeted him when they saw each other. "Where were you when the call came in?"

"Just bought Marina a cone at the DQ and were on our way out to do some off-roading," Ron said. He was the quarterback and captain of the football team with Brad, taller but not as beefy as Brad, with big hands, a thin face that looked even thinner because of a thick football player's neck, and narrow eyes.

"Was she pissed?" Brad asked.

His initial expression told Brad that she was, but Ron shrugged it off. "Who cares?" he replied. "If she wanted to nag on me, she could do it in my rearview mirror. She knew better. I dropped her off and geared up. What do you know?"

"Plane went down northwest of here," Brad said. "I'll bet they'll put us on a Hasty team."

"Maybe we'll get to see victims."

"You're a sicko."

"Beats those stuffed scarecrow things they put out on SAR-EXs."

A few moments later, another young boy came up to them, stood in front of Brad, and saluted. "Cadet Sergeant Markham reporting, sir," he said. He was fifteen years old but looked about ten, with a round face and body, a nose way too small for his freckly face, and big green eyes.

Brad returned the salute. "You don't have to salute indoors, Ralph," he said, "and you don't have to report to me—you report to the IC or whoever's signing us in."

"Sorry, sir," Markham said.

"Don't apologize either. Did you sign in?"

"Yes, sir."

"And you don't have to 'sir' me unless we're in formation," Brad said. But he knew that Ralph Markham liked the military formalities and wasn't going to stop. "They'll probably put us together on a Hasty team. Got all your Seventy-Two gear?"

"Yes, s—Brad," Ralph said. "Out by the van ready for inspection."

"Who's closer to level one?" Brad asked the others. He turned to Ron. "Did you get your advanced first aid at the last SAREX?"

"No, I came in late, so they put me at the base on the radio."

"Then make sure you ask Bellville or Fitzgerald to be lead medic so you can get a sign-off and take the practical exam," Brad said. "That okay with you, Ralph?"

"I've already got my advanced done, sir," he said proudly.

"Excellent," Brad said. "The practical too?"

"Mr. Fitzgerald gave it to me last week."

"So what do you need for your level one?"

"Tracking and DF, sir."

"They said they're getting an ELT signal," Brad said, "so they put me on DF, and I'd like to stay on it to help out if they need me. But if we're on foot, I'll have you organize a line search and take us through some tracking procedures. Remember, verbalize what you see to the rest of the strike team and take lots of pictures or drawings. If you get a sign-off, we'll do some tracking practice on our own and get you ready for your practical exam. The DF sign-off will have to wait for another actual or SAREX next month, unless you can go to the California Wing's summer camp in two weeks."

"I can't," Ralph said. "I have summer school."

"Bummer," Brad said. Ralph was an enthusiastic cadet and loved the challenges of the Civil Air Patrol, but his reading was several grade levels lower than his classmates', and he needed a lot of extra time to do the simplest reading assignments. "No problem. You know your stuff—we just gotta get you some practice and a senior to observe you. You'll get your first class before you know it, and I think you'll skate through Urban DF too. You could be up for officer promotion." Ralph looked as if he was going to explode with pride. Brad turned to Ron. "You gotta get busy on getting some sign-offs, Cap. You've been a second class for, what? A year?"

"Hey, BJ, I'm busy, okay?" Ron spat back irritably. Brad's face turned stony. Ron Spivey was probably the only person who could get away with using that pejorative nickname, and only if he used it *very* sparingly. "I got two lousy part-time jobs that don't pay shit—"

"Watch the language around the younger cadets and the seniors, bro."

"—football practice twice a day," Ron went on, ignoring Brad's remark, "and a girlfriend who thinks I'm her personal chauffeur and cash machine. I'll do the stuff when I can get the time."

"I'll help you, Ron, but you gotta make the time," Brad said. "When this is over we'll go online, I'll take a look at your SQTR progress record, and we'll figure out—"

"I said, I'll do the stuff when I get the time, McLanahan," Ron said, and turned on a heel and walked away.

A few minutes later, all of the senior and cadet members who had arrived took places around the conference table. "Thanks for coming so quickly, everyone," Rob Spara began. He gave a time hack, then began: "This is an actual search-and-rescue mission. Approximately forty minutes ago, the Air Force Rescue Coordination Center was notified by Salt Lake Air Traffic Control Center that a Cessna 182 with three souls aboard was lost on radar and presumed crashed in heavy thunderstorms. A commercial airliner flying in the vicinity picked up an emergency locator transmitter beacon on VHF GUARD frequency about fifty-five miles northwest of here. The Air Force notified the Civil Air Patrol National Operations Center, who called Nevada Wing headquarters, and the colonel made me the incident commander.

"The storm system has blown through and clear skies with gusty winds are expected in the recovery area," Spara went on. "Several airliners have picked up the ELT, and air traffic control actually put together a pretty good triangulation based on signal fade. The plan is to launch the 182 and begin a search grid at the approximate location given by the airliner. Unfortunately, the ELT is an old-style transmitter and isn't picked up by satellite or doesn't transmit its position, so we do a search the old-fashioned way. General McLanahan will be mission pilot, with de Carteret as observer and Slotnik as scanner.

"Because we got an ELT signal and we might have a mostly intact plane with survivors, I'm going to deploy a Hasty team immediately," Spara went on. "Bellville will be the ground-team leader, with Fitzgerald as deputy team leader, driver, and comm, McLanahan as DF, and Spivey and Markham as medics. Repeater setup will be Romeo-17." Everyone wrote that designation on their briefing cards. The repeater network—a series of FM radio towers on several mountain peaks throughout remote areas of Nevada,

California, Oregon, Washington, Colorado, Montana, Wyoming, Idaho, and Utah—would allow the incident commander to communicate with air and ground units simultaneously, even if in a remote area or not in line of sight. "Be sure to carry medical equipment and supplies for three victims.

"Unfortunately the GA-8 ARCHER is undergoing its one-hundred-hour inspection, so it's not available until Tuesday, but I'm hoping to find this objective before then." ARCHER, which stood for airborne real-time cueing hyperspectral reconnaissance, was the most sophisticated nonmilitary airborne ground sensor in the world, capable of detecting fifty different wavelengths of electromagnetic energy in a single pass. It could detect tiny pieces of metal, disturbed earth, or even spilled fuel. ARCHER could not be operated at night and had difficulties seeing through dense trees or deep snow, but in the deserts of the western United States, it was an ideal sensor to help locate downed planes. Because of its capabilities, ARCHER, mounted aboard an Australian-made Gippsland GA-8 Airvan single-engine plane, was borrowed quite often by other CAP wings; it flew so often that it underwent a hundred-hour inspection about once every three months.

"Our Cessna 206 is on its way back from Las Vegas," Spara went on, "and it should be available tomorrow if necessary. Elko and Reno squadrons are issuing alert notifications but I haven't heard if they have backup planes available yet, so for right now, we're it. Cell-phone signal forensics hasn't picked up anything yet." The Civil Air Patrol had the capability to triangulate a person's cell-phone signals to help locate that person, even if the phone wasn't in use—depending on the number of cell towers activated, the position could be determined within a few miles. "Questions?" He waited a few moments, then said, "Conduct your task-force and team briefings, then head on out. Good luck, good hunting."

The air and ground teams got together for a joint briefing. "Based on approximate positions of aircraft flying overhead and relayed to us from air traffic control, the IC picked grid SFO 448 to search," Bellville began, pointing to a topographic chart that had been overlaid with hundreds of numbered rectangles. "I suggest we start on the southwest corner of the grid. We'll plan on driving west on the interstate to Exit 234, north on Grayson Highway, north on Andorsen Road, and go off-road at Andorsen ranch. Hopefully the 182 will have spotted the objective by the time we get there. Fid?"

"The Andorsen family has already given us permission to access their land at any time," Michael Fitzgerald, the deputy team leader but a much more experienced Nevada high-desert outdoorsman, said. Fitzgerald, a Nevada Department of Wildlife field agent and firefighter, was a tall, imposing guy, with long hair and whiskers, definitely not military-looking—and he delighted in that. "I have my charts marked pretty well with gate locations. We've lucked out because the grid is relatively flat, with the east face of Adam Peak in the northwest corner the only high terrain to worry about. I just hope the ground isn't too soggy."

Patrick made some notes and checked his sectional chart, which had been marked with the same grid lines as on the topographic briefing chart, then nodded. "Sounds good, Fid," he said. "We'll enter the grid on the southwest and try to steer to the ELT—if we're lucky, it'll still be emitting. If not, we'll contour-search Adam Peak, then do a parallel search course in the grid, half-mile tracks, at one thousand feet AGL. Based on sun angles, I'll do a north-south track and hope we can pick up some good contrasting shadows. I know our target is a Cessna 182—any details about the three passengers?"

"The fixed base operator at Elko said it was two adults and one young boy on board that plane," Bellville said. Patrick couldn't help but look over at his own son, and Brad looked back at him with sorrow on his face. They had flown together for many years— Patrick was a flight instructor, but in these tough economic times,

Brad was usually his only student—but the thought of losing Brad in a plane crash was almost too awful to think about.

"If the ELT is still on," Patrick said, swallowing hard and shaking off the thought of Brad being in that situation, "they may have survived the crash, and they may be trying to signal us. I feel good about this one, gang."

"Same here, sir," Bellville said. He and Patrick exchanged more information, double-checking radio repeater channels and charts so they could communicate and have common references in case anything was spotted, then shook hands. "Good luck, sir."

"Same to you, Dave," Patrick said, and the air and ground teams broke up to do their own team briefings.

"A few more thoughts, and then we'll mount up," Fitzgerald said to the ground-team members. "Looking at the objective area, we might be able to stay on the wash, but the thunderstorms that moved through the area might make it impassable. Hopefully the ground will have had a chance to dry out by the time we get there. It's fairly flat, but we might have a few deep gullies to traverse. In any case, our job is to move fast to help any survivors. We'll try to drive in as far as we can, but be prepared to do some quick hiking."

Bellville referenced a data card given to him by Spara. "We're on the lookout for a Cessna 182, the same type of plane as Three-Double-Echo, which I know you've all flown on, white with blue stripes," he went on. "Three souls on board. The flight originated from Elko en route to Carson City, so it might have lots of fuel still in its tanks, so be careful of spilled fuel and fire."

Bellville paused, then looked at Spivey and Markham, the two youngest members of the ground team—Spivey was seventeen and a bit younger than Brad, and Markham was fifteen. "Guys, let me and Fid approach the scene first, okay? I know you guys have been on actual missions, but you've never seen accident victims before, right?" Both cadets shook their heads, their eyes wide. "I know you guys are fully qualified in emergency services, first aid, and field operations, but encountering victims of a plane crash is a whole 'nuther world. You've got to ready yourself for some pretty awful sights. I'm not going to push you away from the scene or keep you from doing your assignments, but I'm not going to shove that horror on you either. Let us seniors check out the scene first, okay?" Both of the younger cadets nodded silently; Brad did not. "Good. Get your packs ready for inspection outside the van and let's move out."

Brad wished he was old enough to fly as an observer or scanner, but as they prepared for inspection, he was starting to get revved up to go out and find these victims. Yes, the air-search guys got all the glory, but the ground teams were the ones to actually make contact and help the victims.

Each team member had a twenty-pound backpack on a support frame called a Seventy-Two Hour pack with a carefully prepared list of items for a three-night encampment, the longest authorized for CAP cadets, including sleeping bags and pads, another set of BDUs, Meals Ready to Eat kits for five meals, and other standard personal camping items. A two-gallon water bladder was attached to the back of each backpack, with a tube attached to the front of the uniform for drinking. They also carried a fanny pack with a personal first-aid kit and other essential items that they could access without having to dig through a backpack, such as gloves, goggles, a compass, maps, a headlamp, sunscreen, and other items. After checking their gear, they inventoried the other items they would take along in the van, including tents, packs of bottled water, more MREs, and cooking equipment. The medical team inventoried their kits and equipment, including splints, burn-treatment kits, stretchers, and bandages, and the senior members checked their radios, charts, and portable GPS receivers and spare batteries.

Brad was in charge of the DF, or direction-finding equipment, and he had to show Bellville that it was working properly. The DF, called an L-Per, was a VHF and UHF radio receiver with an oblong directional antenna mounted on a six-foot-high mast, which was attached to a vehicle or could be carried on a special harness if they had to go in on foot. The receiver would pick up the electronic beacon from a downed aircraft and, by monitoring the signal strength as the antenna was turned, point the way to the beacon. The device was powered by two nine-volt batteries, and Brad made sure he had plenty of fresh spares—there wasn't anything worse than to lead a team miles and miles into the desert and run out of juice before reaching the objective.

Once Bellville had inspected everyone's gear, it was all loaded into the back of the ten-passenger blue-and-white four-wheel-drive van, and the team piled in. The van had a special FM radio operating on the Civil Air Patrol repeater network that would tie in all of the teams on that channel, including, air, ground, and base units, along with a cellular amplifier that could pull in distant cellular signals to allow cell phones to be used farther from civilization.

The ground mission was under way.

At the same time Patrick was at the hangar entrance with the squadron's blue-and-white Cessna 182R and the other members of his flight crew, Leo Slotnick and John de Carteret. Leo was in his midthirties, a former U.S. Air Force aerial refueling tanker pilot and currently a Nevada Highway Patrol sergeant and pilot from Battle Mountain, who had only been a member of the Battle Mountain squadron for five months. John de Carteret was just the opposite: he was in his early sixties, a retired captain in the U.S. Coast Guard, and was the co-owner of a gas station and convenience store in town just off the interstate with his wife, Janet, also retired Coast Guard and a CAP volunteer. He had been in the Civil Air Patrol since he first came to Battle Mountain eleven years earlier and was qualified in numerous emergency-services specialties, both ground and flying. Even though he was a pilot, he preferred to be a mission observer and act as copilot and mission commander. Slotnick could qualify for mission pilot after flying a few more actual or exercise sorties as a mission scanner and taking another flight check.

Rob Spara came over with several forms. "Flight release and weight and balance," he said. To the entire crew he asked, "How's everyone feeling today? No one popping open any brewskis early on a hot Saturday afternoon?"

"A couple hours later and I might have," Leo admitted.

"No late nights last night, no allergy medications?"

"A late night for me is eight P.M., Rob," John said.

"I'm right with you, John," Spara said. The "IMSAFE" check, which stood for illness, medications, stress, alcohol, fatigue, and eating/hydration, was a required briefing element to be sure each crewmember was fit to fly. Since none of them was on alert and they all led normal lives, being suddenly thrust into a flying assignment meant that the aircraft commander and flight-release officer had to be sure everyone was ready to fly. "How about you, General?"

"I feel good, no meds, no alcohol, and things are so slow here on the base I can't be stressed," Patrick said.

"Good." Spara tapped some instructions into a BlackBerry, waited a few moments; then: "You're released. Good luck." He wrote their release number on the flight-release form. "I'll see you on the radio."

Patrick opened up the airplane maintenance logs. "Okay, last crew reports they filled the plane to the tabs, so we have plenty of gas. Open discrepancies . . . loose copilot's armrest . . . and left rearmost window is crazed. Let me know if you think it's too bad to look out of, Leo."

"Will do, sir."

"No other glitches." Patrick filled out log sheet from data on the flight-release form, closed it, then referred to a mission briefing card he had filled out after getting a mission briefing from the operations and planning officers. "Okay, guys, we'll head on out directly to the southwest corner of grid SFO 448, and hopefully we'll get a few ELT bearings. Altitude will be one thousand feet AGL, which will be around five thousand five hundred feet MSL in that area. Thirty minutes out and thirty back will give us three hours on station with an hour fuel reserve—hopefully we won't need that long. We might have enough daylight when we get back to return, refuel, and relaunch if necessary. With the front blowing through, we might get some turbulence, so let me know if anyone feels queasy. Flat terrain except for Adam Peak, good visibility, and a half-mile track separation gives us a probability of detection of eighty-five percent, so let's get this one. Questions?" Leo and John shook their heads. "Okay. I'll do an airplane preflight. You guys preflight the radios, camera, and DF, copy the airplane hours into the logbook and the mission forms, and get a good radio check with the IC and ground team."

Patrick put on a pair of Nomex fireproof gloves and began to work on preflighting the four-seat Cessna, working with a plastic-laminated checklist. John met up with him a few minutes later. "Comm is good," he said, "and the DF self-tests okay."

"Which means it'll be almost useless?" Patrick deadpanned.

"If you talk badly about the DF, it will hear you and act badly," John deadpanned back. "I thought 406 megahertz satellite ELTs were required on all planes."

"They are," Patrick said. "But everyone is cutting corners to cut costs these days, and ELTs are one of those things that you never think you'll ever use. The owner was probably waiting until his ELT battery replacement was due before buying the new one."

"Well, hopefully it'll keep on working long enough to get a good steer," John said. He nodded to Patrick. "I'm always amazed watching you work, Patrick."

"Why?"

"You're the guy who's flown all sorts of heavy iron, from B-52s to spaceplanes," John said, "and here you are, preflighting a plane that probably weighs less than one of the bomb-bay doors on a

B-52, and you're using a paper checklist. You can probably pre-flight a Cessna 182 blindfolded."

"I probably could," Patrick said, "but when I think I know it all, that'll be the time to quit flying."

"True enough," John said. He paused for a moment, then commented, "I . . . I'm not sure if I've said this to you before, Patrick, and if I have, I apologize, but . . ."

"What?"

"I just can't believe *you* are here," John said, his eyes filled with unabashed wonder—one might even describe it as amazement. "I mean, *you* are Patrick McLanahan. *The* Patrick McLanahan. It seems like one day you're leading a group of bombers against Russia to avenge America for the American Holocaust, then the next you're on the space station, and then you're in Iraq stopping a major war from breaking out between Turkey and America. The next day, you're in little Battle Mountain, Nevada, flying Cessna 182s and 206s for the Civil Air Patrol. With all due respect, sir . . . what in *hell* are you doing here? I mean, *here*?"

"I explained this to the squadron when I first joined, John," Patrick began. "I retired from the Air Force—"

"You mean, you were *forced* to retire."

"President Phoenix put his political life on the line during his campaign when he supported me and stood against President Gardner prosecuting me for the Aden and Socotra Island incidents," Patrick said. "I felt I had no choice but to retire. President Gardner still decided to prosecute the others and myself. I was lucky: the case hadn't gone to the jury by the time President Phoenix was sworn in, and he pardoned me."

"The others weren't so lucky."

"I know," Patrick said somberly. "A lot of good people had their lives turned inside out because of the orders I issued, even though no one spent any time in prison." He straightened his shoulders. "Okay, let's get our heads back in the game, John."

"But wait, Patrick," the retired Coast Guard officer said quietly. He put a hand on Patrick's arm in earnest. "You still didn't answer my question: Why *here*?"

"I explained that," Patrick said. "Battle Mountain is still a vital bomber, spaceport, UAV, and joint air facility. It's been downgraded to part-time status, but there's no money in anyone's budget for a large support staff. I'm familiar with Battle Mountain and all the Air Force and Space Defense Force activities here; the high school has a good football program for my son, and he likes being part of the Civil Air Patrol. Probably most important: I can work for a dollar a year and live pretty well off my retirement, government housing, and expense reimbursements. I run a small caretaker staff, keep the networks and communications systems alive, and keep the lights minimally on and support the few missions we fly out of here until the economy recovers, and we can start rebuilding the force. It's that simple."

John's expression was skeptical, almost disbelieving, and he looked as if he was going to continue questioning him, but Patrick's expression told him to back off. "Well, General," he said, "I'm proud and pleased that you're here." He touched the silver eagle insignia on his left shoulder. "And I'm sorry you have to wear a bird instead of stars. It seems like an insult to me, given your service to our country."

"They offered an honorary lieutenant-general's rank and position—I declined," Patrick said. "I'm a crew dog, John, plain and simple. I wanted to fly, not give speeches and have my picture taken with politicians who *say* they support our mission and us. I couldn't fly for CAP wearing three stars. Enough already, Observer. There may be people on the ground who need us. Let's stop chitchatting." John gave him a pat on the arm and let him get back to his preflight.

A few minutes later, the crew climbed aboard. Patrick was in first in the left-front pilot's seat, and then he rolled his seat forward so Leo could get in the left-rear seat. Leo carried a flight bag with charts, his own personal headset, and other gear, and another padded canvas bag with a digital telescopic camera for recording pictures for upload to the Civil Air Patrol National Operations Center after their mission was over. John got in last and strapped in. "Ready, John?" Patrick asked.

"Ready," John said, retrieving a laminated checklist card from a pocket near his right leg. "Preflight, completed. Crew brief."

"Seat belts and shoulder harnesses on all the time," Patrick said, reciting from memory. "Fire extinguisher is up here between the front seats. Sterile cockpit in the terminal area and in the grid—no unnecessary conversations. Evacuation order will be Leo first out the left side, then John out the right, then myself, and I'll grab the survival kit after exiting if the plane's not on fire. Remember you can pop the windshield out as an emergency escape, and the rear baggage door is unlocked so you can climb over the backseat and get out that way if necessary. Questions?" He didn't wait for a response—he knew his crew was experienced enough that *they* could give *him* the briefing. They continued with the checklist, got the plane's engine started, the radios and navigation systems on, and minutes later they were taxiing for takeoff.

It was a long taxi to the run-up area, a wide portion of the taxiway where small planes could pull out of the way to make room for other planes while the pilot finished his preflight. Patrick ran through the final engine checks and pretakeoff items. He then ran the Cessna's engine up to takeoff power, leaned the engine until it was just starting to run rough, enriched the mixture until the cylinder-head temperature was 125 degrees cooler, then pulled the power back. Meanwhile, John entered their grid entry coordinates into the plane's satellite navigation system, which gave Patrick his direction of flight after takeoff.

"Takeoff briefing," Patrick began. "John, back me up on engine instruments; Leo, watch for traffic. Engine failure during takeoff roll: throttle to idle, max braking as needed, flaps up, secure the engine. Engine failure after takeoff but less than one thousand feet aboveground: trim for seventy-five knots, full flaps, secure the engine, land straight ahead; if above one thousand feet, we'll attempt a turn back to the runway, but we have lots of better options for an off-airport landing—if the airplane breaks, it belongs to the insurance company, not us. Any questions?" No reply. "Everyone ready?"

"Observer."

"Scanner."

"Here we go." Patrick taxied to the runway hold line, got takeoff clearance from the Battle Mountain control tower—actually a series of cameras and sensors all around the airfield, with controllers indoors watching on monitors—taxied onto the long reinforced concrete runway, and made the takeoff. The runway was so long that he could have made two more takeoffs and landings and still not have been in any danger of running out of concrete.

"CAP 2722, airborne," John reported on the FM radio.

"Battle Mountain Base, roger," Spara replied.

A REMOTE DESERT PLAYA, CENTRAL NEVADA

A SHORT TIME LATER

The landing on the hard alkali desert surface was one of the worst the workers had ever seen, and they were sure they'd see the big twin-engine plane flip upside down or spin out of control across the playa. But the pilot managed to keep it under control, and soon the King Air was taxiing across the three-inch-deep alkali dust toward the drop-off point.

"Thought you'd ground-loop her for sure, Carl," one of them said after boarding the King Air and making his way to the cockpit. The engines were still running at idle power, and a cloud of white dust swirled inside the plane. "You still got the touch, though. I shoulda warned you that the winds were squirrelly, but I didn't want to—"

The man stopped, and a chill ran up and down his spine. The pilot named Carl was slumped over the control wheel, still strapped in his seat, which was covered in bloody diarrhea, urine, and vomit. At first he thought Carl was dead . . . but a few moments later he saw him raise his head and look back. "Carl?" the man asked. "You look like shit, man."

"Funny," Carl breathed. He coughed up more bloody substances, smiled, and sat up. "I feel like hell, not shit."

"You gonna make it, Carl?" the man asked. "The commander said to unload all the casks if you don't think you'll make it."

"I'll be okay," Carl breathed. He wiped his mouth, looked at the bloody mess covering his legs, floor, seat, and most of his instrument panel, then shook his head. "Just great. A perfectly good breakfast, wasted."

"You want me to clean all that up, Carl?"

"Screw it," Carl said. "Won't matter anyway." He seemed to doze off, then reawaken with a start, look around as if regaining his bearings, then turn back toward his comrade. "You got any whiskey, Joe?" he asked.

"Thought you weren't supposed to fly and drink," Joe said even as he thought, What a stupid thing to say, quoting FAA regulations at a time like this. But before Carl could repeat his request, he nodded. "You got it, Carl. Sit tight and relax."

About ten minutes later, the worker named Joe returned to the cockpit with a plastic canteen. Another worker was maneuvering one of the casks behind him. "Here ya go, Carl," Joe said. "A little Black Jack for ya." Carl took the canteen and drank—most of it dribbled out of his mouth, but he didn't seem to notice or care. "We got the payload up here for ya too." Joe dropped a ratcheting wrench onto the copilot's seat, then said apprehensively, "I . . . I can loosen a few of the bolts if you need."

Carl looked at Joe's taut face, smiled, and shook his head. "No reason for both of us to get zapped, Joe," he said. "I can handle it." He held out an emesis-stained hand. "Thanks, brother. For the True Republic."

Joe hesitated for a heartbeat, but swallowed his fear and took Carl's hand. "Good luck, Carl. For the True Republic. See you in Asgard, brother." He turned and made his way out of the aircraft and closed and dogged the door shut.

For several minutes, Carl sat in the cockpit, staring at the floor, trying to remember what he was supposed to do. But one look at the large steel-and-concrete cask sitting beside him reminded him of the task before him.

On the handheld GPS navigation system attached to the control yoke, he called up Flight Plan Nine, the flight plan he had developed and tweaked over the past several weeks for this mission. He had rehearsed it several times on a desktop-computer flight simulator, even using real-world satellite and three-dimensional street-level photographic images to get the most detailed preview of the final moments of the flight. But that was before the diseases ravaging his body began destroying his vision, lungs, and nervous system, and he wondered if he had the strength to do it after all his hard work. It would be so easy, he thought, so peaceful, to just let go of his sense of duty and responsibility, accept the horrible death that had been imposed on him, and let the inevitable happen.

But then, just as his spirit was waning to the point of surrender, he looked out the cockpit window. One of the soldiers had brought an American flag out onto the playa so Carl could see the wind direction and strength. He reached behind the copilot's seat and withdrew his own flag: the flag of the Knights of the True Republic of America. It was a Stars and Stripes flag but with the coiled snake from the Gadsden flag, the original flag conceived by South Carolina army officer Christopher Gadsden and adopted by the colonial American Navy and Marine Corps, in the stripes field. But instead of a coiled timber rattlesnake shaking its rattle and warning others to stay away as on the Gadsden flag, the flag of the True Republic of America showed the rattlesnake striking. The symbology was plain: those who carried this flag would no longer be warning our enemies not to oppose us, but its followers were ready to attack.

The persons he was working for weren't members of the Knights of the True Republic, but it was clear that they shared the same ideas and vision, and he was happy to contribute his flying skills for them. There were armies of men, women, and even children throughout the West, willing to risk their liberty and even their lives to stand under the Knights' flag, willing to do whatever it took to wake up a comatose American public, warn them of the danger of those bureaucrats and politicians who wanted more government and more taxation, and call on others to follow them into battle against those who were driving the nation into the ground. But it was not enough to rally around the flag—someone had to carry it into battle.

This flag was special: he had fashioned it out of material from old uniforms. He hated to soil it with his own blood and vomit, but a flag carried into battle would naturally be soiled with the stain of battle. The important thing was not to make sure the flag stayed clean, but make sure that the world, and especially the enemy, saw the flag at the front of an advancing and angry army. That was his mission: to carry the flag in the Knights of the True Republic of America's next and greatest offensive.

He started the right engine of the King Air, manipulating the controls more by rote memory and feel than by sight, then taxied forward onto the playa. It even seemed as if the winds cooperated and died down right at that moment so he had his choice of which way to go, so he decided to head directly northwest toward his objective. Making sure he didn't apply any brakes so he wouldn't drive the nosewheel into the sand, Carl smoothly advanced the throttles and pulled the yoke all the way back to his stomach with trembling muscles. The nosewheel popped off the playa, helping the big turboprop accelerate. As soon as the King Air left the ground at best-angle-of-climb airspeed, Carl pushed the nose forward, flying just a few feet above the playa in ground effect, being buoyed by the plane's wingtip vortices reflecting off the ground. He retracted the landing gear, staying in ground effect until reaching normal climb speed, then raised the nose, incrementally retracted flaps, and performed a normal climb.

His mission was finally under way. It might be his final mission, but, he reminded himself, it was the first for the Knights of the True Republic of America.

NORTHWEST OF BATTLE MOUNTAIN, NEVADA

THAT SAME TIME

"We lucked out—I'm still getting an ELT," John de Carteret said on intercom. He had set the L-Tronics emergency beacon locator to search for both VHF and UHF beacon signals and was monitoring a tiny needle mounted atop the glare shield. The GPS navigator—an older model, not updated for several years, but with the essential CAP info still valid—showed a series of rectangles with numbers designating their grid identification. "Ten miles to the grid entry point."

"Good deal," Patrick said. He pressed the radio transmit button on his control yoke and spoke: "Battle Mountain Base, CAP 2722 on Romeo-Seventeen, five minutes to grid entry, still receiving an ELT. Do you want us to start homing or continue to the entry point? Over."

"CAP 2722, Battle Mountain Base, start homing right away," Rob Spara radioed back. "I'd hate to lose the signal and not get a good bearing to it. We'll log you in the grid at this time and turning onto an ELT bearing."

"CAP 2722, roger," Patrick said. On intercom: "I'm descending to fifty-five hundred, crew, flaps ten, fifteen inches," reciting the power settings and flight-control settings aloud for everyone's information. "Let's go get 'em, John."

"Roger that," John said. "Right fifteen degrees." He copied the latitude and longitude readouts from the GPS receiver, marked the coordinates on her sectional chart, took the magnetic heading from the compass once Patrick rolled out, matched the magnetic heading to a nearby radio navaid compass rose, and drew a line on his chart. That was the first search bearing—their target was somewhere along that line on the chart.

Unfortunately, the ELT signal was not very strong, and the directional needle refused to stay steady. Patrick made a few course corrections, trying to average out the swings in the directional indications, but it still refused to stay in the center of the dial. He made a few adjustments in the signal gain and volume, trying to get the needle to stay steady, then shook his head in frustration. "I'm chasing that needle too much and not getting a true bearing," he said. "Let's try a wing shadow and see if we can get a bearing." He made a slight right turn so Leo could clear for traffic on the left, then said, "Coming left."

"Clear left," Leo said.

Patrick began a fifteen-degree bank left turn, and they all listened to the emergency locator beacon's *PING! . . . PING! . . . PING!* sound. Just before completing a circle, the signal stopped. As they continued the turn, the signal returned. The Cessna's wing blocked the ELT's signal from reaching the antenna atop the plane, which indicated that the ELT was somewhere off the right wing when the signal went dead. "Got it," John said. "Bearing zero-five-zero."

"Roger that," Patrick said. "Zero-five-zero." He turned to that heading, and both John and Leo searched out their windows. John punched up the GPS coordinates, marked the spot on his chart, then drew a line corresponding to the wing-shadow bearing to the ELT. "Let's get this sucker, guys."

But after ten minutes on that heading, nearing the edge of the grid, they hadn't seen a thing. "I'll go south and we'll try another wing shadow before that ELT dies," Patrick said. "Coming right." He flew five minutes on a southerly heading, then set up another orbit.

The signal faded again—much quicker this time, indicating that the ELT's battery was quickly dying—and John computed another bearing: "Now I have three-zero-zero bearing to the ELT, Patrick," he said. He drew a large circle on his sectional chart where his two bearing lines crossed. "It's there, plus or minus five miles."

"Sounds like my early days in celestial navigation in the B-52," Patrick said as he began a turn to the new bearing. "If I was within four miles of actual position after an hour of taking celestial sextant shots, I was 'king of the wing.'"

"'Celestial navigation'?" Leo remarked. "You mean, navigation using the sun, moon, and stars? Are you kidding me?"

"Long before the days of GPS, we flew bombers all over the world using nothing but a calibrated telescope shoved up a hole on top of a bomber or tanker, celestial precomputation tables, a watch, and a compass," Patrick said. "Just two generations removed from Sir Francis Drake circumnavigating the globe, and one generation from Curtis LeMay in World War Two, leading hundreds of bombers across the Atlantic. The idea was to get close enough to your target to see it visually, or at least on radar, if you had it and it was working. We're doing the very same thing now. Relay the coordinates of the center of that circle and we'll have the Hasty team head that way."

"Battle Mountain Hasty copies those coordinates," Bellville radioed after John had transmitted the coordinates on the FM repeater channel. A moment later: "Looks like it's at the southeastern edge of the Townsend ranch. Can you give them a call and get us permission to go on their land, Base?"

"Roger that," Spara replied.

"We'll get him this time," Slotnick said as they rolled out on the new heading. Leo began a series of visual scans, starting at the top of the window he was looking out of, then traveling down toward the bottom of the window in a series of stop-look-scan, stop-look-scan segments, then starting at the top again but shifted slightly in the direction of flight. Stopping and looking at the ground for brief moments was the best way to spot a target, because in continuous scanning, the human brain would fill in fine details of the terrain, so important details such as debris could be missed.

But after thirty minutes of searching both bearings they had computed, Patrick could tell Slotnick was getting frustrated. "How's it looking, Leo?" he asked.

"Nothing," Leo said. "It's clear as a bell, there's no vegetation or anything blocking the view, but I don't see anything—no smoke, no signs of disturbed ground, nothing."

"We're losing the ELT," John said. "The needle on the DF is just flopping around. Maybe we should go to the center of the grid and search from there."

"I'm not ready to give up on it just yet, John," Patrick said. "I think we had a good position. It's the best clue we've got. How are you doing back there, Leo? Need a break yet?"

"Five minutes would be good," Slotnick replied, rubbing his eyes.

"I'll start a right-expanding box search around the intersection of those two bearings," Patrick said. "You got it, John." John programmed the GPS receiver with the starting coordinates and a right-expanding-box-search pattern, then started his own search scan out the right window as Patrick reversed course and began flying the box-search pattern with shallow right-hand turns—Patrick had to make shallower turns because otherwise the lowered right wing would block John's view out the window.

Meanwhile, the ground team was approaching the original search reference point. The ground was muddy but drivable using four-wheel drive. "Okay, guys, we're coming up on the original intersection spot," David Bellville said to the others in the van. "The air team reports that the ELT signal is fading and might not be reliable, so we're going to proceed to the intersection spot and get ready to respond if the air team makes contact. While we're waiting, we'll search for any signs of a crash. Let's get sunscreened up and ready to go fast and hard."

Just then, they heard on the repeater radio: "Battle Mountain Hasty Team, this is CAP 2722, we're starting an orbit over a possible objective sighting, stand by." A moment later, John read off the geographic coordinates from the plane's GPS navigation device.

Bellville quickly plotted the coordinates on his county map. "About seven miles northeast," he said. "The Andorsen ranch. Do we have standing permission to go on their property, or do we need to give them a call first?"

"We have standing authorization," Fitzgerald said. "He's offered to lend us some of his ranch hands in the past—a stand-up guy. Want to head that way?"

"A-firm," Bellville said. He checked his portable GPS receiver. "Need a steer to the nearest gate, Fid?"

"I know every inch of this desert, Dave—I don't need no stinkin' GPS."

Bellville just shrugged and shook his head—he could never tell when Fitzgerald was kidding or not.

Several minutes later they reached the gate plotted on Fitzgerald's chart, only to find it padlocked. "It's locked!" Fitzgerald exclaimed. "Since when does Andorsen lock his remote gates?"

Bellville read the large sign mounted next to the gate. "It's not just a 'No Trespassing' sign—he's warning intruders of the use of deadly force! What's going on?"

"I don't know, but the CAP are not freakin' trespassers," Fitzgerald said. "We have standing permission to enter his property. Let's just cut the lock off and get going."

"We can't cut locks, Fid, and you know it," Bellville said. "But we do have standing permission, so I think we'll be okay if we climb the gate and go in on foot. Meanwhile we can have Battle Mountain Base call the Andorsens and have one of their hands drive us to the crash site."

"I'd rather just buy Mr. Andorsen a new padlock," Fitzgerald grumbled. But he turned to the cadets in the back: "Looks like we're going in on foot, guys. Let's hustle."

"Shallow up the bank angle a tad, Patrick . . . good, right there," John said. He had drawn a circle on the window with a grease pencil and was directing Patrick's orbit over his sighting so the object he was looking at stayed in the circle. Meanwhile, Leo had a pair of binoculars out and was scanning the area out the right-rear window in short cycles, being careful not to give himself vertigo. "Still can't make it out, but it's definitely not natural."

"I'll set up an orbit," Patrick said. "If it's a good target, your eyes will come back to it in the scan. Pick out details around it in case we have trouble picking it out."

"Roger."

"CAP 2722, this is Battle Mountain Hasty, we're inside the gate and en route to the contact," Fitzgerald radioed. "We had to go in on foot because the gate was locked, so we're about thirty minutes out. What do you got?"

"Still trying to make it out, Hasty," Patrick radioed back.

"Tell Slotnick to stop trying to superanalyze it and just report," Fitzgerald radioed impatiently. "First impression is always the best. Is it a crash or not?"

"Leo?"

"It looks like an abandoned pickup or some farm equipment, not a plane," Leo said, lowering the binoculars, clearing his eyes, then focusing again. "It's too small to be a plane." But his voice implied he still wasn't sure. "Can you go lower, Patrick?"

"Sure. I'll switch to a left orbit. John, eyes off the target, back me up on altitude and airspeed, and you got the radios. Report we're going to five hundred AGL for a closer look."

"Roger," John said. On the repeater, he radioed, "Battle Mountain Base, CAP 2722 leaving one thousand AGL for five hundred for a closer look at a target."

"Roger, 2722," Spara radioed back. "Advise when you're climbing back to patrol altitude."

"Wilco."

Patrick started a shallow descent while reversing the direction of orbit. He took a peek at what he was orbiting over every now and then while continuing to monitor his bank angle, altitude, and airspeed. "Still hard to tell," he said, "but I think you might be right, Leo—I don't think it's a plane."

"I'd expect our objective to not be busted up so bad if the ELT is still working," Leo said.

"Try not to create any expectations," Patrick offered. "We're looking for *evidence* of a downed plane, not a downed plane. Don't decide ahead of time what it's going to look like. Crashed airplanes almost never look like airplanes."

"Roger." Leo used his telescopic digital camera to study the scene. "Nah, looks like an old hay baler or something, with pieces of tarps lying around," he said. "We can go back up to patrol altitude, Patrick."

"Roger," Patrick said. "John, report that we're—"

"*Stand by!*" Leo suddenly shouted. "I saw a glint of a reflection, like off a windscreen! Possible target contact, eight o'clock!"

"Keep it in sight, Leo," Patrick said, forcing himself to not get too excited and forget about flying the plane—every mission had dozens of false sightings. "I'll do a shallow left turn and stay at five hundred."

Leo was straining to keep the target in sight out of the left-rear window. "It's about fifty yards south of the hay baler—I fixated on the hay baler and stopped scanning," he said. "It's lying on its left side. No wings, but the cockpit and cabin look in pretty good shape. Hot damn, I think we got it!"

"Everybody calm down and relax," Patrick said. "Let's stay heads-up and keep on doing our jobs until we set up an orbit around it. John . . ."

"Got it," John said. On the repeater, he radioed, "Battle Mountain Base, CAP 2722, maneuvering to investigate a possible target contact, remaining at five hundred AGL."

"Roger, 2722."

"Battle Mountain Hasty copies, and we have 2722 in sight on the horizon," Bellville radioed. "We're about twenty minutes away."

A few minutes later, Patrick had set up his orbit around a blue-and-white light aircraft. The belly was badly crumpled, as if it had pancaked in at a high rate of descent; the landing gear and wings were gone, and soon they saw that the engine and propeller were ripped off the fuselage too. "Call it in, John," Patrick said. "Good job, Leo."

"With pleasure, sir." On the repeater, John radioed, "Battle Mountain Base, CAP 2722 has made target contact, fuselage of a white-and-blue light plane, undercarriage, engine, propeller, and wings missing, no evidence of fire, no sign of any persons yet."

"I got one," Leo said as he snapped pictures. He saw the grisly sight of a body half protruding from the right side of the wind-shield, bent backward along the right side of the fuselage at a very unnatural angle. "I see one victim sticking out through the wind-shield." John called it in.

"Base, this is Hasty, we found a section of wing," Fitzgerald radioed a few minutes later. They passed by the crumpled piece of aluminum without stopping. "Marking the position. We're ten minutes out. We copy the report of a victim."

"Okay, guys, you heard it," David Bellville said, stopping to address his cadets and let them rest. Each member of the team was carrying his Seventy-Two Hour pack; Brad and Ron were carrying the canvas bag with the medical equipment, while Ralph and Michael were carrying the water and camping equipment. They all immediately doused their heads with water while David spoke: "We have at least one victim. Fid and I will check the scene first for survivors. If there are any, we'll have you come in, and you'll have to do your best to work around the victims. If there are no survivors, we'll photograph the scene, then talk about what we see until the rescue helicopter and sheriff arrive. No one has to go near the victims if you don't want to—"

"But doing so will teach you a lot and help you do your jobs in the future," Fitzgerald cut in. "We're not going to force you, but do a gut check right now and stay part of the team." Bellville looked at Fitzgerald, silently telling him to shut up, but he said nothing. Fitzgerald noticed the expression. "They're level twos, and McLanahan is a level one—they're expected to go on in and stay as a team." Again, Bellville said nothing. He actually agreed with Fitzgerald, but Civil Air Patrol regulations never required anyone to go near a crash scene with victims, especially cadets. After a few minutes, they continued on toward the circling Cessna in the distance.

Soon enough they arrived at the scene. Brad was surprised at how clean it looked—no postimpact fire, no billowing smoke, no big crater in the ground—just a white-and-blue piece of battered aluminum lying in the desert, as if someone had dragged it out there and discarded it rather than its falling from the sky. But soon they could also make out the person sticking through the windscreen.

"Oh, *man* . . ." Ralph whispered.

"Looks like it shot through the windshield, then got caught in the slipstream and bent all the way backward, still stuck in the glass," Ron said. "Wicked. Looks like a chick, too—all her clothes ripped off."

"Button it, Ron," Brad said quietly after he noticed Ralph's wide eyes and face almost drained of color. "Make yourself useful and take pictures of the scene." When Ron left, he turned to Ralph. "You can wait back here, Ralph."

"N-no, I want to help," the younger cadet said. "I'll get the medic gear ready just in case."

"Good idea," Brad said. "Keep hydrated and listen up on the radios."

"Yes, sir."

Brad grabbed his camera and approached the aircraft. It was indeed a woman protruding from the windscreen, he noticed, but she was so badly mangled by the crash and so completely covered with dirt and sand that she was hardly recognizable as human.

"McLanahan . . ." Bellville started.

"I'm okay, sir," Brad said. "Spivey is taking pictures, and Markham is back in the van getting the medical kit out."

Bellville nodded, giving silent approval to stay.

"Good on you, McLanahan," Fitzgerald said. "It's part of the job." He continued his careful inspection of the aircraft. "I see the pilot underneath," he said. "Looks like he's been crushed." He bent down for a closer look. "I've seen victims look worse than this who were still alive, but he has no head that I can see."

Brad decided to stay on the right side of the fuselage—he wanted to participate, he told himself, but only if the victim needed help, which obviously that one did not—but in reality, he admitted finally, he just didn't want to see a crushed human body. The dead woman sticking out through the windscreen was pretty horrible too, but he wasn't afraid—he just felt sorry for her.

"Can you see an ELT shutoff switch in there, Brad?" Bellville asked.

"Stand by, sir." Brad strained to look behind the front passenger seat, which had left its rails, and scan the instrument panel. Most newer planes had a manual-activation and shutoff switch for the emergency-locator transmitter. "I can't see one, sir, but the left side of the panel is pretty busted up." He apprehensively looked in the rear of the plane, expecting to see yet another horrific sight . . . but he didn't see what he expected. "Sir?"

"Yeah, Brad?"

"The third soul is missing."

"What?" Fitzgerald asked.

"The third passenger is missing, sir."

Fitzgerald looked at Bellville, and Bellville turned to Brad. Brad immediately understood his silent command. "Sergeant Markham!" he shouted.

"Sir?" Markham replied immediately.

"Examine the area around the plane for a child's tracks, then organize a line search immediately."

There was a brief hesitation, but a few moments later he heard Markham reply, "Yes, sir!" and Markham trotted over. He was careful not to step any closer to the plane than he needed to, but now that he was there, he was frozen in place, uncertain as to what to do next.

"You know exactly what to do, Ralph," Brad said quietly so the senior members couldn't hear. "Think about it, then verbalize what you need to do." Markham was still unsure. "Let's get with it, Sergeant," he said, a little louder this time. "We have a missing child. Tell me what you want to do."

Ralph still seemed confused, but that slowly seemed to fade away. "Lieutenant Spivey!" he shouted.

"What do you want, Markham?" Ron shouted from across the crash scene.

"Pr-prepare a go-pack for a line search," Ralph said rather weakly. "St-stand clear of the—"

"I can't understand what the heck you're saying, Marky."

Ralph looked at Brad, silently imploring for help, but Brad said nothing—he just looked back at Ralph, telling him without words that he had to take charge, and do it quickly. "I . . . Lieutenant, I need you to—"

"I'm busy over here, Marky," Spivey said. "Don't bug me right now, okay?"

Brad looked at Bellville, who shook his head, silently telling Brad to take charge and get the search going. But just as Brad was going to speak, Ralph shook his head, looked over at Spivey, inflated his lungs to full volume, then shouted, "Lieutenant Spivey, get a go-pack and stretcher ready for a line search, *right now*! And don't you screw up any tracks in my crash scene!"

"What?"

"You heard him, Lieutenant," Brad said. "This is an actual line search for a missing boy. Sergeant Markham is in charge." Ron was still standing there, confused. Brad finally went over to him and said impatiently in a low voice, "Jeez, Ron, what's your major malfunction? Ralph is trying to set up a line search to find the third victim and get his tracking sign-off. The seniors are waiting. Get with the program, would you? This is not an exercise."

Ron finally seemed to catch on. He nodded at Brad, then said, "Well, why didn't you say so, Sergeant? I'll get the medical go-pack."

"Okay, Sergeant, we've wasted enough time," Brad said. "Sing out. What do you see?"

"Stand by, sir," Ralph said. He quickly scanned the ground, starting at the right-side door. "The plane obviously slid quite a distance, judging by the smooth sand. I see your footprints right near the door . . . and I see a smaller set, soft-soled, not combat boots, and not as deeply set. Could be a child's footprint." He scanned the area. "They . . . they lead toward the victim in the windshield, close but perhaps not within touching distance, then . . ." He looked around, almost in a panic. "The prints are gone. I don't see them anymore. I lost him."

Ralph was obviously starting to panic a bit. "Easy, Ralph," Brad said. "They couldn't have just disappeared. What's the boy thinking right now? Put yourself in his place." He could see Ralph's eyes grow large in horror and his lower lip tremble a bit. "Verbalize, Sergeant. We're not mind readers." The young cadet hesitated, his mind's eye still filled with a horrific image of his own making. "You can do it, Ralph."

"N-no, I can't," he said.

Brad nodded. "It's okay, Ralph," he said. "This is an actual, and it's a bad one. We'll wait for a SAREX or encampment to get your sign-off. No worries. Ron, take Ralph's place and conduct the search."

Just as Spivey started to move forward, the younger cadet said, "No . . . no, I'll do it, sir."

"You sure?" Brad asked.

Ralph looked at Brad warily, then nodded his head and looked off into the distance. "He's . . . he's just seen his dead mother," he said in a low voice after a short silence. He closed his eyes and took a deep breath, immersing himself again in the image of the crash scene coalescing in his mind. "He's probably already seen his dead father. Maybe he tried to awaken him, then realized he was dead. He didn't recognize his mom at first, but he can tell something awful has happened to her. He climbed out of the plane. Now he can see his mom, or what's left of her. He's scared and alone, surrounded by death. They were . . . were swatted out of the sky by the angel of death, but he somehow survived, and . . . and he's wondering how? Why? Why was I allowed to survive—"

"For Christ's sake, Ralph," Ron said perturbedly, "let's not get so *Twilight* here, okay?"

Brad held up a hand to silence his friend. "He's doing it his way, Ron," he said. He turned to Ralph. "What else do you see, Ralph? What's happening?"

"He didn't stay with the plane," Markham said curiously. "Why wouldn't he stay? The plane wasn't on fire, and except for the farm equipment, there's no sign of civilization within sight. His parents are dead, but they are still his parents. Why didn't he stay? Why . . . ?"

Ralph swallowed, and Brad saw a tear run down his cheek. "He thinks it's his fault his parents are dead," he said weakly. "He's running because he's scared and . . . and he doesn't want to be found."

"What?"

"He thinks it's *his* fault," Ralph repeated. "He thinks he'll get in trouble, maybe be arrested and put in jail if he's found, so he ran and now he's . . . he's hiding."

"What a load of crap," Ron sneered.

"We need a direction, Ralph," Brad said after shooting Ron another "shut up" glance.

Ralph scanned the ground, his head darting back and forth—Brad thought he looked like a golden retriever hunting for a faint scent. Finally, Ralph looked toward the west, away from the hay baler, and held out his arms out to his sides. "This way, sir," he said. "Away from the crash site and civilization."

"Verbalize what you want, Sergeant," Brad prompted him again.

"Line abreast, six paces between," Ralph shouted. He got out his compass and took a bearing on a distant mountain peak. "Initial bearing will be two-six-zero."

"Let's go," Bellville said. They lined up, with Brad in the middle.

"Make a report to the air team, sir," Ralph said. "We may have a survivor that doesn't want to be found—that'll make it more difficult."

"Good call," Bellville said, impressed with the young cadet's procedures and growing confidence. He pulled out his portable FM radio. "CAP 2722 and Battle Mountain Base, this is Battle Mountain Hasty, we're beginning a line search for the third soul, a boy. We believe he's running and may be hiding from searchers. Initial heading from the crash site will be two-six-zero."

"How confident are you in that bearing, Hasty?" Rob Spara radioed from base.

Bellville looked at Ralph, then smiled and nodded. "Very confident," he replied.

"Very well, proceed," Spara radioed. "CAP 2722, suggest you begin an expanding-square search just in case that's not a good bearing."

"Two-seven-two-two copies," Patrick radioed from the Cessna orbiting overhead. John programmed the GPS aboard the plane to begin the search from the crash site, which would describe a square-shaped pattern that started at the crash site and got larger after each leg was completed.

Meanwhile, on the ground, the team began to move westward, staying roughly in line and carefully scanning the ground. After about a hundred yards, Ron shouted, "I spot a sneaker, and it looks fairly clean. How about that? Marky guessed right."

"Good call, Ralph," Brad said.

"Is it a left or right sneaker?" Ralph asked.

"What the hell difference does that make?" Ron asked.

"He'll be favoring the other foot, which means he might start turning in that same direction," Ralph said. "He'll be taking longer strides with his right foot, which means he'll be turning left."

"Where'd you learn that, Marky—on a cornflakes box, or from a comic book?" Ron sneered.

Ralph looked hurt and didn't reply, which made Brad immediately come to his defense, although he had never heard of that theory either: "It makes sense," Brad said. "Which is it, Ron?"

"The left one, O great white lucky-ass tracker," Ron replied.

"Alter the track ten degrees to the left," Ralph said. "New bearing two-five-zero. Sir, radio the search plane that we have found an artifact from a survivor, we are altering the search track to two-five-zero, and recommend they switch to a creeping-line search along that track." The creeping-line search would fly one mile on either side of the track, going back and forth away from where the sneaker was found.

"Roger that, Sergeant," Bellville said, after a slightly stunned nod of his head and an impressed smile.

"Way to kick butt, guys," Patrick said cross-cockpit. On intercom he said: "We're switching to a creeping-line search, one mile each side of track, quarter-mile spacing—the ground team found a sneaker along the track they predicted." John reprogrammed the GPS for the new search pattern. A creeping-line search was a series of turns perpendicular to the search bearing, moving outward along the search bearing from a known point such as a crash site, road, or runway—useful when a target's direction of movement or travel was known.

"Fitzgerald brought his A-game today," Leo commented.

"It's not Fid—Cadet Sergeant Markham is leading this search," Patrick said.

"You mean 'Little Marky'?"

"You bet," Patrick said. "He may act a little mousy now, but he's sharp as a freakin' tack. I predict 'Little Marky' may be leading this squadron in a few years."

Reno-Tahoe International Airport

That same time

"Cactus Two-Zero-Three-Three, Reno Approach, roger," the air traffic controller radioed after receiving the check-in call from an inbound airliner. "Descend and maintain one-three-thousand feet, Reno altimeter three-zero-zero-one. There's VFR traffic inbound to Reno at your eight o'clock, six miles, primary target only, and I'm not talking to him yet, so I'll have to keep you a little high for now."

"Three-three passing seventeen descending to thirteen," the airliner first officer responded. "Negative contact on the traffic."

The controller hit a button on his panel that connected him instantly to Oakland Center controllers: "Oakland, Reno Approach, I'm looking at a primary target fifteen miles southeast of Mustang. He's doing about two-sixty. Was he talking to you and missed a handoff?"

"Stand by, Reno," the other controller responded. A moment later: "Negative, Reno, everybody's checked in."

"Copy, thanks, JT," the Reno controller said. He punched a button for his supervisor, and a moment later the shift supervisor came over and plugged his headset into the console. The controller pointed to his screen: "Ted, this guy is blasting straight in for the runway and he's not talking to anyone," he said. "I'm going to have to send this Southwest flight into holding over Mustang and back up the other inbound GA flights until he's clear."

"Did you try raising him in the clear and on GUARD?" the supervisor asked.

"That was my next move." The controller hit a button on his console that allowed him to talk both on his assigned frequency and on the UHF and VHF GUARD emergency frequencies. "Aircraft on the one-five-zero-degree radial and fifteen DME from Mustang, airspeed two-six-zero, heading two-eight-zero, this is

Reno Approach Control on GUARD," he radioed. "If you can hear me, turn to a heading of one-eight-zero to remain clear of Reno Class-C airspace and contact me on this channel or switch to one-one-niner-point-two. There is traffic at your two o'clock position, less than four miles." No reply; he repeated the instructions several times, in between vectoring other traffic away from the unidentified airplane. "No answer, Ted," the controller told his supervisor. "He's going to bust right through the Class C."

"Everyone out of his way?"

"Yes."

"What do you think he'll do?"

"He's got to be NORDO or a pinch hitter," the controller replied. NORDO meant "no radio," meaning the pilot was unable to talk to anyone on the radios; a "pinch hitter" was someone other than a pilot at the controls. "I'm betting he'll see the runways Reno or Stead and try to make a landing, or just circle and decide what to do."

"This is not good," the supervisor said. "He could close us down for hours." He punched a button on the console: "Tower, TF, we've got a NORDO inbound, about eleven miles to the southeast."

"We've got him on the scope," the Reno Tower controller responded. "He's at seven thousand eight hundred and level, just southeast of Dayton Valley."

"We've got him at two-fifty knots airspeed now."

"Same up here."

"Okay, I've got the Southwest flight set up to orbit over Mustang, and I'll keep all of the other inbounds outside of the Class C until this guy either calls or zooms through," the approach controller said. "I'm hoping he'll see a runway and go for it."

"I'll activate the crash net here and at Stead, just in case," the tower controller said. "This could be a mess."

Carl was relying on the King Air's autopilot and his extensive rehearsals for the last few minutes of this mission, because his vision was all but gone and the cramps in his stomach and back were making it impossible to concentrate on flying. He had flown this route a hundred times in the past couple months, using desktop-PC flight simulators and Google Earth to study the terrain and obstructions.

Once clear of the mountains around Virginia City southeast of Reno, Carl started a slow descent to 4,600 feet, just a hundred feet above the Truckee Meadows. Letting the autopilot handle the flying tasks for now, he used the socket wrench to start loosening the bolts atop the large canister in the aisle beside him. The ground crew must have already loosened the bolts, because they were easier to turn than he anticipated, especially in his weakened state. There were a dozen bolts securing the top; he managed to remove half of them before he had to turn his full attention to flying.

Only seconds to go now . . .

"Holy shit!" the tower controller cried, and he involuntarily ducked his head as the King Air zoomed past, missing the control tower by less than two hundred yards, flying no higher than the tower cab itself. It was in a slight left turn and appeared to be maneuvering to stay away from both the control tower and the Grand Sierra Resort casino just north of the field. "Is that pilot *insane?*" He picked up the telephone handset marked *CRASH.* "Aircraft is overflying the field at about a hundred feet AGL, heading northwest at two hundred knots, gear and flaps retracted. He missed the tower by less than a couple hundred feet! Somebody call the police and fire departments—if that guy doesn't climb, he's going to hit something right in downtown Reno."

Once he was past the control tower, the Grand Sierra Resort, and the Peppermill Casino, there were no other tall buildings or obstacles around him until reaching his objective. The lid was loosened as much as he could loosen it on the canister, and he could feel something that felt like an exposed lightbulb being held close to the right side of his face.

The mission could not have gone better. All of his preflight preparation, study, and careful consideration of every possible problem ensured success. After the series of bad thunderstorms threatened to cancel the mission, the weather cooperated. Even the old autopilot on this bird worked. The Lord was indeed guiding him, endorsing this mission with great weather and working components, and allowing him to live long enough to see the mission's end.

The target was in sight. It was the first high-rise structure he would encounter on this heading in the downtown Reno area, so he wouldn't have to weave around other buildings, and its distinctive curved shape made it easy to spot. The coordinates he had programmed into the GPS—refined, remeasured, and triple-checked several times over the past few months—were dead on, but he still put his hands on the control yoke, not to correct for any errors but so he could feel the autopilot's servos making tiny corrections in the plane's heading . . .

. . . and then Carl noticed through his cataract-infested eyes the blinking yellow "AP" light on the instrument panel and realized that *the autopilot had disconnected itself*! He didn't remember doing it. But how in the world could the plane have flown so precisely by itself? He was certainly in no condition to sit upright, let alone fly an airplane!

It was as if God Himself were steering his weapon of war, he decided. This truly was a message that his was indeed a blessed mission, ordained by God. The war was on, and God was indeed on their side.

One last task. He switched to the Reno control tower frequency, pressed the "XMIT" button, and spoke: "Live free or die. The Lord has spoken."

Northwest of Battle Mountain, Nevada

That same time

They had walked another two hundred yards or so in the new direction without any more signs. "Whaddaya say, Marky?" Ron Spivey shouted. "We got nothing. We should've stayed on that original track. Now we need to start over."

Brad looked at Ralph Markham. "Sergeant?"

Ralph appeared indecisive, but only for a few moments: "Another hundred yards," he said. Ron groaned. Ralph made some quick calculations in his head. "Then we'll turn right to three-four-zero, go for . . . for forty paces, turn back to one-seven-zero, and search back toward the crash site."

"Where in heck did you come up with all that, Marky?" Ron asked. "Why do we have to do all that?"

"He's putting us back on the reciprocal of the original search bearing," Brad explained with a smile. "The one-in-sixty rule. We go out six hundred feet and change heading ten degrees, so we've offset ourselves one hundred feet, or about forty paces. Ralph's plan should put us right back to where we found the sneaker, on the original search bearing."

"So why don't we just do that now?" Ron asked.

"Because I want to search another hundred yards on this bearing," Ralph said. "Line up and let's go."

Ron rolled his eyes in exasperation but did as he was told.

Brad was starting to get a little tired slogging through the damp, uneven ground, and he could feel the sunburn building on the back of his unprotected neck. The terrain was getting a bit more rolling, and now they came across a wide wash that had a thin rivulet of water flowing through it from the recent thunderstorms. This last hundred yards was going to be tougher than the previous two hundred.

"I say we jog now, before we have to cross this wash," Ron said.

"It's not so bad," Ralph said. "Just sixty more yards."

Ron said something under his breath but pushed on.

Every now and then Brad would glance up at the search plane overhead. He was so close to becoming a senior member and flying that plane, he could almost taste it. Ground-team work was okay, but where he really belonged was . . .

Just as he descended from the wash's embankment and started to look for the best place to cross the water, something made Brad turn around . . . and there, half buried in the embankment, covered in dust, mud, and insects, was a young boy!

RENO, NEVADA

A SHORT TIME LATER

"We are at the scene of a horrible airplane crash here at the Bruce R. Thompson United States Courthouse and Federal Building in downtown Reno," the female reporter began. "The crash happened about fifteen minutes ago and is the worst air accident in Reno's history. My cameraman Jerry Fleck is with me and he'll be providing you shots of this unfolding tragedy."

The camera panned to the southeast face of the building. Thick smoke and flames were still shooting out of the hole in the building, and the entire structure appeared to be tilting away from the camera. "As you can see, the plane hit almost directly in the center of the ten-story building here on the four-hundred block of South Virginia Street," the reporter went on. "We do not know who the pilot was, how many passengers he had on board, or what kind of plane hit the building, although some observers say it is a medium-size turboprop used mostly by small companies. We have a call in to air traffic controllers at the Reno-Tahoe International Airport to find out if they were in contact with the pilot and what could have caused this terrible accident.

"We have been told that the fire department has just upped the response to this accident with a fifth alarm. The plane did not appear to crash all the way through the building, but the force of its impact blew out its north and northwest sides, spreading fire and debris onto the Bank of America office complex across Virginia Street, the U.S. Bank office building across Liberty Street, and onto residents and visitors on the streets below. Fortunately, most workers were not in those buildings during the weekend. The police have cordoned off two blocks in all directions, and they ask that you should not try to come downtown for any reason and allow police, firefighters, medical personnel, and investigators to do their jobs."

The reporter touched her earpiece to listen closer, then said breathlessly, "I have just been given word by my producer, John Ramos, in the truck that, according to a spokesman for the FAA air traffic control facility at the Reno airport, an aircraft called a Beech King Air, which is a medium-size civilian turboprop air-craft, overflew the airport minutes ago at very high speed and very low altitude. We must conclude that it was the same airplane that hit the Thompson Federal Building. There is no speculation from the FAA as to whether the plane was trying to land at the airport and the pilot became disoriented, or if this was a deliberate act. It is simply too early to—"

The reporter stopped and again listened into her earpiece while the camera moved away from her and zoomed in on the shat-tered building. Off-camera, she said in a whisper, "What do you mean, we're getting out of here? We're two blocks away—it's safe! We're . . . John? John?" A moment later, a man wearing head-phones ran up to the reporter and pulled her away, briefly crossing in front of the camera. "John, *what are you doing?* I'm on the air!"

"I know you are," the man said. "We're getting out of here, *now*! Jerry, pack it up!"

"I'm not going anywhere!" the reporter whispered angrily. "This is the biggest story of my life! I'm staying with it for as long as—" The producer whispered something in the reporter's ear as he dragged her toward the crew's truck. "What? What did you say, John?"

"Radioactivity!" he replied.

"What . . . !"

The producer grabbed the microphone. "U.S. Secret Service investigators have detected large levels of radioactivity at the crash site," he said. "The plane that crashed into the Thompson Federal Building was carrying some sort of nuclear device or weapon. The entire downtown district of Reno is being evacuated."

TWO

Youth is wholly experimental.

—Robert Louis Stevenson

Northwest of Battle Mountain, Nevada

That same time

"Holy crap . . . contact! Contact! Over here!" Brad shouted excitedly.

The boy, huddled in the embankment of the desert wash, made a sound that was a combination of a howl, scream, and moan, and he tried to scamper to his feet. Brad rushed over to him. "Easy, guy, easy," he said. "I'm with the Civil Air Patrol. We're here to take you home."

"No! No! I don't have a home! I don't have *anyone!*" the boy shouted in a hoarse, cracking voice. Brad started brushing ants and beetles off the poor boy's face and arms as Fitzgerald and Bellville rushed over. His head and face were covered with a combination of mud, sand, and blood, his lips and eyes were swollen and blistered, both feet were bare and badly cut up, and he appeared to have a broken right arm. "You're here to arrest me! Get away from me!"

"No one's going to arrest you," Brad said. He pulled out a bottle of water and started pouring it over the boy's head, trying to wash the horrific muck from his scratched, sunburned face. "We're going to get you out of here."

"Battle Mountain Base and CAP 2722, this is Hasty, we've located the third person, and he's *alive*," Bellville radioed happily. He turned to Markham. "Great job, Ralph." He pulled out his GPS receiver and started copying their location's geographic coordinates to relay to responders, then said to the others, "C'mon, guys, you have a victim that needs first aid. Let's get busy and help him until the medevac helicopter and sheriff arrive."

"The cadets are doing an outstanding job—I think they can help this survivor just fine," Fitzgerald said with a rare smile on his face. "Spivey, Markham, get busy and help McLanahan."

The cadets donned rubber gloves and got out their first-aid kits. "Assessment first, guys," Brad said. "What do we got?"

"He's pretty messed up," Ron said. "Looks like a drowned rat."

"Real helpful, Ron," Brad said. "Ralph?"

"Airway is open, he's breathing, but he's bleeding from somewhere," Ralph said, going through the ABCs of first aid—airway, breathing, and circulation. Starting at the top, he examined the boy's head. "What's your name?" he asked. The boy didn't answer, but looked at Ralph with relief. "Can you tell me your name?"

"J-Jeremy," the boy said finally, allowing himself to trust the younger boy rather than the older ones. "Jeremy Post."

"Hi, Jeremy. I'm Ralph." He nodded over his shoulder toward the others as he worked. "That's Brad, that's Ron, and the adults are David and Michael. We're with the Civil Air Patrol from Battle Mountain, and we're here to help you. I'm going to look at your head. Tell me if it hurts." Jeremy didn't say anything, but winced as Ralph pressed. "Possible fractured skull in the forehead area," he said. He pulled out a flashlight and checked Jeremy's eyes. "Left pupil is blown and unresponsive. Possible concussion." He smiled at Jeremy. "You're hurt, Jeremy, but you must be a pretty tough kid to come all this way without your sneakers. We're going to get you to a hospital and have the docs take a look at you."

"I don't want to go to a hospital."

"I don't blame you, Jeremy—I don't like hospitals either," Brad said, kneeling beside the boy. "But you're hurt pretty bad. We're going to make sure you get fixed up." Jeremy started to sob. "Don't worry, Jeremy. You'll be okay."

"But my folks . . . my mom and dad . . ."

Brad nodded and clasped the boy's shoulder as Ralph continued his examination, thankful for the distracting conversation. "We're going to make sure they're taken good care of, Jeremy," Brad said.

"They're dead, aren't they?" Jeremy whispered.

"Yeah," Brad said. He remembered what Ralph had said when the search began and added, "But it's not your fault."

"I shouldn't have been talking," Jeremy said. "I should've kept quiet. My dad always told me not to talk at certain times in the flight, and I did, and we crashed. It's *my* fault."

"No, it wasn't your fault," Brad said. Ralph was right, Brad realized: Jeremy blamed himself for the crash, and he was so afraid of being punished that he ran off across the desert, hoping never to be found. "The weather was pretty bad in-flight, wasn't it?"

"Yes."

"What were you trying to tell your dad?"

"That . . . that the compass was twirling and the ball was all the way to the right," Jeremy said. "I could see the altitude indicator, and it was twisting around. We were in a spin, but my dad was too busy to notice it, so I tried to tell him."

Brad smiled. "Are you a pilot?"

"I'm too young," Jeremy said, "but I want to be a pilot. My dad lets me fly all the time, and I've watched a lot of his flying training videos and played his flight simulator on his computer."

"That means you're almost a pilot," Brad said. "I'm almost a pilot too."

"You *are*? Have you soloed?"

"Not yet, but soon, I hope," Brad said. "So you know what I think? I think your warning helped your dad spot the spin and correct it in time to make a controlled crash landing."

"But my mom and dad are dead."

"Yes," Brad said in a soft but firm voice, "but he saved the plane in time to save you, didn't he?" Jeremy lowered his head and nodded, then started to weep quietly. Brad thought there had been enough talking about his dead parents, so he looked over at Ralph. "All done with the assessment, Ralph?"

"Yes, sir," Ralph replied. "Possible concussion, possible fractured forehead, broken right arm, multiple contusions and lacerations all over his body, dehydration, sunburn, and insect bites." He smiled at Jeremy. "But he's one tough kid, that's for sure. He'd make a good CAP cadet."

Bellville was writing all of it down. "Good work, Ralph," he said. "I'll call it in and update the medevac helicopter's ETA."

"Let's get Jeremy out of the wash and protected from the sun," Fitzgerald said. "Then we'll have to pick out a landing zone for the chopper."

Bellville keyed the mike on his portable FM repeater transceiver: "Battle Mountain Base, this is Hasty, I've got a medical report for the EMTs inbound," he said. "Also requesting ETA for the medevac helicopter."

"Stand by, Hasty," Spara replied.

"Hasty, this is CAP 2722," Patrick radioed. "We've just been ordered by the FAA to land immediately!"

"*Land?* What for?"

"Guys, you won't believe this, but they're clearing out *all* the airspace over the U.S.—the FAA is ordering all planes to land!" Patrick exclaimed. "Every aircraft has to be on the ground within fifteen minutes or they risk being intercepted!"

"It sounds like freakin' 9/11 again!" Fitzgerald said. The cadets wore blank expressions on their faces. They were young when the Islamist terror attacks of 9/11 had occurred. Even though they saw videos of the collapsing World Trade Center towers, the hole in the Pentagon, and the crash site of United Airlines Flight 93 in Shanksville, Pennsylvania, they had little appreciation for the true sense of horror that gripped the nation that day and for several months beyond.

"The wing is talking with the FAA and the National Operations Center," Spara radioed. "They can make an exception for CAP flights and medical emergencies." But several minutes later, the news was not good: "No exceptions until the airspace is cleared, and then FAA will clear flights only on IFR flight plans," Spara said. "It's chaos out there. We'd better do what they say before the fighters start launching. RTB right away, Patrick."

"To hell with that, sir," Patrick said. "We've got a survivor and a Hasty strike team out in the middle of nowhere, and it'll be dark in a couple hours." He thought for a moment; then: "I'll land at the Andorsens' dirt strip and get help from them."

"We tried calling Andorsen to get permission for us to drive onto his property—there was no answer."

"Then I'll land, find a vehicle, and do it myself."

"You can't do that, Patrick," Spara said. "The Hasty team will be fine until the sheriff and an ambulance makes it out there. RTB, *now.*"

"I can go back to the van, cut off the lock on the gate, and drive the van back," Fitzgerald radioed.

"Everybody, just shut up for a minute," Spara said. "I'm not going to split up a ground team, especially with a survivor with them. Dave, prepare to keep the survivor comfortable until help arrives. Keep your team *together.* Patrick, RTB *right now.*"

"I won't make it back to Battle Mountain in time to meet the deadline, Rob," Patrick said. "The closest landing strip is the Andorsen ranch. I'm heading that way now."

"Negative, McLanahan," Spara said. "Return to base. We'll advise ATC of your destination and ETA."

Patrick reached up and shut off the FM radio. "Damn FM," he said on intercom. "It's so old, it goes out all the time, just when you really need it." He looked around at John and Leo. "Doesn't it?"

John looked back at Leo, then turned at Patrick and shrugged. "It seemed to be working fine, and all of a sudden—poof, it went out," he said.

"And that's not all," Leo said. "I distinctly heard that engine running a little rough all of a sudden."

"I was going to mention that too," John said with a smile.

"Well then, we'd better get this thing on the ground and check it out," Patrick said. He looked around outside for his landmarks, then made a turn to the right. "I have the Andorsen ranch strip in sight. I think we should land there immediately. And while we're waiting for further assistance, we can help the ground team."

"Sounds like a good plan, sir," Leo said.

John patted Patrick on the shoulder, smiled, and nodded. "That's the Patrick S. McLanahan I've always heard about," he said. "Looks like the Mac is back."

After making a low pass over the strip to check for any hazards—it was by far the nicest dirt strip any of them had ever seen, as clean, flat, and straight as an asphalt runway—Patrick landed the Cessna. Being careful to keep the power up and the control yoke back without braking, all to avoid digging the nose tire into the dirt, he taxied over to the parking area next to two fuel tanks and a storage-and-pump building. Beside the fuel farm was a half-mile-long asphalt road leading to what looked like the main house; on the other side of the asphalt road was an aircraft hangar.

"Nice little airport Andorsen's got here," John commented.

"Andorsen owns a large percentage of the land in northern Nevada not owned by the government," Leo said. "He's probably got a half dozen of these private airstrips scattered all over the state. They may be dirt, but they're built to handle a bizjet. Ever meet him? Great guy. Throws parties and fund-raisers for law enforcement all the time."

After climbing out of the plane, Patrick searched around and found a bicycle propped up next to the pump building. "I'll be back as quick as I can," he said, and he pedaled toward the main house.

The main house was a large, attractive, single-story building with a comfortable-looking wraparound porch, surrounded by desert landscaping. A three-car garage was adjacent, and a pickup truck was parked beside it. The place was deserted except for a couple dogs that came up to him, sniffed, decided he was no threat, and went back to search for some shade. Patrick knocked on the door and waited for an answer—nothing. He went over and looked through a window into the garage and saw one Hummer SUV inside, along with a dressed-out Harley-Davidson Road King and Harley Softail Deluxe motorcycle, all in immaculate condition considering they were in the middle of the desert. The garage was locked. Patrick then went to the pickup and found it unlocked and the keys tucked in the driver's-side sun visor—perfect. He pulled his Form 104 mission briefing card out of a flight-suit pocket, wrote the phone number of the Battle Mountain squadron on it, stuck it in the front door of the house, then started up the pickup and drove back to the airstrip.

"No one home?" Leo asked.

"No," Patrick said, "but I'll bet he's got security cameras all over the place, so I'd expect someone will be along shortly. I left my Form 104 in his door. Grab the survival kit and your flight bags and let's go." They pulled the twenty-five-pound orange survival kit and their personal flight bags from the plane, along with all the bottles of water they had in the cockpit. Patrick found tie-downs and secured the plane, and they clambered into the pickup, with

Patrick driving. All three crewmembers had small portable GPS receivers in their flight bags, so it was simple for them to punch in the coordinates of the ground team to get a bearing and distance, and they headed off across the desert.

The long, bumpy, dusty drive was less than fifteen miles but lasted almost an hour. It was getting dark and decidedly cooler by the time they reached the ground team. Patrick was surprised when Bradley ran over to the truck and wrapped his arms around his father as soon as he stepped out of the pickup. "Dad!" he exclaimed. "You're here!"

Patrick hugged him tightly in return—it had been a long, long time since they had embraced like that. "I'm glad you're okay, Brad," he said in a low voice. He took a look at his son's sunburned, dust-streaked face and smiled, remarking to himself how much taller and more mature he looked just since they spoke back at the base a few hours ago. "You've had a really big day, haven't you, big guy? Congratulations on finding the survivor."

"Colonel Spara is *really* pissed at you," Brad said with a wide grin. "I don't think he stopped yelling on the radio until a few minutes ago."

"I wasn't going to leave my son out here in the desert," Patrick said in a whisper. "The colonel is wacky if he thought I'd just fly back to base and leave you behind." They walked back to Bellville and Fitzgerald. The cadets had set up two dome-shaped tents. They had been eating from self-heating bags of military MREs when they arrived, but now they excitedly ran over to the newcomers. The survivor was resting on a stretcher, covered with a silver space blanket, his head and face bandaged. "Is that the *survivor,* Dave?" Patrick said to David Bellville with surprise after shaking hands. "The sheriff hasn't shown up yet?"

"No, and we don't know what the delay is," Bellville said. "I can't believe you landed out here, sir."

"*I* can believe it," Fitzgerald said, striding up and pumping Pat-

rick's hand enthusiastically. "Damn commanders always kowtow-
ing to the regs and ignoring the real situation on the ground. But
not this guy!" He thumped Patrick on the shoulder hard enough
to tilt him onto one foot. "This is Patrick freakin' McLanahan, the
guy who kicked the Russians' butts after the American Holocaust.
He wasn't about to leave his mates behind. About time someone
said to hell with the damn book and looked out for his troops."
He turned to Spivey and Markham and jabbed a thumb toward
Patrick. "He's a real war hero, you guys, and don't you forget it."

"Thanks, Fid," Patrick said. "Dave, how's the survivor?"

Bellville turned to Markham. "Ralph?"

"His name is Jeremy, sir," Ralph said. "Same condition as previously reported. We're letting him sleep but waking him every hour
or so as a precaution because of his possible concussion. He's alert
and responsive. He hasn't eaten but has had a little water."

Patrick was very impressed, and now he wished he spent more
time with the cadets than he normally did: this cadet was extraor-
dinarily bright. "Thank you, Ralph," he said. "Good report."

"Thank you, sir," Ralph said. "I'll go back and watch over him."
Again, Patrick was impressed.

Bellville held up his portable FM transceiver. "Colonel wants to
talk to you, sir."

Patrick nodded, then walked away from the group before key-
ing the mike: "McLanahan here."

"McLanahan, I am going to kick your ass when you get back
here—I don't care if you are a retired three-star general," Spara
said angrily. "Did you deliberately shut off the repeater?"

"Something happened to it, Rob. We can discuss it when I get
back."

"You violated your flight release and landed at another airport
without permission."

"Leo and John both said they thought they heard the engine
running rough. I made a precautionary landing at the first avail-

able airport. Besides, I'm allowed to land at different airports as long as I don't alter the crew composition."

"Not on an actual mission you can't," Spara shouted. "And *was* the engine running rough? *You're* the damned mission pilot, not Leo!"

"We can discuss that face-to-face too, Rob."

"Jesus," Spara breathed. "You know you were on the hook for that plane and the lives of your crew the minute you touched down on Andorsen's ranch, don't you? Except in an emergency, if you're off the flight release during an actual mission, you might as well have stolen the plane."

"We were ordered by the FAA to land immediately," Patrick said. "If I didn't and tried to return to Battle Mountain, I would have risked being intercepted and shot down. I think I made the better decision, don't you?"

"It won't be up to me—it'll be up to the regional commander, maybe the national commander or even the Air Force," Spara said. "They're likely to boot us all out of CAP."

"I'm fine, the crew is fine, the ground team is fine, Jeremy the survivor is fine, and the plane is fine, thanks for asking, Rob," Patrick deadpanned.

"Why, you son of a b—" Spara began . . . but then he started to chuckle. A moment later: "All right, hotshot, I'm glad you're all fine," he said.

"Thank you. What's going on with the sheriff's department?"

"No idea yet," Spara said wearily. "They keep telling me someone's been dispatched, but that's all they'll tell me."

"I have one of Andorsen's trucks."

"So you stole a vehicle too? Great," Spara said even more wearily than before. "Oh well, might as well go out with a bang. How long did it take you to drive out to the ground team?"

"About an hour."

"It'll be dark soon. We'll stick with the original plan: camp out tonight and await the sheriff and ambulance or medevac helicopter."

"What's happened? Why is the FAA shutting down airspace?"

"It's unbelievable, Patrick: it looks like a terrorist flew a plane filled with nuclear material into the federal building in Reno."

"Nuclear material!"

"They're ordering the evacuation of one hundred thousand residents of Reno," Spara went on. "The downtown part of the city is completely empty."

"Was it a bomb?"

"They're starting to report now that it might have been just a large amount of low-grade medical radioactive waste," Spara replied. "But no one is believing that yet. They're showing video of thousands of people madly running or driving like crazy in a full-throttle panic, as far away as Las Vegas and Sacramento. Same all across the country: people are fleeing any cities that have federal office buildings."

"My God . . ." Patrick thought of his family in Sacramento, friends in Las Vegas and Houston, and colleagues in Washington—and, selfishly he realized, he was thankful he and Bradley were out in the middle of nowhere in north-central Nevada.

"I expect the panic to subside quickly as long as there's not any more attacks," Spara said. "As soon as the airspace is reopened, I imagine CAP will be tasked with surveillance, transport, and SAR missions around Reno. But for now, you guys sit tight and wait for help. Let me know when the sheriff arrives, and try not to violate any more regulations tonight, okay, General? Battle Mountain Base, out."

Patrick returned to the group and gave the transceiver back to Bellville. "Pretty incredible, eh?" Bellville remarked. "I filled John and Leo in. Anything more?"

"They're saying it was a large quantity of radioactive medical waste, not a bomb," Patrick said to the entire group, especially the cadets, "but the airspace is still closed. Folks are panicking all around the country."

"That's exactly what the attackers want: get the people good and scared," Fitzgerald said acidly.

"Well, it's working," Bellville said. "Our plans change?"

"Not before the sheriff arrives," Patrick said. "We have ourselves a campout until daybreak."

Bellville nodded. "If an ambulance or medevac helicopter doesn't arrive by then, we'll take Jeremy to the nearest hospital in Andorsen's truck," he said. "We should make contact with Andorsen by then, and we'll ask him to help us get our van so we can take the ground team back to base. You can take the 182 back to Battle Mountain as soon as the airspace is reopened."

"Sounds like a good plan."

"So you get to camp out with us tonight, Dad?" Brad asked excitedly. "It's the first time camping out with the CAP, isn't it?"

"First time camping out *ever* except for Air Force survival school and maybe once or twice in the backyard when I was a kid," Patrick said. "I'll just sleep in the truck."

"Nah, Dad, you gotta sleep out under the stars with us," Brad said happily. "You'll love it. You can tell us war stories."

"Okay, okay," Patrick said. "But it better not rain on us."

There were thunderstorms in the area, with tremendous flashes of lightning brightly illuminating the horizon and an occasional rumble of thunder rolling across the desert, but the group had clear skies and unusually gentle breezes that evening. Patrick told stories until almost midnight while the rest of them ate MREs and drank water, with hardly a word uttered by anyone. Even Jeremy, occasionally awakened on the stretcher, listened intently.

Bellville finally called the storytelling to a halt and organized the camp for the night, setting up sleeping areas, a latrine, the camp perimeter, and night watches; all their food and anything that might attract animals was stored inside the truck. The cadets took the first hour-long watches, patrolling the area around the camp with their headlights and flashlights to ward off curious coyotes and warmth-seeking snakes. Everyone else slept outside except Jeremy, who was placed in one of the tents, with Ralph steadfastly refusing to leave his patient's side.

Bradley had taken the first perimeter patrol. When his shift was done he went over to Ron. "Wake up, Ron," he whispered.

"I'm not asleep."

"Then get up, jerk-off. Perimeter patrol. You wake up Mr. de Carteret at zero-two-hundred."

"I know, I know," Ron said. He shook off his sleeping bag, found his boots and headlamp, and struggled to his feet.

"Don't leave your sleeping bag open like that, Ron," Brad said. "You'll have half the bugs and lizards in the desert inside by the time you go back in."

"I know, I know," Ron repeated irritably. "I was going to zip it up. Just go to sleep, A-hole." He zipped the sleeping bag closed, turned on his headlamp and flashlight, and took the portable FM radio from Brad.

"Don't forget check-ins at fifteen and forty-five past . . ."

"Jeez, McLanahan, I'm not a goober like Marky," Ron hissed. "Lay off, all right?" and he stomped off.

Brad went back to where his father was sleeping under his unzipped and folded-out sleeping bag. He took off his boots, being careful to stuff spare socks inside to keep bugs and snakes from crawling in, then knelt on the ground. He was surprised to feel his sleeping pad beneath his knees. "You asleep, Dad?" he whispered.

"No," Patrick whispered back.

Brad lay down, then sat up again. "Why aren't you sleeping on the pad, Dad?" he asked.

"I saved it for you. It's too small for both of us."

Brad chuckled. "But you're old," he said, "and the ground is very rocky."

"I'm not old, you young fart, and the ground is just fine."

Brad snickered and settled back down under the sleeping bag. After a few minutes, he whispered, "Is this what it felt like after 9/11, Dad? Scared, but you're not sure why?"

"Yes," Patrick replied solemnly. "And the American Holocaust. No one knew what was going to happen next, or where or when the next attack would be. The Holocaust was far worse. Everyone slept in basements and air-raid shelters for weeks afterward, even after . . . after the counterattacks." He paused, then said, "Lots of sleepless nights."

Brad didn't say it aloud, but he thought it: *Your* counterattacks, the ones *you* planned and led, Dad. But all he said was, "Good night, Dad."

"Good night, big guy."

Because Patrick was flying the Cessna and was the highest-ranking officer, he was the last to take a patrol shift so he could get the most sleep. David Bellville touched his shoulder. "Time, sir," he said. "You get any sleep?"

"An hour or so altogether, maybe."

"That's an hour or so more than me," Bellville said. "I have relatives that live near Reno."

"I know," Patrick said. "I'm sure Rob is checking. Anything?"

"Poor Jeremy crying in his sleep every now and then, and Fid snoring away like an old hound dog," Bellville whispered. He handed Patrick the portable FM radio. "Otherwise good. We'll get everyone up at six."

"Roger." Patrick donned his headlamp, used the latrine pit, then started his patrol. He pretended he was flying an expanding-square search: First he started at the center of the camp, checked every cadet, then checked on Ralph and Jeremy—both were thankfully asleep. Then he checked every senior, checked the ration cache in the pickup's cab with John, then started walking the perimeter, shining a flashlight on every bush, hole, rock, and crevice, trying to scare away any critters.

The shift went by quickly. The stars were amazing, and Patrick had never seen so many shooting stars before. He checked in ops-normal with Battle Mountain Base at fifteen minutes and forty-five minutes after the hour, just as he did on every mission or exercise. As the end of the shift approached, dawn was quickly approaching, and the eastern sky was ablaze with red and orange. Yes, he was here because of a disaster, but the opportunity to see this incredibly beautiful vista was . . .

. . . and as the light on the horizon brightened, he saw it: a Jeep Wrangler, top down and doors off, with two men sitting in the front seat—both armed with what looked like military rifles! It was no more than forty yards to their campsite—how in the world could these guys get so close without being heard by anyone?

Patrick decided to find out, and he walked over to them. The two men never looked over toward him as he approached, but straight ahead, even when Patrick pointed his flashlight in their faces. "Who are you guys?" he asked. No reply. Patrick saw the words ANDORSEN AND SONS painted on the side of the hood. "You work for Andorsen?"

"Mr. Andorsen will be by shortly to speak with you," the man in the passenger seat said, still not looking at Patrick. Patrick could see several radios in the Jeep, including a police-band scanner and VHF aviation-band radio; he could also see that the scopes on their AR-15 rifles were low-light telescopic sniperscopes, able to intensify starlight enough to see in the dark. "We don't talk to trespassers and thieves."

Patrick decided these guys weren't going to answer any questions, so he walked back to the camp and woke up the adults. "We have visitors," he told the senior members.

"What?" Fitzgerald thundered. He followed Patrick's outstretched hand. "Those guys have been watchin' us, and they got *guns*? I'll straighten them out!"

"Negative, Fid," Bellville said. "Stay put; get the cadets up and the camp packed up." Fid turned, glaring at the newcomers.

"They said Andorsen will be out shortly," Patrick said.

"What else?"

"Nothing. They weren't very chatty—or friendly."

"Another Jeep to the south," Leo said, lowering a pair of binoculars. "A little better hidden than the others."

"Looks like Judah has had us under surveillance all night," John said.

"Judah?"

"Judah Andorsen," John explained. "Fourth-generation rancher out here. Good customer of mine at the store. I've known him for years." He fell silent; then: "I wonder why he didn't come in."

"Or why he didn't report us to the sheriff, and why the sheriff isn't here," Patrick said. "You think Andorsen wants to handle this situation by himself?"

"We'll find out pretty soon," Bellville said, "because I hear a chopper." Sure enough, a minute later a Bell JetRanger helicopter approached, flying low. It stirred up a cloud of dust as it settled a few yards away from the Jeep to the east. Through the swirling sand, a tall, broad-shouldered man emerged and strode purposefully toward the camp, flanked by one of the men from the Jeep, carrying the rifle at port arms.

When he was a few paces away from the CAP members, the man shouted over the subsiding roar of the helicopter's turbine engine, "Who the hell is McLanahan? I want to know which one of you is McLanahan!"

"I'm McLanahan," Patrick replied.

"So you think you can steal one of my trucks and leave *this* as some kind of IOU?" the man said. He was waving the CAP Form 104 Patrick had stuck in the ranch house's door. The man was wearing a leather flying jacket, jeans, cowboy boots, and leather ranch hand's gloves. "I've got news for you, bub: we don't do that out here in Nevada on my land. I think it's time to teach you a little down-home respect for . . ." As he got closer to the group, he looked at the others and froze. "John? Is that *you*?"

"Good morning, Judah," John said with a smile. "You're in quite a state this morning, aren't you?"

"You're with this group of thieves, John? Are you all right? What are you wearing?"

"A flight suit, Judah," John said. "I'm a mission observer for the Civil Air Patrol. We're out here on a mission."

"A mission? Civil Air Patrol? Why, I don't . . ." He continued to scan the group, and they could see his eyes widen in surprise again. "Trooper Slotnick?"

"Morning, Mr. Andorsen," Leo said.

"What in hell is going on out here?" Andorsen asked. "Are you making an arrest, Trooper? Why didn't you call and—"

"My mission base has been trying to contact you for the past eighteen hours, sir, but there's been no answer," Bellville said.

"Who are *you*?"

"David Bellville, Civil Air Patrol ground-team leader. We're on a search-and-rescue mission."

Andorsen seemed to relax a bit. "Oh yeah . . . the crashed plane we saw coming out here," he said, nodding. "You looking for that plane? It's about three hundred yards back that way."

"We found the plane," Bellville said. "We were out here looking for a survivor."

"A survivor? From *that*? No way in hell."

"Mind keeping your voice down, Andorsen?" Fitzgerald asked in a low growl. He jabbed a thumb back toward Jeremy's tent. "The *survivor* is sleeping."

Andorsen first scowled at Fitzgerald—obviously unaccustomed to being spoken to like that—but then nodded. He turned to McLanahan. "You fly that plane onto my airstrip?"

"Yes."

"And steal my truck?"

"I didn't steal your truck. I borrowed it to make contact and assist the ground-search team. I left that form so you could call our mission base and we could explain what was happening."

"On my land with my property I prefer to get answers for myself," Andorsen said, "and out here, *I* decide what is stealing and what's not." He looked more carefully at Patrick, then glanced at the Form 104. "What'd you say your name was?"

"McLanahan."

"Unusual name," he said. Andorsen read the name and information on the card, then Patrick's leather name tag on his flight suit. "*Patrick* McLanahan? *The* Patrick McLanahan? But you're wearing colonel's rank. The real Patrick McLanahan was a three-star Air Force general."

"In the Civil Air Patrol, I'm a colonel," Patrick said.

Andorsen's eyes slowly grew wider and wider in sheer amazement. "*You're General Patrick McLanahan? No shit?*" he exclaimed.

"The one and only, Judah," John said proudly. "He's a volunteer for the Battle Mountain squadron, just like us. That's his boy over there."

"I don't believe it!" Andorsen said, mouth agape. He reached over and extended his hand. "It is an honor to have you on my ranch, sir, a real honor." Patrick took his hand, and Andorsen pumped it enthusiastically. "I'm sorry about getting in your face there, sir, but we get a lot of trespassers and thieves these days, what with the economy going to shit and all. The sheriff is doing his best, but this is a big county and a big ranch, and his department's been slashed to the bone . . ." He waved a hand in his own face, interrupting himself, then said, "I apologize, sir, but I'm babbling. You need someone flown to the hospital? If you can put him in the chopper, I'll fly him myself. Otherwise I'll have the boys at the house bring out the Hummer."

"I think he'll be better off in the chopper," Bellville said. "John, Leo, get him ready." They hustled off.

"So you're out here doing a search-and-rescue, and you find the crash, and then you find a survivor who walked away from the crash," Andorsen said. "Amazing work. I'm proud of you guys. And you're *volunteers*. That's even more amazing. I've always believed in the spirit of the volunteer, the person who doesn't expect to be paid for service to his community and country. Real proud of you." He shook his head as he looked at each one of them with a smile. "What else can I do for you?"

"Our van is parked next to your gate number twenty-three," Fitzgerald said. "The gate was locked."

"Like I said, we've had a lot of trespassers over the past couple years," Andorsen said. "Even had some cattle rustlers a while back."

"And you like to deal with them yourself, instead of calling the sheriff?" Fid asked. He nodded. "Sounds like the way it should be done."

"Bet your ass," Andorsen said. He looked Fid up and down. "Do I know you?"

"I've been on your ranch many times for open-range fire drills with the Department of Wildlife air and ground teams," Fitzgerald said. "You've been extremely generous with your time and hands. You've donated help and land for CAP cadet campouts also. I have all of your gates mapped out."

"Happy to do it," Andorsen said, nodding approvingly. "You and your kids need a ride to your van?"

"Yes, sir."

"Take the pickup, and my boys will tag along and take anyone that doesn't fit, then drive the pickup back," Andorsen said. "You'll probably need one adult to stay with your survivor when we drop him off at the hospital." He turned to Patrick. "I'd be honored if you'd fly along with me, General. I'd like to chat and show you my ranch before you fly off."

"We're grounded for now," Patrick said.

"Grounded? The plane not working?"

"The FAA has grounded all flights around the country," Bellville said. "The plane crash in Reno?" Andorsen wore a blank stare. "The plane that crashed into the federal building in Reno carrying radioactive material?"

"*Radioactive ma* . . . are you *shitting* me?" Andorsen retorted.

"You didn't hear about that?"

"Son, my ranch is over fourteen thousand square miles across five Nevada counties," Andorsen said. "I operate a thousand crop circles, fifty thousand head of cattle, eleven mines, and two thousand workers. I go eighteen hours a day, every day; I'm in the air at least three hours a day. I don't have time to watch TV." He looked concerned. "But I've got offices in Reno, and they should've alerted me. Same as that plane crash on my land—someone should have noticed that, and noticed you flying around out here. I'm gonna look into that too." He saw John and Leo two-man carrying Jeremy toward the helicopter, followed closely by Ralph. "That the survivor? Damn lucky kid. Well, let's get rolling."

"I'll stay with Jeremy until next of kin or child protective services show up," Bellville said. "Fid, you head back to base with the cadets."

"Can I stay with Jeremy, sir?" Ralph asked.

" 'Fraid not, Ralph," Bellville said. Ralph looked dejected, but nodded assent. Bellville turned to Andorsen and explained, "Cadet Markham here led the ground-search team right to the survivor, and he's been the survivor's medical attendant since moment one."

"So why can't he ride along?" Andosen asked. "I got plenty of room."

"Because we need at least two adults together with at least two cadets, unless it's an emergency," Bellville explained. "Liability and child protection regulations." Andorsen nodded, saying nothing but wearing a puzzled expression on his face. "Patrick, do you need John or Leo to fly the 182 back to Battle Mountain? I need one of them with Fid and the cadets."

"I'll take Leo and give him some stick time," Patrick said. He saw Brad's anxious expression, wanting some stick time too or at least a ride in the plane, but now was not the time.

"Then John will go back to base with Fid and the cadets in the van," Bellville said. Patrick nodded. "I'll call it all in."

It was a half-hour flight to Battle Mountain, where Andorsen himself landed on a nearly empty parking lot next to Battle Mountain's small hospital. He had already radioed ahead to report the situation, and a nurse and paramedic were waiting outside with a gurney. They carefully placed Jeremy on the gurney and strapped him in while Bellville got out. He shook hands with Patrick and Leo. "See you back at base, guys," he said.

"Roger that," Patrick said. He and Leo stayed by the helicopter while Andorsen went into the hospital with the nurse and paramedic. More hospital staff members came to the door to greet him. "Popular guy," Patrick observed.

"Notice the name of the hospital?" Leo asked. Patrick searched and found the sign that read ANDERS G. ANDORSEN MEMORIAL HOSPITAL. "Judah's grandfather," Leo explained before Patrick could ask. "The Andorsens have their names on most of the public buildings all over north-central Nevada."

"I've worked out here for years and never noticed," Patrick said.

"Just like most folks out here had no idea what the military was doing out on the base for decades," Leo said. "Even now, it's the same: the greatest wartime general since Norman Schwarzkopf is living right here in our little town, and no one has a clue." He looked at Patrick's neutral, faraway expression and smiled. "I was referring to *you,* sir."

"Thank you, Leo," Patrick said. "I'm not feeling very heroic these days."

Andorsen came out a few minutes later and climbed into the JetRanger, with Patrick and Leo scrambling to catch up with him. "Looks like the poor kid's being taken good care of," he said. "Let me give you a tour of the ranch, and then get some breakfast back at the house."

"Aren't all aircraft still grounded, sir?" Leo asked.

"I'm sure that don't apply to local flights below one thousand feet aboveground, Trooper," Andorsen said. "No interceptors will be flying around the boonies—they'll be setting up over the big cities. We'll be okay." He started the engine and lifted off. "That Bellville guy really seems to have his shit together," Andorsen remarked. "That Fitzgerald guy too. I'm gonna have to pay a visit to you guys someday and see what you're all about."

"That would be great, sir," Patrick said.

"Please, call me Judah, General."

"Only if you call me Patrick."

"I'd be honored to, Patrick," Andorsen said.

"Thank you." Patrick noticed they were flying right toward Joint Air Base Battle Mountain, whose controlled airspace extended ten miles in all directions from the surface to five thousand feet above the surface. "Better be careful of the Class-C airspace, Judah," Patrick said. "Do you have the approach control or tower frequency handy?"

"The guys in the tower know my chopper," Andorsen said, "and as long as I stay away from the approach paths, we're good."

Both Patrick and Leo looked at the control tower in the distance, and they could clearly see alternating red and green laser light gun signals from the remote video-tower controllers, indicating "EXERCISE EXTREME CAUTION." "I see red and green light gun signals from the tower, sir," Leo said. "Better stay away from the base."

"With all the shit happening in Reno, I'm not surprised," Andorsen said nonchalantly. He turned slightly east but was still going to break the ten-mile limit. "I can't believe I'm flying with *the* Patrick McLanahan. How long have you been in the area, Patrick?"

"Almost six months on this posting," Patrick said, carefully scanning the sky for aircraft and taking another nervous look back at the warning lights from the base. He knew Battle Mountain had very sophisticated air-defense weapons, but he wasn't familiar with their status and guessed they had probably been deactivated when the drawdown began. "I spent two years here commanding the base previously."

"You know about the underground hangar at the base, of course."

"Of course."

"My grandfather started that project, you know," Andorsen said proudly, "and my father finished it. We've always been a family of miners—everyone in my family can work and live just as easily be-lowground as we do above. I was taken through the complex many times when I was a kid—of course, I was sworn to secrecy, and the threat of commies and saboteurs was so great back then that I was too scared to even think about talking about it to my friends. It was considered one of the eight technical marvels of the modern world back then."

"I couldn't believe it when I was first taken through it," Patrick said. "It still amazes me that we can park B-52 bombers down there."

"And what do you do now, Patrick?" Andorsen asked.

"Officially I'm a reserve Air Force lieutenant-general in com-mand of the Space Defense Force," Patrick replied, "although there really is no Space Defense Force and the planned upgrades to the space-defense systems have been put on hold. In actuality, I'm a caretaker. If a contingency takes place, I'm there to make sure that the place is ready to support aircraft and spacecraft operations when a real commander and battle staff arrive."

Andorsen scowled at him. "You're a *caretaker? You?* Why aren't you out there on the lecture circuit, or a consultant for some de-fense contractor? You could be pulling in some big bucks."

"I might just do that later on," Patrick said, "but if the Space Defense Force languishes in this recession, it might not survive when things recover. Someone needs to be the advocate. I'm happy to do it for my retirement pay."

"You don't even get *paid?*" Andorsen asked incredulously. He shook his head. "How screwed up is that? General Patrick McLanahan, working for *nothing?* Unbelievable."

Andorsen continued to chat about landmarks and features of his expansive ranch, flying this way and that. Patrick listened, but in reality he was looking at the VHF radios, itching to switch one to the Battle Mountain control-tower frequency, Battle Mountain Approach Control, or the GUARD emergency channel. Andorsen had the radio set to some personal frequency that Patrick didn't recognize.

"And this here is our Freedom-3 mine," Andorsen went on. The mine was an immense open-pit area encompassing several hundred acres and several hundred feet deep. "My great-great-grandfather opened it way back after the turn of the century. He found mostly copper back then, but over the years we've found a little bit of everything there: silver, lead, bauxite, even a tiny bit of gold. Look there and you can see—"

Patrick couldn't stand it any longer: "Judah, if you don't mind, I'm going to flip your number two comm to GUARD," he said as he switched radio frequencies and selected the proper button on the audio panel to monitor the frequency. "With all the stuff going on, I want to monitor GUARD. Hope you don't mind."

"No, no, go ahead, set it for anything you want," Andorsen said a bit perturbedly. "Just leave me comm one so I can talk to my boys if I need to."

"You got it." Patrick switched frequencies and hit the COM2 button on the audio panel, and immediately they heard, " . . . fifteen miles south of Joint Air Base Battle Mountain, warning, warning, you have violated controlled airspace during an air-defense emergency. Repeat, unidentified helicopter nine miles north of Joint Air Base Battle Mountain, you have violated controlled airspace during a national air-defense emergency. You are instructed to depart Class-C airspace immediately and contact Battle Mountain Approach immediately on GUARD or on one-two-six-point-four. Be advised, you may be intercepted and fired upon without warning if you remain in Class-C airspace. Unidentified helicopter, if you hear this message, respond immediately on any channel."

"They're talking about us!" Leo exclaimed.

"What in Sam Hill are they getting so wrapped around the axle about?" Andorsen exclaimed. "They know it's me."

"That doesn't matter in an air-defense emergency, Judah," Patrick said. "They may have deployed interceptors to Battle Mountain in case of more attacks in the area. Let me talk to them."

"Fine by me," Andorsen said irritably. "Go ahead."

Patrick quickly switched the audio panel to COM2, hit the mike button on his cyclic, and spoke: "Battle Mountain Approach, this is Sierra Alpha Seven aboard JetRanger One Juliet Alpha on GUARD, fifteen miles south of JAB Battle Mountain. I was previously mission pilot aboard CAP 2722 that launched yesterday. Requesting permission to land at the CAP hangar."

"What's that Sierra Alpha Seven nonsense?" Andorsen asked.

"My call sign at the base—I'm hoping that'll turn down the tension here," Patrick replied. Andorsen snorted and shook his head but said nothing.

"Negative, One Juliet Alpha, negative," the controller replied angrily. He directed Patrick to switch to his regular VHF frequency to clear the emergency frequency, then said, "You are directed to keep clear of Class-C airspace and land immediately. Acknowledge."

"Fine, fine, fine," Andorsen said. He turned the helicopter to the northwest. "We'll head back to the house."

"That's about twenty minutes away, Judah," Patrick said. He

quickly scanned outside, then pointed to the left. "That rest-area parking lot looks empty. You can set it down there."

"I'm not landing on no parking lot!" Andorsen said. "I'm heading away from the base, we've made radio contact, and my ranch is less than twenty minutes away. I'm not threatening anyone." He flipped over to COM2. "Listen, Approach, this is Judah Andorsen on One Juliet Alpha. We're heading straight back to the ranch. I've been helpin' out the Civil Air Patrol with a rescue, so don't get all riled up about—"

At that instant they heard a tremendous screaming *WHOOOSH!* and the helicopter was tossed around the sky like a leaf in the wind. When Andorsen finally got the craft back under control, they all clearly saw what had caused the upset, because it had missed them by less than a hundred yards: an Air Force F-16C Fighting Falcon, banking steeply right in front of them. *"What in the hell . . . ?"*

"That was to get our attention," Patrick said. He switched COM1 to the VHF GUARD channel and spoke: "Air Force F-16, this is JetRanger One Juliet Alpha on VHF GUARD, go ahead."

"JetRanger One Juliet Alpha, this is Saber One-Seven, Air Force F-16, on GUARD," came the reply. "Turn left heading two-six-zero. You are instructed to land at Valmy Municipal Airport."

"I ain't landin' at Valmy—that place has been shut down for twenty years!" Andorsen said. "There isn't anything out there!"

"Judah, you'd better turn to that heading," Patrick said. "If we're not responding, he'll get permission to shoot."

"Shoot? You mean, *shoot me down?"*

"I do, and after what happened in Reno yesterday, he'll do it." Andorsen shook his head but turned to the heading. Relieved, Patrick switched to COM1. "Saber One-Seven, this is JetRanger One Juliet Alpha, requesting permission to land at the owner's private airstrip at our four o'clock, forty miles. We will remain clear of Class-C airspace."

"Negative, One Juliet Alpha," the fighter pilot replied. "You are instructed to land as directed and await law enforcement. Do not attempt to take off again. I will be circling overhead and I may be directed to fire upon you without warning if you attempt a takeoff. Remain on this frequency."

"Why, this is the biggest load of crap I've ever heard!" Andorsen thundered. "What does he mean, 'law enforcement'? What in hell did I do?"

"We're not supposed to be flying, Judah," Patrick said. "Don't worry—once they find out who we are, they'll let us go once the emergency is over."

"I'm not going to wait," Andorsen said. He switched COM2 to his own discrete frequency. "Teddy, this is Judah."

"Read you loud and clear, sir," came a reply moments later, with a remarkably clear transmission, as if the responder was very close by.

"I'm in the JetRanger," Andorsen said. "There's an Air Force fighter jet forcing me to land at the old airport in Valmy. Send some boys out there. Then tell Cunningham to meet us out there too. They may try to arrest us. They may use the Highway Patrol or Humboldt County sheriff before the feds arrive."

"Roger that, sir, I'll tell him."

Andorsen nodded. "They think they're hot shit because they got a jet fighter?" he snapped cross-cockpit. "They ain't seen *nuthin'* yet."

After overflying the deserted field and selecting the least weed-choked area he could find, Andorsen set the JetRanger down with an irritated *thud* and a swirl of tumbleweeds, shut the engine down, and exited the chopper. He scowled at the noise of the F-16 overhead. "Bastard," he muttered. "Intercepted by the damned Air Force, and I haven't even had breakfast yet."

Patrick pulled out his cellular phone. There was no cellular service out here in this remote area, miles from Battle Mountain. But he did have Internet access, thanks to the Space Defense Force's network of mobile broadband satellites that provided high-speed

Internet access to most of the Northern Hemisphere. "Brad, this is Patrick," he said after he had connected via Voice-over IP to the Battle Mountain CAP Base.

"Where are you?" Spara replied. "You missed a check-in."

"We're with Judah Andorsen," Patrick explained. "He was flying us back to his ranch in his helicopter after dropping the survivor and Dave off at the hospital in Battle Mountain."

"He was *flying*? The entire national airspace is still shut down except for medical and law enforcement. From whom did he get permission?"

"No one."

"So you're at his ranch?"

"Not exactly. We were intercepted by an F-16 and ordered to land at Valmy Airport."

"There's an airport at Valmy?"

"Abandoned. We're okay, but we were told to wait for law enforcement. The F-16 is orbiting overhead to make sure we don't leave."

"Great," Spara said with a sigh. "I'll report it to the National Operations Center. I'll ask them to explain to the FBI that Andorsen was helping the Civil Air Patrol, but that might take some time. You might be in the pokey for a while. If they place you under arrest—"

"I know," Patrick said. "Name, address, and Social Security number only, remain silent about everything else, and call the National Operations Center. Number's on my ID card."

"Correct. Remind Leo. Maybe he can pull some strings with the Highway Patrol."

"I think they will want to cooperate in every way with the FBI," Patrick guessed. "I'll try to keep in touch." He put the phone away. "Did you hear that, Leo? If they put us under arrest, we don't answer questions unless we have a CAP-appointed lawyer present."

"They wouldn't *dare*," Andorsen growled.

"The FBI's going to be on the warpath, Judah," Patrick warned. "A suicide terrorist just attacked their offices in Reno with a dirty bomb. I wouldn't mess with these guys until everybody has had a chance to calm down. Once they figure out we're not terrorists, everyone will dial down the volume quickly, but at first things might be tense."

About a half hour later, they saw and then heard a vehicle going Code Three down Interstate 80, and soon it turned off, raced down the frontage road, and headed south to the abandoned airport. It was a Humboldt County sheriff's cruiser. It stopped about twenty yards from the chopper, and a lone deputy got out. "All three of you," he shouted, "put your hands in the air and turn around!"

"Now just wait a damned minute, Deputy . . . !" Andorsen shouted, jabbing a finger at the deputy.

"Do it, *now*!" the sheriff's deputy shouted, placing a hand on his sidearm.

Patrick and Leo did as they were ordered. "Do it, Mr. Andorsen," Leo said. "Don't argue."

Andorsen puffed up his chest as if he was going to start shouting again, but he shook his head, raised his hands, and turned. Patrick noticed his arms trembling; Andorsen looked at Patrick and said, "Old shoulder injury from Vietnam." He raised his voice and said loudly, "I can't hold my arms up like this long, Deputy."

The deputy ignored him. "Man closest to the nose of the helicopter, take five steps toward me, backward," he shouted.

Leo did as he was told, then said, "I'm a Nevada Highway Patrol officer. My ID is in the lower right-leg pocket."

"Are you armed?"

"I'm flying with the Civil Air Patrol today. CAP is never armed."

"I said, are you armed?" the deputy repeated.

"No."

"Hands behind your head, lace your fingers." Leo complied. "Kneel down, cross your ankles." Leo complied again, and the deputy put him in a pair of handcuffs, then took him to his patrol car. He did the same to Patrick, putting both men in the backseat.

"If you expect me to kneel down, buddy, you're loco," Andorsen said acidly when the deputy approached him. "My knees are so old, they will crack like kindling. And I can't hold my arms up like this—the pain gets too much."

"I'll help you up, sir," the deputy said. "Hands behind your head, lace your—"

Patrick could easily sense what was going to happen next: Andorsen whirled, his hands knotted into fists, and he hit the deputy on the side of his head. The deputy must have sensed it also, because he almost managed to dodge away from the swing and received a glancing blow only.

"I told you, boy, I can't hold my arms up like that!" Andorsen shouted.

The deputy's SIG Sauer P226 semiautomatic sidearm was in his hands in the blink of an eye. *"Don't move!"* he shouted, the gun leveled at Andorsen's chest. *"Turn and get down on the ground!"*

"I told you, son, I can't get down like that—it hurts too much," Andorsen said, holding his hands out in plain sight but not raising them. "My name is Judah Andorsen. Get on your damned radio and tell your boss that—"

The deputy grabbed Andorsen by the front of his jacket and tugged backward, and as soon as Andorsen resisted by pulling away, the deputy put one leg between Andorsen's legs, shoved forward, and placed a toe behind Andorsen's heel, tripping him. As the deputy fell on top of Andorsen, he made sure one knee was in Andorsen's groin when they hit the ground. With Andorsen doubled up in pain and clutching his groin, it was easy for the deputy to holster his sidearm, grab a wrist, spin the man over on his stomach, wrestle the other wrist around, and snap handcuffs in place.

"Dispatch, Unit Five," he radioed using his portable radio,

breathing heavily, but more from excitement and adrenaline rush than exertion, "three in custody, Valmy Airport, notify FBI—"

And at that moment a black six-pack dually pickup truck raced up the dirt road toward the deputy, tires kicking up dirt and stones. It was followed by a Cadillac sedan. The dually screeched to a halt in a cloud of dust beside the police cruiser, the doors flew open, and six men jumped out and ran toward the deputy.

"Freeze!" the deputy shouted. He knelt next to Andorsen and again put a hand on his sidearm. "Humboldt County Sheriff's Department making an arrest! All you men, get back in your truck, *now*!"

The six men stopped but did not retreat. "We're right here, Mr. Andorsen," one of the men said. "What do you want us to do?"

"Tell these men to raise their hands and back away," the deputy ordered.

"Back on up, Teddy," Andorsen said into the dust. The six men immediately stepped backward to their pickup, their eyes on the sheriff's deputy and their boss the whole time.

"Dispatch, Unit Five, requesting backup, Valmy Airport," the deputy radioed.

"Damn it, what do those guys think they're doing?" Leo asked from the backseat of the deputy's cruiser. "Were they trying to—"

"Holy shit!" Patrick said between clenched teeth. He looked over to the pickup . . . and noticed AR-15 assault rifles with sniperscopes being passed out from within the pickup, shielded from view. "Those guys have *guns*!"

"This is not good," Leo whispered.

Patrick thought for a second, then shouted, "Judah, this is General Patrick McLanahan. Tell your men to put down their rifles."

The sheriff's deputy leaped to his feet, dashed around the nose of the helicopter, drew his sidearm, pointed it toward the six men, and shouted, *"Show me your hands! Now!"*

In a flash, the six men spread out about six yards apart from one another and dropped to the ground. Patrick counted four AR-15 rifles pointed at the deputy. These guys looked professional all the way, he thought. "I think it's your turn to drop your weapon and show us your hands, Deputy," the man named Teddy shouted.

THREE

If you will just start with the idea that this is a hard world, it will all be much simpler.

—Louis D. Brandeis, U.S. Supreme Court justice

VALMY, NEVADA

"Are they *crazy?*" Leo said. "They're drawing down on a sheriff's deputy!"

During this time, the Cadillac had pulled up to the scene, and a lone, short, balding man in a gray business suit got out and walked toward the helicopter, unbuttoning and then removing his jacket. *"Freeze!"* the deputy shouted.

The newcomer dropped his jacket to the ground and raised his hands. "I'm not armed, Deputy," he said in a remarkably calm voice. "My name is Harold Cunningham, and I am Mr. Andorsen's attorney and counsel." He looked up into his right hand, in which he was holding a cell phone. "I'm expecting a call from Sheriff Martinez, District Attorney Cauldwell, and County Commissioner Blane any minute now, Deputy, and you'll be receiving a call from the sheriff explaining what this is all about."

"You just stay where you are and keep your hands where I can see them!" the deputy shouted back.

"Unit Five," came the message from the deputy's portable radio.

The deputy keyed the mike button on his left shoulder: "Dispatch, Unit Five, three in custody, holding seven at gunpoint, repeat, *seven,* multiple weapons visible, request immediate backup, covers Code Three." His voice was clearly fearful.

"Five, this is Sheriff Martinez," came a different voice on the channel. "Mark, relax. This is all a big fat mix-up by the feds. That's Judah Andorsen you got there."

"Sir, I've got four guys with rifles and two with handguns aimed at me," the deputy radioed back to the obviously known person on the radio.

"They're Mr. Andorsen's security guys," Martinez replied. "The feds have got everybody believing we've got terrorists running amok in Humboldt County. Just relax."

"I'll relax as soon as these motherfuckers lower their guns, sir," the deputy named Mark radioed.

"I'm on my way out there now, son," Martinez radioed. "Just don't do anything until I get there."

In the next ninety minutes, as the day grew hotter and hotter and thunderstorms began to build around them like sand monsters rising from the high desert, more and more cars arrived. After each new vehicle arrived, the man named Cunningham dialed another number, and more cars arrived. Before long, two FBI special agents showed up and took charge of the scene. By then, Andorsen's men had gotten back to their feet and had joined their boss around the helicopter, with their weapons in holsters or slung on their shoulders. The FBI agents stood by their car with sidearms leveled. "This is the FBI," one of the agents shouted. "All of you men, drop your weapons and raise your hands."

"I'm sorry, Special Agent Chastain," the man named Cunningham said, "but I'm expecting a call from the deputy attorney general and the U.S. attorney in Reno. He'll straighten all this out for you."

"How did Cunningham know his name?" Patrick asked in a low voice. He and Leo were still handcuffed in the back of the now-sweltering-hot sheriff's cruiser. "Neither FBI agent identified himself yet, right?"

"This is bizarro," Leo said. "They've got everybody except the governor of Nevada and vice president of the United States out here."

"I said, drop your weapons and raise your hands!" the special agent repeated. It was a surreal scene to Patrick: the Humboldt County sheriff and several deputies, the district attorney, a county commissioner, a high-ranking official from the Nevada Highway Patrol, and someone from the state of Nevada Attorney General's office, along with Andorsen's armed employees, were all standing around Andorsen's helicopter, being confronted by two FBI agents! The officials with Andorsen, Patrick noted with shock, were not only *not* arresting anyone, but were openly protecting and shielding him from federal law enforcement officers!

"You should be getting a call from Washington or the Nevada U.S. District Court any minute now, Special Agent Chastain," Cunningham called out. "It should straighten this whole ugly incident out right away."

"I'm warning all of you, drop your weapons and raise your hands!" the agent named Chastain repeated. But it was obvious that he was distracted by something.

"Boys, go ahead and put your guns down so Agent Chastain there can answer his phone," Andorsen said with a wide grin. His men immediately laid their weapons on the ground so the FBI agents could clearly see them. "I'll bet it's a real important call. Don't you worry none about any of us, son—we ain't gonna move a muscle."

With the other agent covering the odd group, Chastain pulled his cell phone out of his jacket pocket—and everyone could see his jaw drop in surprise when he read the caller ID. "Chastain," he said. "Go ahead, sir . . . Yes, I'm in charge of this incident, the airspace violation and the . . . Excuse me, sir? . . . You're saying there was no violation because the airspace in this area had been cleared because of the Civil Air Patrol search-and-rescue operation?" Patrick could see Andorsen's grin become even wider. "But, sir, I was advised that the entire national airspace system is still shut down and . . . What, sir? . . . I see . . . All the airspace *except* for this particular area. So there *never* was any violation, even though the military controllers at Battle Mountain had . . . Yes, sir . . . Yes, yes . . . Yes, sir, right away." The call ended abruptly. The agent named Chastain half turned to his partner and spoke in a low tone, and moments later he holstered his weapon.

"Sorry for the misunderstanding, sir," Chastain said. "Have a nice day." And just like that, both FBI agents climbed back into their car and drove off.

"Well, I'm glad that's taken care of," Andorsen said as his men picked up their weapons and headed back to their truck. "Deputy, mind takin' those cuffs off my friends?" The deputy hustled to comply, and finally Patrick and Leo returned to the helicopter, rubbing sore wrists. "I apologize for the mix-up, guys, but it's all good now," Andorsen said. He turned to the officials behind him. "I'm going to fly these gents for a little meeting back at the ranch, Patrick, so if you don't mind, I'm going to ask the deputy to drive you back to the ranch to get your plane. Don't worry about the airspace—you shouldn't have no more problems." He stuck out a hand, and Patrick shook it. "It was a real honor meeting you, General, a real honor. I'll see you soon." He shook hands with Leo and offered seats in his helicopter to the county and state officials by his side.

Patrick and Leo retrieved their flight bags—they had been unceremoniously dumped out of the helicopter by one of Andorsen's men—and walked in silent confusion back to the cruiser that they had been locked up in for the past two hours. Neither they nor the sheriff's deputy said anything for the ninety-minute-long ride back to Andorsen's airstrip. The helicopter was already there, as were a number of official-looking vehicles parked outside the ranch house.

"What just happened back there?" Patrick finally asked after they had been dropped off beside the CAP Cessna 182.

"I knew Andorsen was a big name around Nevada," Leo said, "but I never realized *how* big. Call the sheriff? His man calls the district attorney. Call the Highway Patrol? He calls the Nevada attorney general. The FBI shows up? He's got the U.S. attorney general on speed dial. It looked as if that special agent saw his entire career flash before his eyes back there."

Patrick shook his head in confusion as he withdrew his cell phone and called the Battle Mountain CAP headquarters. Spara answered the phone. "Rob, sorry I couldn't check in, but—"

"Just get back here, Patrick," Spara interrupted. "No flight release, no pilot pro stuff, no special clearance—just get back here ASAP. The Class-C airspace is all yours—hell, just about all the airspace over northern Nevada belongs to you."

"What's going on?"

"The phone has been ringing off the hook all morning, and I'm expecting to hear from the frickin' president next," Spara said wearily. "Your new buddy Andorsen is one connected dude, and that's putting it *mildly*. Get back here soonest." And he hung up.

The oddities continued after Patrick took off from the dirt airstrip. The F-16C Fighting Falcon interceptor was gone, but it had been replaced with a Nevada Air National Guard HH-60 Pave Hawk helicopter, which moved into position on the Cessna's left side. Its pilot did not respond to any calls on GUARD or approach control frequencies. Patrick was cleared for immediately landing at Battle Mountain when still fifty miles away from the airport, and was instructed not to change frequencies, even after he landed. Base security vehicles—including an AN/UWQ-1 unmanned Avenger air-defense and ground-security vehicle, and a driverless Humvee carrying eight Stinger heat-seeking missiles and a .50-caliber radar-guided machine gun—escorted the Cessna to the Civil Air Patrol hangar.

It seemed as if the entire squadron was there to greet Patrick and Leo after they climbed out of the Cessna. Rob Spara was standing at the left entry door when Patrick got out. "Don't worry about putting the plane away, Patrick," he said. "They want to do a debrief. Now."

"Who's 'they'?" Patrick asked.

"Hell, General, dip your spoon into the alphabet-soup bowl ten times and you'll come up with a dozen different answers," Spara said. "We've got every agency in the book out here, and several I've never heard of—and I expect those are the ones *you* created."

Base Air Force Security Forces airmen were there to control the crowd around Patrick and Leo, but Bradley was able to break free of the squadron members being corralled away from the arrival and meet up with his father. For the second time in a day, Patrick enjoyed an unexpected hug from his son. "Hey, big guy," he said. He couldn't think of anything else to say except, "You made it back okay."

"I'm glad you're back, Dad," Brad said, hugging his father tightly. He held his father for several precious seconds, then released him and said breathlessly, "They put us in the break room and wouldn't let us talk to anyone. Then they let us out, but we had to stay in the hangar. Then we had to go back to the break room, and they took away our cell phones. There are weird guys talking into their sleeves everywhere. Man, everyone is freaking out around here!"

"Things are tense, big guy," Patrick said. "A major terrorist incident just happened."

"But what do *we* got to do with it?" Brad asked. "They're acting as if we had something to do with it!"

"It's just a coincidence," Patrick said. "Reno is nearby; we had a violation of restricted airspace; we didn't respond the way they wanted—"

"What?"

"Never mind," Patrick said. "You're home, I'm home, no one got hurt, you got a find and a save—those are the important things. Let me talk to these guys real quick and then we'll go home."

There were six men and a woman in the small break room when Patrick, Leo, and Rob entered. They had laptop computers set up on the countertops. As soon as they entered the room, one of the men began frisking them, and not gently either. To Patrick's surprise, the lead agent was the same one who had confronted them at the abandoned airport at Valmy! There was also a very attractive female agent whom Patrick had not seen before.

"I'm Special Agent Philip Chastain, FBI," the lead agent said, still working on his laptop while the inspection continued. He was tall and young-looking with thick dark hair and a square jaw—Patrick thought he looked like a Hollywood actor portraying a federal agent. Chastain gestured over his shoulder with a pen at the others. "That's Special Agent Brady and Agent Renaldo of the Department of Homeland Security. Empty your pockets on the counter here." Patrick and Leo did as they were told. Chastain examined Patrick's documents first and typed more instructions into his laptop; Patrick could see a small flare of surprise when some information came in. "General Patrick McLanahan." The jaws of the others in the room dropped and their eyes widened in surprise.

Chastain quickly shook away his initial reaction and assumed a very serious expression. "Both of you are being video- and audio-recorded. What were you doing flying in that helicopter toward the base?"

"Aren't you going to read me my rights first, Agent Chastain?" Patrick asked.

"Considering what happened yesterday in Reno and the seriousness of your violation, I assumed you'd waive your right to an attorney, cooperate fully with this investigation, and agree to answer my questions."

"You assumed incorrectly, Agent Chastain."

"Everyone else has been answering questions, including your son and the other ground-team members."

"I'll warn my son against talking to law enforcement officials without his father present," Patrick said, his voice low and his eyes boring directly into Chastain's, "and I'm warning you against speaking with him again unless I'm present. He's still a minor."

"You're in serious trouble, General," Chastain said, matching Patrick's warning gaze. "If I were you, I'd do less warning and more cooperating."

"Bring my attorney here and let me talk with her, and then I will cooperate," Patrick said. "I want my attorney."

"We have the chief counsel of the Civil Air Patrol on the line," Chastain said, motioning to a phone with a flashing hold button. "He's authorized everyone in your squadron to talk to us."

"That's fine, but I still want my attorney first."

"I'm very surprised at this attitude of yours, General," Chastain said, looking at Patrick suspiciously, then shaking his head in confusion. "I thought you'd want to do everything in your power to advance our investigation. Instead, you seem to be doing everything you can to hinder it."

"I want my attorney," was all Patrick said.

Chastain glanced at the woman beside him, then shook his head again as he went through Leo's identification. "Fine," he said resignedly after several minutes. "You and Trooper Slotnick will be placed under arrest until she arrives." The agent named Brady who had frisked Patrick and Leo made them turn around and place their hands behind their backs, and for the second time that day they were in handcuffs. "You're charged with violating Homeland Security executive directives and entering controlled airspace without permission." Chastain's fingers poised over his laptop. "What's your attorney's name?"

"Darrow Horton."

Chastain looked up from the keyboard, and all of the agents began another round of surprised stares. "Darrow Horton?"

"You've heard of her?"

"You mean, *former attorney general* Darrow Horton?"

"That's the one. Need her number? Her Washington office is just a couple blocks from the Justice Department."

Chastain nodded at his agents to silently tell them to take the handcuffs off. "Of course," he said. "She represented you when the Gardner administration indicted you for ordering attacks against noncombatants, disobeying lawful orders, and dereliction of duty, correct?"

"I want my lawyer," Patrick repeated.

Chastain smiled. "Tough guy," he said. "Too bad the tough-guy act is blinding you to how much shit you're in." He turned back to his laptop. "No phone calls are allowed for now, but we'll contact Miss Horton for you. You can go." He turned next to Leo. "Trooper Slotnick, I hope you'll be much more cooperative than the general."

"I want my lawyer," Leo said, giving Patrick a wink as he walked past.

In the hangar, Patrick met up again with Rob Spara, who was with David Bellville and Michael Fitzgerald. "That was quick," Rob said. "We were in there for a lot longer."

"I refused to answer any questions and lawyered up," Patrick said. "They couldn't do much with me after that except arrest me."

"Good on you, General," Fitzgerald said. "I told them to kiss my ass too until I get a lawyer—they weren't too interested in talkin' to me after that. Which was good, because I have no friggin' idea how to get a lawyer."

"I don't know if that's such a good idea, Patrick," Spara said worriedly. "I spoke with the CAP attorney from headquarters, and he told everyone to cooperate fully."

"That's maybe good for CAP, but not necessarily for you," Patrick said. "I'll let my attorney straighten things out."

"If they ever let us call anyone," Bellville remarked. "How long can they keep us here incommunicado like this? They took our cell phones and even the squadron's computers."

"They said we couldn't use cell phones," Patrick said. "Let me see what I can do." He motioned to Brad to follow him, then walked over to an isolated corner of the hangar as far from the break room as he could. "Keep an eye out for guys talking into their sleeves," he told his son. He raised his right hand, then activated his personal satellite Internet portal, his artificial lens monitors, and his virtual keyboard.

His first VoIP phone call was to Darrow Horton in Washington. "Patrick!" Darrow said excitedly. Darrow—named after famed libertarian and criminal attorney Clarence Darrow, a distant relative—was a bit older than Patrick, tall and slender, with long dark hair and sparkling blue eyes, an avid outdoor-sports enthusiast as well as a brilliant attorney. At that moment she was outdoors on a video-enabled laptop—obviously not in her Washington office. "Things are a little busy since the attack in Reno, but it's nice to hear from you. Wish I could see you. Your webcam not working?"

"Hi, Darrow," Patrick said, pronouncing her name "Darra" in the proper North Carolina way, which was where she was originally from. "No, I'm on a . . . different machine right now. This is a business call."

"Uh-oh," Darrow said. "What did you do now?"

"I'm here in Battle Mountain, Nevada," Patrick explained. "I was airborne during the nationwide airspace closure, and now I'm being detained."

"Ouch," Darrow said. "Homeland Security—that's going to be

tough until things calm down, if they ever do. Where's Battle Mountain?"

"North-central Nevada."

"Good. I'm up in Friday Harbor, Washington, on vacation, so it won't take that long to get to you. Who's got you? FAA? Homeland Security? Customs and Border Protection?"

"FBI."

"Another ouch." He could see her thinking, planning strategies; then: "Okay, I'll get my staff on the case back in D.C., and I'll get a car and start heading in your direction. I should be there in a couple days. What in the world is in Battle Mountain, Nevada?"

"What's left of the Space Defense Force, and my son."

"How's Bradley doing?"

"He and his Civil Air Patrol strike team found an airplane-crash survivor yesterday," Patrick said proudly. "He's turning into a young man. You won't recognize him when you see him."

"And Gia?"

"MIA."

"Again?" Patrick wasn't sure, but he thought Darrow didn't really sound concerned or empathetic. She spent as much time on canoeing trips and rock-climbing expeditions as she did in courtrooms—Patrick knew few men who had a chance in keeping up with her, including himself. Darrow did not like weakness, in herself or in others. She always felt that Gia Cazzotto had been too quick to blame others for her downfall, and it left a bad mark on all women. But men were a different issue. Patrick always felt that Darrow wasn't looking for a man who could keep up with her, but one who was strong in other areas. "Sorry. We'll have a chance to talk when I get there."

"Thanks. I'm looking forward to seeing you."

"Dad?" Brad touched his father's shoulder. "Someone heading this way."

"Gotta go, Darrow. Thank you." He terminated the call and

turned. It was the female FBI agent who'd been with Chastain in the break room. Patrick got to his feet as she approached. She was a bit taller than he was, probably about ten years younger, with long dark hair, dark eyes, and an athletic body. She wore a dark gray suit with a low-cut cream blouse under the jacket that accentuated her breasts very well. Her eyes were narrow and inquisitive as she crossed the hangar, but when she noticed Patrick standing, she immediately put on a friendly smile.

Patrick held out a hand to her as she approached. "We were never introduced," he said. "Patrick."

"Everyone knows who you are, sir," she said. She took his hand and shook it with a very firm grip. "Special Agent Cassandra Renaldo, U.S. Department of Homeland Security, antiterrorist unit. Everyone calls me Cassie."

Patrick smiled as she released his hand. "That must be your shooting hand," he said with a smile, shaking his hand in mock pain.

"Sorry," she said, rolling her eyes. "I spend too much time with guy agents who do that to me all the time."

"My son, Brad," Patrick said, putting a hand on his son's shoulder.

They shook hands, and she saw it immediately: that adolescent smitten expression. Brad McLanahan was in love. She gave him a big smile and an appreciative glance. "You're in the Civil Air Patrol too?" she asked, admiring his camouflage field uniform. "I think that is so exciting for a young man." Brad didn't answer, but continued to gaze at her, casting glances at her cleavage. Cassandra gave him another approving smile, then turned back to Patrick. "Both of you, working together. How cool is that?"

"Agent Renaldo . . ."

"Cassie, please," she said. She gave him her best contrite expression, then said, "Honest, Patrick, I'm not trying to get you to talk to me . . ." She gave him a sly smile, then added, "Although I *was* sent over here to ask you again if you would talk to us."

"I want my attorney first, Cassandra."

"That's what I told them you'd say, but I had to ask first." She then shrugged and added, "And, I *did* want to meet you. I couldn't believe it when Special Agent Chastain called up your info. We thought it was a mistake." Patrick smiled and nodded but said nothing. Cassandra looked sheepishly at him and Brad, then said, "So. A little father-and-son talk over here?" No response. "Brad, I heard you found a survivor from a plane crash, *alive*. Congratulations."

"Thank you," Brad said. He squared up his shoulders and added, "My team and I found him. I was the cadet strike-team leader."

"Wow. You're a hero. Pretty cool. What a great story." She turned to Patrick. "You must be very proud of him, sir."

"I want to speak with my—"

Cassandra held up her hands. "I'm sorry, I'm sorry, Patrick—I don't mean to pressure you or chat you up in hopes of getting you to talk to us," she said. "I . . . I really did want to meet you. You're a hero to a lot of us." She held out a hand again, then said, "When this is over, I hope we have a chance to get together and get to know each other." She gave him a slight smile when he shook her hand, then nodded respectfully. To Brad, she held out her hand. "Very nice to meet you, Cadet McLanahan."

"Call me Brad," he said quickly. Patrick blinked in surprise at that invitation but said nothing.

"Okay, I will, Brad. And you can call me Cassie." She gave him one last smile, turned, and headed back to the break room.

"Hey, she was nice," Brad said after Renaldo departed.

"I guess," Patrick said noncommittally.

Brad looked at his Dad carefully. "You don't think she's nice? I think she's great."

"I really don't know her, Brad," Patrick said. "I've seen an awful lot of folks doing and saying strange things this morning, and I don't feel like trusting anyone just yet." He turned back toward the wall and logged back online once again, with his son guarding his back—so he didn't notice Brad's eyes following Cassandra Renaldo as she walked across the hangar.

Renaldo returned to the others in the break room. Chastain was finishing another cup of coffee. "Well?" he asked.

"Like I thought: he stayed lawyered up," Renaldo said.

"Losing your touch, Renaldo?" one of the other agents quipped.

"My job is to track down extremists, Brady, not to bat my eyes and shake my ass at suspects," Renaldo said acidly. The agent named Brady gave her a "yeah, right" expression. She turned back to Chastain. "I still don't think he's working with any extremist groups, sir," she said.

"Based on?"

"Gut feeling right now," Renaldo admitted. "Plus, he's Patrick McLanahan. Everyone thought he was going to run for president last year."

"David Duke ran for president too," Chastain said. "There are plenty of extremist groups who would welcome McLanahan as their leader, even as a spiritual figurehead."

"Like an American Osama bin Laden," the agent named Brady interjected.

"You're comparing Patrick McLanahan to Osama bin Laden, Brady? Are you insane?" Renaldo asked. "Sir, I don't think we should abandon our investigation, but I just don't feel it. He's not the target."

"Anyone who lawyers up right away like that sets my alarm bells off, Renaldo," Chastain said. "The guy's been through hell fighting off the Gardner indictment, and he could be angry at the government for sticking him in this shithole assignment. When a disaster like the attack in Reno happens, most everyone cooperates,

but not McLanahan. And what in the world is he doing out in
the middle of nowhere at Battle Mountain? There's nothing out
here—a few buildings, a skeleton staff, not many aircraft. Hell, the
Space Defense Force doesn't *really* exist. And what was McLanahan doing flying around when he knew the airspace was closed?
Things aren't adding up."

"McLanahan wasn't flying—Judah Andorsen was," Renaldo
said. "I can't wait to have a chat with *him*."

"The guy has been talking with investigators since he flew
home," Chastain said. "He's giving statements to everyone, and so
far he checks out. The guy is cooperating, which is more than I can
say for McLanahan."

"Well, I don't think McLanahan is going to talk before his lawyer shows up."

"We've already heard from his damned lawyer," Chastain said.
"I can't figure out how a D.C. law firm found out we had one of
their clients in Nevada, but Washington is already ordering us to
charge McLanahan or release him."

"I thought I saw McLanahan in a corner working on a laptop
with his son, but I checked and he didn't have one," Renaldo said.
She thought for a moment, then said, "McLanahan's son."

"What about him?"

When Renaldo didn't answer right away, the agent named
Brady smiled and nodded. "You couldn't get to the old man . . . so
you got to his teenage *son*?" He chuckled. "That's the Renaldo I
know and love!"

"I didn't go after the son—he was after *me*."

"Then he must like older women," Brady said. Renaldo
scratched the tip of her nose with an upraised middle finger. "But
the boy wasn't flying with the father."

"If the old man is involved with any extremist groups, the boy
may be able to tell us," Chastain said. "There's no way McLanahan
is going to let you near his son in here, and if we arrest him he'll

tell his son to keep quiet. You'll have to approach the son some other time."

"No problem," Renaldo said. "In the meantime, I still want a crack at hunky Trooper Slotnick. Give me the letters from his boss and his union, and maybe he'll talk to me about what McLanahan was doing out there." Chastain handed her a folder with several faxes from different agencies and courts, ordering all personnel to cooperate with the FBI and Homeland Security. "At least maybe I can chat him up and find out more about him that I can use later."

"They don't call you the 'Black Widow' for nothing, Renaldo— you have your way with your victims, then eat them," Brady said. "It's fun to watch a person who loves what they do."

"The one thing I hate more than smart-ass FBI agents like you, Brady, is extremists and terrorists," Cassandra Renaldo said. "There are extremists nearby in this stinking-hot desert—I can smell them. Even if it turns out to be a genuine national hero like Patrick McLanahan, I'm going to make it my business to throw his ass into a supermax prison as fast as I possibly can."

THOMPSON FEDERAL BUILDING, RENO, NEVADA

THE NEXT DAY

Smoke still billowed out of the stricken Thompson Federal Building and in several other nearby buildings as well. Investigators and searchers wearing biohazard suits were still being kept three blocks away from the crash site, and other responders were being kept six blocks away because of lingering radioactivity.

In the early-morning stillness, a V-22 Osprey tilt-rotor aircraft flew over the crash site in airplane mode, then transitioned to helicopter mode and cruised slower over the area. Minutes later, as it made a third pass over the building at one hundred feet aboveground and thirty knots, the rear cargo ramp opened and two figures dropped out.

The figures landed upright about a half block from each other in front of the federal building. Each humanoid figure was twelve feet high, medium gray in color. Its trunk and shoulders were large, but its arms and legs were little more than hydraulic pistons, and its head was a dark low-profile dome with sensor arrays behind protective dielectric windows arrayed all around it. They each carried two large bags.

"CID One, on the ground," Lieutenant Colonel Jason Richter, piloting the first robot, radioed. The robot, called a CID, or Cybernetic Infantry Device, was a manned robot that used advanced materials and systems to enable its pilot to do functions and tasks equal to a large armored fighting vehicle. "Check."

"Two," Charlie Turlock, piloting the second CID, responded. She looked up at the gaping hole in the building where the King Air had entered. "My God."

"Radiation levels are lower than reported," Richter said. "Our time on station should be about an hour. Let's go."

They approached the rear entrance to the building, and Jason kicked the reinforced door open. The security area was still intact, but he could see that the floors above had collapsed and the hallway beyond security was impassable. "Can't go this way," he radioed.

"From the outside, then?" Turlock suggested.

"You want to climb the outside just to show off," Richter said.

"Damn right," Turlock said. "Follow me." On the outside of the building, she examined the best route up to the hole. Looping one pack on her back by its carrying straps, she merely reached up and, floor by floor like a ladder, climbed up the outside of the shattered building, punching her armored hands and feet through cracked walls and windows. On the ninth floor, which was the lower edge of the hole, she smashed through the walls and windows as easily as brushing away cobwebs and climbed inside.

"Looks like the plane punched almost all the way through the building, then collapsed a bunch of floors down below," Turlock radioed. "Radiation levels are much higher up here—I might only have another thirty minutes."

"Roger, then we can switch."

"Roger," Turlock said. She started scanning the devastation around her. The right wingtip of the King Air had sliced an entire hallway wall open, and at a desk in one of the offices, Turlock found a young woman, half burned, still sitting at a reception desk. "One casualty found. I'll set up the sling." She withdrew a large sling, cable, and pulleys from her bag, rigged the pulley up on a support beam, looped the cable through the pulley, recovered the body of the young woman, put her in the sling, and lowered her to Richter on the ground. He carried the body over to the rescuers in hazmat suits outside the cordon while Turlock pulled the sling back up.

She found no one else as she carefully made her way down the ripped-apart hallway, then down one collapsed floor to where the

burned hulk of the King Air rested. "I'm at the plane," she radioed. "Radiation levels are very high here. I'm going to take a peek
inside, and then I'll probably have to get out."

"Roger," Richter said. He was watching a video feed from Turlock's CID unit. "Be careful—that floor looks very unstable."

"Yes, Dad," Turlock responded. She was able to climb up the
left side of the fuselage. The entry door was partially unhinged,
most of the glass throughout the entire plane had shattered, and
the cabin of the plane was charred and melted—but, surprisingly,
the cockpit appeared to be in better condition. "Hey, we may have
lucked out—I think the pilot is still in here, and mostly intact! I
might be able to get him out . . . or pieces of him, at least. Stand
by—I'm going to open the door." Turlock grasped the air-stair
hatch in her armored hands and pulled. The door broke free . . .
and then the entire fuselage rolled left and fell about three feet.
Turlock was able to twist away, narrowly missing being trapped
between the fuselage and the crushed concrete floor.

"You okay, Charlie?" Richter asked.

"Yeah, but the entry door is blocked now," Turlock replied. She
checked forward. "Okay, I'm going to try one more thing, and then
I'll have to get out." She moved forward and stood over the pilot's
windshield. The remains of the pilot were barely recognizable as
human—the body was badly burned and half smashed against the
control wheel and instrument panel. "The pilot is one crispy crit-
ter, but I think he was wearing a fireproof flight suit, because most
of the torso is intact. Let's see if I can yank him out." Turlock first
used her powerful armored fingers like the Jaws of Life to cut the
control wheel free, then reached through the windshield, grasped
the pilot's seat and as much of what was strapped onto it as she
could, and pulled . . .

. . . and as she did, the fuselage and the smashed building roared
like an angry lion and the floors gave way. The plane dropped
straight down two floors, then slid forward twenty feet, crashed

through the front of the federal building, and fell the remaining six floors to the street.

"Charlie!" Richter shouted. He used every erg of energy in his CID unit to dash around to the front of the building. The plane was underneath a mass of rubble. Richter began furiously digging through the debris, appearing as if he were wading through waist-deep water, throwing chunks of concrete and steel in every direction until he reached the plane. The fuselage was upside down—he couldn't see Turlock, and her video feed was dark.

Like a scrap-cutting machine gone berserk, Richter began plunging his superhydraulic hands and arms through the underside of the nose section of the King Air, ripping pieces of steel and aluminum away in large sheets and chunks. In seconds he had torn through the entire left side of the plane and, like a wrecking crane, ripped away the entire nose section. He finally found Turlock's CID unit underneath what was left of the cockpit and instrument panel. "Jesus, Charlie, can you hear me? *Charlie* . . . ?"

"I'm . . . I'm okay," Turlock responded several tense moments later. "Wow, what a ride!" She raised herself up to a sitting position and threw the pilot's seat and pieces of the instrument panel away. Richter pulled more debris from her legs and tried to help her up, but she stopped him. "Wait . . . oh, *yuk!*"

"What the hell is it, Charlie?" he asked.

"It's the pilot."

"The pilot?" Richter looked around. "I don't see anyone."

Turlock motioned to the thick mass of charred debris covering the entire front of her CID unit. *"This* is the evidence we were looking for," she said. She pulled a piece of fireproof flight suit off her armored chest. "Looks like they're going to have to swab *me* for *his* DNA."

FOUR

*I don't think change is stressful. I think failure is
stressful.*

— Bob Stearns

The White House, Washington, D.C.

Later that day

The president of the United States, Kenneth Phoenix, strode into
the press briefing room, followed by the vice president, Ann Page,
and the director of the Federal Bureau of Investigation, Justin
Fuller. The reporters assembled in the room shot to their feet,
wearing surprised expressions—they had not been told that the
president himself would be attending the daily press briefing.

"Good afternoon, ladies and gentlemen," Phoenix began.
"Please take your seats." The president was just forty-nine years
old, tall and ruggedly handsome, but the past year had taken a
toll on him, and he looked much older. Ken Phoenix's career—as
a former Marine Corps attorney, U.S. attorney general, and vice
president of the United States—had, to say the least, been a se-

ries of challenges. He was always able to overcome them, but the
journey had never been easy for him and his family. His face told
everyone that the hard journey was still under way.

"I know that you had been briefed that Vice President Page and
I were at secret undisclosed locations until the full examination of
the attack in Reno was concluded," Phoenix began, "but that was
not the case. Our responses had to be immediate, and although
we have very good emergency facilities all across the country, Vice
President Page and I, who as you know serves as both my chief of
staff and my national security adviser and press officer, decided to
stay in Washington.

"Let me give you the latest information that I was just given by
FBI director Fuller. Based on his investigations and the fact that
there haven't been any more attacks, the FBI is recommending to
the Department of Homeland Security, U.S. Northern Command,
which is in charge of the defense of the continental United States,
and the North American Aerospace Defense Command, which
is in charge of the air defense of the United States and Canada,
that the airspace around the United States be reopened, with strict
limitations. All aircraft will be required to be on flight plans filed
on the ground. Any aircraft not on a flight plan may be attacked
by ground or airborne air-defense units without warning. These
limitations will be relaxed as the investigations proceed, but I agree
with the director that we exercise an abundance of caution.

"Next: The radioactive material detected at the Reno crash site
was iridium-192, used in medical radiography as well as industrial
nondestructive testing facilities," the president went on. "It was not
a nuclear bomb . . . I repeat, it was *not* a nuclear bomb. Iridium-192
is relatively widespread in industry and medicine and has a short
half-life, which means its toxicity degrades in a matter of days, and
decontamination procedures are common and well known." He
paused for a moment, then said, "The source of the material was
positively identified as part of a shipment of radioactive materi-

als stolen from the FBI by suspected domestic terrorists yesterday morning."

The room erupted into sheer bedlam, with every reporter leaping to his or her feet trying to ask a question. Phoenix held up his hands and spoke in a soft voice, which forced the reporters to quiet themselves so they could hear the president's remarks. "It was my decision not to reveal the theft, in order to prevent a panic," Phoenix went on after the reporters took their seats again. "The materials were stolen in an FBI sting gone bad north of Sacramento, California. Several FBI agents and deputy sheriffs were killed." A ripple of shock and disbelief swept through the room. "FBI director Fuller briefed me and outlined a plan for an investigation and arrest of known terrorist leaders, and I approved the plan. Unfortunately, no arrests could be made that could have stopped the attack on the federal building in Reno, Nevada.

"I want to assure the American people that I am in Washington and I'm in constant contact with the FBI and other law enforcement agencies across the country, and we are on the hunt for the terrorists who launched this horrible attack," Phoenix went on. "I am personally overseeing the government response, and it is my highest priority. We have no way of knowing if there will be more attacks, but since the other stolen materials haven't been recovered yet, we are operating on the assumption that the terrorists intend to use them. We will do everything in our powers to stop them from doing so."

The president paused, then waved a hand as reporters started to raise their hands with questions. "I'm not going to take questions right now. I'm going to say one more thing before I get back to work. At first, I was concerned about creating a panic, so I didn't want any information released until we were further along in the investigation. I realize now that was a mistake. Instead of worrying about the American people panicking, I should have enlisted your help in tracking down the terrorists.

"So this is what I'm charging all Americans to do right now and well after the terrorists are captured: be vigilant, be safe, be wary, be suspicious. We possibly could have caught the terrorists if I had released the info on the theft sooner, so don't make the same mistake I did. Call the police or the FBI if you suspect something—don't be afraid of bias, discrimination, or paranoia. That's all for now. Vice President Page and Director Fuller will take a few questions, but I have plenty of work for both of them as well, so it'll be short. Thank you." And the president left the dais and headed for the Oval Office.

Because of all the cutbacks in every level of government following the severe double-dip recession of 2012, the West Wing of the White House was a much quieter place these days than it was during the Martindale and Gardner administrations under which Phoenix previously served: no staffers constantly running in and out of the Oval Office, no ringing telephones, no queue of cabinet officials waiting for yet another meeting. The Oval Office was actually a haven again. Ken Phoenix took off his jacket, hung it up on the stand behind the door to his private study, poured himself a mug of coffee, and turned on the four hidden Oval Office high-def wall monitors—no one around to do all those little things for him anymore.

One satellite news channel was showing Vice President Page's and FBI director Fuller's press briefing—it looked to the president as if Ann was winding it up quickly, as they agreed to do beforehand—but another monitor was showing more coverage of the search for survivors in the wreckage of the Thompson Federal Building in Reno by the two Cybernetic Infantry Device manned robots. The president winced when he saw the video of the plane crashing to the ground with the one robot clinging to the front of it, and he breathed a sigh of relief—he had seen the replay a half-dozen times now, but he always had the same reaction—when he saw the second robot pull the first out, and they walked away apparently unharmed.

Minutes later there was a knock on the door to the Oval Office, and a moment after that Ann and Justin walked in. "I know you'd be willing to do a longer press conference, Director," Ann was saying as they came in, "but believe me, less is more. Save the longer briefings for when you have something good to report."

"I agree with her, Justin," Phoenix said as he watched his monitors.

"And may I suggest, Mr. President," Ann said, "that you not be quite so anxious to apologize for any executive decision you make. You made a tactical decision not to release any information about the FBI operation or stolen materials, and you had no way of knowing that the materials stolen would be used so soon after being stolen, or if public observation and reporting, however accurate or timely, could have helped stop the attack. You have nothing to apologize for, and you end up writing your critics' copy for them."

"I believe the American people want honesty and sincerity from their leaders in times like this," Phoenix said. "My critics don't seem to have any problem writing copy about me, with or without my help." Nonetheless, he nodded to Ann that he understood her recommendations, which she silently acknowledged, then motioned to his monitors. "Man, I never get tired of watching that video of those robots in action," he said. "Wish we could afford an entire brigade full of them."

"What video is that, sir?" the director of the Federal Bureau of Investigation, Justin Fuller, asked. Fuller was a twenty-five-year veteran of the FBI, with a very similar background to Phoenix's: former U.S. Marine and law degree before joining the FBI. He looked at the flat-panel TV, which was normally hidden behind a painting on the Oval Office wall. "Oh, the CID robot units. Yes, sir, amazing technology."

"They all but succeeded in stopping the Turks in Iraq, and just two of them destroyed that Russian base in Yemen," Phoenix said. "But I think those two in Reno are the only ones left." He stood and shook hands with Fuller. The FBI director was a few years older but looked considerably younger than the president. Phoenix motioned Fuller to a seat, muted the monitors, then took his place at the head of the conversation area, where Ann was already seated. "Okay, Justin, what's the latest on the investigation of the attack in Reno?"

"Another HRT officer has died of his wounds," Fuller replied somberly. "Fifteen-year FBI veteran. Father of two."

"My God," Vice President Page breathed. Ann Page was in her early sixties, a physicist and engineer, former two-term California senator, and a veteran astronaut; in the trimmed-down Phoenix White House, she acted as chief of staff and national security adviser as well as performing her duties as vice president. "What an incredibly brazen and violent attack. Any suspects, Director?"

"We're looking at a number of extremist groups in the West, ma'am," Fuller said. "The pilot of that King Air made a radio call to the Reno Airport control tower and used the phrases 'live free or die' and 'the Lord has spoken.' We're back-checking those phrases to see if they're associated with any particular groups. The use of the King Air, the direction of flight, and the target are all being factored in as well. The search teams we sent to the crash site also found a homemade flag belonging to a well-known extremist group."

"Who are they?" the president asked.

"They call themselves the Knights of the True Republic, sir," Fuller said. "They're based in a fairly isolated part of northwestern Nevada near the town of Gerlach. They're led by a minister named Reverend Jeremiah Paulson. It's a collection of old-timers, military veterans, bikers, ranchers, outdoorsmen, miners, and even Native Americans. They claim to be a community of like-minded so-called sovereign citizens that oppose federal, state, and county government interference in local affairs. We've made some arrests and are conducting searches of members' properties—nothing yet.

Paulson was questioned, but the community is compartmentalized enough that they know very little about the terrorist side of the organization. But eventually someone who lost a loved one in Reno or is fearful of the leadership will drop a dime."

"You don't sound very hopeful, Director," Phoenix observed.

"It takes time to infiltrate one of these groups, sir," Fuller said, "and there are hundreds of such groups in the western states alone. Most are very small and isolated and don't resort to any sort of violence; this one obviously wants to prove they have the will and the resources to take on the federal government. We've been after them for months. We got them on tape buying weapons and explosives and were about to take them down until they asked about large quantities of radioactive material. We decided to delay the arrests. We took a chance, hoping to nail more members or associates and uncover more plots. The plan backfired."

"Can you round them up again?" Ann asked.

"We may be able to, ma'am, but they've scattered," Fuller said.

"When do you hope to take this group down, Director?" Ann asked.

Fuller spread his hands. "We're almost at square one with the Knights, ma'am," he replied. "It took several months to get a confidential informant close enough to make a buy for the radioactive materials, and now he's dead. Local law enforcement is plainly scared because of the group's power and reach—the sheriff's department lost more men than the FBI that morning. They destroyed four helicopters and killed twelve officers."

"God," Phoenix said under his breath. The president paused, then rubbed his temples in frustration. "And all this because of my economic austerity programs. People are out of work, and there is very little or no government to help them, so they resort to banding together to share whatever little they have. And if they feel they're not getting enough protection from the government, they turn to violence."

Ann looked to the FBI director, giving him a silent order. Fuller caught the glance and said to the president, "If there's nothing else, sir, I'll get back to work."

"Of course, Justin, of course," Phoenix said. He stood and shook hands with Fuller. "Let me know when the funerals for your agents will be—I'd like to attend."

"Of course, sir," Fuller said, then turned and left the Oval Office.

"What a loss he's suffered," Phoenix said somberly after the FBI director departed. "It's got to be crushing him."

"I'm more worried about *you*, Ken," Ann said directly. "You're blaming *yourself* for what this nut-job group did yesterday? Are you insane?"

Phoenix's eyes flared at his vice president's words. "These extremist groups didn't exist before my austerity programs went into effect, Ann . . ."

"Of course they did, Ken," Ann snapped. "But law enforcement went after them more than they do today. How? By borrowing trillions of dollars, raising taxes, or printing money, that's how. Your programs, your decisions, your leadership stopped the destructive financial practices that were driving local, state, and the federal government into the *ground*. Less government. Across-the-board spending cuts. Across-the-board tax cuts. No bailouts for failed institutions or irresponsible actions. All of that has been good for the country. Right-minded folks can see real hope out there.

"But there will always be whack-jobs and extremists who see the continued unemployment and the disparities between the haves and the have-nots and conclude that government isn't working and they need to take the law into their own hands," Ann went on. "You can't reason with them or try to understand them, and you certainly can't look at their murderous actions and blame yourself. The only thing you can do is use every resource at your command to stop them."

She went over to Phoenix and softly put a hand on his shoulder—an unexpectedly gentle gesture, Phoenix immediately thought suspiciously. As if verifying his doubts, she then said sharply, "So snap out of this funk, Ken. I know you well enough to know this is unlike you. I know as former attorney general that you're close to law enforcement in general and the FBI in particular, but you can't let those cops' deaths keep you from forgetting to *lead*. I don't want to see you wallowing in self-pity, Mr. President— I want to see you *act*."

He looked directly into her eyes and recognized exactly how serious she was, then nodded and said, "Sometimes I regret giving you permission to always respond openly, honestly, and directly to me, Ann . . . but this is not one of those times." She slapped him on the side of the shoulder, pleased with his response and with the return of his positive attitude. Phoenix returned to his desk. "We need to give the FBI all the resources they need," he said. "If Fuller's got hundreds of extremist groups spread out over the West, he's going to need unmanned aircraft, surveillance equipment, sensor operators . . . all the stuff we were using in Iraq to monitor the borders."

"I'm sure the Air Force and Army would love to assist the FBI," Ann said. "I'll call a meeting and get it set up."

"I remember that defense contractor Dr. Jon Masters had the equipment to be able to provide precise surveillance of several hundred thousand square miles of varying terrain in Iraq from one aircraft," Phoenix said. "Find out if he can assist. I'm not sure if there's any money in the budget to pay him anything, but maybe he'd be willing to make a donation." Ann smiled, nodded, and made notes to herself on her PDA. While she did this, the president's attention was drawn back to his computer monitors, one of which was still playing a replay of the Cybernetic Infantry Devices' incredible activities at the crash site in Reno.

"Ann, I need you to contact the Justice Department and the solicitor general and get a ruling on something," Phoenix said.

"Regarding what, Mr. President?" When he didn't reply right away, Ann turned toward him, then followed his gaze to the computer monitors. "The robots? What about them?"

"I know they've been in action in the Middle East and Africa, but do you remember the last time they were used inside the United States?"

"Of course I do: San Diego, during the implementation of the guest-worker identification program. They were afraid of mass riots and violence on both sides of the border against the Nanotransponder Identification System, so the robots were deployed around the city."

"And?"

"It was a *nightmare*, that's what," Ann said. "People were more afraid of the robots than of the rioters." She paused in thought, then said, "I'm not sure if the president issued an executive order banning their use within the United States, but I remember the hue and cry against them was pretty intense after that. Why?"

"The FBI needs help in taking on these extremist groups," Phoenix said. "The FBI's budget has been cut by fifty percent, just like everyone else's budget, and that Knights group seems much more heavily armed and just as connected as the FBI. Maybe it's time for the FBI to get some additional firepower. Why stop at UAVs and sensors?"

"Give the *robots* to the FBI?" Ann asked incredulously. She thought about it, her expression seeming to indicate a firm rejection of the idea . . . and then after a few moments, she nodded. "Send them out west, into more isolated parts of Northern California and Nevada . . ."

"If they go into the cities, they can do humanitarian assistance stuff like they're doing on TV," Phoenix said. "I think most folks like to watch those things searching that building—I know I can't stop watching that replay. I'm so amazed that one robot got up out of that wreckage and walked away as easily as if he had jumped into a haystack. But we keep them operating in the countryside, far from population centers, unless they're needed. They have excellent speed and maneuverability."

"But no weapons," Ann said. "I think the thing that freaked people out most in that San Diego deployment were those weapon packs they wore—once people realized they were carrying enough machine guns and missile launchers to take on a squadron of tanks, they were scared. The FBI has plenty of firepower—the robots can be their equalizers."

Phoenix wore a pained expression. "I hate tying their hands, Ann," he said after a moment's consideration. "I think it would best left as a judgment call by the task force commander. If he's faced with threats like advanced weapons or dirty bombs, the robots should be armed appropriately."

"That might be a hard sell to Congress or the American people," Ann observed. "But after the attack in Reno, maybe they'll be open to giving the FBI and Homeland Security more gadgets."

"Agreed. I think the robots would have a much smaller footprint than the Army or Air Force."

"I'll put together a proposal and send it up to the leadership in Congress," Ann said. "Of course, they'll tweak it to make it sound like *their* idea."

"Fine with me."

"Speaking of Reno and reopening the airspace: Director Fuller passed on an interesting tidbit of information to me," Ann said with a sly smile. "There was an airspace violation east of Reno the morning after the attack."

"There *was?*" the president asked incredulously. "Does he think it was connected to the attack in Reno?"

"No, although they are still investigating," Ann said. "But guess who was involved?" Phoenix shook his head—he knew Ann Page hated guessing games, and now that she was indulging in one with him, it got his attention. "Patrick McLanahan."

"*Patrick?* You're *kidding!* What in hell happened?"

"Apparently our friend is a pilot in the Civil Air Patrol out of Battle Mountain, Nevada, and he was involved in a search for a missing plane when the attack in Reno occurred," Ann explained. "Patrick's son is also a member, and he was actually part of the ground team that found the missing plane and rescued a passenger. It was all over the national news this morning."

"Unbelievable! Good for little Bradley—although I'll bet he's not so little anymore. But how did Patrick violate the airspace?"

"The owner of the land where the rescue took place flew the survivor to the hospital, and afterward they were cruising around the local area close to the military air base out there."

"That doesn't sound like something Patrick would do."

"It wasn't. The pilot of the helicopter is a big-time mucky-muck rancher that I guess owns half of Nevada."

"Doesn't matter. Homeland Security and maybe even the Justice Department should put the fear of God into that guy."

"Fuller said they tried, but the rancher has more friends in high places than Billy Graham," Ann said. "He said even Attorney General Caffery got a call. Fuller said that because they were involved in a Civil Air Patrol rescue, everyone decided to back off, but they're continuing their investigation deep in the background."

Phoenix nodded, then shook his head in amusement. "I thought Patrick would just retire and take it easy out there," he said. "I should have known he'd be doing *something*, keeping his hand in the flying game. He'll never change."

"I could sure use him here in Washington, sir," Ann said. "He's the only guy still advocating for the Space Defense Force, and there's that rumor of a bill before Congress to ramp up defense spending again."

"Do that," the president said. "If he's working for living expenses only out in Nevada, I'm sure he'd be willing to do the same in Washington. Besides, Battle Mountain is closing next year, if

I'm not mistaken—they're moving everything to Fallon Naval Air Station."

"Is that . . . situation of his still an issue?" Ann asked.

"Unfortunately, yes, and it'll probably stay like that until President Truznyev of Russia is out of office," the president said. Patrick McLanahan was the head of a secret nongovernmental military operation that had attacked Russian commando and space operation forces in Africa and the Middle East, and since then the Central Intelligence Agency and Federal Bureau of Investigation counterespionage units had intercepted hit squads, supposedly sent by Truznyev, that were intent on assassinating him. "CIA and FBI still say they can spot a hit squad easier if he's isolated rather than in Washington."

"Maybe so, but I'd like him back in Washington," the president said. "We can protect him. I just wish we could pay him what he's worth, but there's just no money in the budget."

"I'll find a place for him, sir," Ann said. "He'll probably want to stay until Bradley graduates from high school, so next summer."

"Put him to work in the meantime. I want a ten-year plan for space forces and long-range strike ready by the time this economy turns around, and he's the guy I want to work on them."

"Will do." She looked at the president, studying him carefully, then said, "I admire you for sticking to this severe austerity plan, Mr. President. But to be totally honest with you, sir, it looks like the pressure is grinding on you. Are you sleeping at all?"

"A few hours a night is all I've ever needed, ever since my years in the Corps," Phoenix said.

"Try not to let the pressure get to you, sir," Ann said. "The programs you put in place *are* working. Unemployment is still high, but it's going down. There's talk that Moody's will restore the U.S.'s triple-A credit rating soon, and the balance-of-trade numbers look very good."

"That's because the dollar is as low as it's ever been in history, commodities are dirt cheap, and no one is buying anything from China and Russia as long as they're continuing their military buildup," the president said. He waved a hand at his vice president. "I know our plan will work, Ann, and I know the folks expect results unreasonably fast. But I see all the suffering out there, and I think if I just loosen the purse strings a little more, I can alleviate some of it. Reduce the cuts we made in Medicare and Social Security by a few percentage points; raise the income level of Medicaid applicants by a little bit; give the states a few more dollars to hire a few more cops and teachers—"

"And we both know what will happen then, sir: they'll scream for more, we'll be forced to borrow and print more money, and the downward spiral will happen all over again," Ann said. "We're moving in the right direction, sir. There's hardship now, but your plans will help everyone in the long run. We need to stay the course."

"Even if we create more of these Knights of the True Republic extremist groups?"

"I would say that the recession helped to create the conditions for these extremists to grow, yes, sir," Ann said, "but they already existed and will always exist, whether we're in prosperity or recession. We need to show the American people that we're not going to tolerate extremism in any form, for whatever reason. I'll get busy right now, draft the legislative proposal for the Army, Air Force, and Sky Masters law enforcement assistance package in the next day or two, we'll go over it, and I'll take it to the congressional leadership right away. So soon after the attack in Reno, I don't think we'll get very much opposition, even from Gardner and his sycophants."

"Joseph Gardner," Phoenix said with an exasperated sigh. "Whatever happened to the rule that former presidents aren't allowed to criticize the current president?"

"That went out with compact discs and free television, Mr.

President," Ann said with a wry smile. She turned serious; the smile disappeared, and she then said, "What we're going to propose is a major counterterrorist offensive against fellow American citizens, sir. We're talking about sending American-manned robots and unmanned aircraft against our own."

"I know that, Ann—"

"I just want to be clear, sir," Ann Page interjected. "We have to stay tough and united on this. It's not going to be popular, not in the *least*. We're laying ourselves open to a lot of criticism—some of it legitimate—that we're creating a state in which the military is used to control and monitor the public. That's not going to sit well with a lot of folks. But in order to guard against more Renos happening, I believe it has to be done." She paused, looking carefully into Phoenix's eyes, then added, "If you don't believe that is true, Mr. President, you should say so now, and tell me to knock it off. We'll quash this, and think of something else to do."

"Frankly, Ann," Phoenix said, after several long moments of thought, "I'm not comfortable with this."

Ann Page's shoulders slumped disappointedly, but moments later she straightened them and said, "Fine, sir. So let's—"

"No, I'm not saying we *shouldn't* do this," Phoenix said. "I don't like it, but I want to shut down the violent extremist groups, and do it *now*. I'm going to hunt those bastards down with all the tools at my disposal—even the military. Draft that legislative proposal and let's get on it right away . . . before those other stolen radioactive casks end up inside another federal building."

THE ARIZONA BORDER, THIRTY MILES
SOUTHEAST OF YUMA, ARIZONA

DAYS LATER

"Freeze!" the U.S. Border Patrol agent shouted in Spanish through his van's public-address loudspeakers. His partner shined a powerful searchlight into the faces of the migrants in front of them, instantly blinding them. "This is the United States Border Patrol. Drop all your belongings and raise your hands!"

The group of about twenty illegal immigrants—they were about eight miles north of the border here in the Yuma Desert, with the closest legal border crossing twenty-five miles away in San Luis—did as they were told slowly and carefully, without a sense of fear or anger. No one panicked or ran—obviously a group experienced in getting caught, the officer thought.

The economy might be in the tank, the U.S. Border Patrol agent thought, and a lot fewer Mexicans were illegally crossing the border because there were no jobs in the United States. But they were still coming, and although the Border Patrol's budget had been cut and a lot of the technology they relied on was in disrepair or simply not deployed, they were still catching them. The Mexicans were all carrying several one-gallon jugs of water looped around their necks with rope, plus backpacks, trash bags, or whatever else they could find to carry their belongings. They ranged in age from the teens to sixties, both men and women, and most looked in fairly good health, which was necessary when making this dangerous border crossing in such hostile conditions, especially in summer.

"Yuma, Unit Eighteen, intercepted a group of twenty," the officer radioed. "Requesting additional transportation."

"Looks like we might finally be getting some decent intel again," the second officer said. "They were exactly where we were briefed."

"Yeah, and remember, they briefed us that we might run into more OTMs," the first officer said. "Let's see if this was the group they talked about." They had been seeing a lot more OTMs—Other Than Mexicans—on these intercepts lately—some were from as far away as China and Africa.

With the van's headlights and spotlight still shining in their faces, the agents had the migrants move away from their belongings except for one bottle of water each, then sit apart from one another. All complied silently. Since it was too dangerous for just two agents to try to handcuff and search twenty migrants, it was better if they just waited for their backup to arrive, so they took their shotguns and stood, walking up and down the line, keeping watch.

The first officer stopped in front of one migrant. Most of them made occasional eye contact with the officers, but this one seemed to purposely look away all the time. Something about him didn't seem right. He was in his midthirties, with several days' beard growth, but somehow he looked out of place. Many migrants wore knit caps even in summertime—at night temperatures in the desert could drop sixty degrees from daytime highs—and many wore layers of clothing so they wouldn't have to carry them. But this one looked . . . different, like a guy *trying* to make himself look like a migrant.

"Jim, I'm going to have a chat with this one," the first officer said.

"What's up?"

"A feeling. Maybe an OTM." He motioned to the man and said in Spanish, "Stand up, sir." The man looked up and pointed at his chest, then did as he was told when he saw the officer nod his head. "Turn around, hands behind your back."

"Wait for backup, Pete."

"Just this one." He was the more experienced officer, so the other agent demurred, but rattled the ammo bandolier on his shotgun to remind the others that he was covering them.

The officer named Pete pulled out a set of plastic handcuffs and locked the migrant's wrists together in a control hold. "Just relax, sir," he said in Spanish. "What's your—"

All he saw was a blur of motion, and suddenly he felt a hand drive into his face just below his nose. He tried to yell, but it came out a bloody gurgle. He then felt a knife-edge hand slam into his throat, then nothing.

"Freeze!" the second officer shouted, and he whirled and leveled the shotgun at the migrant from his hip. But with amazing speed three other migrants shot to their feet, pulled the shotgun skyward, and knocked the officer to the ground. They quickly armed themselves with the officers' sidearms and backup weapons . . .

. . . then, at a nod from the first migrant, began shooting the officers and the migrants on the ground, one shot each to the head.

"Twenty more miles to the pickup point," the leader of the hit squad said in Russian. "I don't know how far away the other Border Patrol vehicle is, but if they're coming from Yuma, we should be good. At the pickup point we split up, then rendezvous as briefed. Let's go." The four assassins picked up their packs and piled into the Border Patrol vehicle. Before driving off, one of them activated a small device that would scramble the GPS tracking signal from the van.

JOINT AIR BASE BATTLE MOUNTAIN

DAYS LATER

It was truly an amazing thing to watch, Patrick thought: a five-hundred-thousand-pound aircraft that seemed to float through the air as gracefully as a blimp. The C-57 Skytrain II—named after the military version of the Douglas DC-3 from World War II fame—was a flying-wing transport plane, resembling the B-2A Spirit stealth bomber but with a thicker bulbous midsection and its three turbofan engines mounted on pylons atop the rear of the fuselage. Originally designed to be a stealthy cruise-missile launch aircraft and aerial refueling tanker, today it could be adapted to various missions by uploading different mission modules in its two large internal cargo bays.

The Skytrain floated across the numbers on Battle Mountain's shortest runway, stopped within two thousand feet, and turned off at the first taxiway. Thanks to its advanced engines and mission-adaptive wing technology, with which tiny computer-controlled micro-actuators could make almost the entire fuselage and wing skin a lift or drag device, the huge aircraft could fly close to the speed of sound at gross weight, as well as half as slow as any other aircraft of its size. The massive plane taxied directly into an empty hangar, and the doors closed behind it as soon as the engines shut down. Patrick parked at his assigned spot on the ramp beside the hangar and waited inside at the Skytrain's belly entry hatch.

"Patrick! Hey, long time no see!" Jonathan Masters exclaimed as he climbed down the entry ladder and emerged from the plane. Jon Masters was chief engineer of Sky Masters, Inc., a high-tech military-systems design firm that invented much of the technology used in the C-57. Just a few years younger than Patrick, Jon Masters still looked like a punkish twenty-year-old whiz kid—tall, skinny, with unkempt hair and gangly features. He shook hands with Patrick with the same limp "cold fish" handshake that always made Patrick smile—it was as if Jon purposely used that weak handshake just to make the other person uneasy, even a longtime associate. "How have you been, my friend?"

"Not bad, not bad," Patrick said. "How's the biz?"

"Believe it or not, hanging in there," Jon said. "Bunch of canceled contracts, like everyone else, but we're in negotiations on a few that might keep the company afloat." He patted the C-57 on its smooth, seamless composite carbon-fiber side. "They gave us funds to finish building the two 'Losers' we had half assembled on the floor, and they might give us money to build a few more if we can demonstrate full mission capability of a few more mission modules."

"Then it's not a 'Loser' anymore, is it?" Patrick said. Jon had called the C-57 the Loser because it had lost the Air Force's Next Generation Bomber competition, which was eventually canceled anyway. "It survived because it's a good multimission design."

"We could still use you down in Vegas, my friend," Jon said. "You'd be flying, not sitting around on your ass in this dust bowl. This place is closing down in less than a year. The Air Force is actually talking about building bombers again, and I know you're more than a little interested in those things. And I might even give you something you've probably had very little of in the past few years: something called *money.*"

Before Patrick could respond, another person exited the C-57, and Patrick turned to greet him. "Welcome to Battle Mountain, Colonel," he said.

"Thank you, sir," U.S. Army Lieutenant Colonel Jason Richter responded, shaking Patrick's hand with a surprised look on his face. Richter was a full head taller and twenty years younger than Patrick, trim and athletic, with dark good looks and an air of supreme confidence . . . and an attitude to match. "I wasn't told you would be part of this project."

"I'm not part of your project," Patrick said, "but I'm granted access to the flight line when certain special air-mission aircraft come in, and the arrival of one of Jon's monstrosities qualifies. Besides, the doc here and I go way back."

"Patrick!" a female voice shouted happily. A young, lithe, strawberry-blond woman sprang out of the Skytrain's belly and fairly leaped into Patrick's arms. "Oh my *God,* the pack is back! How lovely to see you again!"

"Same here, Charlie," Patrick said. Charlie Turlock—her real first name, not a nickname—was Jason Richter's longtime assistant design engineer in the Army's Infantry Transformational Battlelab, designing high-tech infantry-soldier enhancements, mostly in the field of robotics. Charlie had left the Army to work with Jon Masters, but Jason had elected to stay in the Army. "Have a nice flight?"

"Very nice flight—until I wandered up to the cockpit and found *no one flying the plane!*" Charlie exclaimed. "A plane that size, *with nobody flying it?* That's insane! I need a little drinky-poo after that."

"That's the wave of the future, Charlie," Patrick said. "Transport, reconnaissance, surveillance, air-defense suppression, resupply, long-range strategic strike—all unmanned. Half the planes that fly in and out of here these days are unmanned, and the military graduates more unmanned-aircraft pilots than manned-aircraft pilots these days. They can't keep up with the demand for pilots and sensor operators, especially with all the military budget cutbacks. Jon has led the way in designing unmanned systems for years, but the pace is definitely accelerating. Any new ideas you come up with, get them into the system as fast as you can. If you don't do it, someone else will."

"Hey, we don't need research or new-product counseling from some old retired guy," Jon Masters quipped. "For some reason the great Patrick McLanahan has decided to check out of the real world and banish himself and his infinitely smarter son to the armpit of the world—which, I believe, used to be Battle Mountain's unofficial designation, no?"

"Don't be bad-mouthing my town, Jon," Patrick said.

"Well, well, look who's here," another voice said, and Wayne "Whack" Macomber emerged from the Skytrain. "The famous disappearing general." A former college football star and Air Force special-operations commando, Whack towered over the others. His face still bore the scars of being held captive and brutally interrogated by the *Glavnoye Razvedyvatel'noye Upravleniye,* or GRU, the Russian military-intelligence bureau, the year before, and he walked with a bit of a limp.

They shook hands. "How are you feeling, Whack?" Patrick asked.

"Better," Whack said. "Thanks for all the visits." Whack had spent several months in a hospital recovering from his injuries, and Patrick had seen to it that he visited him at least once a week; his former private security firm paid for his hospital bills and rehabilitation. "Thought I'd tag along with Charlie and Richter on this deal—hangin' around the house and doin' nuthin' but rehab was driving me batty."

"You bring one of the Tin Man units?"

"Of course," Whack said. "Masters still wants to sell a bunch of them to the government, so I'll demo it if they want. Actually, I kinda like wearin' the long undies these days—the exoskeleton is like a whole-body brace."

"Glad to see you up and around," Patrick said. He turned to Jason and Charlie. "You guys are all set in this hangar—everything you asked for is right here. If you need help with housing, just ask, but the trailers are the best we have right now. The base is shrinking every day. We once had over six thousand here—now we're down to less than a thousand. But we're still—"

"I think I can take it from here now, General," a voice said behind Patrick. He turned and found FBI special agents Chastain,

Renaldo, and the other federal agents walking up behind him. "Thank you for parking the plane."

"That's my job," Patrick said. To Jon and the others he said, "I'm just a phone call away if you need me, and if you'd like to explore the town later—"

"I think we may be very busy for the next few nights, General," Chastain interjected. "Thanks for the offer." His body language and tone definitely suggested that it was time for Patrick to depart, so he did. After he left, Chastain said to Masters and Richter, "He's not to be hanging out around here except in his official capacity."

"He's a good friend, Agent Chastain, but I know how to protect classified programs," Jon said. "I assure you, if the general wanted to be attached to this project, he could do it with one phone call."

"I highly doubt that—at least, not with me in charge."

"Same for me," Richter muttered acidly.

"He would probably *be* the one in charge . . . if not your boss's boss," Jon said, giving Richter an exasperated expression. This was his first time working with the gifted Army engineer, who was all of his reputation and more: as irritating as he was brilliant. "How many times have you piloted a CID? Patrick's been in combat inside one several times."

"Let's take a look at one of your robots, Colonel," Chastain said, ignoring Jon's remarks. Jon went up inside the C-57, and a moment later the left cargo bay opened and a container was lowered outside. At the same time the landing-gear struts extended, allowing the container to be pulled directly out from underneath the plane.

Richter went over to the container and unlocked the door, and he and Charlie pulled out an odd-looking gray object a little larger than a refrigerator—although it was a very large object, Chastain noticed neither of them had any trouble carrying it. The object resembled several dozen boxes of different shapes and sizes haphazardly stuck and stacked together. "That's *it?*" Chastain asked. "It has to be assembled first?"

"Not exactly," Charlie said. She turned to the box she had just helped unload. "CID One, deploy."

All of a sudden the object seemed to come alive. Piece by piece, the boxes shifted, folded out more pieces, shifted again, refolded and shifted yet again, and quickly it reconstructed itself into a twelve-foot-tall robot. When it finished unfolding itself, it adopted a sort of low crouch, like a hunter warming himself before a fire.

"The Cybernetic Infantry Device, or CID, version five," Richter said. "We made it a bit taller but made it ten percent lighter, made the armor both stronger and lighter, increased the pressure in the microhydraulic system to boost actuator strength and performance, and miniaturized and improved the sensor suite. Battery life is slightly improved, and—"

"I don't need to hear the sales pitch, Colonel," Chastain interrupted. "Let's see it work."

Richter nodded at Charlie, who almost giggled with excitement as she spoke, "CID One, pilot up." At that command the robot stood, crouched forward with its right leg stuck out straight behind it, and extended its arms backward. At the same time a hatch opened on the robot's back. Charlie climbed up the extended leg, using the leg like a ramp and the arms like railings. She then knelt down on the robot's back just outside the hatch, then started to enter the robot, legs first, followed by arms, and finally her head. When she was fully inside, the hatch closed. Nothing happened for several moments . . .

. . . and then suddenly the robot stood up, and it started hopping up and down, shaking its shoulders, and shadow-boxing with its immense arms and knotted fists like a boxer warming up and getting ready to step into a boxing ring. Chastain couldn't believe how fluid and humanlike it moved—it was nothing like any other robot he had ever seen in his life.

"Pretty cool, huh?" an electronically synthesized voice said. It had Turlock's phraseology, but definitely not her voice. "How do you like me now, Agent Chastain?"

"Amazing," Chastain said. "How does she . . . er, *it* move like that?"

"Thousands of microhydraulic actuators being operated at increased pressure, acting like muscles and ligaments on multiaxis joints, responding to haptic commands using advanced processors," Richter said. Chastain scowled at Richter, who was obviously trying to show up the FBI special agent. "A conventional robot might use one or two large hydraulic actuators to move a limb in one axis—up or down, left or right, in or out. The limbs on the CID are mounted on joints connected with powerful microhydraulic actuators that work completely different from human muscles. The CID has so many of these microactuators that some of its limbs can move in unhuman ways." To demonstrate, Charlie rotated the lower part of the CID's left leg around in a complete circle.

"How strong is it?" one of the other agents asked.

"Let's find out," Charlie said. She walked over to the C-57 Skytrain and carefully placed the CID's hands under the center of the left wing.

"Don't break my plane, Charlie," Jon Masters warned.

"I'm doing it on the jack point, Jon, don't worry," Charlie said. Moments later, they could all see the left strut begin to extend. Charlie moved the plane about four inches up before carefully letting it back down. "It registered about twenty thousand pounds before I got a limit warning."

"It just lifted *ten tons?*" the agent exclaimed.

Charlie climbed out from under the wing. "How about I direct some of that power downward this time?" The CID crouched a bit, then flew upward about fifty feet, grasping onto the steel trusses overhead. "Hey, I think I can see my house from up here!" she deadpanned before dropping back to the concrete floor.

"The CID has survived drops from an aircraft exceeding two hundred feet in altitude and two hundred knots airspeed," Richter said. "The previous version has survived RPG rounds and even thirty-millimeter cannon hits. It can operate underwater up to a hundred feet, and in a chemical, biological, and even radioactive environment for short periods. We can increase its effectiveness with packs that contain different weapons, sensors, even unmanned aircraft. It can—"

"Absolutely no weapons," Chastain said firmly. "Director Fuller made that exceptionally clear, and I concur with his directive: the robot is not to be armed with any weapons. In fact, I don't even want it out in the open unless involved in an actual operation against armed extremists or terrorists and it's been determined that our capabilities might not be superior to theirs. As far as I'm concerned, it's for heavy lifting, and that's all."

"That's a big mistake, Agent Chastain, but it's your call," Richter said. He nodded to the robot, and in a few minutes Charlie had dismounted and stowed the robot back into its self-molded container. "The CID has thousands of advanced capabilities that can easily—"

"Richter, do me and yourself a big favor and shut the hell up," Chastain interrupted. "I don't need your robot or its 'thousands of advanced capabilities.' The FBI uses its own resources to investigate crime and make arrests, and if we use any outside agencies at all, they are directly controlled and supervised by the FBI, and function in a support role only."

He looked at Whack. "You Macomber?" Whack nodded and scowled at Chastain. "You're here with the other setup, that electronic armor or whatever it is?"

"We call it 'Tin Man,' " Jon said. "Armor made of a special material that—"

"Masters, you just can't shut it off, can you?" Chastain interrupted. He looked at Whack dismissively. "I don't think we'll be needing it at all, if the robots work as advertised." He looked at the folded-up robot. "Normally I wouldn't even accept military hardware, but with loose radioactive materials around, I will." He motioned to one of the agents behind him. "That's why you will train Special Agent Brady in how to operate the CID."

Both Richter and Turlock looked at Brady. "He's a little big for the CID," Charlie said, looking directly at Brady's waistline. "It'll be a tight squeeze." She motioned toward Renaldo. "She'll fit much better."

"She's Homeland Security, not FBI," Chastain said. He looked back at the other agents. "Savoy, front and center." An agent stepped up beside Brady. He was much more trim, about a head shorter, and ten years younger than Brady, wearing rimless spectacles that made him look like a middle schooler. "You're going to train to operate the robot."

"I'm C-Four-I, sir," Savoy said, looking apprehensively at the folded-up robot. "I'm in charge of communications and computers—I don't know anything about robots."

"You're the gadget geek, so you're going to learn. Besides, you get to work with Miss Turlock here." Savoy gave Charlie a nod and a toothy grin. Chastain turned to Jon. "Now, what about the drones, Masters?"

"We're unloading them now and we can have them airborne tonight," Jon said. "The Sparrowhawk series of unmanned aircraft are small, lightweight, but very capable—"

" 'Sparrowhawks'? What in hell are they?" Chastain asked derisively. "I thought I was getting Predators. I've been trained in Predator deployments for years."

"Predators? Are you kidding me?" Jon responded with an incredulous roll of his eyes. "Predators were hot *five years* ago. True, they set the stage. But the technology has advanced way beyond Predators." Chastain's expression told Jon he obviously didn't believe him. "Sky Masters, Inc., manufactures the next generation of unmanned aerial vehicles—smaller, lighter, easier to deploy, easier to manage, more autonomous—"

"I'm not interested in your sales pitch or the sweetheart deal you obviously got from your buddies in the White House or the Pentagon," Chastain said. "Tell me what I have to work with here, or get them out of my face and away from me so I can do my job."

"With pleasure, Special Agent," Jon said. "The Sparrowhawk is designed for medium-altitude, high-resolution, long-range, long-endurance surveillance. It is small, easy to deploy, easy to program and flight-plan, and all-weather capable. You'll love it."

"All I want is for it to be where I want, when I want, and look at what I want to look at," Chastain said. "Let me know when they're ready to fly."

"They'll be ready for a test flight tonight and should be ready to start patrolling tomorrow morning."

Chastain blinked at this information, obviously not expecting them to be ready so soon—and not sure if he should believe Masters. "We'll see. Keep me informed." He spun on a heel and walked away, followed by the others except for Savoy, who stayed with Charlie.

"So . . ." Savoy said uncomfortably. "I'm . . . ready to get started, I guess. Do you have a manual or training video I can use?"

"First things first," Charlie said, "I need to know your first name."

The FBI agent looked rather uncomfortable for a moment, then responded, "Randolph."

"Randolph?" Jon asked.

"What do your friends call you, Randolph?" Charlie asked.

"Randolph." He looked at the growing smiles of those around him and scowled, which made Jon's chuckling even more pronounced. "Is there a problem?"

"Not at all," Charlie said, choking down her own snickering. "Randolph it is. Are you married? Single?"

"What does that have to do with training on the robot?"

"We're a small and pretty close-knit group here, Randolph," Charlie said. "We like to know a lot about the folks that are assigned to work with us."

"Do I get to know everything about you?"

"Of course. Ask away."

Savoy looked skeptically at those around him, then said with a sigh of exasperation, "About those training manuals and videos, Miss Turlock?"

Charlie looked at Jon and Jason, shrugged, and put an arm around Savoy, turning him toward the folded-up CID unit. "We don't use no stinking books or videos like they did in the olden days, Randolph—we believe in on-the-job training around here. CID Four, pilot up," she said. The robot immediately assumed the boarding stance. "If you're your unit's gadget guy, you should learn how the CID operates in . . . about a day."

"A *day?*"

"Only if you're paying attention," Charlie added with a smile. "Otherwise, it might take as long as two days. Now, if we were going into combat, everything might take an extra day or two to learn, but since you won't be using weapon packs, you should be fully checked out by this time tomorrow." She motioned to the open hatch on the CID unit's back. "Hop on up there, Randolph, and let's get started."

FIVE

There comes a moment when you have to stop revving
up the car and shove it into gear.

—DAVID J. MAHONEY

JOINT AIR BASE BATTLE MOUNTAIN

A FEW DAYS LATER

Ron Spivey strode into the Civil Air Patrol hangar wearing a football jersey, shorts, running shoes, and carrying a backpack. He found Bradley McLanahan and Ralph Markham at a table. Ralph was in a CAP camouflage field uniform, but for the first time he saw Brad wearing a green Air Force–style Nomex flight suit. They had a stack of manuals on the table, along with sign-off forms. "Where the hell were you, McLanahan?" Ron shouted as he came over to the table. "You're the only guy on the defensive squad that didn't show for the workout."

"I told you, Ron—I couldn't make it because I'm getting my first ride as mission scanner," Brad replied. "With the current air emergency, we got an 'A' mission number, so I get to go for real."

An "A" mission was one assigned and paid for by the Air Force for a specific task.

"Oh yeah—it's your birthday today. Happy birthday," Ron said tonelessly. "You get to start training to fly as a scanner for real. So why aren't you flying?"

"I'm waiting to be briefed. I thought I'd help Ralph with his reading assignments for summer school."

"Why doesn't Marky do his own reading?"

"You know he has a little trouble reading," Brad said. "But if you read it to him first and then help him through it, he picks it up pretty quick."

"We'd all like someone to spoon-feed us," Ron said. "But you're still a cocaptain on the football team, so you've got to set a fucking example. You gotta do five miles every day plus wind sprints, and an hour in the weight room until football training-season starts. No excuses. And we train as a damned team. If you don't show up, other guys won't show, and pretty soon everyone is fucking around doing their own so-called training routine, which turns out to be nothing but *dick*."

"I know," Brad said. "I won't miss any more. But I didn't want to miss out on an 'A' mission."

"Well, get your fucking priorities straight," Ron said acidly. "I was at practice, and now I'm here, and tonight I'll be on the FedEx ramp in Elko loading and unloading planes, and after that I'll be at the AM/PM out there in Elko hoping I won't get held up and the drunks won't set the gas pumps on fire."

"You got a job at the AM/PM in Elko too? You have *two* night jobs?"

"My mom's boyfriend knows somebody," Ron said. "It doesn't matter. If I can do it, you can fucking do it. Just get your rear in gear and do what you said you'd do, or get the hell out of the way." And he stormed off.

"Wow, he was sure mad," Ralph remarked.

"I didn't realize he was working so much," Brad said. "He's

probably beat, driving all the way out to Elko and back. He works part-time afternoons at the Walmart too, at least until school starts."

"Why is he working so much?"

"Helping out at home, I guess," Brad replied. "He doesn't talk about it much, after his Dad left and all. I know he likes to take his girlfriend out a lot too."

"I'm never going to have a girlfriend," Ralph announced.

"You say that now, but in a year it'll be totally different," Brad said.

"*You* don't have a girlfriend. You're a pilot, and you're on the football team, but you don't have a girlfriend."

"I have friends that happen to be girls," Brad said, surprised at how uneasy he felt, "but . . . I don't know. Lots of reasons. Girls don't like special-team guys like they do quarterbacks and line-backers; I'm not a private pilot yet, so I can't take girls on rides; I'm fairly new in school, and . . . I don't know, dating is just not high on my list right now. I'm thinking about college, and scholarships."

Ralph sighed. "I wish I could go to college."

"You can. We just need to work on your reading. You're a smart guy—you just don't learn like other kids."

"I get tested every year in school. They say I'm like a fourth grader."

"That's compared to other students in school," Brad said. "But how many kids you know can do all the first aid, orienteering, and fieldwork you do? How many kids can pick up a complex adult video game and figure out how to ace it in just a couple hours? Heck, how many kids do you know that have any idea what the one-in-sixty rule is?"

"But that's easy."

"It wasn't when you started. I remember when I first tried to teach you land navigation and how to read a map and compass—you just didn't have a clue. But you're a visual learner."

"What's that?"

"You find it easier to learn by watching and doing rather than by reading a book or listening to a lecture," Brad explained. "We tried to teach you map reading in a classroom for weeks and you never got it—you gave up several times. But once we took you out in the field, you learned to visualize the map with the actual terrain features, and once you got a compass in your hand and laid it on a map in the field, it all clicked. Same with video games or computers: you can read the instructions for a week and never get it, but we sit you down in front of one and just let you explore it, and soon you have it down cold."

"But games and computers are easy," Ralph repeated. "So why is school so hard?"

"Because traditional school is the same as it was in ancient Greece thousands of years ago—it's listening to lectures in a classroom and reading books," Brad said. "But that's not always the best way to learn. You think the Paiute Indian boys learned how to hunt in a *classroom?* The braves took the young boys out in the hills and showed them how to hunt elk and bighorn sheep. If they failed, they didn't get an F—the tribe didn't eat. You have to find the best way to teach a person, and it's not always in a classroom. It depends on the student and the subject matter, I guess."

Ralph nodded, then said, "I remember the land-navigation courses you taught. They were prerequisites for the fieldwork. I never passed any of the exams."

"No, you didn't."

"Then how did I get to go into the field?"

"Because I signed you off anyway."

"You did? But why?"

"Because I had a feeling you could learn that stuff if we just got you out there and showed it to you," Brad said. "I'm kind of a visual learner too. Take flying: I can muddle through the classroom stuff and squeak by on the exams, but I really don't learn anything about flying until I get behind the controls. Then all the classroom stuff makes sense. If you didn't pick it up in the field, I'd go to the squadron commander and explain what I did. But you did it."

Ralph nodded and was silent for a few moments, then asked, "So if you're a visual learner like me, sir—why do you want to go to a traditional college?"

Brad opened his mouth to reply . . . then realized he didn't have an answer. But thankfully just then Jon Masters came up to the table. "Hey, there's the birthday boy!" he greeted him loudly. Brad stood and held out a hand. Jon shook it, then spun Brad around and spanked him eighteen times, plus a last hard one for good luck. "I'm not too old, and you're not yet so big, that I can't give you a proper birthday greeting!"

"Thanks, Uncle Jon," Brad said. "Uncle Jon, this is Cadet Markham. Ralph, meet Dr. Jon Masters."

"The one that led the search and treated the survivor of that plane crash? Very nice to meet you." They shook hands. "They tell me you're quite the video-game expert."

"I'm a visual learner, sir," Ralph said proudly.

"I see," Jon said. "Well, hopefully while I'm here I can show you some stuff that you might just find is right up your alley."

"Like what, Uncle Jon?" Brad asked.

Jon put a finger to his lips and winked. "Hush-hush, need-to-know, super-duper secret, all that happy horseshi—well, you get the idea," Jon said. "I could tell you, but then I'd have to kill you."

"Really?" Ralph gasped.

"Not really, Ralph, but I like saying that," Jon said, smiling. "But, I am here to tell you that your sortie this afternoon has been canceled." Brad's shoulders slumped. "I feel bad, because my stuff has something to do with it, and I know it was going to be your first mission as the guy who sits in back and looks out the window for stuff."

"Mission scanner."

"Right. So to make it up to you, I got you a present. I gave it to your dad."

"Thank you!" Brad said excitedly. Jon Masters's gifts were always weird, highly unusual, and one-of-a-kind high-tech gadgets. "When do I get it?"

"As soon as your dad gets off the computer, which might not be until you're thirty," Jon said with a smile. "In the meantime, if you guys are done here, why don't you show me your Civil Air Patrol plane."

"Sure!" Brad said excitedly. He ran to the communications room and retrieved the airplane's keys, then escorted Jon and Ralph to the Cessna 182 parked outside. "This is a Cessna 182R Skylane, built in 1984," he began proudly as they walked up to the red, white, and blue airplane. "It is a four-place, high-wing, single-engine monoplane, constructed mostly of aluminum with some fiberglass components. It is powered by a two-hundred-and-thirty-horsepower normally aspirated piston engine. It has a max gross weight of about three thousand pounds, cruises at about one hundred and forty knots, and has a maximum endurance of about four hours with an hour's fuel reserve."

"'Normally aspirated piston engine'? 'One hundred and forty knots'?" Jon Masters asked incredulously. "Who uses piston engines anymore? It runs on avgas? I didn't think there were any planes that ran on avgas anymore! And I have unmanned aircraft I can carry in a backpack that can fly twice as fast!"

"The 182 is a good aircraft for the mission, Uncle Jon: good-weather, short-range, short-endurance, low-altitude, low-speed search-and-rescue, flown by civilian volunteers," Brad said. "We have other planes that fly other missions. The Civil Air Patrol is the largest single operator of 182s in the world, with a fleet of more than five hundred."

"A fleet of dinosaurs, if you ask me," Jon said. "The plane is almost thirty years old!"

"They're introducing newer planes into the fleet as the older ones reach a certain airframe time limit," Brad said. "We were slated to get a glass-cockpit turbo 182 this year. That was canceled because of the economy and all the cutbacks. Maybe we'll get it when the recession is over."

"Or maybe get something better," Jon mused.

"There's nothing better than a trusty 182—maybe a turbo 182 with a glass cockpit," Brad said. He unlocked the pilot's-side door, then opened the passenger-side door from inside. "We still use the original instruments."

"Holy cats—I'll say you do!" Jon exclaimed, his eyes wide in wonder as he scanned the faded Royalite plastic instrument panel. "I can't remember the last time I saw round steam gauges!" He pointed at the GPS device. "Jeez, that GPS manufacturer hasn't been in business in fifteen years! And . . . and is that an FM simplex radio?"

"The radio operates both in simplex and repeater functions," Brad explained. "CAP operates about five hundred repeater stations around the country to provide communications over a wide area, hostile terrain, or when conventional communications like telephone and the Internet are knocked out."

"Wow—I didn't realize you guys did what you do with such . . . outdated stuff," Jon exclaimed. "I guess your major tool is the old Mark One eyeball, eh?"

"We have a Gippsland GA-8 with the ARCHER hyperspectral sensor—that's probably the most high-tech plane in the fleet," Brad said. "Back in the Vegas squadron they were able to send digital photos from the planes via satellite, but we don't do that here."

"It would be easy enough to do," Jon mused again. Brad could always tell when his uncle's mind began working a problem, same as his dad: they got this faraway look, as if they were looking through the earth back onto their lab bench or computer, already experimenting and planning. "The transceiver weighs less than a sack lunch. You could even do two-way voice, data, and text."

"That would be cool," Ralph said.

"Look at that—vacuum-powered gyroscopic gauges . . . a wet compass . . . carburetor heat . . . my God, an L-Tronics Model LA direction finder," Jon muttered in disbelief. "Those were built in

Santa Barbara, California, by hand practically by one guy, years ago. He was my hero. The guy literally transformed the nation with his gadgets."

"Most of the time the stuff works pretty well," Brad said. "And the plane flies great."

"You've flown it?"

"You bet I did," Brad said. "Ralph too. Every CAP cadet gets five powered and five glider orientation rides. It's part of CAP's aerospace education program. We're not allowed to do takeoffs and landings in CAP airplanes, but I've done steep turns, stalls, and slow flight."

"I didn't realize the Civil Air Patrol did all that stuff with these planes," Jon said. "Actually, I never thought about it. So when do you get to pilot one of these hot rods, Brad?"

"Not for a while," Brad said. "I'll train to be a mission scanner, get two supervised flights, then train to be a mission observer. Meanwhile, I have to get my private pilot's license and get a hundred and fifty hours of pilot-in-command time. Then I can train to take a CAP Form 5 check ride, which is like an annual flight review. Once I pass that, I get two supervised flights in the left seat with a crew, followed by a CAP Form 91 evaluation."

"Sheesh, it sounds worse than the Air Force," Jon remarked. "They really make you jump through some hoops, don't they?"

"I'll be flying two other crewmembers in an Air Force airplane on an Air Force–assigned mission—they want us up to speed," Brad said. "I don't think it's jumping through hoops at all."

"You sound just like your dad—who, speak of the devil, here he is now." Jon shook hands with Patrick as he walked up to the Cessna. "Brad was showing me his high-tech piece of machinery here. Are you sure flying one of these isn't taxing your aging flying skills too much?"

"Jon, even *you* could pilot one of these," Patrick said with a smile. "How are you, Ralph?"

"Fine, sir. Brad was helping me with some reading."

"Good for you, Brad. How's Jeremy doing?"

"Released from the hospital to his grandparents in Sparks, sir," Ralph said. Patrick knew the boy would know the details. "He's doing fine and has asked about joining the CAP."

"I think he'd be a great cadet," Patrick said. "So. Are you guys done?"

"Yes, sir."

"Then I have a birthday surprise for my son, thanks to Uncle Jon here," Patrick said. "Unfortunately your first scanner flight was canceled, but I have something else I think you'll enjoy. Climb on out of that flight suit." Eyes dancing in anticipation, Brad locked up the Cessna, put the keys away, then returned in a flash in civilian clothes.

"Drive us over to the hangar," Patrick said, tossing him the keys to the Wrangler. Brad happily drove to the other side of the base, where the civilian aircraft were parked, the smile not leaving his face.

"Are we going flying, Dad?" Brad asked excitedly after parking beside Patrick's hangar.

"We are," Patrick said. "Dr. Masters owns the airspace around the base for his special project today, and he's not using it for the next two hours, so he got us permission to use it. It won't be a cross-country—we have to stay within thirty miles of the base—but you'll be able to get some air work and some landings in."

"Great!" Brad shouted. His smile dimmed a bit. "But . . . I can't afford to fly the 210, even half. I'd be just as happy flying the 172." Brad had been training for his pilot's license in a rented Cessna 172 Skyhawk, saving money and doing odd jobs around town and the base to pay for fuel and flying time; Patrick was his flight instructor.

"That's the second surprise," Patrick said. "Dr. Masters is paying the tab for this flight. Happy birthday."

"All *right*!" Brad cried. "Thank you, Uncle Jon!" Brad had to contain his excitement and, as his father had taught him, put his pilot's brain in gear as he proceeded to unlock the hangar and get the turbine Cessna P210 Centurion ready to fly.

Patrick had downsized his airplane from the twin-turbine-powered Aerostar to a single-engine airplane, but it was just as high-tech. Thanks to Jon Masters's tinkering, this Cessna pressurized single-engine airplane had an advanced turboprop engine that propelled the plane at a top speed of more than three hundred miles an hour for over 1,500 nautical miles at altitudes up to twenty-five thousand feet. It was equipped with two wide-screen electronic flight displays, dual GPS navigators, a NextGen datalink for weather and traffic, side-stick controllers, single-lever engine control, and a host of other features and upgrades. Its advanced electronic ignition system allowed it to burn any kind of liquid fuel available, from automotive gasoline to the latest biofuel.

"I'm going to let you do everything," Patrick said. "I want to see if you've gotten rusty. Take your time."

"Yes, *sir*!" Patrick watched as Brad pulled the plane out of the hangar, drove the Jeep inside, and began a preflight.

The exterior preflight mostly consisted of draining the numerous fuel tanks and sumps to check for water or contamination, checking that the flight controls were free and clear, and checking for any signs of leaks or damage. When the walk-around was completed, Patrick climbed into the front passenger seat first, followed by Brad in the pilot's seat, and he closed and dogged the entry door tight. The interior preflight was even easier: the computers mostly did everything, under Brad's watchful eye. Engine start was stone-cold simple: turn on the battery switch, command the engine start on the touch-screen electronic controls, watch the engine displays, and watch for any hot-start anomalies that weren't caught by the computer. Within minutes they were airborne.

"Three of the most dangerous stalls you can do," Patrick said once they were at their operating altitude, "is an approach-to-landing stall, a departure stall, and a traffic-pattern or accelerated stall, so that's what we're going to practice first. Run through those for me."

"Roger," Brad said. "Clearing turn, coming left." He performed a clearing turn left and right to check that the airspace around them was clear of other traffic, then said, "The approach-to-landing stall simulates stalling with the plane in landing configuration. Flaps ten, then the gear." He lowered the first notch of flaps, then the landing gear. "As the airspeed decreases I'll pitch up to landing attitude. Flaps twenty . . . flaps thirty. Power back, nose stays up . . ." A few moments later, the stall-warning horn sounded and they felt the first rumbles of disturbed air over the wings, the sign of an impending stall.

"Recover," Patrick said just as it felt as if the plane was going to nose over. Brad released the back pressure on the side-stick controller and fed in full power. When the plane reached takeoff speed, he raised the landing gear and the first notch of flaps and waited until he had a positive rate of climb.

"Good job—minimal loss of altitude, nose straight, positive rate of climb," Patrick said after Brad had completely recovered from the stall and reconfigured the plane. "Next: departure stall."

Like the first, Brad verbalized his procedures, then executed them. The departure stall was done in the takeoff configuration with full power, simulating a stall right after takeoff; the third was a stall while turning in the traffic pattern.

"Very good," Patrick said after the last one was finished. "Remember, keep those controls centered and use rudder to keep the nose straight as you approach the stall—a stall with one wing down is a spin, and the P210 is not a spin-friendly plane at all."

"Got it, Dad."

"Good. Let's do some landings. This plane has prop beta and reversers, but let's not use any of that—just watch your airspeed. Normal configuration, then half flaps, then no flaps. Watch your descent rates with each flap setting. After that, we'll go over to the other runway and do a crosswind landing."

Brad's landings were very good with the winds right down the runway, but when they switched runways, it was slightly different story. Brad had never been a big fan of crosswind landings. The Cessna P210 Centurion had thin tubular main landing gear and small tires, which necessitated a crabbed approach to an airport in crosswinds instead of a wing-low approach. A crabbed approach meant angling into the crosswind until just before touchdown, and then "kicking out the rudder"—quickly transitioning to a wing-low approach and using the rudder to keep the wheels aligned with the runway centerline to avoid excessive side loads on the landing gear, all done just moments before touchdown.

Brad had trouble gauging when the crab should end, and on touchdown it felt as if they'd shoot off the side of the runway. Patrick's hands were ready to grab the throttle and controller, but Brad kept the plane on the runway. "Good recovery," Patrick said as they taxied off the runway. "Use more nose-up trim to help you keep that landing attitude, and be aggressive with your rudder inputs. Let's taxi back and do a crosswind takeoff, then another crosswind landing, and that'll be enough of a workout for you. Verbalize everything you do."

When they were cleared for takeoff, Brad said, "Okay, crosswind takeoff. I've got lots of power and runway, so I'm not going to use flaps."

"The plane will be on the ground at a higher speed, which is usually bad for landing gear and tires," Patrick said. "Tell me why you're not using flaps."

"Because with flaps the plane will have a tendency to weathervane into the wind, which makes it tougher to straighten out with the rudder," Brad said. "The extra speed will make controlling it easier too."

"Exactly," Patrick said. "Now the crosswind is not that strong, so if you wanted to you could use ten degrees flaps, but you are correct that we have plenty of runway and power. Continue."

"Because the winds are coming from the left, I'm going to start the takeoff on the right side of the runway and aim for the opposite corner, so I have less of a crosswind component," Brad went on. "Emergency stuff briefed as before: engine failure before takeoff is power to idle and braking as necessary to stay on pavement; engine failure after takeoff but below five hundred feet is best glide speed of eighty knots, flaps full, land straight ahead with minimal turns to avoid obstacles; engine failure above five hundred feet is best glide speed, attempt to return to the runway, gear and flaps when the runway is made."

"Good," Patrick said. "Remember to put in full aileron into the wind until your rudder is effective." Brad made the takeoff, being careful to put in firm aileron and then rudder inputs to maintain runway alignment. "Good takeoff," Patrick said after they made the turn onto the crosswind leg. "Let's see how you do on this landing. Keep positive authority on those rudder pedals."

Patrick could feel that Brad was indeed being more aggressive on the pitch trim and rudder pedals as he lined up with the runway, established his crab angle, lowered the flaps and landing gear, and approached the runway. Normally Patrick's hands would be ready to take the controls as soon as he felt something amiss, but Brad was reacting well to every change in the winds or every altitude correction. When it was time to flare and kick out the rudder, it was almost a nonevent—Brad pressed in plenty of right rudder to align the plane with the runway centerline, dipped the left wing into the wind to correct for the crosswind, and eased the controller just enough to let the nose come carefully up. As soon as the stall-warning horn bleeped, the main landing-gear wheels kissed the runway in a satisfying *SQUEAK SQUEAK* of rubber hitting the runway. He put in a tiny bit of power so he had enough airspeed to fly the nose gear onto the runway instead of letting it drop because of a lack of airspeed.

"Excellent job," Patrick said after they taxied clear of the runway. "You definitely felt like you were in charge of your plane, anticipating rather than reacting. How did that feel?"

"It felt great, Dad," Brad said. "I think I'm getting used to cross-wind landings. They always got me so nervous."

"It's the same with just about every pilot in the world," Patrick said. "No one likes crosswind takeoffs or landings, and a lot of takeoff and landing accidents happen when crosswinds are involved. It just takes practice. Had enough for today?"

"Heck no," Brad said. "I wish we could go somewhere, but I'm ready to go flying, even if it's just around the airport. Let's do some more."

"Unfortunately, I've got stuff to do, and they're restricting everyone unless they're on an IFR flight plan," Patrick said. "Let's head back to the barn." Brad's face registered a hint of disappointment, but he steered the Centurion back to its hangar without complaint. When they arrived, they noticed Jon Masters, Rob Spara, David Bellville, John de Carteret, Ralph Markham, and Michael Fitzgerald standing in front of the hangar.

"What's going on?" Brad asked. "Did we get another alert?"

"I have no idea," Patrick said. "Park it out front and let's find out." Brad parked the Centurion in front of the hangar, accomplished the shutdown checklist, and stepped outside, with his father following closely behind.

"So, how did he do?" Jon asked.

"He needed a do-over on the crosswind landing," Patrick said, "but he did good the second time around, and otherwise he's good to go."

"I had no doubts," Jon said. "If you're good, I'm good."

"Thank you, Jon," Patrick said. He turned to his son. "Hop back in, big guy. Three landings with a full stop in between, then bring it in."

NYE COUNTY ADMINISTRATIVE OFFICES AND SHERIFFS SOUTH AREA SUBSTATION, PAHRUMP, NEVADA

THAT SAME TIME

The express delivery truck turned left onto Kittyhawk Drive and was met by a crew with a tractor, which was lifting three-foot-high concrete jersey walls into place on the side of the street. The truck driver had to stop to let the tractor pass. He slid his door open and asked a nearby worker, "What's going on?"

"The county is closing off Kittyhawk and Vaqueros Streets and the parking lot in front of the administration building," the worker replied. "Added security, I guess, although it's not going to protect anybody from another damned plane."

"Well, who'd want to attack the county building in Pahrump?" the delivery driver asked. The worker just shrugged. "So where do I make the deliveries?"

"You can go ahead for now around to the loading dock—we haven't closed the streets off yet," the worker said. "But after this they'll be setting up the vacant lot across the street for parking. I don't know about deliveries—they'll probably be inspected before being allowed in."

"The times we live in, I guess," the driver said. As soon as the street was clear, he proceeded on. He took a right onto Vaqueros Street, then another right toward the parking area marked DELIVERIES. He let a security guard see his delivery manifest, then let him peek inside the truck. "All these here in the back," the driver said, pointing to several large boxes and one wood-framed crate. "Copiers, paper, and office furniture."

"I thought there was a recession going on," the security guard grumbled. "Who has the money for all this stuff? The security staff gets cut by half, but some suit gets all-new office stuff?" The guard initialed the manifest. "After today, you guys will have to park across the front parking lot in the vacant lot for inspection."

"I heard. I'll pass the word." The guard handed the driver his manifest, and the driver drove to an empty bay at the loading dock. He took his electronic clipboard inside to the receiving office. Just as he reached the receiving clerk's window they heard an electronic siren followed by the words, "A FIRE ALARM HAS BEEN AC-TIVATED. PLEASE EXIT THE BUILDING THROUGH THE MAIN ENTRANCE IMMEDIATELY," followed by the same message in Spanish.

"What's that?" the driver asked.

"It happens about once a week," the disgusted receiving clerk groused. "Someone's pissed because they've been laid off or had their hours reduced, so they pull a fire alarm or call in a bomb threat."

"You're kidding!"

"Unfortunately, no," the clerk said. "Follow me."

"Why don't we go out this way?" the driver asked, pointing toward the loading docks.

"Security wants everybody to go out the front so they can be counted and ID'd," she said. "Did you leave the keys to your truck in the ignition?" The driver nodded. "If it's the real deal, the fire department will move it." She looked at her watch. "It was almost time for my cigarette break anyway." The driver followed the clerk through narrow hallways that led to the main forum, which further branched out into the different departments. No one seemed to be in any great hurry or panic at all. The driver noticed uniformed court bailiffs leading some men out in handcuffs. "I'm going to meet up with my friend in the sheriff's department," the clerk said. She pointed toward a wall of glass doors. "Head right out those doors. Someone will tell you where to go next."

The parking lot was filling with workers gathering together

in small knots while at the center of the lot a security officer had formed a checkpoint and was yelling at folks to get in line to show ID. The driver retrieved his company ID card and clipped it to his uniform pocket. No one seemed to want to line up—they obviously expected the alert to expire soon—so the line moved quickly. After just a few minutes' wait, he was next in line. "Making a delivery?" the security guard asked.

"Yep," the driver said. The guard glanced at the ID card, then at the driver, and nodded. But something caught his eye, and he ran a finger along the edge of the photo on the badge. With just a tiny bit of effort, the photo started to peel away from the badge!

"Wait a minute—is this *your* ID badge?" the security guard asked.

The driver shook his head, smiled, and replied, "No, it isn't"— and at the same moment he lifted a device in his left hand and pressed a button. There was an intense burst of light, followed by an earsplitting explosion that shook the ground. People screamed and scattered in all directions as what seemed like a mile-wide fireball erupted from the back of the administrative building, followed by a huge black cloud of smoke and debris.

Joint Air Base Battle Mountain, Nevada

That same time

Brad McLanahan's face turned into a mask of sheer disbelief. "Wha-*what?*" he stammered.

"Time to solo, son," his father, Patrick, said confidently. "You're more than ready. Go for it. I'll be on the portable radio in case you need me." Patrick was expecting him to be more excited than this. Brad looked completely stunned. "You okay, big guy?"

"S-sure," Brad said. "Three landings. Got it." He stepped hesitantly back to the Centurion, looked around inside for a moment, then climbed in. Patrick listened for the entry door to be fully latched and looked for seat belts hanging out. He then waited for the strobes to come on and the starter to start winding up, but Brad just sat there. After a few long moments, Patrick went over to the passenger-side emergency-exit window. Brad reached over and opened it, still wearing that same blank expression. "What, Dad?" he asked in a low voice.

"You okay, Brad?"

"I . . . guess," Brad said. "I mean . . . the cockpit looks so much bigger with no one else sitting here."

"You can do it, Brad," Patrick said. "You're the pilot in command now. You do everything you just did and you'll be fine. Remember what I said: when you step near the plane, you put your pilot-in-command brain on until you lock the door to the hangar after you button up the plane. Right?"

Brad nodded, then looked past his father at the others. "Are they all going to watch me?"

"You might as well get used to it: pilots watch other pilots all the time, and everyone's a critic. Try not to think about it. Fly the plane like I know you can do. Put your pilot-in-command brain on. Have a good one." Patrick closed the window, stood there to make sure Brad locked it from the inside, and then stepped back.

It took another few long moments, but at last Brad reached up and took the checklist in his hand, and finally his nervousness began to subside. Reading the checklist items and then touching the proper switch, lever, or readout helped to pull him back into the routine of flying, and soon he forgot that it was his first solo flight and he was alone . . .

. . . until he was ready to taxi. He was so accustomed to leaning forward to look around his father to see out the right window, and when he did so again he realized he didn't have to do that, and he remembered he was alone. He had to wipe his sweaty palms on his jeans.

"Centurion Two-Niner Bravo Mike, Battle Mountain Ground."

Brad couldn't find the mike button for a few moments, but he finally managed to key the button: "Niner Bravo Mike, go ahead."

"Message from Sierra Alpha Seven: Taxi on out or park it."

Brad looked out the window and saw his dad waving his cellular phone at him. The others with him had smiles on their faces but were looking a little concerned—all except Ralph, who gave Brad a big excited smile and two thumbs-up.

"I can do this, damn it," he said aloud to himself. "I know what I'm doing, I know what I'm doing." He took a deep breath, then keyed the mike again: "Roger, Ground, Centurion Two-Niner Bravo Mike ready to taxi from the south hangars with information Tango."

"Niner Bravo Mike, information Uniform is current, winds three-two-zero at eight, altimeter three-zero-one-zero," the ground controller reported—Brad had forgotten to get the current Automatic Terminal Information System data. "Two-Niner Bravo Mike cleared to taxi to Runway three-zero."

"R-roger," Brad responded nervously. "Taxi to Runway three-zero, Niner Bravo Mike." Wiping his sweaty palms on his pant legs again, he turned on the taxi light, released the parking brake, and started rolling.

It was a long and lonely ride to the runway, even though he had done this dozens of times. Brad had to consciously remind himself to use beta and low power settings to avoid tapping the brakes. Everything seemed louder, and every bounce or sway was cause for alarm. What was that vibration? Was that rattling from the nose gear normal? He found himself checking every millimeter of the electronic displays, looking for some indication of a problem, and then he found himself swerving too much across the taxi line.

"Get it together, shithead," he said aloud to himself. "You're the damned pilot. Be the pilot, or park it. When you're taxiing, you concentrate on taxiing, not on looking around the cockpit. Be the pilot, or park it."

He taxied to the run-up area and completed the "BEFORE TAKEOFF" checklist. He couldn't believe how nervous he was: he actually *forgot what to do next*! The checklist jumped to the "AFTER TAKEOFF" items, but what was he supposed to do now? Maybe I'm really not ready to . . .

. . . and at that moment he was startled from a blur of motion in front of him. It was an XS-19A Midnight single-stage-to-orbit spaceplane, coming in for a landing at Battle Mountain! In all his confusion about what to do next, he had never even noticed the radio transmissions between it and the control tower!

The Midnight was the most incredible aircraft in the world: it could take off and land from almost any airport in the world, but once it refueled after takeoff, it could launch itself into Earth orbit. It could take passengers or supplies to and from Armstrong Space Station, fly around the planet in just a couple hours, re-trieve and deploy satellites in orbit, and even launch antisatellite and antiballistic-missile interceptors or ground-attack weapons.

That's what I want to do, Brad told himself: I want to fly a spaceplane. I want to go on missions to the space stations, orbit Earth hundreds of miles up, fly around the planet in less than two hours, and defend America with weapons fired from space . . .

. . . and the first step to doing all that: make three takeoffs and three landings solo in this little air-breathing Cessna Centurion.

And like that, everything came together. He switched radio frequencies on the right multifunction display like he always did and spoke: "Battle Mountain tower, Centurion Two-Niner Bravo Mike, ready for takeoff Runway three-zero, staying in the pattern." When cleared, Brad released the parking brake, cleared the approach end of the runway, taxied out, and made his first solo takeoff.

The three landings and takeoffs were over before he knew it, and he taxied the Centurion back to the hangar, after acknowledging a "Good job, new solo pilot," from the tower controller. After shutting down and securing the plane, his father and the others greeted him to applause. As soon as he stepped away from the plane, the others ran up and doused him with water from plastic bottles, and his father ripped half of the back of his shirt off. "Gotta have someplace to write about your first solo," he said. "Every new pilot-in-command gives it up. Congratulations, Brad."

Brad hugged his father tightly as the others continued their applause. "I wasn't sure if I could do it," he admitted. "I couldn't even remember what to do after I finished the checklist. But I saw the Midnight come in, right in front of me, and it all came back."

"Good for you, son," Patrick said. "You'll be flying a Midnight before you know it. Your uncle John is going to kick in with us for the rest of your flight training, right up to your check ride. By the time you get your cross-country flights, night flights, and instrument time, you'll have enough hours to do the check. And since I just got my authorization as an FAA designated examiner in the turbine P210, I'll be giving you your check ride."

"Awesome!"

"I'll be ten times worse than any other check pilot," Patrick said
with a smile, "but I know you can do it. You'll be a licensed pilot
before you know it. Now, you're in charge of putting the plane
away, because I need to run over to the other side of the base and
find out why the Midnight is in. Congratulations again, son." He
hated to leave the celebration, but the sudden appearance of the
XS-19 was unexpected.

"Sierra Alpha Seven, Alpha," he heard on his secure subcutaneous transceiver. The transceiver was a leftover from his days with
the top-secret High Technology Aerospace Weapons Center at
Elliott Air Force Base; although it was capable of global two-way
communications, it was mostly used for regular UHF and VHF
radio transmissions these days. "Alpha" was the base commander
of Joint Air Base Battle Mountain, Air Force Brigadier-General
Kurt "Buzz" Givens, a former bomber navigator and operations
officer when Patrick commanded the base.

"Go ahead, Alpha," Patrick responded.

"I'm going to put 'it' in Uniform." Both men knew exactly
where "it" was.

"Roger," Patrick responded. "I'd like to meet up with it and the
crew."

"Approved." There were six secure aircraft hangars aboveground, but the Uniform secure area was sixty feet underground.
The belowground aircraft storage and servicing area—big enough
for several B52 Stratofortress bombers—was a leftover from Battle
Mountain's Cold War days.

Patrick drove over to the secure aircraft parking hangar. The
XS-19 Midnight spaceplane had just been directed to park inside a
large aircraft shelter, and Patrick followed it in and parked beside
it. A few aircraft handlers and maintenance officers were standing
ready and waiting to assist the crew, but no one could get near the

ship for several more minutes because the skin was still too hot to touch—just minutes earlier it had been reentering Earth's atmosphere, flying thousands of miles an hour, and even the ultracold upper-air molecules acted like billions of keys being scraped against a sidewalk, turning the carbon-carbon composite skin red-hot.

The floor of the aircraft shelter was actually a giant elevator. As soon as it was safe to do so, the Midnight spaceplane was secured with chains, and the ship, Patrick's Wrangler, and the handlers were lowered underground. It took twelve minutes to go six stories—part of the security of the underground facility were ultra-slow elevators that allowed security forces to get into position to repel attackers—but finally they reached the floor.

"Hey, General!" Patrick heard a voice shout. The entry hatch to the spaceplane's cockpit had opened, and Hunter "Boomer" Noble, the vice president of engineering for Sky Masters, Inc., appeared in the opening. Not quite thirty years old, roguish good looks, a bit taller than most astronauts, and always with an above-average air of excitement and humor about him, Boomer was one of a generation of young, idealistic, limitless creative dreamers whom Jon Masters liked to surround himself with at Sky Masters. He was wearing one of the newer Electronic Elastomeric Activity Suits, or EEAS, a tight-fitting garment that used electronically controlled filaments to apply pressure on the body instead of a traditional bulky space suit, which used breathing air under pressure. "I heard you were here at BAM again! How are you, sir?"

"Doing okay, Boomer, doing okay," Patrick replied. They had to talk at a distance because the spaceplane was still too warm to put up a boarding ladder. "How was the flight?"

"Excellent—except for the finish."

"What happened?"

"You haven't heard? It just happened about twenty, thirty minutes ago."

"I was out flying with Bradley. He soloed today."

"Little Bradley? Congrats to him. But you haven't heard what happened?"

"No." Patrick felt a sudden pang of loss—he was getting very, *very* tired of being out of the loop.

"There was another terrorist attack on a government office in Nevada," Boomer said. "The Nye County administrative office in Pahrump was attacked with a truck bomb." Patrick's mouth dropped open in surprise. "Twenty-one people were killed. All flights in and out of Las Vegas, Nellis, Henderson, and as far away as Riverside were diverted. That's why I'm here."

Patrick was thunderstruck. "Did they detect radioactive materials?" he asked.

"Yes," Boomer said. "I don't know what it was, but it's apparently a lot nastier than the stuff used in Reno."

Patrick's transceiver beeped. "Sierra Alpha Seven," he responded.

"This is Alpha," Kurt Givens radioed. "Gizmo and Nutcracker want the airspace cleared and want immediate launch authority." "Gizmo" was Jon Masters's call sign, and "Nutcracker" was Special Agent Chastain's, picked by Patrick himself—both appropriate call signs, if he did say so himself. "Is 'it' secure?"

"Affirmative," Patrick replied.

"Roger. Make sure the Centurion knows his airspace access is terminated. Alpha out."

Patrick put in a call to Bradley's cell phone to make sure the plane was put away—it was, and Brad was already back at the Civil Air Patrol squadron, in utility uniform, awaiting a briefing on the new terrorist attack—then turned to Boomer, who had finally joined him on the deck. "Jon and the FBI have full control of the Class-C airspace, and they're going to close it, so you're our guest for the immediate future," he said.

"Fine with me," Boomer said. He motioned to a young woman standing beside him. "You remember Gonzo, don't you?"

"You mean Major Faulkner? Of course," Patrick said, extending a hand. Jessica Faulkner was one of the more experienced astronauts in the U.S. Space Defense Force. A Marine Corps F-35 Lightning II fighter pilot before the program was canceled, the petite red-haired, green-eyed woman was also wearing an EEAS, which accentuated her curves very, very well indeed. She shook hands. "How are you, Major? Or is it Colonel by now?"

"I took an early retirement a few months ago, sir," Jessica said. "I'm with Sky Masters, Inc., now. They're practically the only ones flying the spaceplanes."

"Well, congratulations on your retirement and new employment," Patrick said. "Boy, Boomer, is there anyone from the Space Defense Force that Jon hasn't hired lately?"

"Just you, sir," Boomer said. "Do you know why they've closed the Class-C airspace, General?"

"No, but I guess I don't have a need to know," Patrick said. "I assume it has to do with whatever Jon brought in the Skytrain."

"The only reason it's a secret is because the FBI is involved—if it was up to me, we'd be telling the world," Boomer said. "The White House gave the FBI a couple of Jon's newest unmanned surveillance aircraft and two CIDs to search for bad guys." He looked at Patrick and added, "The most qualified guy to deploy UAVs and CIDs is standing right beside me, sir. Why aren't you assigned to this?"

"I'll tell you when it's safe to tell you," Patrick said.

"So there's a reason other than you decided to move to Nowhere, Nevada, and babysit what's left of the Space Defense Force?"

"Keep it to yourself," Patrick said. He nodded at the XS-19 Midnight spaceplane. "Anything fun in the jet?"

"Boy, you really are unplugged out here, aren't you, sir?" Boomer remarked. He turned to Jessica. "Hey, Gonzo, how about getting out of the EEAS and we'll meet up with you in a few."

"Sure, Boomer," Jessica said. She understood: Go away, be-

cause the grown-ups want to talk. "Nice to see you again, sir." She
gave Boomer a warning glare but said nothing as she turned and
walked out of earshot.

"She's a cutie," Patrick said.

"Jon only hires the cute ones," Boomer said. His expression
started to turn much more serious. "Jon doesn't keep you informed
of what's going on in the company, does he, sir? You still have a
top-secret clearance, don't you?"

"I do, but if I don't have a need to know, I'm not entitled to a
briefing," Patrick said.

"That's Air Force and Department of Defense policy," Boomer
said. "I'm talking about company policy."

"I don't work for Sky Masters," Patrick said. "Besides, what's
the difference? Sky Masters is a major defense contractor. They
should follow DoD guidelines for operational security."

"For DoD programs, yes, sir," Boomer said. "But what if it
wasn't a DoD program?"

"I'm not following you, Boomer."

Boomer thought for a moment, then nodded toward the cargo
bay. "Let's go up and take a look, sir."

"Am I cleared?"

"As far as I'm concerned you are," Boomer said. "Heck, after all,
it was *your* idea—Jon just took all the credit for it, of course."

Boomer ascended the boarding ladder, and Patrick followed.
The Midnight's cargo-bay doors atop the fuselage had been opened
to help ventilate residual heat from reentry. Boomer climbed up
onto the fuselage and motioned inside the cargo bay. "It was meant
as a subscale test article for a nonreusable booster, but it's been
working so well that Jon told me to rewrite the entire proposal and
submit it for spaceplane use. Remember the 'Serviceman' idea you
developed?"

"What?" Patrick remarked, peering inside the cargo bay in surprise. What he saw resembled a large silver propane tank, with

thruster nozzles on each end and two visible grappling arms on top. "That's 'Serviceman'?"

"That, sir, is a one-hundred-and-ten-million-dollar Navy—not Air Force, not Space Defense Force—contract to build three demonstration units of an autonomous, reusable satellite refueling, rearming, and space-debris cleanup system—the very one *you* proposed when you were still working for Sky Masters," Boomer said stonily.

"I knew nothing about it," Patrick said.

"Jon got the contract less than six months after you left the company," Boomer said. "I think it became a Navy project because of Joseph Gardner . . . and because if it was Air Force, you might find out about it sooner."

"Me?"

Boomer nodded solemnly. "Yeah . . . or about the two-point-seven-five-million-dollar bonus that belongs to the design team—in this case, *you*." Patrick looked up at Boomer, who was looking back at him with a deathly serious expression. "Nowhere in the project proposals or design specs does it mention your name, but we both know you came up with the idea. I don't know where the money is, but I don't think *you* have any of it, do you?" Patrick said nothing—which was all the response Boomer needed. "If this goes to full deployment, I estimate it'll be a two-billion-dollar contract over five years. That's an additional *fifty million dollars,* if I'm not mistaken . . . and I'm *not*. And if the government doesn't buy the system and we decide to set up our own service and space-debris cleanup system for other countries or companies, it could be worth hundreds of times more than that."

"That's not cash money, Boomer—that's usually put right back into the company," Patrick said.

"True, sir," Boomer said. "Most of us take a small portion of it, pay the taxes, and then take stock or stock options on the rest and hope the capital-gains taxes remain at zero like they are now. Did

Jon offer any of that to you?" Patrick said nothing. "I didn't think so. Sir—"

"Enough," Patrick said, holding up a hand. "Jon and I are friends. We go back a lot of years. He's been bugging me for years to go back to Sky Masters—maybe he was going to bring it up then. Maybe he invested the money back into the company, knowing that's what I'd do, or thought it would be better not to have it while I was going through the legal issues with the government." Boomer lowered his head and nodded, not wanting to argue. Patrick took another look at the device in the Midnight's cargo bay, then stepped toward the ladder. "Secure that cargo bay, Boomer," he said as he headed down, "and let's go find out what in hell's happening topside."

THAT SAME TIME

"Jesus, Masters, I thought you said we'd have this thing airborne this morning!" FBI special agent Chastain shouted as he strode into the hangar. "What's the holdup *this* time?"

"No holdup—we're ready to go," Jon replied anxiously, clearly agitated that this first flight was way behind schedule. He waved to his ground crew, and one of them hit the switch to open the hangar doors. Inside the hangar was an unusual-looking vehicle on spindly landing gear. As the hangar doors opened, Jon gave another signal, and ground-crew members began to tow the vehicle out of the hangar.

As they pulled it forward, the vehicle started to transform itself: wings began to unfold from each side of the fuselage; from within each wing a turboprop engine unstowed itself; and from around each engine, propeller blades unfolded as the wings extended their full length. In less than two minutes, the ungainly vehicle had become a tilt-rotor aircraft. But unlike other tilt-rotor aircraft that had their engines on the wingtips, the turbo-diesel engines on the RQ-15 Sparrowhawk were mounted on swiveling mounts that connected the inner and outer portion of the wings, which gave the Sparrowhawk a much longer wingspan. The engines remained tilted at a forty-five-degree angle, allowing the propeller blades to clear the pavement.

"It's about time," Chastain said. "It's finally looking like a real damned airplane."

"It has twice the endurance and twice the payload of a Predator or Reaper, with the same airspeed," Jon said. "If necessary, it can hover—that's something the first-generation UAVs can't do. Plus, you don't have to disassemble them to transport them in a cargo—"

"You just can't stop the snake-oil-salesman pitch, can you,

Masters?" Chastain said. "Just get the damned thing airborne, will you?"

"Let's go to the control room," Jon said. He and Chastain went to the "control room"—a desk set up with three large-screen laptops, surrounded by partitions to block out ambient light. "Everything is done with the touch-screen laptops," Jon said. "The Sparrowhawk has already been programmed with the airfield's runways and taxiways, so it will steer itself to the proper runway for takeoff. After climb-out, you just touch the map on the laptop screen to tell it where to go—no need for a pilot or flight plan. If you see a target you want to look at closer, you just tell it to orbit or hover by touching the image on the screen."

"So get it going already," Chastain said irritably. "I want plenty of imagery on the Knights to see if we can link them to this new attack." Jon nodded to his technicians, and moments later the turbo-diesel engines started up and the Sparrowhawk taxied away. As it started down the long taxiway to the active runway, Chastain shook his head. "Why in hell do you need to drive that thing all the way to the end of the runway? If you say it can hover, why not just take off right now?"

"Because it's been programmed for all of the taxiways and . . ." But he looked at Chastain's impatient face, then said to his technician, "You have enough taxiway there, Jeff?"

"I think so, Jon."

Jon checked the engine readouts to make sure the engines were at operating temperature, then said, "Launch it from the taxiway, Jeff, and let's get this mission under way." The technician stopped the Sparrowhawk and entered commands into the center laptop's keyboard. A few moments later they could see the taxiway rushing out of view, and the Sparrowhawk was airborne. It took a bit more taxiway than anticipated—they caught a glimpse of the blue taxiway lights missing the nose gear by just a few feet.

AT THE CIVIL AIR PATROL HANGAR

THAT SAME TIME

Michael Fitzgerald was testing the radios in the rear of the Civil Air Patrol's communications trailer parked beside the hangar when he heard a booming voice say, "Well, well, look at all this fancy gear." He turned to find none other than Judah Andorsen, dressed as he was the first time they met—leather flying jacket, work gloves, boots, and cowboy hat.

"Mr. Andorsen," Fitzgerald said, surprised. He got out of the trailer and they shook hands. "How are you today, sir?"

"I'm doin' just fine . . . uh, the name's Fitzgerald, right?"

"Yes, sir. Michael Fitzgerald. What brings you out here?"

"I just got done with another chat with the Homeland Security folks, including a hot and sassy agent who I'd let frisk me all day long, if you get my meanin'."

"Cassandra Renaldo. She didn't give me the time of day."

"Renaldo. That's the one."

"I told her and her FBI pals to kiss my hairy ass until I got a lawyer," Fitzgerald said.

"I know I shouldn't be talkin' to no federal agents without a lawyer, but what the hell, I don't have anything to hide, so I just . . . *holy bejeezus,* what in hell is that?"

Fitzgerald turned to follow Andorsen's surprised gaze and saw the Sparrowhawk flying across the airfield. "I don't know planes myself, sir," Fitzgerald said, "but if you hang around this place long enough, you'll see all kinds."

"It looks like it's unmanned—I don't see no cockpit on the thing!"

"It's probably a surveillance aircraft, like a really big Predator," Fitzgerald said. "They fly a lot of unmanned planes out of here, although I don't recall seeing that one before." He jabbed a finger toward one of the hangars surrounded by a tall barbed-wire fence off in the distance. "Came from one of those hangars over there, in the restricted area, I think."

"Is that right?" Andorsen watched the Sparrowhawk until it flew out of sight, then shook his head and turned his attention to the trailer. "So, what do you got here?"

"This is our Civil Air Patrol communications trailer," Fitzgerald said. "It's a thirty-foot 'toy hauler' that we converted into a mobile incident command post." He stepped inside. "This is a high-frequency radio; those two are tactical VHF base stations; that's a VHF airband base station; that's a computer terminal that we can link up with the global satellite Internet network; and we carry several portable radios. The front of the trailer has a galley, latrine, bunks, and a small planning area, big enough for two guys. We have a telescoping thirty-foot antenna mounted on the roof for the radios, and we can pull in satellite broadcasts as well. We have enough fresh water, power generators, propane, supplies, and gray water storage for two men to deploy for as long as a week without any hookups. We can communicate with just about any local, state, or federal agency even with power knocked out." Fitzgerald tapped a wood-and-brass plaque attached to the bulkhead over the desk. "In fact, sir, we have *you* to thank for the trailer—you donated it to Civil Air Patrol a couple years ago."

"You don't say!" Andorsen exclaimed. "When you get to be my age, you forget a lot of stuff. I'm happy to help out." He was silent for a few moments, then said, "You spend a lot of time with the Civil Air Patrol, do you?"

"More nowadays," Fitzgerald said in a low voice. "I got laid off from the Department of Wildlife."

"Sorry to hear that, son."

"They said it was 'budget cutbacks,' but I'm sure the FBI complained to my boss that I wasn't answering their questions, and told them to can me," Fitzgerald said bitterly. "Now that I can't afford a lawyer, the FBI probably thinks I'll talk. They can kiss my ass." He jammed his hands into his pockets. "Fucking feds. They don't give a shit about personal freedom or individual rights—they just want answers, and they'll do whatever they feel like, and fuck the Constitution. I was less than a year from retiring from the department. I'm screwed. I got no savings, and now no retirement, thanks to the feds."

"Sounds like you might have a case against the Department of Forestry, son," Andorsen said. He pulled out his wallet and handed Fitzgerald a card. "Call that number. I set up a legal defense fund for Nevada and California ranchers to help them keep their land if they're getting foreclosed on or if the state or county comes after them for back property taxes. I'm sure they can help you, or if they can't, at least get you pointed in the right direction."

"Thank you, sir," Fitzgerald said, looking at the business card in awe. "I appreciate that very much."

"It's my pleasure, son," Andorsen said. "Us folks gotta stay together in these tough times, especially when the government thinks they can run roughshod over us."

"Damned right," Fitzgerald said.

"And if the Department of Forestry doesn't do right by you," Andorsen said, "I'll make sure my people tell me. I might have a position for someone with your skills in my organization."

"Working for *you*?"

"No promises," Andorsen said, holding up a hand in caution, "but you seem like a squared-away guy that has his priorities straight: tell the government to back off, and get busy taking care of the things that matter. You volunteer your time for the Civil Air Patrol when most guys out of work would either be out breaking into houses, beating their wives, kids, or girlfriends, or drinking themselves into a stupor. I like that attitude, and I try to surround myself with men and women that have that same can-do, will-do attitude."

"Yes, sir, that's me," Fitzgerald said. "Screw the government. Hardworking guys can take care of their families and communities just fine."

"Amen," Andorsen said. "Hey, Fitz, I gotta go. Nice to talk to you." He shook hands with Fitzgerald. "Give my folks a call. They'll help you out. And thank you for doing this Civil Air Patrol stuff. It's pretty darned cool."

SIX

In nature there are few sharp lines.

— A. R. AMMONS

THAT SAME TIME

As the Sparrowhawk unmanned aircraft turned on course, Chastain pointed to a spot on the left laptop. The screen displayed a sectional chart that showed details of landmarks on the ground— roads, power lines, terrain, and cultural points. "Zoom in on that," he said. The technician did so, and Chastain pointed to a tiny square at the base of a mountain marked simply *ranch*. "This is highly classified," he said. "That's the ranch I want pictures of." The technician hit a function key on the center laptop and touched the left screen, and a magenta line indicated that the Sparrowhawk's course was set. "The Knights have expanded that ranch considerably over the past year and a half. They started out with two families and a half-dozen hands residing there—now it's sixty families and almost a hundred hands. They add another two or three families almost every week."

"What do they do there?" Jon asked.

"It's like a commune: whatever income they have goes to the collective; they contribute skills and manual labor for food and water," Chastain said. "The ranch hands act as security. Several of the hands are ex-military, and we believe they have the skills to pull off these attacks."

"Jon, we're going to have to move the orbit to the northwest or southeast a little to keep the Sparrowhawk off the airway," the technician named Jeff said. He studied the sectional chart for a moment, then said, "About four miles southeast looks best, with a northeast-southwest orbit."

Jon nodded. "Go ahead and—"

"Negative, Masters," Chastain interrupted. "I want an orbit right over the center of the compound."

"We can't do that, Agent Chastain," Jon said, pointing at the sectional chart. "The compound sits almost directly under the center of this Victor airway."

"What in hell is that?"

"It's a charted electronic corridor that pilots flying under eighteen thousand feet use," Jon explained. "It guarantees radio- and navigation-aid reception at or above certain altitudes."

"So?"

"It's dangerous for unmanned aircraft that can't look for other aircraft to fly on an airway," Jon said. "We just offset ourselves four miles away from the center of the airway, outside the corridor. It's not a problem—the Sparrowhawk's sensors can scan the entire compound on one leg easily from that distance. Then we'll switch sides of the airway and scan it from the other direction so we can—"

"That's bullshit, Masters," Chastain snapped. "I want it orbiting right *over* the compound."

"That's not safe."

"I don't give a rat's ass, Masters," Chastain said. "First of all, there's not supposed to be any other aircraft out there unless they're on an approved flight plan."

"That's not true," Jon said. "Only aircraft flying in or transiting within fifty miles of Alpha-, Bravo-, or Charlie-controlled airspace have to be on IFR flight plans. If you're flying under eighteen thousand feet and not flying into or near busy controlled airspace, you can still legally fly anywhere."

Chastain pointed to the right laptop, which was displaying a radar traffic display similar-looking to an air traffic control system. "Isn't this supposed to tell us if there are any other planes in the area?"

"This only shows us the aircraft that are on IFR flight plans or are using air traffic control flight-following advisory services," Jon said. "If there are other planes out there not using FAA radar services, we won't see them."

"Aren't these planes supposed to have beacons or something to locate other planes?"

"Some do, but small light planes or light-sport aircraft that don't fly in controlled airspace probably won't," Jon said. "Besides, those beacons interrogate other planes' beacons to locate them, and you ordered the Sparrowhawk's transponder shut off."

"Because *you* told me anyone on the ground can identify an aircraft flying overhead with that beacon on the Internet, or even with a camera phone!"

"That's true."

"So I'm not going to reveal the drone's position with a beacon on the wild-ass off chance that another aircraft might be in the exact same location and altitude," Chastain said. "That'll tip off the Knights that they're under surveillance for sure. Besides, pilots are supposed to be looking out for other planes, right? What are the chances of two planes colliding?"

"If the drone is on an airway below eighteen thousand feet, the chances are much greater," Jon said. "That's what I'm trying to tell you: if you put the Sparrowhawk right on the airway, the chances of a disaster are greatly increased. If you move it just a few miles away, the chances don't go to zero, but they are much, much more favorable."

"So even if we turn on the beacon and move the drone away, it can still be hit by another plane?"

"Unlikely . . . but yes, it . . ."

"Masters, I think the odds of something happening are much lower than you're telling me," Chastain interjected. "The drone is out in the middle of nowhere, more than a hundred miles from the nearest city; people aren't flying anyway because of the shitty economy; and even if they were, the odds of two planes being at the same spot at the same time are astronomical. You people that whine all day about safety, safety, safety drive guys who are trying to get the job done, like *me,* absolutely *crazy.* Now quit your damned bitching and orbit that compound."

Jon finally gave up, and he nodded to Jeff to have the Sparrowhawk orbit the ranch. "Make the altitude seventeen thousand feet," he told his technician. "If they're on an IFR flight plan, they'll be at either sixteen or seventeen, so we should be able to see them on the FAA feed."

"Is that too high?" Chastain asked. "I want detailed imagery of that compound."

"The sensors on the Sparrowhawk are optimized for ten thousand feet aboveground, which is fifteen thousand feet above mean sea level," Jon said, "but the resolution is perfectly fine at—"

"Then put the damned drone at fifteen thousand," Chastain said. "Why in hell would you have it fly higher?"

"Because . . ." He was going to say, *It's safer,* but it was obvious that Chastain didn't much care for the "safety" argument. Jon turned to Jeff. "Put Sparrowhawk at fifteen thousand," he said. "Let's notify Oakland, Seattle, and Salt Lake Centers of the altitude change."

"Do what?" Chastain asked.

"We coordinate all flight activities with Seattle, Oakland, and Salt Lake air traffic control centers," Jon said. "They don't disseminate the information without telling us first, but we have to tell them. They can see most primary-target traffic on radar so they—"

"Primary targets?"

"Radar returns that don't have transponder data such as altitude and identification codes."

"Speak English, would you please, Masters?"

"It's important we coordinate with them," Jon said. "If they're in radio contact with other traffic, they can advise them of the Sparrowhawk's position so they can help them avoid it."

"Fine, fine," Chastain said dismissively. "As long as they don't interfere."

This was incredibly risky, Jon thought, but he issued the orders to put the Sparrowhawk at fifteen thousand feet, then put in a call to air traffic control facilities in Sacramento and Salt Lake City, advising them of the Sparrowhawk's orbit.

Jon was soon able to relax as the day went on. It looked like Chastain was probably going to be correct: there was very little traffic in the Sparrowhawk's orbital area. Only once did they have to steer the unmanned aircraft off the airway for a bizjet descending into Reno, and the two aircraft passed well clear of each other without the bizjet's crew having to turn to avoid the UAV.

They were getting excellent images of the suspect's entire desert facility, and it was indeed very impressive. It resembled a medieval town, with crop circles and groves of fruit trees in the outlying area, stockyards and maintenance buildings inside that, a variety of housing units from cabins to tents next, then a tall chain-link and stone fence surrounding the main compound. Inside the main compound were several houses, barns, warehouses, storage tanks, and an outdoor meeting area large enough for perhaps five hundred people. They saw several small sheds that many persons walked in and out of, way out of proportion to its size—that had to be entrances to an underground facility.

"All of that activity is being recorded and analyzed by our computers," Jon said. "Then over time the computers will compare activity at certain times in different locations. If there's a change in activity—a sudden marshaling of vehicles, or a large movement of people that's out of the ordinary—the computer will alert us."

"My agents have been doing that for decades, Masters—it's called 'police work,'" Chastain said dismissively, taking a sip of coffee and carefully studying the monitors. "Again with the sales pitch. Do you mind? We're trying to work here."

Jon held his hands up in surrender and departed.

ANDORSEN PARK, BATTLE MOUNTAIN

LATER THAT AFTERNOON

Talk about coming down from an extreme high, Bradley thought: this morning I was soloing a high-tech turboprop airplane—now I'm scrubbing toilets for six dollars an hour, and thankful I'm doing so.

Brad picked up his cleanup kit and headed out of the men's room at the city park's rest facilities. It was still very warm, so the park was empty, but closer to sunset, folks would come out to barbecue or hang out. Brad was a sort of part-time security guard as well as janitor and maintenance man: if there were any problems, such as drug, alcohol, or hooker issues, his job was to call the police and get help; otherwise, his job was to clean the johns and urinals, empty the trash bins, and wipe down benches. After finishing the men's toilets, his job was to scrub the women's toilets, so he put out all the "Cleaners Working" and "Use Caution—Wet Floors" signs on his way to mucking out the ladies' room.

A few minutes into his labors, he heard a voice say, "Hey, I know you." He turned and found Department of Homeland Security special agent Cassandra Renaldo alone in the bathroom with him.

"Hello," Brad said. Jeez, he thought, she looked hotter than ever. "What a . . . surprise."

"Why, it's Cadet Bradley James McLanahan, the Civil Air Patrol rescue hero," Renaldo said. "Fancy meeting you here. Remember me? I'm Cassandra. Cassandra Renaldo."

Oh yeah, I damn well *do* remember, he thought, checking out her breasts once again. He could see her hard nipples through her thin blouse from all the way across the bathroom. "I work here," was all Brad could say, swallowing hard.

"You do?" Renaldo said.

"Just part-time."

"Why, I think that is very diligent of you," Renaldo said. "What a weird coincidence. I was heading out to Salt Lake City for a staff conference tomorrow morning, and I left the base without . . . you know, without stopping, and I spotted the park and decided to stop here. I was thinking of you. I thought, you are such an impressive young man. And suddenly poof, here you are, all by yourself, in the flesh. How lucky can I get?"

"Uh-huh," Brad heard himself say.

"I think it's so incredible that young men like you step up and get the training and perform the services you do in the Civil Air Patrol," Renaldo said. "The whole world is changing, and young men like you are taking the lead in protecting your country and saving lives. You are *so* incredible, Bradley. Thank you so very much for your service."

"You're welcome." He couldn't seem to manage to get more than two or three words out at a time.

"So," Renaldo said, putting her hands together, "are you . . . going to be done soon?"

"Oh!" Brad said, looking at the scrub brush and the gloves on his hands as if he forgot he had them on. "I'll just get on out of here and wait . . . until . . . you know . . ."

"Okay." As he walked toward the door, she put out an arm to stop him. "Brad? Can I call you Brad?"

"S-sure."

"And you can call me Cassie." She lowered her eyes. "I have a confession to make."

"W-what?"

"I didn't just happen to stop here on my way to Salt Lake City," Renaldo said, looking deeply into his eyes and taking a deep breath, which only accentuated her breasts even more. "I knew you were going to be here."

"You did? How?"

"It's my job to find out things like that," she said. "But the thing is . . . I learned that not because of business, but because I wanted to see you." She lowered her eyes again. "I could lose my job if anyone found out."

"Found out what?"

"That . . . that I'm turned on by you," Renaldo said. "You're a hardworking, dedicated guy, but"—she put a hand on his chest—"but you're also great-looking, and you have this hard young body, and I'm just plain turned on by you. I know I could lose my job if anyone ever found out I followed you here, but right now I don't care. And I saw the way you looked at me back on that first day in the hangar. I was flattered. That makes me even hotter for you." She stepped closer to him. "Brad, can . . . can I kiss you?" All he could do was stand there and sweat. "I know you just turned eighteen today, so you're a man, and that turns me on even more. I love hard, strong young men." And she lightly touched his lips with hers, with the very tips of her nipples pressing against his chest.

"I knew you would have soft lips," she murmured. "Hard-body guys always have soft lips." She backed away, her eyes still closed, and she smiled when she opened them and saw Brad frozen like a statue in front of her. She pressed a card into his hand. "Call me sometime on my cell when we can . . . be alone," she said. "And please, Brad, keep this a secret. My career depends on your discretion." And she turned and walked out.

Brad stood there, still frozen, until he heard Renaldo's car door slam and the engine start up . . . and when he was able to move, he found his legs as weak and rubbery as straws.

How in the world, he thought after a long breathless moment, am I going to get anything else done today . . . with no damned blood above my *waist*?

JOINT AIR BASE BATTLE MOUNTAIN

FOUR DAYS LATER

"I'd say that was a very successful first deployment," Jon Masters said. He had just ordered the first Sparrowhawk remotely piloted aircraft back to base, and the second was en route to take up the surveillance orbit. "Almost five straight days on station, and we gathered a ton of useful data on the routine in that compound."

"But we don't know anything more than we did five days ago," Special Agent Chastain grumbled.

"We know a *lot* more," Jon said. "If there's any meaningful change in the routine, we'll know about it right away, and we can launch a Sparrowhawk to follow up. Any change in the number of residents, new vehicles, large meetings, new construction, any new fortifications, even changes in temperature of individual buildings—the computer will notify us."

"I wish we could identify some of those individuals down there," the agent named Brady said.

"We're working on face-recognition capabilities for some of our remotely piloted aircraft," Jon said. "Ten thousand feet and overhead is not a good position to get a good shot of a face, but an unmanned plane at a lower altitude and standing off would have a better angle at a face. After that, it's just biometric comparison done by computer—we've been doing that for years."

"You're always with the damned sales pitch, Masters," Chastain snapped, "but we've been sitting here for four damned days and we haven't seen a thing that helps our investigation." He studied the laptop monitors. "If we flew the drone lower, we'd get better resolution on these pictures, right?"

"The sensors are optimized for ten thousand feet aboveground," Jon replied. "The resolution will always be better the lower you go, but usually we go for the best resolution at a higher altitude, not lower. The lower you go, the more likely it is for your target to spot the aircraft. We also have problems with data transmission and interference from local radio and TV broadcasts, not to mention having to think about terrain and obstacle avoidance. We usually—"

"I'm not interested in what you 'usually' do, Masters," Chastain said. "I'm only interested in results. Fly the drone at ten thousand feet."

"But . . . that's less than a mile aboveground," Jon said. "Most folks can see large aircraft quite easily if they're less than a mile up."

"No, they can't."

"And ten thousand is the minimum en route altitude for the Victor-113 airway," Jeff the aircraft control technician chimed in. "Any small aircraft flying the airway heading southwest will pick ten thousand feet."

"We've been flying the drone right on the damned airway for five days and we've had to move it . . . what, twice?" Chastain argued. "And even if we didn't move the drone, it would've missed the other traffic by miles. There's no traffic up there we need to worry about. Fly the drone at eleven thousand."

"That puts it right at the altitude that northeast-bound traffic flies," Jeff said.

"Then add five hundred feet, or six hundred, I don't care, just *do it*!" Chastain snapped. "I'm tired of you eggheads arguing with me. Change the altitude, and do it *now,* or I'll recommend to Washington that we get someone else to do the job." Jon nodded to Jeff, who put in the commands on the laptop. "When does the first drone return to our airspace?"

"In about twenty minutes."

"Make sure the airspace is closed down again, and fly the thing so it stays away from populated areas," Chastain said. "We'll have it orbit inside protected airspace until dark, then land it." Jeff selected North Peak, about fifteen miles west of Battle Mountain and clear of all airways, to orbit the Sparrowhawk, and he was careful to turn on its transponder beacon to help air traffic control steer other aircraft away from it. Jon contacted air traffic control and advised them of the orbiting unmanned aircraft.

Time passed much as it had done the previous four days. With both Sparrowhawks flying, Charlie Turlock was able to use the interior of the hangar during the daytime to help Agent Randolph Savoy train in the Cybernetic Infantry Device robots, and as she expected, he was a very fast learner; at night, they trained outdoors. Wayne Macomber watched, but kept to himself most of the time, using rubber cables to keep up with his rehabilitation exercises. "Any questions, Randolph?" Charlie asked after their last session ended.

"None," Savoy said. "You were right: it's pretty intuitive and straightforward to learn how to pilot these things." The other agents looked over and shook their heads at the sight of the two massive mechanical humanoids conversing in electronic voices, as if they were acquaintances who had just met on the street.

"The whole idea was to issue CID robots to young, qualified soldiers right out of basic training, so it had to be easy to learn," Charlie said. "Combat training is a whole different story: the basic combat course is two months, and each weapon backpack is another two weeks, plus range time. But if we had the funding, we could field an army of CIDs." She stepped over to the storage container, climbed out, then initiated the refolding and stowage sequences, and Savoy did likewise. "Now I guess we wait to see what they find at that Knight compound."

The images from the second Sparrowhawk orbiting at the lower altitude were indeed much better, and now the federal agents crowded around the wide-screen laptop, studying the compound carefully. "Look at the heavy weapons those guys have in there," the agent named Brady said, pointing at the screen. "There's at least four machine-gun squads right there."

"Looks like they're getting ready for something," Chastain said. "Looks like we might need the robots after . . ." Just then, the image went blank. "What happened?"

"I told you that might happen," Jon Masters said. "The lower altitude means more interference." They waited, but the image did not reappear.

"Jon, we might have a problem—I'm not getting flight data from Sparrowhawk Two," Jeff said. "We might have lost satellite contact."

"What the hell does that mean, Masters?" Chastain asked impatiently.

"It's no big deal," Jon said. "It'll orbit the area until satellite contact is restored. If it's not restored within two hours, it's programmed to return to the airport."

"Send the other drone back over the compound," Chastain said. "The Knights looked like they're getting ready for something—I need to know what's going on."

"It'll have to fly higher than ten thousand."

"But we were getting great shots at ten thousand," Chastain said.

"We don't know where the second Sparrowhawk is," Jon said. "We can't fly it at the same altitude as the first."

"Then fly it at nine thousand."

"That's only four thousand feet aboveground!"

"I don't care. Just do it."

"It can't stay on station for very long," Jeff reminded them. "It's already been airborne four days."

"How long can it stay?"

Jeff turned to the first Sparrowhawk's flight-data screen . . . and his mouth dropped open in surprise. "Uh, Jon . . ." Jon looked . . . and found the flight data on the first Sparrowhawk blank as well!

"What the hell happened?"

"Not now, Chastain," Jon said, pushing Jeff out of the way and frantically typing instructions into the laptop. He waited for a few moments, then pounded the desk in frustration. "Get Bidwell and Henderson out there to check the satellite uplink and network connectivity, *now*," he shouted, jabbing a finger at Jeff. "If they don't find anything wrong, have them hardwire the computer interfaces with the uplink and antenna instead of using the wireless routers. Reboot the computers and run the network and I-O diagnostics before reinitializing the software. Call Las Vegas and have the entire staff stand by—no, better yet, have them send the entire Sparrowhawk team up here."

"Masters, what's going on?"

"We've lost contact with both Sparrowhawks," Jon said, staring at the blank data readouts in complete bewilderment. "Losing one is bad, but it happens—losing both at the same time is a freakin' disaster." He looked at his watch. "We've got two hours until they start heading back to base. Make sure the airspace is clear. I'll talk to air traffic control and see if they have primary radar hits on either one of them."

The next two hours was a flurry of activity inside and outside the hangar. As they got closer to the arrival time, Patrick drove Jon and Special Agent Chastain in the airfield operations truck to the taxiway intersection closest to the approach end of the arrival runway and started scanning the sky for the Sparrowhawks. It was not yet sunset, but the eastern sky was dark enough to prevent seeing any aircraft unless its position and landing lights were on. "What did air traffic control say, Jon?" Patrick asked.

"None of your business, McLanahan," Chastain growled as he swept the sky with binoculars. Jon lowered his binoculars, looked at Patrick, and shook his head. "How much longer, Masters?" the FBI special agent asked.

"Any minute now."

Chastain's cell phone rang. "Chastain." He listened for a few moments, his eyes growing wider by the moment. "Oh, *shit*. I'll be right there . . . find a TV."

"In my office," Patrick said.

"What happened?" Jon asked.

At first Chastain wasn't going to say anything with Patrick there, but he decided Patrick was going to find out soon anyway: "There are news crews at the Knights' compound," he said. "The drone crashed."

"What . . . ?"

"There are pieces of another plane out there too—they're saying there was a midair collision," Chastain said. "It's all over the damned news."

They raced back to Patrick's office and turned on the television. They expected to see pictures of the crashed drone, but instead they were looking at what appeared to be a large area of scorched desert just south of a multilane divided highway that appeared to be Interstate 80. "What is *this*? They're reporting on a brush fire?" Chastain asked.

They found out soon enough: the caption on the bottom of the screen read: *Scene of the second unmanned aircraft crash near Battle Mountain, Nevada.*

"What in hell . . . !"

"Both Sparrowhawks crashed?" Jon Masters said in a low, stunned voice, almost a whimper. "My God . . ."

Chastain's cell phone was in his hands in a flash. "I want those crash sites cordoned off and all news helicopters kept away," he said.

"I've got to get out there," Jon said tonelessly, his eyes wide with disbelief and despair. "I've got to find out what happened."

"You're not going anywhere, Masters," Chastain said, putting a hand over his cell phone's microphone. "This is still a classified operation." He turned back to his cell phone. "Jordan, Chastain here. I want . . ." He fell silent, listening, then veins started to pop out on his forehead. He jabbed a finger at Patrick, then at the door, silently ordering him to get out. After Patrick departed, Chastain yelled, "Get HRTs Four and Five loaded up and on their way out to that compound *now*. I'll get Los Angeles and Seattle to send their teams."

"What happened?" Jon asked.

"The damned Knights are dragging pieces of the drone inside their compound," Chastain said. "The news crews are going in with them. They say they're expecting the government to respond with force, and they say they're going to defend themselves and repel all attackers."

"You mean *they're stealing my Sparowhawk?*" Jon cried out.

"Shut up about your damned drones, Masters," Chastain said. "They're evidence, and I'm going to get them all back, you can count on *that*."

"Send in the Cybernetic Infantry Device robots," Jon said. "The robots will get them back."

Chastain thought for a moment, then redialed his cell phone. "Richter, I'm going to brief you and Savoy on a mission. Meet me at the drone control desk. We'll deploy by helicopter in fifteen minutes."

They drove back to their hangar, where they met Jason Richter, Charlie Turlock, Wayne Macomber, and FBI agent Randolph Savoy at the Sparrowhawk control center. "Flip back to the last images of the compound," Chastain ordered. He waited until the right images were displayed. "Okay, here's where the drone crashed, about two hundred yards outside the main fenced part of the compound, at the edge of one of their crop circles." He pointed to the machine-gun squads. "Here's where the terrorists are setting up machine-gun nests, behind cover of these buildings outside the fence. It's been more than two hours since these pictures were taken, so we've got to assume they've moved some of these nests closer to the crash site." He turned to Richter. "Can you pull the wreckage away from the compound?"

"I'm sure we can," Jason said. "But if the terrorists are armed with machine guns, we'll be going into a combat zone. Randolph's not trained for that, and we have no defensive weapons. Charlie and I will do this mission."

"You're not *supposed* to have *any* weapons, Richter," Chastain said. "First of all, this is an FBI operation, so Savoy goes. That's what he's been training for."

"Let me go in," Whack said.

"Get out of here, Macomber—this isn't for you," Chastain snapped. Whack backed up a step; Chastain was going to order him out, but one look at Whack's dark scowl made him decide to just turn and ignore him.

"I'll go in the second CID," Charlie said. "Randolph and I have been working together all this time—it's best to keep us together." Jason thought about it for a moment, then nodded.

"Second, I don't want you to engage with them," Chastain said to Charlie. "What I'm asking is: Can the robots provide you with enough protection from machine-gun fire to allow you to get in there and drag the wreckage away from the compound so those terrorists can't take all of it?"

Charlie thought for a few moments, studying the frozen Sparrowhawk images. "What kind of guns are those, Whack?" she asked.

"They look like M60 machine guns," he said after studying the screen for a few moments. "I see a couple others that might be M16s, but bigger. AR-18s on a bipod, maybe."

"Well, Turlock?" Chastain urged.

Charlie turned to Savoy, a look of concern on her face. "The CIDs can take 5.56- and 7.62-millimeter fire at all ranges, even full auto," she said directly to Savoy. "They can't hurt you, but you *will* feel them. It can get really distracting, even disorientating, like bugs or bats flying around your head. You need to—"

"I can do it, Charlie," Savoy said. "Let's go."

"If it's a heavier caliber, like a fifty-cal or twenty-millimeter, at close range with sustained automatic fire, it could damage a muscle joint or sensor, especially in the head," Charlie went on. "If they use heavier weapons—and your sensors will alert you to the weapon size, direction of fire, and range—you'll have to protect your forward sensor with your forearms. Try not to use just your hands, because the armor's not as tough. If you feel heavy automatic fire on you, you have to move right away so you don't get sustained impacts on one section of armor. The robot's sensors will tell you if you're taking damaging fire . . . sheesh, we've hardly talked about the sensors and helmet warning and malfunction readouts—"

"I understand them pretty well," Savoy said. "I'm ready."

"We haven't talked *at all* about a helicopter insertion." She turned to Chastain. "We can't do this, Chastain. He's not ready."

"I *am* ready," Savoy repeated.

"Is he ready or not, Turlock?" Chastain growled.

Charlie looked at Savoy with concern, but nodded. "I'll be right beside you," she said. "The best thing to do if you get pinned down by several nests is to run away."

"Got it, Charlie," Savoy said. "Let's go."

Charlie looked at him carefully once more, then nodded at Chastain. "Let's go."

While Charlie and Savoy mounted inside their CIDs, an Army National Guard UH-60 Black Hawk helicopter was flown over to the hangar. The UH-60 was a long-range medevac model with an external fuel tank on a short pylon on each side mounted above the entry doors, plus protective skids surrounding the landing-gear tires. With the helicopter hovering, Charlie showed Savoy the exact place to hold on to the pylon. "You can fend yourself away from the landing gear," she radioed to him, "but don't squeeze the pylon, because you'll snap it right off. Grab onto this cross-member on the pylon, circle your fingers around it, and keep your fingers closed. Don't squeeze."

Minutes later, they were airborne—and the moment they lifted off, Charlie heard a loud *CH-CHUNK!* on the other side of the helicopter. "Randolph? You okay?"

"I might have grabbed the pylon a little too hard," he admitted.

"You copy that, pilot?" Charlie radioed. "You might lose the left fuel tank."

"They're both empty," the pilot radioed back.

"Roger," Charlie said. "If you feel it coming loose, Randolph, just let it bounce off your back." She hesitated for a moment, then added, "And if you fall . . . well, have a nice ride down. You should be okay when you hit."

"'Should be'?"

It was a short flight to the Knight compound. From a hundred feet aboveground and two miles away, Charlie could easily see the Sparrowhawk's crash site through her telescopic imaging infrared sensors. The residents had several pickup trucks surrounding the crash, with headlights helping workers pull pieces of wreckage free and throw them into the trucks. "Base, looks like they've just about got the whole thing—we're too late," Charlie said. "There's four pickups around the crash site full of debris, and it looks like they're loaded up and getting ready to head back. I recommend we—"

At that instant Charlie saw a long, thin flash of yellow fire winking from a few dozen yards west, followed by another several yards north. *"Ground fire!"* she shouted. "We're taking heavy machine-gun fire! Pilot, *break right!"* The Black Hawk swung hard to the right at sixty degrees of bank . . .

. . . and as it did, the entire left pylon snapped from the sudden g-loads and broke free, disappearing into the darkness.

"We lost Savoy!" Charlie shouted, and she let go of the right pylon and fell to earth.

Her landing on the desert surface wasn't her best, because the helicopter had been in such a violent turn when she released, and she rolled and skidded across the hard-packed sand and dirt for about twenty yards before regaining her armored feet. She crouched low and scanned the area. The machine guns were still firing into the night sky. Seconds later, her electronic sensors located Savoy, just fifty yards away, and she dashed toward him. He was facedown, motionless, his arms and legs splayed in unnatural directions.

"I've located Savoy," Charlie radioed. "Randolph, can you hear me? Damn, he looks hurt." No response. She checked his physiological readouts. "He's alive but unconscious." She picked him up in a fireman's carry, then scanned the area. Several pickup trucks were heading from the west toward them, headlights bouncing wildly as they raced across the desert. "They're after me. I'll move east away from these jokers."

Just as she started to run, her sensors picked up a burst of heavy machine-gun fire on her armor. "Those bastards have a heavy machine gun mounted on one of those pickups!" she radioed. "Might be a fifty-cal!" The fire was pretty sustained considering she was running and the trucks were bouncing all over the place—those pricks were pretty good gunners, she thought. Savoy, on top of Charlie's shoulders, was taking most of the hits. "They're catching up to me," she radioed. "These guys are driving like maniacs."

"We've got you in sight," the Black Hawk pilot radioed. "Keep on coming." Charlie spotted the Black Hawk in front of her, not more than thirty feet aboveground, heading straight for the pickups.

"They've got a big machine gun," Charlie radioed. "Break off!"

"Just keep coming," the pilot said, as calm and cool as if he were sipping a beer. Moments later, the Black Hawk zoomed overhead, flying better than eighty miles an hour.

Charlie could hear the machine gun open fire, but no rounds were hitting her. Were they firing at the helicopter? They must have night vision to be able to see it! Just then she saw a flare of light similar to the machine-gun muzzle flashes, but this one was directed *down* at the ground. Moments later in the sky she saw a burst of fire, followed by a brief trail of fire and loud pops of metal. The roar of the Black Hawk's engines seemed to surge, then hesitate, then surge again. "Are you guys okay?" she radioed. "Are you hit?"

"We took some hits—that last one felt like a missile or RPG," the pilot radioed, still as calmly as before, "but I got it, I got it, I—" And at that second there was a brilliant flash of light, an earsplitting explosion, and a sharp vibration that rolled through the earth under Charlie's armored feet. She turned and saw a massive fireball blossom across the sky.

"Oh *God* . . ." She ran in the direction of the crash, less than half a mile away, even though she began receiving "POWER 50 PERCENT" warning messages. But as she got closer, she could see the Black Hawk fully engulfed in flames. Soon several pickup trucks surrounded the wreckage, and men began shouting and shooting automatic weapons in the air in celebration.

"One cannon backpack—that's all I need," Charlie said. Angrily, reluctantly, she turned away from the wreckage and the extremists and headed across the desert to safety.

WASHINGTON, D.C.

THE NEXT MORNING

"This is without a doubt one of the most flagrant and outrageous misuses of power since Japanese internment camps during World War Two," former president Joseph Gardner said. Gardner, a tall and impossibly handsome character bred for politics, was a long-time Washington power player—secretary of the Navy and ardent sea-power advocate, who parlayed his steep buildup of naval forces after the American Holocaust into a successful campaign for president of the United States on a strong national defense platform.

"Who would have believed," Gardner went on, "that Ken Phoenix would order the FBI to use military hardware to secretly spy on American citizens, over American soil?" Gardner went on, deliberately not using Phoenix's title when talking about him. "And then, in an even greater assault on personal freedom, they send two of those manned robots in to attack that community. It's *unthinkable*."

"Why do you say it's military hardware, Mr. President?" the morning talk-show interviewer asked. "Unmanned aircraft are used by police and Border Patrol agencies, not just the military."

"Both drones were built by a company called Sky Masters, Inc., which is a small but well-known developer of military hardware of all kinds, including weapons, satellites, and aircraft," Gardner said. "The drones that crashed were called MQ-15 Sparrowhawks. They are capable of carrying up to a thousand pounds of sensors or weapons, including laser-guided missiles, and they've been used in Afghanistan, Pakistan, and Iraq. That Ken Phoenix actually ordered the FBI to fly potentially armed aircraft over the United States to target innocent American citizens is criminal. And those robots belong to the U.S. Army and are armed with cannons and missile launchers—clearly, military technology, designed to kill. Someone has to be held accountable for this outrage, and the buck stops right on Mr. Phoenix's desk."

"A spokesperson for the Department of Justice said that suspects residing in the compound where the drone crashed were linked to the recent attacks in Reno and southern Nevada," the interviewer said. "Shouldn't we be using all the resources we have to investigate such extreme terrorist activity, Mr. President?"

"Where's the evidence backing this claim?" Gardner said, spreading his hands. "Let's see the evidence. Besides, the FBI has its own resources—*legal* resources—to investigate crime. Why did Phoenix give the FBI military hardware?"

"So you oppose using drones and these manned robots to conduct surveillance on suspected terrorists?" the interviewer asked. "As I understand it, it is not against the law for the U.S. military to *assist* law enforcement, as long as they don't make arrests or attack civilians."

"How would you like a military spy plane flying over your home taking pictures and sending them to gawkers in the FBI and White House?" Gardner asked. "And what do you think those robots were doing out there—taking pictures? It's crazy. This is America, not Soviet Russia. And where's the warrant authorizing these drone flights? Who was the judge that signed the warrant? Or did Phoenix himself order the surveillance, without a warrant? And what if there *was* a midair collision, as the residents there claim? Did Phoenix kill innocent civilians with this dangerous and possibly illegal surveillance? We need answers to all these questions, and so far the Phoenix administration has been slow and extremely reluctant to provide them."

"That's a load of crap, Gardner," Vice President Ann Page said acidly at the television she was watching from the Oval Office.

She muted the sound, but continued to watch as the cable news network showed a low-light camera image of the Cybernetic Infantry Device robot running across the desert, carrying another robot. "I've put out a press release detailing the entire operation, including the name of the U.S. District Court judge that signed the warrants."

"I know, Ann, I know," President Ken Phoenix said. "President Gardner is just spouting off. Point out all of his inaccuracies in the daily press briefing and folks will start to ignore him."

"Don't worry, I will," Ann said heatedly.

The computer on the president's desk beeped, and Phoenix hit a button to put the secure videophone call on speakerphone. The screen was split, with Attorney General Jocelyn Caffery on one half and FBI director Fuller on the other. "General Caffery, Director Fuller, this is the president. How are you?"

"Good, thank you, sir," Attorney General Caffery replied. "Director Fuller has an update for you."

"Go ahead, Justin."

"Thank you, sir," FBI director Justin Fuller replied. "I'm en route to Nevada to oversee the investigation on those two drone crashes and the Black Hawk attack. Here's is the latest:

"There are five casualties: two U.S. Army National Guard pilots and one National Guard crew chief—all volunteers assisting the FBI—and one FBI agent died in the Black Hawk crash. Another FBI agent piloting the Cybernetic Infantry Device robot died about thirty minutes ago of trauma from his fall from the helicopter and wounds from heavy machine-gun fire that pierced his armor. The pilot reported to one of the CIDs that he thought he had been hit by a missile or a rocket-propelled grenade. The FBI and Army are on the scene of the helicopter crash, and the residents of that compound are not interfering, but I ordered all investigators to stay away from the compound."

The president nodded his assent.

"The wreckage of the drone that crashed near the interstate has

been taken to Joint Air Base Battle Mountain for forensic examination," Fuller went on. "With your permission, sir, I've ordered
the National Transportation Safety Board not to convene an accident panel until the FBI completes its investigation."

"Approved," the president said, "but I'd like you to turn over
any unclassified findings to the NTSB as soon as possible."

"Yes, Mr. President. We did have a very interesting development
regarding the first drone: an eyewitness who was hunting in the
vicinity south of the crash site claims he saw what he described as
a contrail."

"Contrail . . . you mean, a missile trail?" Ann asked.

"The witness couldn't be sure," Fuller said. "He said the trail
was pretty straight, and motor smoke from a man-portable air-
defense missile is usually not. We're investigating. We should be
able to tell once we get a look at the wreckage."

"Domestic terrorists, armed first with radioactive materials . . .
and possibly now with antiaircraft missiles?" Ann breathed. "It's
too scary to think about."

"Let's not get too far ahead of ourselves here," Phoenix said.
"Director Fuller, who authorized the robot action against the extremists?"

"Special Agent Philip Chastain, special agent in charge of terror
investigations, out of the San Francisco office."

"He should have asked for permission to deploy those robots."

"He made a tactical decision, sir," Fuller said. "He was given the
robots to use as part of this investigation of extremist groups, and
he acted when he saw that drone being captured by the extremists.
I can't fault him, sir. I stand behind his decision."

Phoenix thought for a moment, then nodded. "Very well," he
said. "You're right: we expect these men to make decisions and act.
And thank you for sticking with your man."

"Yes, sir. Chastain is one of our best."

"So we may never know if it was involved in a midair collision,
like the extremists claim?"

"We've been in contact with the FAA and they say that there were no other aircraft in the vicinity of the second drone, sir," Fuller said. "However, that's inconclusive because of radar limitations—they might not see small or low-flying aircraft—but the claim that there was a midair collision might be untrue. They are extremely rare, even with unmanned aircraft. We won't know until we examine the wreckage."

"Which leads us to the big question, sir: what to do about those extremists," Caffery said. "They've dragged all the wreckage of the second drone into their compound; they fired on our helicopter and the CID units with heavy automatic weapons; and they may have used antiaircraft weapons against our surveillance planes."

"I've got two Hostage Rescue Teams standing by to enter that compound and make arrests, with two more on the way to assist," Fuller said. "We've set up long-range ground-based surveillance of the compound, and in a few days we'll have a clear picture of exactly what we're up against there."

"I don't want anybody entering that compound," the president said. "Surround it, prevent anyone from entering or leaving unless it's a humanitarian necessity. Collect intelligence, and start negotiating a surrender of those responsible for shooting at the helicopter. I'm not going to have another Branch Davidian disaster televised for the entire world."

"Yes, Mr. President."

"I'll be waiting to hear more about the results of the investigation into the first drone," the president said. "Anything else for me?"

Attorney General Caffery looked a little uneasy, but said, "About former president Gardner, sir."

"I heard him this morning," Phoenix said, rubbing his eyes wearily. "He's entitled to his own opinions."

"But not his own facts, sir," Caffery said. "What he's saying is not only untrue, but I'm afraid it could spark more violence if he scares the American people into believing that the government is using the military against them."

"We'll deal with that if and when we have to," the president said. "But we'll expose the former president's untruths in the daily press briefings—the more he fabricates the facts, the faster he'll marginalize himself."

Joint Air Base Battle Mountain

That same time

Patrick McLanahan was driving by the parking lot outside the hangar being used by the FBI, and he saw Special Agent Chastain getting out of his car. He stopped and got out of the car, which immediately attracted Chastain's attention. "I'm very sorry about your men, Agent Chastain," Patrick said. "Agent Savoy was extremely brave for going on that mission."

"He was doing his job," Chastain said flatly. He stepped toward Patrick, looking at him carefully. "I'm sure you know already," he said, "but the U.S. attorney has decided not to charge you."

"Yes, I heard."

"But I still don't get you, General," Chastain said. "I spoke with the Pentagon. They say you are retired, period. You still have a security clearance, but it's 'confidential' only, like most retired flag-rank officers. You are permitted virtual unfettered access to the base, not because you have any official duties but because of your rank and because you were once the commander here. Along with your retiree benefits you receive temporary base housing in lieu of cost-of-living adjustments and not because you're part of the staff. Yet you keep on telling me and everyone that you work for the Space Defense Force as some sort of liaison or facility manager."

Patrick shrugged. "I guess I feel deep down that I do have a role here," he said. "Frankly, being retired is the pits. I don't recommend it. It's a way I can keep involved with the Air Force and space operations, and at the same time I have time to spend with my son."

"Like the Civil Air Patrol thing," Chastain said.

"Exactly," Patrick said. "I get to fly, contribute my skills, and wear a green bag, just like the old days. I'm with a great bunch of locals and we like to tell stories and teach the cadets about the military and service to the community and the country." Chastain just nodded—Patrick thought he was just plain uninterested. "Again, I'm sorry about your men." They shook hands, and Patrick drove off.

Inside the hangar, Chastain found Brady and Renaldo around the Sparrowhawk control table, going over the video they recorded from the reconnaissance flights, along with photos of the compound obtained by agents using telescopic high-resolution digital cameras. "What do you have?" he asked.

"The Knights are really getting cocky, the sons of bitches," Brady said. "They're out in the open, still celebrating, still going in front of the media telling the world how evil the FBI and U.S. military are, setting up defenses, and doing target practice with automatic weapons. They must have a shitload of weapons and ammo out there, because dozens of them have been doing target practice for hours, with a whole range of weapons. We're identifying about a half-dozen new residents an hour." He looked at Chastain's distracted expression. "What's up?"

"I just spoke with McLanahan."

"You did?" Cassandra Renaldo asked. "You mean he actually *talked* to you?"

"Condolences for Savoy and Eberle," Chastain said, "but he was unusually chatty after that. I told him that I checked him out and found out he's really not the manager of anything around here, and he didn't seem to care. He seemed to be . . . feeling pretty relaxed, considering the shit that happened here last night."

"That's weird," Brady said. He nodded toward the images on the laptop screens. "Kinda like these jerk-offs here, celebrating the fact that they killed five fellow Americans, shot down three aircraft, and are flaunting their illegal automatic weapons in front of federal and state authorities."

Chastain looked at the pictures, and his eyes flared. "Are you putting together files on these people?"

"Of course."

"How many of them belong to the Civil Air Patrol?" Chastain asked.

"I haven't drilled down to nonpolitical affiliations yet," Brady said. "The support staff is doing basic background, aliases, employment, criminal history, and military experience on about a hundred and forty individuals and counting."

"Start looking into Civil Air Patrol membership," Chastain said. "I had a bad feeling about McLanahan the moment he refused to talk, but I couldn't figure out why a guy like him would be involved with domestic terrorists. The Civil Air Patrol could be the common thread. A lot of ex-military, a lot of patriotic wave-the-flag rhetoric, a lot of old guys wearing military-style uniforms . . ."

"I'm on it," Brady said excitedly.

"I'm still not so sure," Renaldo chimed in. "I don't get that feeling about him. Now, a couple of the guys I've interviewed in this CAP unit like Fitzgerald, Slotnick, and de Carteret, yes, they could be extremists; McLanahan, no."

"I want to keep searching," Chastain said. "My radar is buzzing, and it's still aimed right at McLanahan and now this Civil Air Patrol unit. What about the son?"

"He's ready to pop—literally, if I do say so myself—any day now," Renaldo said with a smile. Brady gave her a leer and a wink. "He'll call me soon, don't worry."

SEVEN

The strongest of all warriors are these two—Time and Patience.

—LEO TOLSTOY

NORTH PEAK, WEST OF BATTLE MOUNTAIN

THE NEXT MORNING

"Remember, you're not looking for anything in particular, Brad," John de Carteret said. He was in the right front seat of the Civil Air Patrol Cessna 182 as mission observer, with Brad McLanahan in the left rear seat as mission-scanner trainee and his father, Patrick, as mission pilot. "Camps are probably the hardest to find, especially from one thousand feet above ground."

"It all looks the same," Brad said. He was using scan techniques, shifting his vision and locking briefly on a spot before shifting and relocking again, and scanning from top to bottom out to the sight line, but it didn't seem to help. To make matters worse, his stomach wasn't feeling quite right. "I mean, it's like I see everything and nothing at the same time."

"The best thing to look for when looking for camps is how the campers get to the site, not necessarily the site itself," John said. "Tire tracks, new trails, disturbed ground, open gates, broken fences—those are easier to see from the air." Brad shifted his attention to those things, but there didn't seem to be anything like them anywhere.

"Need to take a break, Brad?" Patrick asked. "I can reverse the turn and contour-search the mountain from the other direction to let John do some scanning." They had been assigned to search North Peak, west-northwest of Battle Mountain, for signs of a missile launch site—the FBI investigators definitely discovered that the first Sparrowhawk had been hit by a Stinger-like missile. Because this was an Air Force–assigned mission, Brad was getting his first of two required actual missions before being able to move up to mission observer. A ground team, led by Michael Fitzgerald with Ron Spivey as the cadet leader, was in the area below searching as well.

"No, I'm good, Dad," although his stomach sure wasn't liking these orbits around the mountain. A contour search started a thousand feet above the highest point of a peak, then two left-turn orbits. Then they would descend five hundred feet and do two more orbits, staying about a half mile away from the mountain's face. After that, they would descend another five hundred feet and do it again.

Working around mountains and ridges always meant turbulence and squirrelly winds, especially in summer, and each bump didn't help Brad's stomach. Now he wished he'd eaten something before this mission, and wished he brought a barf bag—the only container he could see within reach was his brand-new flight-gear bag and the case for the digital camera, and he didn't want to throw up in either one.

"I'm really glad Colonel Spara let us fly together, Brad," Patrick said.

"Me too," Brad said uneasily. He took a sip of water, but it didn't help his stomach much.

"I think it's because there's a whole lot less guys hanging around the squadron these days, after the attack on the FBI guys," John said. "It's getting harder every day to put a crew together. Leo is busier than ever with the Highway Patrol. I think there's just one other pilot I've seen around, other than Rob and you."

Just as they were circling the northeast side of North Peak, Brad saw it—two black circles, one small, like a campfire area, and the other much larger. "Dad, I think I see something, nine o'clock."

"Pick out things around it that will help steer your eyes back to it," Patrick said. "What do you see?"

"A couple black spots on the ground, right beside a trail," Brad said. He had to look farther down and back to keep it in sight, and that was even more disorientating.

Patrick scanned out his window, but he knew he couldn't get too distracted from flying the plane. "I didn't see it," he said. "I don't have enough room to keep turning left, but I'll loop around to the right and bring you right back to it on the same heading. Coming right." He made a right turn away from the mountain, perhaps a bit more sharply than he intended . . .

. . . but Brad wasn't ready for it, and when Patrick turned, Brad couldn't stop it—he put his head between his legs, pulled the headset microphone away from his lips just in time, and threw up on the floor of the Cessna.

"Brad!" Patrick exclaimed, rolling wings level. "Are you all right?" His question was answered with another heave. "Brad?"

"I'm . . . I'm okay." But he followed that announcement with a third heave.

Patrick and John pulled their overhead vents open all the way to let in as much fresh air as they could, but it was no use—the smell wafted up to the cockpit, and now it was everywhere, impossible to ignore. Patrick looked over at John, who was already starting to turn a little pale. "John . . . ?"

"I think I'm done for a while too, Patrick," he said uneasily.

"I'm sorry, Dad," Brad said. "I should've eaten something. It's all the turning, and looking sideways and downward, and the turbulence . . ."

"Don't worry, Brad," Patrick said. "Either it's happened to every pilot, or it soon will. We're heading back to base." John radioed Rob Spara at the squadron to report that they were exiting the search grid and gave them their ETA back to base.

As they were approaching the traffic pattern, John looked and saw a group of about ten cars on either side of the road to the base. "What's going on down there?" he asked.

Patrick looked himself. Two lines of individuals carrying signs were walking down the road toward the main entrance to the base. "Why, they look like protesters!" he exclaimed. "Looks like they're going to demonstrate outside the base!"

"I hope they *stay* outside," John said. There was really no outer gate to Joint Air Base Battle Mountain, just a light chain-link fence designed to keep out tumbleweeds, and a cattle guard on the road to keep out stray farm animals on the nearby open ranges. All of the base security was electronic, using laser, infrared, and millimeter-wave sensors for all-weather precision scanning, with responses made by unmanned and then manned vehicles. "I haven't seen a protest march since the Vietnam years."

Patrick made the landing, brought the plane back to the hangar, then helped clean out the back. Afterward, they checked in with Rob Spara and described what they saw, including the protesters outside the main gate. "Yeah, they warned us about that," Rob said. "Base security said if it gets bigger they might have to escort folks in and out." He turned to Brad. "You feel okay, Brad?"

"I'm much better," Brad replied. He had a packet of cheese and peanut-butter crackers and a ginger ale. "I just needed to eat something. I didn't really have breakfast. I was too excited." He turned to Patrick. "Sorry for messing up the plane, Dad," he repeated.

"Don't be. It's okay. Feel like giving it another try?"

"Yes!"

"Sure you want to push it, Brad?" Rob asked. "It's not going to get any less bumpy out there."

"I still want to go," Brad said.

Rob looked at Brad carefully, then glanced at Patrick. But Patrick just put a hand on Brad's shoulder. "He's an adult and a senior member now, Rob," he said with a smile. "He can make his own decisions."

Rob hesitated. "I'd say airsickness is an 'illness' in the 'IM-SAFE' checkoff that would ground you, Brad," he said. "But I have a ground team in the field and no other crews to fly the 182." He turned to John. "You feeling okay, John?"

"Yeah," he replied. He too was munching on crackers and washing them down with ginger ale, both believed to be good nondrug remedies for airsickness. "I got a little green around the gills when the smell first hit, but I'm good now."

Rob thought about it a little more, but he finally nodded. "Okay, guys," he said, punching flight-release information into his computer. "You're released. Make contact with the ground team and see if you steer them over to that sighting you made." After Patrick got a bite to eat himself—with a bottle of ginger ale too, just in case—they refueled the plane, preflighted, loaded up, and were off.

But it was soon obvious that Brad's stomach was not going to cooperate. They were on the downwind leg of the departure, still in the climb and not yet at pattern altitude, in smooth air, when Brad said, "I don't feel so good again, Dad."

Both air vents were already wide open. Patrick leveled off at about five hundred feet aboveground and reduced airspeed to smooth out the ride. "Try looking out the front window instead of the side window for a while, Brad," John suggested.

"I tried that," Brad said. "I think it's sitting in the back. I feel all cooped up back here. I never got airsick when I sit in front or when I'm flying."

John turned to look at Brad, and he saw how miserable he

looked. "I think we better put it down, Patrick," he said. "Brad's not—" And at that moment they heard a loud *PRRING!* and felt a sharp metallic impact vibration from the left wing. "What was that? Did we hit a bird?"

"Didn't feel like a bird," Patrick said. "Back me up on altitude while I look, John."

"Roger."

Patrick searched the leading edge of the wing for the source of that noise. "I don't see any—"

"I see a hole in the wing!" Brad said suddenly. "Out by the tip, just forward of the aileron! Fuel is coming out!"

Patrick saw it a moment later. "Now, how in heck did that happen?" he asked no one in particular. He turned the control wheel slightly, then scanned the instrument panel. "Everything feels okay, and the engine instruments look—" And at that instant they felt and heard another sharp rap on the airplane, this time from somewhere on the tail and rear fuselage. "What the hell . . . ?"

"Hey, the back window is broken!" Brad exclaimed. They all turned and saw the rear Plexiglas window with numerous spiderweb-like cracks emanating from a deep round hole near the upper edge! "It looks like a bullet hole!" Brad said.

"Holy crap, I think someone's shooting at us!" Patrick shouted. He mashed the microphone button: "Battle Mountain Tower, CAP Twenty-seven-twenty-two, declaring an emergency, requesting immediate landing clearance."

"CAP Twenty-two, Battle Mountain tower, roger, cleared to land, any runway," the tower controller responded immediately. "State fuel and souls on board and the nature of your emergency."

"CAP Twenty-seven-twenty-two, three souls, four hours' fuel on board," Patrick replied as he banked steeply toward the northeast-southwest cross runway. "I think someone hit us with gunfire."

There was a momentary pause; then: "CAP Twenty-two, *say again?*"

"I think someone on the ground hit us with gunfire," Patrick said. "They put a hole in our left wing and back window."

"Roger," the controller said, obviously trying to remain calm. "Do you require men and equipment?"

"Affirmative," Patrick said. "I'm going to land on Runway zero-three. Advise any other aircraft to remain clear of the protesters outside the main gate—I think one of them might have a rifle."

Outside the Main Gate to Joint Air Base Battle Mountain

A short time later

The appearance of the two squat remote-controlled Avenger air-defense armored vehicles inside the main gate of the air base, with their Sidewinder antiaircraft missile-launcher tubes and twenty-millimeter cannons aimed forward and elevated in a definitely menacing position, only served to enrage the protesters even more. The crowd of about thirty chanted, *"Hey hey, ho ho, the killer robots have got to go!"* and *"Spy planes spy planes, what do you see? Innocent citizens living free! Spy planes spy planes go away, if you come back, you will pay!"*

Just then they heard sirens behind them. A convoy of six Nevada Highway Patrol vehicles, sirens and lights on, moved slowly up the road to the main gate, led by a vehicle that somewhat resembled the armored vehicles inside the base. *"This is the Nevada Highway Patrol,"* a voice on a loudspeaker blared. *"You are blocking a public thoroughfare without permission and interfering with freedom of travel. Please disperse immediately. Thank you for your cooperation."* The convoy stopped just a few yards away from the crowd of protesters.

"We're not going anywhere until they shut down the robots and spy planes!" someone shouted.

"Your grievances will be forwarded to the Department of Defense and the governor and attorney general of the state of Nevada," the voice on the loudspeaker said. *"Be assured, all of your grievances will be promptly addressed. But you are still blocking a public-access thoroughfare and creating a disturbance. Please return to your vehicles and leave the area so free access to this public roadway can be restored. Thank you for your cooperation."*

"We're not going anywhere until the governor or the president orders all the spy planes and robots out of Nevada!" someone in the crowd shouted. "This is bullshit! You're flying weaponized planes and operating armed robots out of this base to terrorize innocent citizens! How do we know you're not looking in on me or my children right now? We want it to stop *right now*! *Right now*! *Right now!*" And the chanting and anger level rose once again.

"Please return to your vehicles and leave the area," the voice on the loudspeaker said over the chanting. *"The public roadway must remain clear. Thank you for your cooperation."*

"Oh yeah?" someone else shouted. "What are you going to do—blast us with that cannon or those missiles, cop? You gonna drop a bomb on us from one of those CAP planes you got flying around?"

"Thank you for your continued support of our community," the voice said. *"The Nevada Highway Patrol is here to assist you. Please return to your vehicles. Thank you for your cooperation."*

It took several minutes, but soon the energy level of the protesters seemed to decrease, and one by one they turned and headed away from the main gate. A few slammed their signs on the armored vehicles and spit on the Highway Patrol vehicle's windshields, but the officers did not react.

"Well, this is definitely a new one for me," Nevada Highway Patrol sergeant Leo Slotnick said. He was standing beside his car, the second in the convoy behind the armored car, talking with his partner. He was wearing a bullet-resistant vest over his uniform that read *NHP* and *POLICE* in large yellow letters, a Kevlar riot helmet with face shield, and heavy Kevlar gloves—his riot baton and cans of pepper spray were inside the vehicle, out of sight but quickly available. Most persons passing by him waved hello—no one seemed to be angry at him personally. "A protest march, way out here in Battle Mountain? I think it's pretty funny. I had to dust off my riot gear—*literally* dust it off."

"Whatever happened to the sheriff's department?" Leo's partner, a relatively new member of the Nevada Highway Patrol named Bobby Johnson, asked. He was outfitted the same as Leo but with a small digital video recorder affixed to his helmet; Leo was his training officer in his first six-month probationary period. "They're a no-show?"

"They said they couldn't spare the manpower," Leo said. "Technically this road is a state highway, so we have jurisdiction, but they should be out here with us. They never showed when the Civil Air Patrol was searching for that downed plane either."

"I heard one of your guys thinks he was shot at by someone in this crowd," Bobby said. "These bastards were shooting at aircraft over the base? Are they nuts? I think we should search each and every one of them for that rifle."

"Bobby, think about it—there's thirty of them, and just twelve of us," Leo said. "If there's a gun in that crowd, we don't want it let loose on us. If they start heading off and going home without another shot being fired, that's a good thing. Next time there's a protest, we'll be ready with more guys." As his eyes scanned the departing protesters, he caught a glimpse of two men, apart from each other but definitely together, walking along with the crowd toward their vehicles but looking as if they were scanning the crowd themselves. "Get a shot of those two tall guys at twelve o'clock," Leo said.

Bobby turned in that direction but couldn't really see whom Leo was referring to. "What's up?"

Leo shook his head. "Just a hunch," he said. "Remember what you were taught at the Academy about the personalities that create a disturbance?"

"Agitator, instigator, aggressor, and . . . and . . ."

"The lemmings—the followers," Leo said. "Who are the agitators here?"

"The guy who organized this march."

"True," Leo said, "but couldn't you also say it was the Air Force when they rolled out those armored vehicles over there? Maybe the crowd wouldn't be so agitated if they hadn't brought those out."

"Well, then couldn't you say that *we* are agitators for bring our armored car?"

"Good point," Leo conceded, "although then you have to think about officer safety, and that's a command decision. Now, the instigator is the one who does the first noncivil action—in this case, maybe the ones hitting the armored car with their signs. But he doesn't usually cause the riot. It's the aggressors that you have to watch out for—the ones who wait for something to happen, then push everyone around them over the top. Then the lemmings do whatever the aggressors and the rest of the crowd does, and the thing turns into a riot."

"So if you can find the aggressors, you might have a chance of stopping the riot."

"Exactly," Leo said. "The agitators are the hotheads, but they're usually just lashing out, not attacking—they get the crowd's attention with an overt act, but the crowd hasn't turned into lemmings yet. The aggressors do the extreme actions that turn the crowd."

Bobby continued searching the crowd, but still couldn't see whom Leo was referring to. "Gotcha."

Leo made eye contact with one of the tall guys he was watching, broke eye contact and scanned the crowd for a few seconds, then came back to the guy—and they made eye contact again. "And the first rule of surveillance?"

"Countersurveillance," Bobby said. "Make sure you're not being watched yourself."

"Either we're being watched, which I doubt," Leo said, "or these guys were on their way to do something else and have now noticed that *they've* been spotted. They're spooked, but they're not running—they know it's the running man that attracts attention." He looked behind him at some of the protesters widely circling his car, but couldn't see anyone else who stood out—there could easily be another pair behind him, but he couldn't make them out. "Weird vibes around here, that's for sure."

When he looked back at the pair, they had both vanished, and no one was running or shoving—they had quite literally disappeared.

"I don't know what to say, Brad," Patrick said as they examined the Civil Air Patrol Cessna. They had pans and buckets underneath the hole in the left wing, collecting leaking avgas. Maintenance crews already had the shattered window off, and they were getting ready to start removing inspection panels and rivets to replace the damaged left-wing sections. "You have about thirty hours total time flying the C-172 and P210, and I don't recall you ever getting airsick. I know you flew in the back of the Aerostar a few times when Gia was with us, but you were a lot younger and you weren't looking out the window—you were usually asleep. Did you ever get airsick flying cadet-orientation rides?"

"I don't think I ever flew in the back," Brad said. "There was never anyone else riding along."

"So today was the first time that you've ever ridden in the back of a light plane with your eyes open and searching out the window," Patrick summarized, "and every time you've done it, you've gotten sick."

"But what does that mean, Dad?" Brad asked. "If I can't ride in the back without getting sick, I can't be a mission scanner, and if I can't be a scanner, I can't be a mission pilot. And that's what I want to be!"

"Let's not get too far ahead of ourselves, big guy," Patrick said. "We'll get you a few rides with you not doing scanner duties but just sitting in back, not looking out the side windows, to get you accustomed to sitting in back; we'll find out about approved medicines or other remedies. You can still be a transport mission pilot—ferrying planes, taking cadets on orientation rides, towing gliders—and a mission observer, and there may even be a way for you to be a mission pilot without being a scanner first. I think the reason they have you qualify for scanner first is to see how well you do in a light plane. But we know you *can* fly a plane without getting airsick—it's just that you get airsick riding in back. We'll start checking out all the options. But just remember, there's more to Civil Air Patrol than flying. You can lead a ground-search team, and you can man an incident command post and put together sortie packages—"

"But I want to *fly*, Dad. I want to be a pilot, in charge of a crew."

"And you can fly . . . just maybe not with the Civil Air Patrol as a mission pilot," Patrick said. "We'll have to see what happens. But don't act like it's the end of the world if you can't be a mission pilot. There are plenty of ways to serve. You'll find that life throws you a lot of obstacles—you have to figure out how to overcome them. That's the fun of being a grown-up."

"Well, so far being a grown-up really sucks," Brad said, and he turned and walked away.

"Amen to that." Patrick turned and saw Jon Masters standing beside him, looking at the damage to the Cessna. "So you think someone took shots at you, huh? He's got to be a pretty darn good shot—you were five hundred feet up, going about eighty knots?" He went over and looked at the hole in the wing. "Pretty good-size hole—maybe a hunting rifle?"

"Or an infantry rifle," Patrick said.

"A military shooter? A marksman with serious military hardware? You mean, someone from the base?" Patrick had no answer. Jon was silent for a short while, then asked, "So what's Brad sulking about?"

"He got airsick when riding in the back of the Cessna as a scanner," Patrick said. "He's okay up front, but not in back."

"I get airsick sitting in the back too, sometimes, but I take a dimenhydrinate and I'm okay," Jon said. "I don't think that's an option if you're a crewmember, though."

"Back in my B-52 days, I had gunners and EWOs who flew facing backward and got airsick all the time, especially when flying low-level," Patrick said. "They were using stuff like scopolamine patches behind their ears for airsickness, but I don't know if that's the case anymore. They have wristbands and neckbands for seasickness, but I don't know if those are gimmicks or not. Gingerroot pills worked good for me if I took them before a space flight. We'll find out. But I don't like to see Brad start to mope around after each and every downturn. He's got to learn to roll with it." He looked at Jon. "So what are you up to?"

"Moping around after my latest downturn—losing twenty million dollars' worth of aircraft in one night," Jon said. "The Sky Masters, Inc., board members hit the freakin' roof."

"Why? The government should make it right. It might take a while, but . . ." He looked at Jon, his eyes narrowing. "Okay, what did you do?"

"We . . . hadn't exactly worked out the details of the contract before the Sparrowhawks were deployed," Jon admitted.

"Uh-oh . . ." Patrick said. "You didn't get a signed contract before you deployed? You *donated* the Sparrowhawks to the government?"

"I have a *draft* of a contract," Jon argued, "so we can argue that it wasn't *meant* to be a donation." Patrick smiled but shook his head ruefully. "The FBI said they were in a hurry, and I wanted to get the aircraft out there before they put the job out for bids. It'll work out, don't worry."

"Sure . . . five years from now," Patrick said. "Well, I guess that's why a lot of the contractors we hire are attorneys."

"Exactly," Jon said. "Our job is to get things done, not worry about stupid contracts. Let the suits work out the details."

"Right," Patrick said. "Besides, you got insurance on the Sparrowhawks, right?" He saw Jon's downcast expression, and his eyes widened in surprise. "Jon, *no insurance* . . . ?"

"I have R-and-D insurance out the ying-yang," Jon said, "but . . . well, I didn't have a government contract—yet—and you wouldn't believe what those insurance companies wanted for these simple little missions. You'd think we were flying armed combat missions over Iraq again!"

"Jon, you can't do stuff like that," Patrick said. "At best you could get fired—at worst, you could get fired, sued, *and* have to pay for the Sparrowhawks yourself!"

"Hey, look who's talking about bending the rules! You practically made an entire career out of it!"

"I did it when I had the discretion as the on-scene tactical commander," Patrick said. Jon looked at him with a skeptical "oh, really?" expression. "And when I did it otherwise, I was either kicked out, forced to retire, or was sued. You work for a private company. The directors and officers make the decisions, not you."

"Well, I'd be worried—if I already wasn't the smartest guy in the company," Jon said dismissively. "They can't fire me or sue me—it'd tank the stock and we'd be lucky to get a contract to provide propeller beanies to Cub Scouts. Don't worry about it." He paused, looking in the direction of where Brad walked off. "I feel sorry for the kid," he said. "What's a scanner do?"

"His job is to search for mission targets or for hazards," Patrick said. "Apparently Brad has trouble when he looks sideways out the window in a turn, or has to look downward or backward—we don't quite know yet what triggers the motion sickness."

"He looks out the window? That's *it*?"

"He'll also take pictures, make records of what happens on a mission, run checklists, maybe talk to mission base or ground teams on the radio, but basically his job is to search outside the plane, from engine start to engine shutdown."

"We have stuff that can more than take the place of a scanner," Jon said. "We've developed sensor balls that can fit easily on the wings of a little bug smasher like your Cessnas. They're a quarter of the size of a Predator's sensor dome but do even more stuff and perform better. Plus, the scanner can operate the sensors from the ground. You save weight, the plane performs better, and you put fewer crewmembers at risk. Plus, once we install the video datalink, you can up- and download voice, data, telemetry—almost anything."

"You know," Patrick said after adopting that "ten-thousand-yard stare" expression for a moment, "the Civil Air Patrol flies missions called Predator Surrogate. They mount a Predator sensor ball on the Cessnas, and they fly around the Nellis Air Force Base ranges. The Army and Marine Corps use them to train sensor operators. It solves the problem of 'see-and-avoid' and loss of control that unmanned planes have—you have two guys in the plane that can look for traffic, and they can take the controls if the aircraft loses contact with remote operators."

Jon was starting to adopt the same faraway expression as Patrick. "But our sensor domes are much better for the job than the Predator's," he said. "All we have to do is stick one on the Cessna . . . maybe one on each wing for better coverage and to even out the drag. Even with two, you'd have lower weight and better performance—"

"Jon, this is the Civil Air Patrol, not the U.S. Air Force or Space Defense Force," Patrick said. "The whole idea of CAP was to have civilian volunteers helping their country by using their planes and skills. It defeats the purpose of the organization to start outfitting the planes like military aircraft. They're—" But Patrick stopped . . . because the idea was starting to make total sense to him. "But . . . it would take years to get approval to put those sensors on the CAP Cessnas."

"Maybe so," Jon said. "So . . . let's stick them on *your* Cessna. The CAP plane here with the bullet holes in it is out of commission, right? Let's use yours, and anyone else's plane who wants some toys to play with."

"What?" But after a few moments, the idea made him smile. "You know, CAP once *only* used a member's plane—they switched to using CAP-owned planes about twenty years ago." But then he shook his head as reality set in. "It would take months, maybe years, to get a field approval from the FAA for that kind of major modification. We'd have to do engineering drawings, do controllability and flutter tests, get authorization for—"

"Blah blah blah blah blah," Jon Masters said, shaking his head. "Sheesh, maybe living way the hell out here *has* softened you up. So you decertify your plane and turn it into an 'Experimental.' You're worried about the FAA? Have you ever *seen* the FAA out here at Battle Mountain? Do they even *have* field inspectors anymore? What are the odds of getting ramp-checked these days? Besides, if they do catch you, so what? They'll make you take the sensors off, so we'll take them off. There are lots of options, Patrick. It seems to me you're coming up with more excuses *not* to do it than ideas on *how* to do it."

Patrick realized that was *exactly* what he was doing, and he nodded his head. "You're right," he said. But he looked at Jon seriously and added, "But we're just going to grab a couple sensor balls from the company, *again,* like the Sparrowhawks? We can't do that."

"You're right, we shouldn't," Jon said. He held out his hand. "Got a credit card? We'll make it a straight-out purchase. The company will be happy."

"But I don't have enough money to—"

"There you go again with the negative waves, Patrick," Jon said with a laugh. "Always with the reasons *not* to do it. C'mon, it'll be fine. I just need the account number—I won't run anything against it. If it works, we'll work something out moneywise. I'll order up the parts and bring a mechanic up from Vegas, and we'll have you flying in no time."

Brad changed out of his flight suit and into civilian clothes, then sat by himself outdoors at a picnic table beside the hangar. My first flight as mission scanner—on an actual mission, no less—and I can't handle being a backseater, he lamented to himself. This really sucks.

He had reserved the entire day for flying, and now he had nothing to do. He pulled out his cell phone and was going to start calling his buddies to find out what they were up to when he found Cassandra Renaldo's business card.

Should I do it? he asked himself. She *was* an older woman, but she was still hot as hell. Was she just stringing him along, being a cockteaser or trying to make a fool out of him, or was she serious about wanting to see him again? He wished he knew more about women, like Ron Spivey did—he always seemed to have a different girl every week, and even when he treated them like crap, they always seemed to come back. How did guys learn how to do that?

I guess this is one way, Brad thought as he commenced dialing her number . . .

"Renaldo."

"It's me. Brad."

Cassandra looked up at Special Agent Chastain and nodded. "Let me finish up here and go somewhere where I can talk. Hang on." She put the call on hold.

"Who is that?" Chastain asked.

"Bradley McLanahan," she said, smiling evilly. "I told you he'd call."

Chastain smiled back. "Reel him in," he said.

She took the call off hold a few moments later. "I'm so glad you called, Brad," she said in her sweetest, most heartfelt voice. Chastain shook his head and smiled at her performance. "I've missed seeing you. How are you?"

"I've been better."

"What's wrong, baby?"

"It's an . . . an airsickness thing. I'm okay when I'm piloting, but not so good when I'm in back."

"Oh no," Renaldo said. "Are you all right now?"

"Oh yes, I'm good."

"Then when can I see you?"

There was a bit of a pause; then: "Well, I was supposed to be flying all day, but that's been canceled . . ."

"I heard—someone shot at a Civil Air Patrol plane," she said. "You mean, *you* were *on* that plane?"

"Yes."

"My God, Brad! How awful!"

"So I'm . . . I'm not doing anything for the rest of the day."

"That's perfect," Renaldo said, giving Chastain a wink. "You're at the Civil Air Patrol hangar now?"

"Yes."

"Perfect. If you walk down Powell Avenue toward the base exchange, I'll pick you up in about ten minutes. We can go to my place. How does that sound?"

"Okay."

"Great. I'll see you soon, baby." She hung up. "He's on the line—now it's time to start landing him," she said to Chastain. She thought for a moment, then asked, "How bad do you want the dad?"

"Badly." Chastain picked up the latest report from Brady's reconnaissance of the suspected terrorist compound. "So far we've discovered that there are nineteen residents of the Knights' compound who are active members of the Civil Air Patrol Battle Mountain squadron. All but two are ex-military. Eight are Iraq and Afghanistan vets, including multiple deployments; four are Desert Storm vets; and two are Vietnam vets. All have combat experience. We're trying to obtain medical backgrounds on them, but I wouldn't be surprised to find some PTSD cases in there, or worse. McLanahan could have his own little strike force in that CAP outfit."

"Then I've got an angle on the son that could really lock him in good," Renaldo said. "I'm going to meet up with him. I'm going to borrow a little something from our drop stash, okay?"

Chastain looked at her seriously. "I definitely see why they call you the 'Black Widow,' Renaldo."

"Nothing evil, I assure you," she said. "I'm not going to hurt him—well, maybe just a little. But if you want him, and the dad, I'll get them for you."

Chastain thought about it for a moment, then nodded. "Have fun," was all he said.

"Oh, I intend to," Renaldo said with a growing crocodile smile. "I intend to."

TEMPORARY HOUSING AREA, JOINT AIR
BASE BATTLE MOUNTAIN

THAT SAME TIME

This was turning out to be a pretty sucky day, Patrick told himself as he headed to his trailer to change out of his flight suit—and it wasn't even half over yet. Like Jon, he felt sorry for Brad. But he was acting more like a ten-year-old than an eighteen-year-old. He would have to make some phone calls to the aerospace physiology folks in the Air Force—the ones who installed an electronic heart monitor in him when he started suffering from heart arrhythmias during space flight—and find out the best way to treat Brad. But whatever the outcome, he wanted to cure the boy of whining and feeling sorry for himself whenever . . .

. . . and it was then, just before he was going to pull into his hard-baked mud driveway beside the trailer, that he noticed the front door to his trailer partly open.

That was not unusual—these were not the best-constructed trailers in the world, not by a long shot—and he or Brad could have failed to close and lock it properly. But alarm bells were going off in his head, and he had learned many years ago that ignoring those bells was extremely unwise.

Patrick activated his intraocular computer monitor and called up the security-camera images from inside his trailer. The security system's readouts showed that the door had been opened by key just a few minutes ago. He could see a person wearing a cowboy hat, blue jeans, a white untucked shirt, and a long black-and-gray ponytail with his back to the camera, going through mail and articles on the dining-room table. The other cameras revealed no other intruders. Patrick then retrieved an object from under his Wrangler's seat that resembled a flashlight, but was actually a launcher that would fire a wireless projectile that would act like a Taser, embedding probes into a person's skin and incapacitating the person with a high-voltage but nonlethal shock.

He stepped quickly to the porch, skipped the steps, pushed open the door, and aimed the launcher at the intruder. *"Stop right there!"* he shouted.

The intruder jumped, a little cloud of mail flying from his hands, and whirled around to face him. "Patrick! You startled me!"

"Oh my God . . . *Gia!*" Patrick cried. He put down the launcher and rushed into her arms. Gia Cazzotto buried her face into his shoulder, sobbing. "You're back, you're finally back!"

"Oh, Patrick, I'm so sorry I left like I did," Gia said after several long moments, "and for not keeping in touch, but . . . well, I wanted to get well before I came back to you." She looked up at him, her brown eyes searching his for any signs of hostility or distrust. Her dark hair was much longer and streaked with a lot more gray than he remembered, and she looked thinner. He didn't smell any alcohol on her breath—that was a major change right there. "Do you . . . want me to go, or—"

"Of course not, Gia!" Patrick said, hugging her tightly again. "I've been waiting for you to come home! I knew you had a key, so I never changed the lock. Sit down, sit down, for God's sake!" He led her to the couch, sat on the ottoman before her, and took her hands in his. "Are you all right? Where have you been?"

"Southern California," Gia said. "I went back to Palmdale to see if I could get work. But with the economy still in the tank, no one was hiring." She lowered her eyes, then added, "Even for jobs that didn't require a security clearance."

"I told you before: just wait another four years, and you can apply for a full pardon," Patrick said. "The president has told me often he'll do that, as long as you don't have any other convictions." He looked at her carefully. "Everything okay in that regard, Gia?"

"Yes," she said softly. "No other convictions." But her voice told him that this wasn't all. After a few moments, she looked up and said, "I met someone."

Patrick felt his heart explode in his chest, and he had to choke down a surge of anger. "'Met someone'?"

"In rehab," Gia said. "He's an alcoholic, like me. He's a building contractor. He's been sober for a few years, and he was helping me, making sure I went to the meetings, making sure I was applying for work and benefits, giving me some part-time work here and there."

There was still something in her voice that said there was much, much more to tell, Patrick thought. "What else?" he demanded, a lot harsher than he intended.

"That's all," she insisted. He didn't believe her, and she could see that in his eyes, and she didn't try to defend herself. "I told him about you, and he said I had to choose, because he knew I still wasn't over you, and he said I had to go back and see you, and—"

"What? Choose between us?" Patrick snapped. "Compare notes?"

"Find out if you still loved me, Patrick," Gia said. "I know I haven't been here for you, trying to deal with my own problems. I wanted to be with you, but I had to leave so I could figure out if I wanted to be sober or not."

"You had to decide whether or not to be sober?"

"You don't understand being an alcoholic, Patrick," Gia said. "I like drinking. I like being able to suppress the rage and the despair as easily as drinking a little Cabernet Sauvignon. I didn't care if I couldn't fully function, as long as I didn't have to feel the anger, the frustration, the helplessness." She paused, then said, "But now I understand who I am, Patrick. I'm an alcoholic. I know now that I was wasting my life dealing with my anger with alcohol, and I want to change that . . . no, I'm *going* to change that."

Patrick let go of her hands and stood. "And . . . *he* helped you realize that," he said.

"The rehab program got me to stop drinking and start dealing with my anger in a positive way," Gia said. "But he was there at the meetings, and he knew I was out of work, and he said he could help, and he did. Now he wants to . . . to take it to the next level, but he said I had to decide about you. But I didn't know how you felt about me."

"How could you ever doubt that I love you, Gia?" Patrick asked, almost pleading. "Brad and I welcomed you back every time you left, without hesitation, without a word. I helped you find treatment programs here. You'd be good for a few weeks, and then you'd be gone again. But when you came back, we always welcomed you."

"I know, I know," she said. "I'm sorry. But you and Brad were . . . were always gone, and I was here alone in this trailer. I tried to make it a home for all of us, but then I didn't know how to suppress the anger any way else but with alcohol, and then I didn't want to be around you and especially Bradley when I was drunk, so I'd leave. And then I'd miss you so badly, and I'd get the courage to come back, and then the whole thing would start all over again."

Patrick sat back down on the ottoman and took her hands again. "It can be different now," he said. "I'm retired, Gia. Maybe I needed to grow up and finally realize that. I pretended I had a job and a function here, but now I know I don't. So I can be with you and help you in any way I can, any way you need."

Gia looked up, touched the collar of his Air Force–style sage-green Civil Air Patrol flight suit, and choked down a sob with a smile. "I find that a little hard to believe," she said with a wry smile. "Somehow I can't see you settling down. If it's not Civil Air Patrol, Angel Flight West charity flying, flight instructing, or meeting up with your space-faring buddies, it would be something else."

"Well, Gia, I guess I'll always do a little bit of that stuff," Patrick said honestly, "but with you and me together, it can be different. We'll move off base, rent until we save up some money, then when

Brad graduates high school and goes off to college, we can pick a place together and move."

"Move off base?" Gia asked. "What about . . . you know, the Russians . . . ?"

"It's been almost a year since we found out about that, and nothing has surfaced," Patrick said. "I think the CIA shut that threat down completely. They've got bigger fish to fry, and I've been under their radar for too long."

"I saw you on TV, on the news, as part of the team that rescued that little boy in the desert," Gia said. "I think you're on the radar again."

"I'm not worried about that," Patrick said. "You're much more important to me than some supposed threat that young Agent Dobson came up with."

CIA agent Timothy Dobson, an adviser to Kenneth Phoenix when he was vice president, had warned Patrick of the threat of Russian assassination squads sent out after him in retaliation for last year's attacks in the Gulf of Aden and Yemen, and had suggested that Patrick move to Battle Mountain to make it easier for the CIA and FBI to detect their approach.

Gia looked into his eyes, saw that he was sincere, and smiled. "Thank you, Patrick," she said. "Let's take a little time to get to know each other again, and find out what Bradley thinks of all this. And my first order of business is to find a meeting place here on base or in town."

"I can find that out for you in the blink of an eye . . . literally," Patrick said. He activated his intraocular monitors, virtual keyboard, and computer network . . .

. . . but Gia put a hand on his arm. "Let's start exploring a new life together . . . by doing away with the high-tech gadgets a little more," she said with a smile. "Frankly, that thing you do creeps me out."

Joint Air Base Battle Mountain

Several Days Later

It was becoming an almost daily occurrence now: mornings around eight A.M., the protesters would return to the main gate. Their numbers were growing, but they were becoming more civilized as well. The Nevada Highway Patrol cars were reduced to just two, with no armored vehicles and no riot gear. The Air Force Avenger units were no longer in sight inside the base either, although they were not far away.

The protests were organized, almost routine, and relatively nonthreatening. The marchers—about a hundred of them today, the biggest number yet—would pile up to the front gate, chanting and singing as they approached, waving signs and banners, surrounded by photographers and crews from news outlets all over the world. A Highway Patrol trooper would order them to get off the highway. Someone with a bullhorn would read off a list of demands, usually right into the trooper's face. The Highway Patrol trooper would repeat the order. The protesters continued to sing and chant, amplified with bullhorns, and a half dozen or so would sit down in front of the gate. The trooper would put one of them in handcuffs, surrounded by the crowd, yelling and screaming while the one person was taken away. Then the one patrol car's lights and sirens activated, and the crowd would slowly move off to either side of the highway. They would stay for another hour or so, then start to leave. The one arrested protester would be allowed to leave as soon as the cameras were out of sight. By nine-thirty, ten o'clock tops, it was over.

It was Leo Slotnick's turn at the front gate. The air was already fairly hot and humid for this time of day, but he still wore his long-sleeved blouse with body armor underneath, and he was already damp with sweat. He had been sure to install a pair of foam earplugs to help preserve his hearing from the noisy crowd with their bullhorns, and he was wearing a pair of black Kevlar knife-proof gloves with steel knuckles. His trainee, Bobby Johnson, was back beside the patrol car, ready to take today's designated volunteer arrestee into custody.

When the protesters approached, Leo let them chant and sing for about fifteen minutes—he thought a few of them were actually looking at their watches, wondering why he was taking so long to confront them. At the next pause between songs, he filled his lungs and shouted, "Ladies and gentlemen, your attention, please. I am Sergeant Slotnick of the Nevada Highway Patrol. I am here to inform you that you are illegally blocking a state thoroughfare and interfering with normal traffic, in violation of Nevada Revised Statute four-eighty-four B point nine-twenty dash one. You are hereby ordered to clear the highway and allow traffic to proceed. Failure to obey a traffic officer is also a violation of Nevada Revised Statutes four-eighty-four B point one hundred, and could result in arrest and detainment. Please clear the highway immediately. Thank you."

Now it was time for the shouting and demands. Leo folded his hands in front of his body—these folks were mostly harmless, but he still had to be ready to protect himself—and he steeled himself to accept the amplified yelling and screaming that was about to occur. Sure enough, the bozo with the bullhorn began shouting just a couple feet away from his ear, and even with the earplugs firmly installed, the bastard was giving him a splitting . . .

. . . and then he saw them: the same two tall guys he had seen at the first demonstration, but this time they were right up front, at the head of the crowd.

He tilted his head so he could talk into his shoulder-mounted microphone: "Bobby, this is Leo. C'mon out here and cover me, will you?"

"Roger," came the immediate reply.

Leo looked directly at the taller of the two men. They returned his gaze, not attempting to retreat or hide at all. Over the blaring bullhorn beside him, he waved two fingers at the man. "You, sir, would you come with me, please?" The man did not move. "I said, *you,* sir, come with me." The crowd, sensing something unknown was unfolding, seemed to back away from the direct line between the two men. "Anyone here know this man?" Leo shouted.

"He has a right to be here!" the guy with the bullhorn shouted. "What's your beef, man?"

"I want to talk with you, sir," Leo said to the stranger. "I want you to come with me."

"What the hell's going on, Leo?" the guy with the bullhorn asked. Leo recognized him as the night-shift clerk at the 7-Eleven in town. "Why are you dissin' this guy?"

"Do you know who he is, Tommy?" Leo asked him. "Have you met him before? Is he from around here?"

The guy with the bullhorn looked at the stranger with a blank expression, but turned to Leo and said, "Hey, Leo, I don't get it. I don't know this dude, but he ain't doin' nuthin'. We don't want no trouble, bro. He's not the one we're going to get arrested today with you, so don't—"

"I want you to come with me, sir, *right now,*" Leo shouted, and he put a hand on his sidearm . . .

. . . and no one was exactly sure what happened first after that:

There was the sound of gunshots, four in rapid succession. Screams, cries of surprise and fear, and an immediate retreat of the dozens of persons crowded around Leo and the stranger at the main gate, as if pushed aside by a mighty gust of wind. Then several loud explosions erupted behind the crowd, followed by an immense billowing mushroom cloud of green skin-burning gas. The crowd of protesters surged forward away from the noxious green chlorine-smelling gas directly at the base's main gate. Almost the entire crowd of over a hundred protesters rushed onto the base, trampling anyone who was overcome by the gas or not quick enough to surge forward or get out of the way fast enough.

NORTHERN NEVADA VETERANS MEMORIAL
CEMETERY, FERNLEY, NEVADA

THREE DAYS LATER

Following the hearse and the limousine carrying the family members of Nevada Highway Patrol sergeant Leo Slotnick were three
dark blue armored Suburbans and several other limousines. Behind the limousines was a truly awe-inspiring sight: a long line
of police cars from all over the United States, stretching for miles
along Interstate 80, with lights flashing, slowly making their way
to the cemetery. The police cars were followed by hundreds of
other cars, some with Civil Air Patrol flags affixed to their roofs.
The Nevada Highway Patrol troopers who were blocking cross-
roads and directing the impossibly long procession of cars saluted
the hearse as it drove past. At Exit 48 on the freeway, the lead
group continued on to the Northern Nevada Veterans Memorial
Cemetery, while the hundreds of police cruisers and Civil Air Patrol members that were part of the procession lined up and stopped
in the number two lane. The passengers got out of the cars, and
they held salutes or hands over their hearts until the hearse was out
of sight.

The flag-draped casket was brought to the center of the visitors'
center, escorted by an honor guard composed of Air Force, Highway Patrol, and Civil Air Patrol officers and cadets. Since the facility was so small, only a small fraction of the thousands of attendees
could be seated inside, but hundreds of others stood outside to
listen to the service on loudspeakers. The family members—Leo's
wife, three young children, his parents, and his wife's parents—
were escorted to their seats, followed by the invited VIP guests: the
vice president of the United States, the secretary of the Air Force,
the governor of Nevada, the commandant of the Nevada Highway

Patrol, and the national commander of the Civil Air Patrol, among
many other dignitaries.

After the service was over, the vice president's motorcade departed first, heading west on Interstate 80 toward Reno with two
armored Suburbans as escorts, where her C-32 transport, a VIP-
modified Boeing 757-200, was waiting at Reno-Tahoe International Airport. "Patrick, it's good to see you again," Vice President
Ann Page said. "You need to come to Washington more often—it
seems I only get to see you at funerals."

"Thank you, Madam Vice President," Patrick McLanahan
said. "It's good to see you too."

"And I never would have recognized young Bradley here,"
the vice president said to Brad, seated beside his father, "although
you're certainly not so young anymore. Congratulations on the
Civil Air Patrol save."

"Thank you, ma'am."

"You know who Mr. Dobson is, don't you, Brad?" the vice
president asked, motioning to the man seated beside her.

"I think so," Brad said, but it was obvious he didn't remember—
and that was the way Patrick had wanted it, at the time, when
Dobson delivered the message that Russian hit men had been sent
to target his father for assassination in retaliation for the attacks on
Russian installations in the Middle East and East Africa. They left
Henderson, Nevada, soon after President Kenneth Phoenix's inau-
guration, went to Washington to support Gia Cazzotto in her trial
and to await Patrick's trial, then moved to Battle Mountain after
Gia's sentence was commuted and Patrick was pardoned.

"Mr. Dobson has some information for your father," Ann said,
"but I thought it was okay if you hear it too, because it concerns both
of you, and I think you're old enough to know everything. Tim?"

"Thank you, ma'am," Timothy Dobson said. Dobson, a fifteen-
year veteran of the Central Intelligence Agency, had served with
then–vice president Ken Phoenix on a panel to rewrite the national

space policy. But when China and Russia began a cooperative plan to attack American space-defense satellites, Phoenix assigned Dobson to work with Patrick on a covert strike plan to destroy the Chinese antisatellite-missile sites and Russian intelligence radar sites that were damaging the American antisatellite-weapon garages. In the aftermath of Patrick's attacks, Dobson had discovered that Russia was sending assassination squads into the United States, targeting Patrick for reprisals.

"We've analyzed photos and videos taken at the demonstrations in front of Battle Mountain air base," Dobson said, "and my team has identified two and possibly four foreign agents that have been moving closer and closer to the air base at Battle Mountain."

"They're getting bolder by the day," the vice president said. "They're moving right to your doorstep. You're not safe."

"We think Sergeant Slotnick detected the agents about two weeks ago at one of the demonstrations," Dobson went on, "and actually confronted one the day he was killed. Most likely it was one of the agents that killed Slotnick, and the backups in the crowd set off the tear-gas bombs that caused the protesters to panic and rush the base."

"The base is still a safe place for you," the vice president said. "The security there is the best in the nation. But it's closing soon, and you'll lose that protection. And I'm concerned about young Brad here. You go to high school off base, and I know you have off-base jobs and activities, and that's where they could get to you. It won't be much of a life stuck on the base." She turned to Patrick. "That's why I want to suggest you come to Washington, Patrick."

"Ma'am . . ."

Page held up a hand. "I understand all about Colonel Cazzotto, how angry she was at President Phoenix for not pardoning her. But have you seen her lately?"

"Yes, I have, ma'am," Patrick said. "In fact, she's at my trailer right now."

Ann turned a horrified expression to Tim, who had a look of concern on his face that made Patrick's fingertips tingle. "The FBI has had her under observation ever since she started applying for work at defense contractors in Southern California, General," Dobson said. "With her felony conviction she can't get a security clearance, and with the bad economy few firms are hiring anyway."

"That's what she told me," Patrick said.

"High-profile individual, highly skilled and intelligent, formerly had a top-secret security clearance but out of work with a federal felony conviction, angry at the government, an alcohol problem, possibly emotional problems—the textbook example of a disgruntled worker," Ann said. "And a woman to boot. A perfect target for recruitment by a foreign or enemy power."

"*What?*" Patrick exclaimed.

"She met a guy in one of her twelve-step meetings that was helping her out, befriending her, hiring her part-time, maybe . . . maybe something more intimate," Dobson said hesitantly.

"She said all that too," Patrick said perturbedly. Dobson paused. "Spit it out, Tim," he said.

"We're having . . . trouble, difficulties, identifying the guy, sir," Dobson said uncomfortably. "His neighbors and acquaintances have the same story about him: he's a building contractor, he's been in the area for years, he's dependable, he's a good guy. His license is real. But when we dig one or two levels lower, we start to lose continuity. His Social Security number and his previous addresses on his contractor's license application don't correlate."

"So what are you saying, Tim?" Patrick asked.

"Agent more-than-polite Dobson here is trying to say that your girlfriend's new boyfriend doesn't check out, and he thinks he's a sleeper agent working for the Russian Federal Security Bureau, targeting Cazzotto to get close to you to set you up for a hit," Vice President Page interjected impatiently. "C'mon, Patrick, wake up and smell the damned coffee. Someone got to your alkie girlfriend for the express purpose of getting close to *you*. Get with the program, will you? You're a former Air Force intelligence chief, for Christ's sake." She saw Patrick's eyes flare in indignation, which only egged her on: "Don't give me that 'I'm shocked! Shocked!' expression, McLanahan," Ann retorted before he could speak. She stuck a finger directly into Patrick's face. "Don't try to tell me you didn't have some suspicions when this woman suddenly turns up on your doorstep after being gone for seven weeks."

"I thought she was just returning home," Patrick said. "This is her home, ever since she left the service . . ."

"Yeah, right—and you thought she was going to come back to the armpit of the world and sit on the porch of your little double-wide trailer in one-hundred-degree desert heat and wait for you to come back from your heroic Civil Air Patrol and Angel Flight West flying missions and snuggle close to her," Ann retorted. "Can you possibly be that blind or galactically stupid, Patrick? In her mind, Phoenix screwed *her,* but saved *you*. That means *you* screwed *her* in her twisted crazy fevered head. With that mind-set, she'll shack up with anyone who wants to get close to you, for whatever reason imaginable. Wake up, damn it. This is serious. Are you paying attention to me, General?"

Patrick didn't answer, which to Vice President Page meant that he was certainly paying attention. "I invited you to ride with me because, in essence, this is a kidnapping—for both of you gentlemen," she said. "Battle Mountain is getting too dangerous for you and Brad. I think you'll both be safer in Washington. The entire District of Columbia is all about counterintelligence and counter-counterintelligence. I think you'd be safer there, no matter how many hoods the Russian Federal Security Bureau sends over. Besides, the president wants to start ramping up the Space Defense Force program again, and he wants you to head that program, be the out-front guy, the face of the entire push for military space. You can't do that from a base that's going to be a ghost town in a few months."

"I don't like the idea of running from these hit-man goons, Madam Vice President," Patrick said. He sat back, thought for a few moments, then looked at Brad. "But the most important thing is your safety, son."

"But what about my friends, my team, the squadron?" Brad asked. "We can't just disappear. And if I'd be in danger, wouldn't all my friends be in danger too?"

Dobson looked at the vice president. "He's right, ma'am," he said. "Any one of Brad's friends—maybe even their entire families—could be targets."

"One problem at a time here, guys," Ann said irritably. "I don't mean to scare you, Brad, but it would be an immense blow to the entire nation to lose your father to an assassin's bullet. I know you'd be missing out on your senior year in high school with your friends, but Mr. Dobson and I feel it would be too dangerous for you to go back. You can enroll in high school in Washington. I know you're accustomed to military moves, so this shouldn't be too much of a shock to your system, right?" She didn't wait for a reply; to Patrick, she said, "In Washington, you'd be working in the White House again as my special adviser for space affairs—unfortunately not a salaried position, but all of your housing would be provided as well as stipends for living expenses." She looked at him carefully. "I don't expect you to go back to Battle Mountain, guys. I'll send some folks to get your things, but you and Brad are coming with me to Washington, *today*."

Patrick thought for a moment, then shook his head. "I appreciate the concern, Madam Vice President," Patrick said, "but Brad is right: if they couldn't get to me through Brad, they'd try it with someone else. And if we moved to Washington, they'd just start the whole hunt over again, and the FBI and CIA would have to start looking all over again. The whole reason to send me to Battle Mountain in the first place was not just to hide out, but to draw the assassins in to a place where it would be easier to detect their presence. And with all due respect, ma'am, I'm not running out on my friends to save my own neck—especially Gia. She's in the greatest danger of all next to Brad, and she's the most vulnerable."

"You're insane, General," Ann said. "You actually think you're safer in Battle Mountain than in Washington?" She shook her head, then looked at him directly. "I could order you to leave, in the interest of national security."

"You wouldn't do that, Ann," Patrick said. "Besides, you know I'm right." She didn't answer him. He smiled at her, which only made her scowl darken. "But I appreciate the try."

"You're wrong—I *would* do that, Patrick, and you know it," Ann said. She leaned forward toward him. "Let me ask you a direct question, Patrick: this woman, the one that left you many times, the one who shacked up with some guy, the one who is probably leading another hit squad up here to target you—you still care about her?"

"I not only care for her, Ann—I love her," Patrick replied. "When she first told me about the other guy, I was furious. But she still came back to me. I wasn't sure if she would stay, but I decided that if she left I'd carry on, and maybe she'd be happier. But now that you've told me this guy might be a sleeper, I know he doesn't really care about her. That just makes me want to help her even more. And if she leaves again anyway . . . well, Brad and I will deal with that later."

Ann Page nodded. "You're a good guy, Patrick," she said. "You are. Sometimes you're dumber than a bag of doorknobs and sappier than a maple tree in the fall, but you're a good guy."

"Thank you, Madam Vice President."

"Bite me, McLanahan," she said with a faint smile. "And you're still coming to Washington—the president has already ordered it. You're working for me, in the White House, to spearhead the charge to get the Space Defense Force fully funded, set up, and running. President Phoenix agreed to wait until next summer, after Brad was on his way to college."

"That sounds fine, Madam Vice President," Patrick said. "I think I'd enjoy working for you."

"You're damned right, you will," Ann said. "You're damned right."

EIGHT

Be good and you will be lonesome.

—SAMUEL CLEMENS

JOINT AIR BASE BATTLE MOUNTAIN

THE NEXT EVENING

"I'm sorry to have to tell you, folks," Squadron Commander Rob Spara said at the Civil Air Patrol seniors' squadron meeting, "but the CAP national headquarters is suspending our squadron's activities until further notice."

There was a rumble of disbelief and surprise around the conference room. "Why in the *hell* are they doin' that, Rob?" Michael Fitzgerald boomed.

"They feel it's too dangerous to come on the base anymore," Rob said. "The protesters, the shootings—frankly, I can't argue with them. The planes have already been scheduled to depart: as soon as the 182 is flyable, it'll go to Winnemucca; the ARCHER is already in Minden; and the 206 will go to Elko. The comm trailer will probably go to Winnemucca too."

"Well, that blows," Fitzgerald grumbled. "What about the cadets? Are we just going to shut down emergency services and all the cadet programs just like *that*?"

"All emergency services are suspended," Rob said, "but cadet aerospace, military, and PT programs can continue away from the base, as long as the cadets don't wear utility or Air Force–style uniforms and aren't seen doing drill-team or marching exercises outdoors. PT and Class-B clothing are okay."

"Don't wear uniforms?"

"National HQ is afraid that extremists that see the cadets in uniform off base will think the military is moving into their communities," Rob said, "and if any of the extremist violence is directed at CAP, they may try to harm the cadets too. I want you and David to get those organized, maybe at the church or at your place, Fid."

"Nothing but spineless wussies," Fitzgerald grumbled again. "You know, this is our town and our base too—it doesn't belong just to the nut jobs. Why don't the cops do something to protect *us*?"

"When was the last time you saw a sheriff's deputy on the street, Fid?" David Bellville asked. "It seems they're all on vacation or something. Ever since Leo was killed, it's as if all the cops are staying out of sight."

"Screw 'em anyway," Fitzgerald said. He patted his right hip. "I'm takin' care of business myself right here."

"Not around the cadets you're not, Fid," Rob said.

"I won't—as far as you know," Fitzgerald said, and it was obvious he wasn't going to debate the issue. There wasn't anything else to talk about, so the meeting soon broke up.

As the seniors were departing, Patrick caught up with John de Carteret. "Hey, John," he said. "Got a few minutes?"

"After that last bit of news we got? Sure, I have *lots* of time now," John said. He followed Patrick to his office, where he found Jon Masters and Gia Cazzotto seated at Patrick's desk in front of two laptop computers.

"John, I don't believe you know these folks," Patrick said. "My good friends Gia and Jon. This is my favorite mission observer, John de Carteret." They shook hands. "I worked with both of them in the Air Force. Gia is a former—"

"I remember you," John said. "The one prosecuted by President Gardner for war cri—" He stopped when he saw Gia's shoulders slump and she averted her eyes. "Sorry to upset you, miss. Jon, good to meet you."

"Take a look at this, John," Patrick said, motioning to the laptop. John studied the display. It showed an overhead view of the Knights of the True Republic's compound, with all sorts of symbology inside the compound itself, and a side window with a legend explaining what the symbology stood for. The detail was astounding: it was easy to pick out individuals walking around the compound, and even easy to make out what they were carrying.

"Is that the extremists' compound—the Knights of the True Republic, or whatever they call themselves?"

"It is."

"Is it recorded?"

"No, it's live," Patrick said.

"Where are you getting this from?"

"This is being downlinked from my Cessna P210," Patrick said. "Jon and I mounted a pair of sensitive all-weather-imaging infrared and millimeter-wave radar sensors on it, plus the hardware to send the images here. The P210 is orbiting about five miles away from the compound at four thousand feet AGL."

"Who's flying the plane?"

"Brad."

"Brad? Cool. But why is he taking pictures of that compound?"

"Because these are the guys who supposedly organized the protests at the front gate, shot at our plane, and may have killed Leo," Patrick said, not mentioning the fact that the ones who killed Leo may have been gunning for *him*. "The FBI is conducting visual surveillance of the compound, but they don't seem to be getting anywhere."

"The FBI? How do you know all this?"

"Jon here supplied some of the technology to the FBI to conduct aerial surveillance."

"You mean, the drones that were shot down? The ones on the news?"

"Yes."

"So the FBI asked you to put those sensors on your plane and start surveillance on that compound?" John asked.

"Not exactly," Patrick said. "This is our project. We're doing our own surveillance."

"Why are you doing that? Why not let the FBI handle it?"

"Because like Fid said, this is our town and our base," Patrick said. "We have the technology to do it, so I'm going to do it."

John smiled. "I said it before, and I'll say it again: that's the Patrick S. McLanahan I've always heard and read about," he said, chuckling. His expression turned serious again. "So why are you telling me all this, Patrick?"

"Because out of all the guys in the squadron except for Leo, I know and trust you the most," Patrick said. "I'm going to start conducting surveillance of the entire area, not just of the Knights' compound. I'm going to assist law enforcement in protecting our community, and if the cops won't do it, I'll organize our community to do it for ourselves."

"You're starting to sound like some of those Knights of the True Republic yourself, Patrick," John said seriously, a look of concern on his face. "You sure that's the smart thing to do?"

Patrick shook his head. "Honestly: no, I'm not sure," he said. "It's probably not legal, and it may not be ethical or my right as a citizen. But something is happening in this community and this entire country, John, and I want to do something about it. I thought the Civil Air Patrol was a good start, but now I don't even have that. So I'm starting this."

De Carteret thought for a moment, then nodded. "Sounds good to me, Patrick," he said. "If you need help, I'm in."

"Great. Who else do you think would be interested?"

"Well, I'm sure all the ex-military guys in the squadron: Rob; David; my wife, Janet; David Preston; Kevan; Bill and Nancy Barton; Rick; Mark; Debbie for sure," John said. "Fid . . . no offense to him, but he's strung a little too tight for my taste."

"That's a pretty good group to start with," Patrick said. "You still fly your Skyhawk, don't you?"

"Not so much these days," he admitted, "but when I get a couple extra bucks saved up, you bet."

"Feel like flying some of these surveillance missions?"

"In your P210? Sure!"

"The P210 . . . and in your Skyhawk."

"You mean, put those sensors on my Skyhawk? Are you kidding me?"

"No sweat, John," Jon Masters said, not looking up from his laptops. "It'll take me a couple days, plus a couple flight tests."

"Wow, that would be cool," John said, sounding more and more like a little kid. "You gonna get field approval from the FAA Flight Standards guys in Elko?"

"This mod . . . isn't going in your logbooks, John," Patrick said. "We've got some of the best mechanics and technicians in the country from Jon's company installing them, and I'll make sure your plane is put back together properly when we're done."

"Hot damn," John said, sticking out his hand. "Can't wait to get started." His eyes were dancing with anticipation. "So tell me, Patrick—is this how it felt when you were getting ready to fly some of your supersecret missions with all the newest high-tech gear? Because I'm telling ya, it's pretty damned exciting."

"This is how it felt, John," Patrick said, taking John's hand and shaking it enthusiastically. "This is *exactly* how it felt."

LATER THAT EVENING

Brad orbited over the Knights of the True Republic's compound for an hour more; cruised around the area about fifty miles around the town of Battle Mountain in a parallel tracklike pattern for another hour so they could record sensor scans of activity on the ground; then did three takeoffs and landings back at Battle Mountain to log some of his required night full-stop landings. Four hours of flying, three of it at night, and not one rumble whatsoever in his stomach—what a great day.

After putting the Centurion back in its hangar, he phoned his father. "Plane's put up, fueled up, windshield's clean, bugs wiped off," he said. "How do the pictures look?"

"Excellent," Patrick said. "Better than we expected. The other scans around the area will be stored by the computer, and we'll compare them to scans we'll take later to look for unusual activity."

"Cool."

"How's your stomach feel?"

"Great. Not even a big burp."

"I was a little concerned with you flying at night—I was afraid the loss of a horizon might bring back the nausea," Patrick said. "But you seemed to do okay when we did our night landings the other night."

"I'm fine, Dad."

"Heading home?"

"I'm going to stop by the bowling alley."

"Drinking age is—"

"I know, I know, no booze until I'm twenty-one. I don't like the stuff anyway, and with Gia back, I don't even want to deal with it. I just want to see if anything's going on, maybe play some pinball."

"I can't believe pinball machines are making a comeback," Patrick said. "We used to play those things for hours when we sat alert in the B-52s." He was getting into reminiscing mode again, Brad thought—that was happening more and more the older he got. "Have fun. Be back by midnight."

"It'll be before then—I've got workouts in the morning, and then I want to fly the P210."

"I'm flying Captain de Carteret and maybe Colonel Spara tomorrow, getting them checked out in the P210. It might have to wait."

"They're going to patrol with us?"

"Yes."

"Cool. It's like our own secret little Civil Air Patrol squadron."

"*Secret* being the key word here, Brad."

"No problem. Okay. See ya."

His next phone call was to Cassandra Renaldo. "It's me," he said when she answered.

"I'm so glad you called, baby," she said. "It has been a long day. I'm still at work."

"I'm at my dad's hangar. I just got done flying."

"You did? Flying at night?"

"I need to log at least ten hours and ten night landings for my check ride."

"How do you feel?"

"Excellent. No problems."

"You didn't have to take any of that medicine I gave you?"

"Nope. I've got it with me, but I didn't need it."

"You should keep it with you, in case you have to fly in the back of the plane again."

"Okay. Can I see you tonight?"

"I would love to see you, but I'm still at work." She hesitated, then said, "But I want to see you *so* badly . . . I think it'll be all right—no one else is here. Do you know which hangar is ours?"

"I think so. One of the hangars on the east side of the field with the big fence around it, right?"

"Yes. You'll see my car parked in front of one of the hangars, outside the fence. If there's another car parked there, I won't be alone, so I'll see you another time. But if there are no other cars, I'll be all alone. The gate will be closed, but I'll leave it partially open so you'll just need to nudge it a few times to get the gate open. Same with the hangar door—just pull, then push a couple times, and it'll open. C'mon in. I might be in the comm room, but I'll be waiting for you, lover. Maybe we'll do it right here on the . . . well, we'll see. Bye."

Man, Brad thought as he hung up, she had that sexy X-rated phone-porn voice that never failed to make the blood run right out of my brain. He had to be extra careful not to exceed the base speed limit as he headed over to the east side of the field.

He found her car in the parking lot outside the row of security hangars, and *yes,* it was by itself. It took more than a little nudge to get the gate open, but he wasn't going to let it stop him. Same with the hangar door, but after putting his shoulder in it a little, it finally came open.

The hangar was dark except for a desk with several laptops on it, illuminated by desk lights. "Cassandra?" he called out. No reply. He went over to the desk. This was definitely her desk—he could smell her fragrance . . . or was that just chronic horniness and the lack of blood in his brain making him imagine it? "Cassandra, where are you?"

Brad decided to wait. He checked out the images on the laptops. There were electronic charts, diagrams of what looked like the Knights of the True Republic's compound, and still photographs of people, obviously taken from very long distance. Each image was marked *SECRET,* but as far as he could tell, he didn't see anything *SECRET* about any of—

Suddenly his arms were yanked behind his back so hard he thought they were going to rip off his torso, and his head was slammed down onto the desk so hard that his vision exploded into a field of stars. *"Freeze! FBI!"* he heard through the sudden roaring in his ears. *"Don't you move!"* His hands were being twisted so hard that he thought they were going to pop off his wrists. His legs were kicked out behind him so even more pressure was on his face and head. He felt cold steel handcuffs being snapped onto his wrists, and then rough hands patting him down from head to foot.

"Ow! You're hurting me!" he protested.

"Shut up!" someone yelled. "Do you have any weapons in your pockets? Any knives or needles?"

"No! Stop twisting my—"

"I said, *shut up!*" He felt his shirt being pulled out of his pants, and then rough hands searching his body right down to the skin. The guy then started going through his pockets, turning them inside out. "Got something," he called out, before resuming his search inside Brad's pants, then right against his crotch. Brad was then spun around and thrust into a chair, and the desk light shined right in his face, blinding him. He felt blood trickling out of his nose, and his shoulder felt dislocated. "Why did you break in here, McLanahan?" the guy shouted.

"I didn't break in!"

"We got it all on surveillance cameras, McLanahan," the guy yelled. "You forced open the outside gate, then forced open the hangar door. It's all on video. It's called 'breaking and entering,' McLanahan, and in a federal facility, it's a federal crime. You could get five years in prison just for that. What are you doing here?" Brad said nothing. The guy slapped him on the side of his head so hard he almost fell off the chair. *"Answer me, you punk!* What are you doing here?" Brad couldn't tell them the truth—Cassandra would get fired for sure.

"Did you come in here to steal our computers?" the guy shouted. "That's burglary, McLanahan—that's another ten years in prison. And you came in here and viewed classified material—that's another ten to fifteen years, along with about a million dollars in fines. You're looking at some hard time, bub, and not in minimum security either. There will be some very big, very bad men who will be anxious to get to meet you up close and personal." The man held up a tiny bag of white powder. "What the hell is this?" he shouted.

"Nothing!"

"What do you mean, nothing?" He handed it back to someone behind him and shouted again, "What is it?"

"It's nothing. It's airsickness medicine."

"Airsickness medicine, huh? That's a new one." A few minutes later, he held up a tiny tube filled with blue liquid that was passed over to him by someone in the darkness. "This is a cobalt-thiocyanate test, McLanahan, and you just flunked it. The stuff in the bag we found on you is cocaine. So you broke in here to steal equipment to buy more coke, is that it, McLanahan?"

"No!" Brad shouted.

"You gonna tell me the stuff isn't yours?"

"No . . . no, it's mine, but it's not cocaine, it's airsickness medicine!"

"Who told you that?" Brad didn't answer. "You're a burglar, a liar, and a doper, McLanahan," the guy said. "You're going to go to prison for a very, very long time. I hope you get some good drug treatment while you're rotting in a cell, you miserable little—"

"That's enough, Brady," a different voice interrupted. The desk light was turned away from his face, and some of the hangar lights were turned on so he could see better. When his eyes adjusted, he could see the head FBI agent seated in front of him. "Good evening, Mr. McLanahan. I'm Special Agent Philip Chastain, FBI. We've already met briefly, if you recall." He turned. "Wipe his face off, Brady, you gave him a bloody nose. I hope you didn't break it. And put those cuffs in front and loosen them—you're making his hands turn purple." The first agent roughly wiped his face with a damp towel, then took off one of the cuffs, brought his hands in front of him, then snapped the loose one back on.

"You're in some serious trouble, Mr. McLanahan," Chastain said in a quiet voice. "Agent Brady wasn't lying about any of this: we've got the video of you breaking through the gate and the hangar door; we've got video of you checking out the computers; and the stuff in your pocket really is cocaine. We've got the entire search and cobalt thiocyanate test on video, so you can't claim it was planted." He inched a bit closer to Brad and lowered his voice: "I even know about you and Agent Renaldo of the Department of Homeland Security." Brad's head snapped up in surprise. "Yep, I'm afraid she's going to be in some trouble, but not nearly as much as you are right now."

"Cassandra wouldn't give me cocaine," Brad said, his voice strained and cracking.

"So it's got to be yours."

Brad lowered his head, then nodded. "It's mine," he lied.

"We thought so," Chastain said. "Possession, sale weight . . . you might be able to get a break if this is your first offense, but even so, with all the other charges, you're looking at serious federal prison time." Brad hung his head, and his shoulders started to shake. "And Agent Cassandra Renaldo is still in trouble . . ." He paused for effect, then added in a quiet voice, almost a whisper: "If anyone else ever finds out about any of this."

It took a moment for his words to sink in, but soon Brad raised his head. "Wha-what . . . ?"

"I'm in a position to offer you a deal, Brad," Chastain said. "It's just for right now, tonight only. If I pick up the phone to my office and tell them I'm bringing in a prisoner, no more deals will be possible with me. It'll be yes or no, right here, right now. Do you understand?"

Brad nodded. "What's the deal?" he asked.

"First of all, you are going to sign a contract," Chastain said in a firm, measured voice. "You're going to admit to everything you've done, and agree to do everything I tell you to do in exchange for me not pressing any charges against you or Agent Renaldo—conditionally. It's a federal contract, countersigned by the U.S. attorney and a federal judge." Brad's face brightened. "You're going to do some tasks for me. You will do them precisely as I tell you, and give me exactly the information I tell you to give me, exactly when I want it, with no excuses. If you fail to do any of this, you will be rearrested, formally charged, and put in jail to await trial." Brad's eyes flared when he heard the word *jail,* and Chastain noticed that right away. The agent produced a typewritten piece of paper with the FBI shield at the top—Brad was too scared to realize that the contract had already been drawn up. "Sign at the bottom."

"What do you want me to do for you?"

"First, sign the contract, Brad," Chastain said. "If you don't, you'll be placed under arrest and taken to my office in San Francisco tonight, in-processed, jailed, then taken in front of a federal judge and formally charged. You're not a minor anymore, so your father won't know where you've been taken until after you've been arraigned, which could take a couple days." Brad's face turned pale, and his mouth dropped open in shock. "By the time you're released on bail, Agent Renaldo will be out of a job, and I'll charge her with conspiracy and aiding and abetting several felonies, and put her in jail too. I'm sure we'll find that she helped you get in here so you could steal the computers and classified materials, and gave you the cocaine as well."

"No! She . . . she didn't do *anything* . . ."

"That's for a judge and jury to decide, Brad," Chastain said evenly. "Unless you sign this contract, I'll have no choice in the matter. You'll be in jail, I can't do anything more, and your life will change forever. Your dad won't be able to help you." Brad hesitated, trying to clear the cobwebs out of his head enough to think. Chastain waited a few seconds, then shook his head and looked over his shoulder. "Brady, cuff him in back again and read him his rights," he said with a dismissive sigh. "Then go arrest Renaldo, and alert the office that we'll be bringing in two prisoners tonight—separately. I'll need the—"

"No, wait! I'll sign it," Brad said, and he snatched up the pen and scribbled his signature at the bottom of the page, with Agent Brady taking a photograph as he did it. "Okay, I agree. I'll do whatever you want. Just don't arrest Cassandra."

"Good choice, Brad," Chastain said. "Your future, and Agent Renaldo's career, are still intact . . . as long as you do exactly what I tell you to do."

"What do you want me to do?"

"Simple," Chastain said. "You will tell me everything your father does, where he goes, and whom he meets and talks with. Whenever possible, you will accompany him and tell me whom he meets with, where, and when."

"My . . . my father . . . ?"

"This is not open for debate or question, Brad," Chastain said. "You do what I tell you to do, or you go to jail, *period*. Where he goes and whom he meets with; go with him whenever you can." He gave Brad a card. "That's my secure text-message and e-mail address. I expect a detailed report three times a day, or more. If I don't get it, you're going to jail, and all the evidence I have gets turned over to the U.S. attorney, along with Cassandra." He motioned to Brady, who took his handcuffs off. "Now get out of here, don't tell anyone about this, don't ever see Renaldo again, and never come near this building again."

Brad leaped out of the chair, stumbled, then started crawling for the hangar door, his legs unable to support his weight. Brady grabbed him by the back of his neck, carried him to the door, and tossed him outside. "So much for the tough football player," he said when he returned, laughing. He theatrically sniffed near the desk. "Why, I think I smell a hint of scared-shitless piss over here."

"He may be eighteen, but he's just a kid," Chastain said. "He's been babied and pampered by his war-hero father his entire life."

"He may be a boy, but he's a very *big* boy," Cassandra Renaldo said as she walked over to the others.

"Good job, Renaldo," Chastain said. "Sorry to take away your new plaything, but it's the best way to see if there's any connection between the general, the Knights, and the Civil Air Patrol."

"He was fun," Renaldo said dismissively, lighting a cigarette, "but business is business. I still don't think the general is up to anything, but young stud muffin Bradley will tell us."

"What if he tells his father what's happened?" Brady asked. "The general has some pretty powerful friends."

"If he did, what's he doing in Battle Mountain, Nevada?" Chastain said. "That's only one of many questions I want answered, and I think the boy will get them for us."

JOINT AIR BASE BATTLE MOUNTAIN

THE NEXT MORNING

Thankfully no one was there when Brad got up. He dressed in workout clothes, had a light breakfast, then picked up his cell phone. "Hey, Dad."

"Hey, big guy."

"I'm going to practice. What are you doing?"

"I'm going to take Captain de Carteret up in the P210 this morning, fly some patrols and take more sensor images, then take Colonel Spara up later," Patrick replied. "There're thunderstorms forecast for this evening, so I don't think we'll be flying tonight. What time did you get in last night?"

"Ten-thirty." Brad swallowed, then said, "I . . . I got into a little fight last night outside the bowling alley."

"*What?* A fight?"

"No big deal, just an argument over a stupid game," Brad lied. "The guy claimed he put money in the machine I was playing on, but he didn't, and I guess him and a friend waited for me outside."

"Are you okay?"

"Just a few bruises. I'm still going to practice."

"Did you report it to base security?"

"No. I . . . I kinda started it."

"'*Started it*'?"

"Look, Dad, it was dumb, and I got what I deserved. I'd rather forget about it."

"Do you know the guys? Were they military?"

"I guess."

"Are you sure you're all right?"

"Yes."

"Was alcohol involved, Brad?"

"No, Dad. I told you, I'm not drinking."

"Stop by the office when you get done with practice and let me take a look."

"I'm okay, Dad. I'm going to practice, and then I'm going to work."

"I'll come over and give you the Wrangler," Patrick said. "I'll take the scooter."

"I'll be fine, Dad. If I don't feel well enough to ride to town, I'll come over and switch. But I'm gonna be late."

There was a long pause; then: "All right, I'll see you tonight. Call if you don't feel good. Be careful driving."

"Okay." Brad hung up, then composed a text message: FLT INSTRUCTING DECARTERET AND SPARA UNTIL DINNER to Chastain's number. Then he put on a jacket, helmet, gloves, and reflective safety vest, looped his equipment bag over his aching shoulders, painfully got on his Genuine Buddy scooter, and headed off to the senior high school for football workout.

"What the heck happened to you?" Ron Spivey asked when Brad jogged over to the team. Brad's face was badly bruised, his eyes were swollen, and he could hardly move his arms. "You get into a fight or something?"

"Couple of guys at the bowling alley," Brad said.

"No shit," Ron said. "You tell your dad?"

"Yeah."

"I hope the other guys look worse than you do," Ron said. "You okay to work out? We were going to do light pads today."

"Red-shirt me," Brad said.

Ron threw him a red pinnie from the equipment bag, indicating that none of the other players were allowed to block or tackle him during practice. "First time I've ever seen you red-shirted," he said.

"First time I ever got beat up like that."

"Do you know who they were?"

"GIs, Marines I think, but I never saw them before."

"We should get a bunch of the guys and lay in wait for *them*."

"Let's just drop it," Brad said, and they started their workout. Brad thought the ride over in the scooter was painful, but now he thought his arms were going to fall off as he started running. But soon the double dose of aspirin he took was kicking in, and he forgot about the pain.

It was the most difficult practice Brad ever remembered since he started playing football, but he made it through it. He limped back to the scooter and loaded up. He seriously thought about skipping work, but he needed the money. A couple more aspirins would probably take the edge off enough for him to make it through work. He started up the scooter, readjusted the equipment bag on his shoulder one more time to find a more comfortable position, headed out of the parking spot toward the exit . . .

. . . and before he could react, a car screeched backward out of its parking spot and crashed into the front of his scooter, traveling about ten miles an hour. Brad was thrown backward off the scooter from the weight of his equipment bag. The car kept on going, backing right over the scooter.

"Hey, asshole!" Ron Spivey shouted, running up to Brad. The car was about fifteen feet away, revving its engine. He saw two guys in the front seat, both wearing sunglasses, both with baseball caps. The guy in the passenger side was yelling something that Ron couldn't understand, gesturing with his right hand like a knife blade at the driver as if he was stabbing him. *"Someone call the cops!"* Ron shouted, and threw his football helmet at the car, cracking the windshield. More players ran toward them, shouting. The car suddenly shifted into gear and roared out of the parking lot. *"Jesus,* Brad, are you okay?"

"I don't know," Brad said, holding his left leg.

"Stay down, Brad," Ron said. "I'm calling 911." He pulled out his cell phone. "Man, that guy was *haulin'* out of that parking space! What in hell was he doing? And he didn't have any license plates either!"

Brad felt a creaking and grinding when he tried to move his left leg, and the pain shot through his entire body all the way to the top of his head. "Shit, I hope it's not broken," he grunted through clenched teeth.

"It's just not your day, hombre," Ron said. "First you get beat up, and then you get run over. What's next for you, pal?"

Brad didn't even want to think about *that*.

Andorsen Memorial Hospital, Battle Mountain, Nevada

A short time later

Timothy Dobson walked into the hospital room, noting that there were no other persons in the room except Patrick and Brad. Patrick was seated on Brad's bed beside him; Brad had his left leg slightly elevated in a temporary cast, his left arm also in a temporary cast, and his torso wrapped. Patrick saw Dobson enter, and his face immediately filled with concern. "Hello, General," Dobson said. "Hi, Brad."

"Tim? What's going on?"

Dobson turned and locked the door. "How are you, Brad?" he asked.

"Okay."

"He's lucky—no broken bones, just sprains, bruises, and scrapes," Patrick said. "They're keeping him overnight for observation. We're waiting for X-rays on internal injuries." Dobson nodded. "What's up, Tim? Do you have information on who hit Brad?"

"Not yet," Dobson said. "We've got a good description of the car from witnesses, and we're checking freeway, intersection, and security cameras. We'll know something soon." He looked at Brad. "Any idea who might have done this, Brad? Ever seen the car before?"

"No."

Dobson nodded, a very somber look on his face. "While you were getting X-rays, Brad, your dad told me about getting beat up at the bowling alley last night." Brad looked down at his hands. "I asked around, thinking the same guys that ran you over might have beat you up . . . but no one saw you at the bowling alley last night."

"Brad?" Patrick asked. "Why the story? Where were you last night?" Brad said nothing. "I said: Where were you?" He was getting angrier by the moment. "Damn it, Brad answer me! What the hell is going on?"

"I can't tell you."

"Why the hell not?" But Brad only kept his eyes averted. Patrick turned to Dobson. "Well?"

"Maybe this is between you two, sir."

"Where was he, Dobson?"

The agent hesitated for a moment, then said, "We tracked his cell-phone signals from your hangar . . . to the hangar the FBI is using on the base."

"What?" Patrick exclaimed. He whirled back to stare in astonishment at his son. "Why in hell would you go there?" Still no answer. "Damn it, Brad, I'd rather hear it from you than from Mr. Dobson, but I *am* going to hear what happened, one way or another. Were you arrested? What were you doing there?" No answer. Patrick jumped to his feet and yelled, *"Answer me, damn it!"*

"I was told not to tell you," Brad said. "They told me I'd be arrested and taken to jail in San Francisco if I told you."

"Jail? What are you talking about? Told me what?"

Brad sniffed away a silent sob. Patrick knotted his fists, fighting to keep his anger in check. He whirled back to Dobson. "Well?"

"His cell-phone records have a call last night to Special Agent Cassandra Renaldo from Homeland Security."

"Renaldo? You were going to meet Renaldo? What for?" Brad didn't answer, but he didn't need to—the whole thing was becoming clear to Patrick now. "Jesus, Brad, you were seeing Renaldo?" Brad nodded. "But you didn't see her last night, did you?" Brad started to cry, his shoulders shaking. "Chastain and Brady? They did this to you?" His son was sobbing, and Patrick's heart broke, spilling red-hot acidic fury through his veins. "What did they do to you?"

"They thought I broke into the hangar and was going to steal their computers," Brad said through the sobs. "They handcuffed me and searched me. Then they found the airsickness medicine Cassandra gave me and told me it was cocaine." Patrick's hands flew up to his eyes in horror. "They told me if I didn't do as they said, they were going to arrest me and take me to jail in San Francisco, and you wouldn't know where I was for days. They said I'd go to prison for a long time."

Patrick sat back down on the bed and hugged his son, letting him weep for several long moments. "What did they tell you to do, Brad?" he finally asked.

"They . . . they told me to tell them what you were doing," Brad said. "I was supposed to spy on you. I didn't want to, Dad, but I didn't want to go to prison, and I didn't want Cassandra to get into trouble."

"It's okay, Brad, it's okay," Patrick said. "You're not going to prison."

"I didn't break into the hangar," Brad said. "I didn't try to burglarize the hangar. And it wasn't cocaine, I swear!"

"I said don't worry, Brad," Patrick said. "Don't worry about Chastain, Renaldo, or Brady. They're going to be gone from here shortly, and you won't have to worry about them again."

"Cassandra?" Brad looked up at his father. "She . . . she was in on it, wasn't she? She didn't like me—it was all a setup to get me to spy on you." He started to cry again. "Why am I such a dork, Dad?" he said, burying his face into Patrick's chest. "I don't know crap about *anything*!"

"It's not your fault, big guy," Patrick said, holding his son closely again. "Brad, there are people out there who just victimize other people, take advantage of them for their own purposes, no matter how badly it hurts others. We have to learn to watch out for people like that and stop them whenever we can." He took a deep breath, then said, "I know I wasn't around for you much when I was in the Air Force and working outside, Brad, and even after we moved here, I wasn't here for you as much as I should have been. I was pretending I was still in the Air Force, flying Civil Air Patrol and Angel Flight West missions, when what I should have been doing is being your dad and teaching you about scumbags like Chastain, Brady, and Renaldo. All that is going to change."

He stood up, touched Brad's face, then laid him back on his pillow. To Dobson, he said, "Can you arrange protection for Brad, Tim?"

"U.S. Marshals should be arriving in a few hours," Dobson said. "I can stay with him until they get here. The vice president wants to move him to—"

"We're not leaving," Patrick said. "We're going hunting." He pulled out his cell phone and started making calls.

Joint Air Base Battle Mountain

That night

Brady and Renaldo were seated at the desk in the FBI hangar, watching the latest images on their laptops being transmitted from the FBI agents conducting video and photographic surveillance of the Knights of the True Republic's compound; Chastain was in the communications room taking a nap. Brady heard a rattle on the main hangar door. "What was that?" he asked.

"Sounds like the thunderstorms are kicking up," Renaldo said. "We're supposed to get some big ones tonight."

"These are nothing," Brady said. "When I was assigned to the Dallas office, we'd get every possible kind of storm—snow, hurricanes, tornadoes, and these huge towering thunderstorms that would hang around for—"

Suddenly they heard the screeching ear-shattering sound of ripping metal, and the two flew to their feet and turned toward the hangar door. A huge twenty-foot-high seam of torn metal opened up right in the center of the hangar door, and like a pair of curtains being opened, the metal seam burst apart . . . and the Cybernetic Infantry Device robot stepped through the newly created opening as easily as a child walking through the curtain onto the stage at a kindergarten recital.

"What the hell are you doing?" Brady shouted. "Who is that in there?"

The robot rushed forward with incredible speed. As Brady and Renaldo scrambled to get out of its way, it reached out, put its armored hands on either side of the desk, and brought its hands together. The desk and computers were squished together into one lump in a shower of sparks and flying wood and metal. It then grabbed Brady and Renaldo by the throat and lifted them off their feet.

"What's going on in here?" Philip Chastain thundered, running from the comm room. "What's that thing doing in here? It's tearing the place apart!"

At that instant the side hangar door flew off its hinges and sailed across the hangar like a leaf tossed about in a hurricane, and a man in a gray outfit whom Chastain had never seen before, with a multifaceted helmet and devices on his waist, stepped through the opening. He walked toward Chastain. The special agent drew a semiautomatic pistol and fired three times at him, but the man kept on coming. Chastain kept on firing until the pistol was empty, but the figure still advanced. It appeared as if it was going to walk right past him, but instead it reached around behind Chastain's neck, picked him up, and carried him over to the CID, suspending him two feet off the hangar floor. Both figures stood with their struggling prisoners, facing the destroyed hangar door . . .

. . . as Patrick McLanahan stepped through the newly created opening.

"McLanahan!" Chastain grunted through the pressure on his neck. The others were desperately trying to chin themselves up the best they could to keep from being strangled. "What in hell do you think you're doing?"

"Issuing you a warning, Chastain," Patrick said. He walked up to Chastain, and the armored figure lowered him down so they were face-to-face. "Your operation here is at an end. You are going to leave this state, or you're going to die."

"Die? You're threatening to *kill me?* Are you *crazy?* I'll see you're put in prison for the rest of your life!"

"I don't think so, folks," Patrick said. The Tin Man commando squeezed Chastain's neck a little tighter, which made his mouth open and his tongue protrude like a drowning victim gasping for air. Patrick shoved a tiny capsule into his mouth, and when the Tin Man relaxed his hold on his neck, Chastain involuntarily swallowed the capsule when he took a gulp of air. Patrick did the same with Brady and Renaldo.

"What the hell was that, McLanahan?" Chastain shouted. "Are you poisoning us?"

"I gave you each a nanotransponder," Patrick said. "It's the same capsule given to legal U.S. guest workers. I can track your position at any time, and you can't stop it, because your body will be filled with microscopic electronic transmitters that will report your position as long as you're alive." He stepped closer to Chastain. "You are going to leave Nevada and terminate your surveillance of the Knights' compound."

"Like hell I will!" Chastain shouted. "I have an operation under way—"

"And you will cancel it as of tonight," Patrick said. "All of your agents will move out of Nevada. If anyone asks, you will tell them that the Knights are not a threat and you will conduct your surveillance elsewhere."

"Like hell I will!"

"If you don't, Agent Chastain, I will kill you, and I will kill Brady and Renaldo too," Patrick said simply. "They will eventually find your decomposing bodies in the desert, perhaps months, maybe years from now, or maybe never. The FBI may eventually trace the murders to me, but by then you will be long dead."

Patrick moved to within a breath's distance from Chastain. "You touched my son, you son of a bitch, and you threatened him, and you hit him," he said, his eyes wide with rage, a vein in his temple pulsing with fury. "I should kill you right now, just for that. I'm within a red cunt hair's breadth of ordering the Tin Man to scrunch you up into a tiny round red ball of goo and drop-kick you across to the other side of the base. I'll gladly trade ten years in prison for the privilege of watching him do that—and, I assure you, he's done it before, with *great* enthusiasm, for a lot less motivation than this. Or, I could just take the videos of you and my son you claim to have to the U.S. attorney, and see what would happen to you. I'd put enough pressure on him and the attorney general to fire you, maybe even bring you up on criminal charges.

"But I'm not going to do any of that, Chastain," Patrick went on. "I prefer to deal with you three directly. It's simple: you leave the state and leave me and my son alone, *forever,* or we'll be back—and it won't be as pleasant for you as it is right now."

Patrick nodded to the CID and the Tin Man, and the three agents were dropped to the floor. "You wouldn't kill anyone," Chastain croaked hoarsely, rubbing his neck. "You don't have the guts."

"I wouldn't kill you tonight, Chastain," Patrick said. "But if you three aren't out of the state immediately, or if you do anything whatsoever to me or my son, I will track you down. You'll go to sleep one night and wake up just long enough to realize I'm standing over you, and then that'll be that. I promise you."

"You're full of shit, McLanahan," Brady said.

The Tin Man reached out and tapped Brady on the shoulder with two fingers, but Brady's body reacted as if he had been hit by a sledgehammer. *"Aaaughh!"* he screamed. "What the . . . shit, *I think you broke my damned shoulder!"*

The Tin Man picked up Brady by the neck, shook him, and watched as he cringed in pain. "The general has killed his enemies face-to-face many times before, I assure you," the Tin Man said in his electronically synthesized voice. "But if he ever hesitated to do it, even for a split second, I'd gladly do it for him—and not with this getup on either." He dropped the agent back to the hangar floor, where he writhed and whimpered in pain.

"What's it going to be, Chastain?" Patrick asked.

"You cowardly bastard," Chastain cried. "You bring your high-tech goons in here to torture and threaten us—you don't have the balls to do it yourself." He jabbed a finger at Patrick. "I'm not done with you, mister. I'll find a way to come after you, and I'm not going to be behind a badge either." He turned and walked toward the side door, leaving Renaldo to help Brady.

"You had me convinced," Brigadier-General Kurt Givens said after he watched the three agents leave. Jason Richter and Jon Masters were beside him. "But I think you've made yourself a pretty powerful enemy. I've got security forces escorting them off the base. What do you intend to do now?"

"Make sure Chastain and the FBI leave," Patrick said, "then resume our searches of the area. There are other extremist groups out there, and I want to get images and movement history on as many as I can."

"You must be made out of money, my friend," Kurt said.

"I'm borrowing it from a friend," Patrick admitted, nodding to Jon, "and I'll figure out a way to repay him—eventually." To Jon, he said, "Can you bring some weapon packs and electromagnetic rifles in for the CID and Tin Man?"

"How many do you want, Patrick?" Jon asked.

"I didn't hear any of that, boys," Kurt said. "Try not to rip up any more of my hangars tonight, okay?" He looked up at the Cybernetic Infantry Device towering over him. "Put the doors back together, will you?"

"Yes, sir," the CID replied in its electronic voice. The CID and the Tin Man got to work repairing the hangar doors, pinching and squeezing the metal back into a sort of solid surface and using their fingers like rivet guns to hang the side door back on its hinges. The CID unit assumed its dismount position, and Charlie Turlock climbed out. "Man, that was fun!" she exclaimed.

"Beating FBI agents up for personal reasons is not what the CID is made for, Charlie," Jason Richter said. "It belongs to the U.S. Army and is loaned to the FBI."

"They haven't been doing a rip-roaring job with them so far, Jason," Charlie pointed out.

"The general seems to feel the CID is his personal property," Jason said, addressing Patrick indirectly. "I have to assure him, he's wrong."

Patrick ignored him. "Charlie's right: we need a better approach to this Knights of the True Republic extremist situation than what the FBI has been pursuing," he said. "We're still going to find and track them, but we don't have the authority to arrest or kill them, and there doesn't seem to be any local law enforcement willing or able to help. And we have to organize our group to start going over all the sensor images we've collected so far. I suggest we get some rest, then meet tomorrow morning to discuss a plan of action."

As they all turned to depart, Patrick said to Richter: "One moment, Colonel." Jason went back, looking directly at Patrick, his hands behind his back in an attitude that was both respectful and dismissive. "Have I done something to tick you off, Colonel?" Patrick asked.

"With all due respect, sir: I object to the way you take things and personnel and act as you please, as if you answer to no other authority but your own," Jason said as matter-of-factly as if he were describing a sunny day. "Dr. Masters's sensors and computers; the CID and Tin Man; Charlie Turlock and Macomber; and all of those Civil Air Patrol people—you treat them as if they've been assigned to you, and you have an unlimited budget to direct them to do anything you wish. And you literally tortured and terrorized those federal agents with the CID and Tin Man, not to mention threatening their lives. I'm just trying to decide if I have a responsibility and duty to report you to someone so a proper authority can evaluate your actions—and stop you."

Patrick thought for a moment, matching Jason's direct glare; then: "Tell me, Colonel: Where do you live?"

"I'm currently assigned to the Army Infantry Transformational BattleLab at—"

"No, I mean, where's your hometown?"

Richter blinked at the question. "I'm from western Pennsylvania, General."

"Still no mention of a hometown," Patrick observed. "I think that's the key to why you don't understand what I'm trying to do, Colonel: you don't seem to have a hometown."

"I'm in the U.S. Army, General," Jason said. "I travel two hundred days a year to bases and laboratories all over the world; I visit a half-dozen defense contractors and engineering firms a month; and the rest of the time I'm working in my lab a minimum of twelve hours a day."

"How about your folks?"

"They live near Wilmington, North Carolina, surrounded by kids and grandkids," Jason said. "I've never been there."

"Interesting. So you don't really have a home, do you?" Jason didn't respond. "But if Fort Polk was attacked by extremists, you'd certainly defend it, wouldn't you?"

"Of course, sir. That's obvious. What's your point?"

"And if there were no military police when the attack began, you'd certainly pick up a gun and do your best to fight off the attackers, right?"

"Yes."

"You'd even climb aboard a Cybernetic Infantry Device and use it to defend the base, correct? Maybe even put on a weapon backpack if you felt you needed it?"

"Yes, sir."

"Even if the Army didn't order you to do anything?" Patrick asked. "Even if the military police were already responding?"

Jason thought for a moment; then: "If the CID could get the job done and prevent loss of life and property . . . yes, sir, I would. It would be crazy to have a weapon system like that and not use it in a crisis."

"But the CID doesn't *belong* to you," Patrick pointed out. "You have access to it, but you don't own it." Again, Jason said nothing. "So what's the difference between you and me, Colonel? Battle Mountain is my home. I live on this base, and my son goes to school in town, and my friends and Civil Air Patrol squadron mates live all throughout this area. I'd certainly do all I could to defend my home, same as you—even convince my neighbors to join me to do whatever we could to stop the bad guys."

Jason still had not responded, so Patrick took a step toward him.

"So get your head out of your ass and get with the program, Colonel," he snapped. "The situation here is real, and it's serious. It's not someone else's problem—it's *our* problem.

"Now, if you want, you can call anyone you feel you need to call, and I'll respond in the same way," Patrick went on. "You can take the CID and leave, and I'll find a way to get the job done without it. But if it's here, I'm going to use it, because I *can*. And I'm not going to let you or anyone else short of the president of the United States stop me, and I might even argue with him over it. Is that clear?"

Jason stared back at Patrick, matching his determined glare—but after a few moments, he nodded. "Yes, General, it's clear."

"Good. Now, why don't you meet with us in my office in the morning and suggest ways we can best utilize the CID. If you don't care to do that, then load up the CID and get the hell out of my face so I can do the job."

Joint Air Base Battle Mountain

Several days later, early morning

Patrick walked into the Civil Air Patrol squadron conference room after flying another sensor shift around the area. Six cadets were seated at the table, using laptop computers and trackballs, with cans of soda or energy drinks ready at hand. On the whiteboard at the head of the room there were drawings of various things to watch for: tire tracks, disturbed earth, days-old campfires, and patterns of debris or discarded objects.

Brad was also there, in front of his laptop, acting as the second senior required in any cadet formation. "How's it going, big guy?" Patrick asked his son.

"Great," Brad said. "I've got some interesting observations."

"How do you feel?" Patrick asked.

"I feel fine—good enough to fly some scans." The bruises on his face had all but gone away, but Patrick could see him still limping in the house when he thought his father wasn't watching.

"It's not my call, Brad—it's the flight doc's," Patrick said. "We'll get you flying again soonest. Until then, I appreciate you helping out here."

"Uncle Jon's sensors and analysis technology stuff is pretty cool," Brad admitted, "but I want to *fly*, Dad. I'm a pilot. Maybe not a licensed pilot yet, but I want to fly."

"And you will, big guy," Patrick said, "when the doc says so." But he was not encouraging a return to flying status one bit, and he'd told the doctor so.

"How was flying?"

"Good," Patrick said. "We've got six pilots trained to fly the P210 Centurion and C-172 Skyhawk. You'll be number seven as soon as the flight doc clears you. Bill Barton's C-182 Skylane is being fitted with Sky Masters, Inc.'s sensors, so we'll have three planes. Dave Preston is interested in having his G36 Bonanza fitted too." He motioned to the images on Brad's laptop. "What are you looking at that's so interesting?"

"I've been assigned to scan the Knights' compound," Brad said, "and there seems to be a lot of people congregating in the main compound—a lot more than usual, outside of their prayer sessions and meetings. Also, I think the irrigation system on a couple of their crop circles has gone out. Wonder what's going on."

"I don't know," Patrick said, "but that doesn't sound good. Rob Spara and David Bellville have been trying to call the leaders of the group, but there's been no answer. What are you up to the rest of the day?"

"Since you don't want me to go to practice or work, and I can't fly yet, I'm going to stay here if they need me," Brad said. "Might as well make myself useful." He paused for a moment, then asked, "Hey, Dad, mind if I ask Colonel Richter and Miss Turlock to check me out in the CID?"

"You want to pilot the robot?" Patrick asked. "Why?"

"I don't know," Brad admitted. "It's still here, right?" Patrick nodded. "And nobody's using it. So I thought I'd give it a try. If I can't fly the Centurion, I might as well learn how to pilot the robot."

Patrick hesitated, but only for a moment. "I don't see why not," he said. "Sure. I'll call Colonel Richter and ask him—it's not my device, but his—and I'll call Charlie to see if she'd be willing."

"Thanks, Dad."

"Have fun," Patrick said. "I'm going to fly the Centurion to-night, if the weather holds. I'll see you tomorrow morning." He went over to an older gentleman who was walking around the table, ready to help when needed, and shook hands with him. "How's it going, Todd?" he asked.

"Slicker'n goose snot, General," Todd Bishop said happily. Even though he was age eighty-one, Todd was one of the more active seniors in the squadron, serving in the incident command center, the comm trailer, and as a glider-flight instructor and cadet-orientation pilot. "Those sensors are flippin' amazing. I caught a glimpse of one of the cadets reading a newspaper through someone's window! I nixed that right away, of course—you know he wasn't just searchin' for newspaper headlines—but I'm amazed we can do that."

Patrick watched one of the fifteen-year-old female cadets named Roxanne study the images taken yesterday. She started with a wide-angle picture of an area about thirty miles southeast of the base, then punched a function key. Immediately there was a series of flashing red icons. She started at the upper-left corner of the screen, rolled the cursor over the icon, and pressed a button. The screen zoomed in to reveal a dirt road stretching from a ranch house westward until it intersected a paved road, which eventually led north to the town of Crescent Valley. "What have you got, Roxanne?" Patrick asked.

"A lot of new activity on this dirt road in the past few days, sir," she explained, taking a sip of Red Bull. "This is the Kellerman ranch, except Mr. Fitzgerald says it's been vacant for quite a while. I've looked at the house, and it doesn't seem to be vandalized or anything."

"Any patterns in the activity?" Patrick asked. "Types of vehicles, or when they come or go?"

"Not really, sir," Roxanne replied. She hit another function key, and the image changed slightly. "This is real time. Most of the activity happens at night, but it's everything from motorbikes to ATVs to pickups. No one seems to stay very long. It's like they're visiting or going out there to get something, but I don't see any activity in the house otherwise. The corrals and barns are empty too."

"So what do you think, Roxanne?" Patrick asked.

She thought for a moment, then replied, "They might be kids just joyriding, or maybe someone looking for the Kellermans—I don't see any sign of a crime being committed. We should call the sheriff's office to take a look on the ground. It'd be best if they were there between eleven P.M. and two A.M., but I don't think the sheriff will put somebody out there for that long, on the off chance of catching someone out there."

Patrick nodded, impressed with her analysis and recommendation. "I'll keep on bugging the sheriff's department," he said, "but they don't seem too interested in what we're seeing." He nodded at her energy drink. "How long have you been here today, Roxanne?"

"Since eight."

"Five hours already?"

"Yes, sir."

"And when do you usually quit?"

"I have to be back home by four so I can finish feeding the animals and cleaning out the stables and pens by six," she said. "Dad always wants dinner right at six."

"What do your folks say about all this?"

"I don't think they care much," Roxanne said. "As long as I do my chores and stay out of trouble, they think it's okay."

"What do they think of you analyzing drone imagery?"

"I don't think they know, or if they do, they don't care," she said. "I tell them I'm going to the squadron to work with you, and they just say, 'Have fun.'"

"And how do you like it?"

"I think it's neat," Roxanne replied. "Mr. Bishop has made it a sort of contest: whoever turns in the most detailed analyses wins a Baskin-Robbins gift certificate. The boys think they can win just because they play more video games than girls, but their reports are nothing but junk—they're just trying to turn in the most reports."

That was interesting, Patrick thought: it wasn't work, but a game. "Thanks for explaining all this, Roxanne," he said. "Good work. Carry on."

"Okay," Roxanne replied, but she was already twirling the trackball and fixating on the next red blinking icon, ignoring the senior beside her.

He scanned around the room. "Hey, you got Ralph Markham here too?" he remarked to Brad.

"The kid's a computer freak, Dad," Brad said. "Uncle Jon hardly had to explain how to work anything—he just sat in front of the computer and started working. He's been here since seven A.M. He actually found a crash site that hadn't been found before. Mr. Fitzgerald went out there and found a victim that had been reported missing for *six years*. Do you believe it?"

"Ralph's a natural Civil Air Patrol guy, that's for sure," Patrick said. He went over to the boy's workstation. "Hi, Ralph." Ralph immediately tried to shoot to his feet, but Patrick held up a hand to stop him. "Carry on, Ralph. This isn't Civil Air Patrol, just us."

"Yes, sir."

"What are you looking at?"

"Las Vegas grids six and seven, sir," Ralph replied. "Right on the border between central Lander and Eureka Counties."

"About as far south as the patrols fly so far," Patrick observed. "Anything happening?" He looked at Ralph's screen. "A lot of flashing icons in this area."

"Those are mines, sir," Ralph said. "A lot of trucks going in and out." He hit some function keys and the display changed. "We don't have a plane in that area right now, so this isn't real time, but less than an hour old, from your last patrol sortie." It was a huge terraced strip mine, probably a mile in diameter and hundreds of feet deep.

"That's one of Judah Andorsen's mines," a voice said next to him. It was Michael Fitzgerald, wearing what appeared to be deer-hunting clothing. "That might be Freedom-7. They all look alike to me." He shook hands with Patrick. "How are you, sir?"

"Very good, Fid. What's happening?"

"Still looking for work," Fitzgerald said. "I was hoping there was something here on the base."

"I heard you got laid off. Sorry. I can check with the base personnel office. I heard they were going to put a bunch of the trailers on foundations to make them more permanent. Sound good?"

"If it pays cash money, Patrick, I'll pick up the trailers with my bare hands," Fitzgerald said. "Thank you, General." He nodded toward the screens. "How's the surveillance going?"

"Pretty good. Congrats on making that find the other day."

"The kids made the find—I just walked to where they told me," Fitzgerald said. "Any more targets you need checked out? Roxanne mentioned the Kellerman ranch. You need that scoped out?"

"If the sheriff won't send anyone, yes, I might have you go on out there," Patrick said. "It certainly looks suspicious." Just then he was alerted to an incoming phone call via his intraocular monitor, and he touched his left ear to answer the call. He spoke just a few words, then logged off. "Ralph's mom is at the front gate, asking— no, *demanding*—she be let in. I'm going to escort her in."

Several minutes later, Ralph's mom, Amanda, was led into the squadron conference room. She went directly over to Ralph. "Hi, Mom," Ralph greeted her. "I'm helping with—"

"Helping with *what*, Ralph?" she demanded. She looked at the images on the laptop, her eyes getting bigger and bigger by the second. "So it's true—you *are* spying on people in Lander County?"

"I'm not spying, Mom," Ralph said. "We're conducting surveillance of the area around Battle Mountain, looking for—"

"I don't care what the military propaganda says you're doing, Ralph—what you are doing is *spying* on American citizens." She whirled on Patrick. "I did not sign Ralph up for Civil Air Patrol to spy on fellow American citizens, General McLanahan," she said angrily. "How can you ask *children* to do such a thing?"

"Mrs. Markham, first and foremost: this is not a Civil Air Patrol activity," Patrick said. "We asked the cadets if they wanted to participate, but this is not authorized or sanctioned by the Civil Air Patrol. Secondly: this is not spying on anyone in particular, but performing surveillance over large areas of Lander, Humboldt, Pershing, Eureka, and Elko Counties, looking for evidence of terrorist and extremist activity. All we do is watch and report. Consider it a high-tech neighborhood watch program."

"With all due respect, General . . . are you *serious?*" Amanda asked. "This sounds like something out of Nazi Germany in the 1930s—asking kids to inform on their Jew neighbors and report them to the Gestapo so they could be rounded up for extermination."

"Ma'am, it's nothing like that at all," Fitzgerald said. "These are private individuals helping their community by staying on watch. You should be thanking them."

"*Thanking* them?" the woman asked incredulously. "This . . . this is *espionage,* against fellow Americans! This is an invasion of privacy! My son will have absolutely no part of this! Ralph, we're *leaving.*"

"But, Mom, I still have two grids to analyze before—"

"Ralph, we're leaving, *now.*" And with that, Amanda Markham towed her son out of the conference room.

Patrick escorted Amanda back to the front gate, then returned to the squadron. "Well, that's the second parent to pull their kid out just this morning," he said, "and the tenth since we started. The word's definitely getting around, and it's not good. I wonder how these folks are finding out about what we're doing? We're certainly not advertising it, especially since we're using improperly modified airplanes."

"We'll do the best we can with what we got, General," Todd Bishop said. "But Ralph was one of our best. The kid's got a sixth sense."

"Some folks just got no clue," Fitzgerald grumbled. "They expect the government to wet-nurse them, and the citizens should do nothing but roll over and play dead. Well, she's in for a rude awakening." He shook hands with Patrick. "Thanks again for checking on jobs for me, General. Much appreciated. Let me know about the Kellerman ranch—I've been there many times before." And he lumbered off.

Patrick thought for a few moments, then returned to Brad's workstation. "Wow, was Mrs. Markham mad," Brad said. "I can call Ron and see if he can take over."

"Okay," Patrick said. He studied Brad's monitor. "So do you have the Knights' defensive positions mapped out?"

"Sure—they're updated on every flight," Brad replied. "Couple guys in each nest, four-hour rotating shifts, and they change nests on every shift. We've even seen kids man those nests. But the big problem is not the machine-gun nests but those guys on the pickups with the heavier machine guns. They're mobile, they're fast, and they do roving patrols that change constantly—"

"And they're deadly," Patrick said. He thought for another moment, then spoke into his subcutaneous transceiver: "Whack? Charlie? Patrick here. Got a few minutes? . . . Yes, over at the squadron, where we set up the surveillance workstations. Thanks, guys." To Brad, he said, "I'm going to have Mr. Macomber and Miss Turlock look at what you have. Would you mind explaining your observations to them when they get here?"

"Sure, Dad. Why?"

"I think it's time to have a talk with the Knights of the True Republic," Patrick said. "The FBI set a confrontational tone with the Knights from day one, and we blindly followed along when we set up our own surveillance. I think it's time for that to change."

A few hours later, Ron Spivey walked into the squadron conference room. Brad was the only one using the laptops. "Hey, bro," Brad greeted him. "Where have you been? I only see you at practice these days. We could use some help around here."

"Working," Ron said wearily. "I gotta leave for the convenience store in Elko in a few minutes. I'm doing a twelve-hour shift there tonight."

"You sure are busting your hump these days."

"Yeah. I'm kinda glad they suspended the squadron's activities—gives me a little time for some rest." He sat beside Brad, but he didn't look at the laptop's screen. After several long moments he said, "Brad?"

"Yeah?"

Ron was silent until Brad looked at him, then said, "Marina's pregnant."

"What?"

Ron nodded. "We . . . actually found out a couple months ago," he said in a quiet voice, "but I wanted a paternity test done. We just found out today: chances are, it's mine. They can't tell you positively, only give you a percentage, but it's a pretty high percentage." He sighed, then said, "I guess I knew it was mine all along. Marina's been faithful. Me, not so much."

"Is this why you've been working your ass off on a dozen different jobs?"

Ron nodded, then looked up at Brad. "Marina wants to keep it," he said, the fear evident in his voice. "She told her parents— they noticed her morning sickness—and they *freaked,* and now my mom knows. I haven't spoken to her yet, but she calls me every ten minutes. What the hell am I going to do, Brad?"

"Sounds to me like you've already got a plan of action, bro—you're working your butt off, saving money for when the baby comes." He looked at his friend carefully. "That *is* what you're doing, right?"

"Well, of *course* it is, ass-wipe," Ron shot back. "What'd you think I was going to do—skip town?"

"It had crossed my mind," Brad said. He saw the hurt and disbelief on Ron's face. "Oh, give me a break, jerk-off. I see you with a different girl almost every day. You may be with Marina most of the time, but you can't say *you're* exclusive."

Ron's face turned crestfallen, then he lowered his head in shame. "I guess I have been a jerk," he said. "Marina didn't sleep around— that was me."

"Well, maybe the fickle finger of fate pointed you in the right direction after all."

"The what?"

"Forget it—old TV-show bit. What I'm saying is: maybe out of all the chicks you aimed your shotgun at, the right one got bagged."

That seemed to brighten Ron's entire demeanor for the first time in many days. "Yeah, maybe you're right," he said. He actually smiled. "Did you know Marina is half Greek and half Apache Indian? Can you imagine a Greek woman going at it with an Apache? She sure is a wildcat in the sack, that's for sure. And she can *actually* cook—not just reheat takeout, but make meals out of just random stuff in the cabinets. She wants to go to nursing school." He fell silent. "Shit, I guess a football college scholarship is out the window."

"You never know," Brad said. "Like they say: when one door closes, another opens."

Ron looked at him in mock disgust. "You been beating off while watching some chick flick again?" Brad laughed. Ron shrugged, still smiling. "Yeah, maybe that's true. I always thought Marina was just another lay—you know, date the high school football captain, trading sex for cash. But she actually saved the money I gave her, and she used some of it to pay for her doctor's bills—she didn't blow it on clothes and stuff. All this time I thought she was just this moody, clingy bitch, when it turns out she was nesting, trying to straighten me out." He was silent for a moment, then looked at his watch. "I gotta hit the road."

Brad smacked his friend on the back as hard as he dared. "Congrats, you SOB. You're going to be a dad. And you've actually got a plan."

"I wouldn't go giving me too much credit," Ron said, shrugging off the sting in his back. "My dad ran out on my mom a long time ago, and I know how tough it's been for her to raise two sons alone.

I'd hate to do that to some little kid of mine." He shook hands with Brad. "Thanks for listening, bro."

"Sure. See you at practice."

He watched Ron's face fall. "I . . . I'm not so sure," he said. "I got a chance for a full-time job at the overnight delivery company warehouse in Elko. I might drop out of high school after I turn eighteen in a couple months."

Brad was thunderstruck. "Are you sure you want to do that, Ron?"

Ron shrugged. "I hate school, Brad, you know that—the only reason I'm there is for football and girls," he said. "At the company I'll get a decent salary, medical and dental, a pension, and they'll help with getting a GED and an online bachelor's degree. After a year I could become a manager. And I actually like working there. I won't just be loading and unloading short-haul planes, but working toward a real career in the express shipping industry." He fell silent, then nodded. "I think it's the right thing to do."

Brad shook his head. "Man, you're freaking me out here, dude," he said. "You're turning into . . . like, a regular *guy,* right before my very eyes."

"Yeah, I know—it's hard for guys like me to be seen as anything else but an Adonis to you mere mortals." They both laughed at that one. "I'll see you soon, bro."

"Congrats again . . . Dad."

Ron nodded his thanks and left.

NINE

Duty cannot exist without faith.

— BENJAMIN DISRAELI

LATER THAT AFTERNOON

Patrick's desktop computer monitor showed the seal of the president of the United States. "Hold for the president, please," the White House operator said after she had initiated the secure video-conference. A few moments later, Patrick saw President Ken Phoenix, seated at his desk in the private study next to the Oval Office. Beside him was Vice President Ann Page, smiling warmly. "Patrick, how are you, buddy?"

"Fine, Mr. President. Good to see you. You too, Madam Vice President."

"It's been too long, Patrick." His expression turned serious. "I'll get right down to it, Patrick: I received a very serious accusation from the Justice Department this morning, something dealing with the FBI agents leading the surveillance operation against the extremists near you."

"The accusations are true, sir."

Phoenix's eyes widened in surprise. "You *threatened* three federal agents with *death?*"

"Yes, sir."

Phoenix sat back in his chair in complete shock. "The attorney general is screaming mad, Patrick. You used the CID robot and a Tin Man to threaten those agents with death? Why would you do something like that?"

"The agent from Homeland Security seduced Brad and lured him into a trap with the FBI," Patrick explained, "and then the FBI agents set up Brad so they could get him to inform on me. I don't suppose they mentioned any of that."

The president rubbed his temples. "Has the entire damned world gone mad?" he murmured. "Why would the FBI want to spy on you?"

"I don't know, sir."

"They said you've been uncooperative ever since violating no-fly airspace a while back."

"My attorney advised me not to answer any questions."

"Attorney General Horton told you that?"

"Yes, sir."

The president leaned forward and looked directly into the camera on his desktop computer. "Listen to me carefully, General," he said. "You will rescind this . . . this *death threat* immediately, and you will guarantee to me that those agents have nothing to fear from you, the CID, the Tin Man, or any technology or weapons you control."

"As long as I'm still free to protect my family, my community, and myself . . ."

The president held up a finger. "No conditions, Patrick. *None.* Agree to this, or I'll send the Marines to come get you, the CID, and the Tin Man. I'm not going to have anyone threaten a federal agent, even you." Patrick still hesitated. "I'm serious about this, my friend. If you have evidence that these agents did something illegal, turn it over to me, and I'll have the Justice Department's internal affairs look into it. But you *will not* go around threatening federal agents as long as I'm president." He paused, the anger level in his face slowly rising. *"Well?"*

"I guarantee no federal agents will be harmed, sir," Patrick said finally.

The president sat back in his chair. "That's better," he said after a few moments. "Just wait until Gardner gets hold of this. It'll be front-page news all around the world in no time. The only reason I don't bust you now, Patrick, is because I believe you will send me clear and convincing evidence of what those agents did to Bradley, and that it was outside their legal authority. I was the attorney general, Patrick, *remember?* I believe the FBI is the finest law enforcement and investigative agency in the world. I'm not going to let anyone threaten an FBI agent, even you."

"I'll have Darrow Horton send you the recordings, sir. I turned everything over to her."

"You do that—*soonest.*"

"She's requested an interview of Special Agent Renaldo of Homeland Security to verify the plan to entrap my son," Patrick said. "Renaldo invoked the Fifth Amendment and refused to cooperate."

"Let them handle it," the president said. "Next: you left a message with Ann saying you wanted to ask me something?"

"Yes, sir. I've been conducting surveillance of suspected extremist compounds in the Battle Mountain area, and—"

"You've been doing *what?*" the president interrupted. "What kind of surveillance?"

"Exactly the same kind that Special Agent Chastain was supposed to be doing," Patrick said, "but instead, he decided to trick my son into informing on *me.*"

"Has that desert heat fried your brain, Patrick?" the president asked. "Using what? The CID and Tin Man?"

"No, sir—Sky Masters sensors mounted on private aircraft."

"First the Iranians, then the Turks, the Russians, and now Americans," the president muttered. "Next you'll be spying on me, I suppose? I regret putting you and Jonathan Masters in the same half of the country again—the trouble you two get into never ceases to aggravate me." He thought for a moment; then: "I can think of a dozen different laws you've broken, but if anyone can keep you out of prison, it'll be Darrow Horton."

"At the risk of eating fruit from the forbidden tree," Vice President Page asked off-camera, "what have you found, Patrick?"

"That the FBI was barking up the wrong tree, ma'am," Patrick said. "I have a plan to try to fix the situation, Mr. President, and I need your permission to do a few things."

THAT SAME TIME

"So the deal is: I teach you how to pilot the CID, and you teach me how to fly," Charlie Turlock said. She, Jason Richter, and Brad were in the FBI hangar with the stowed Cybernetic Infantry Device. "Deal?"

"I'm not a licensed pilot yet," Brad said, "let alone a flight instructor. But I'll take you flying anytime as soon as I get my license, and as soon as I become a CFI, I'll teach you."

"Good enough," Charlie said. "Okay, before we get started, we have some programming to do so the CID will respond to your—"

"Already did it this morning with Colonel Richter, just before I asked you if we could train together," Brad said. "Voice prints and brain scans too. CID One, deploy." To Charlie's amazement, the CID unit began to unstow itself, and seconds later it had assumed its low crouching standby position.

"You did all that in just two hours?" Charlie remarked. "Usually it takes all day and a couple test runs to get it to respond properly."

"We did it in less than an hour," Brad said. Charlie turned to Jason in surprise, and Jason shrugged—he didn't understand why either. "Colonel Richter said they need to study me at the Battle-Lab to figure out why I can program so fast."

"I couldn't believe it myself," Jason said. "I thought we were just going to do a preliminary scan to get the input parameters set. We ended up running the entire routine."

"Let's see if it took. Keep going."

"CID One, pilot up," Brad spoke. The robot immediately assumed the boarding position, and the entry hatch opened on its back. Brad climbed up and slid inside as if he had been doing it all his life, as evidenced by the hatch closing on the robot's back as the haptic interface connected Brad's brain to the computers and sensors inside the robot. Moments later, the CID was up on its feet.

Brad looked at his hands and body like a frog that had just been turned into a prince. "Man, this is *incredible*!"

"Not so loud, Brad," Charlie said, smiling. "Well, this is a milestone. Savoy took two days to interface. Stand in the center of the hangar so you don't go crashing into things." Brad stepped forward, and Charlie saw no evidence of Brad's feet or legs hitting each other, as was common in new CID pilots. "It takes a while for the haptic interface to adjust for the differences between where you think your hands are and where the robot's hands are really—"

"Charlie, let's see if it was a fluke or the real deal," Jason said. He went over to the hangar wall and retrieved a cart with four bowling balls on it. "This is my favorite demonstration of the CID, Brad. Care to give it a try?"

"You *bet,* sir." Brad came over to him, and Jason tossed him one of the bowling balls. It landed on his right hand, but slipped out before he could close his composite armored fingers around it.

"Feet and legs are one thing, but fingers are another," Charlie said. "We have an exercise routine that'll help with programming the haptic interface to—"

"Wait a second . . . I call a do-over," Brad said. He picked up the bowling ball on the hangar floor with his fingers.

"Not too tightly," Charlie warned him. But Brad was definitely getting the hang of it. He tossed the bowling ball up in the air and caught it with one hand. "Not bad. Try . . ." But Brad began tossing the ball between two hands, then doing it faster, and then higher. Then he took another bowling ball and juggled the two in one hand, tossing one up while catching the other.

"Know how to juggle three balls, Brad?" Jason asked.

"No . . . but I can do hacky sack," Brad said . . . and to Jason and Charlie's amazement, he dropped one of the bowling balls on the instep of his right armored foot, held it there for a moment, then began flipping it up and down. In moments he was using every portion of his foot to kick the ball back in the air. Still carrying the second bowling ball, he then kicked the ball back and forth between his feet, bounced it off his chest and back onto his feet, kicked it up onto his head and balanced it there for a moment, then even kicked it back over his head, spun around, and caught it with a foot again. Before long Brad was prancing around the hangar, bouncing the bowling ball off his feet, his thighs, his chest, and his head as he moved.

"A-*mazing*," Jason breathed. "The guy's a natural."

"What else can you say: he's a McLanahan," Charlie said. "Definitely his father's son. He can fly, and he's a gadget nut."

"Let's bring it in, Brad," Jason said.

"Can we do some outdoor training tonight?" Brad asked in his electronically synthesized voice. "I can't wait to *really* open this baby up!"

"We're going to use it tonight," Charlie said. "And you have some studying to do on the electronics, electrical system, microhydraulics, sensors, and communications gear."

"Okay," Brad said. He stopped at the place where the CID was going to be stowed, flipped the bowling ball up into the air one last time, held his arms out straight with the second bowling ball in his left hand, then caught the first in his right hand without even looking. "Ta-*daaa*!" he cried out . . . then crushed both bowling balls in his armored hands, the balls exploding into clouds of dust with a loud *BAANG!*

"Definitely a McLanahan," Jason said.

KNIGHTS OF THE TRUE REPUBLIC'S COMPOUND

THAT EVENING

"Intruder inbound! Intruder inbound!" the loudspeakers through-out the compound blared. Men, women, and even children ran to preplanned response positions inside and outside the fenced inte-rior part of the compound. Men, women, and older boys carried weapons of all kinds, from small revolvers to heavy machine guns; children helped by carrying ammunition, lights, radios, and even water buckets in case they had to fight fires.

A lone four-door three-ton crew-cab pickup truck moved up the dirt road leading to the main entrance to the compound, stopped outside the cattle guard at the outer perimeter, and Patrick McLa-nahan got out of the driver's side. Several spotlights were trained on him. "You're on private property," a man with a bullhorn spoke. "You are trespassing. Turn around and go back to the main high-way immediately."

"My name is Patrick McLanahan. I want to speak with Rever-end Paulson."

"The reverend doesn't speak with strangers in the middle of the night. Go away."

"Tell the reverend that I was responsible for the FBI pulling out of the surveillance of your property," Patrick said. "Tell him I want to talk and make an offer to the residents of this compound to ter-minate the hostilities between you and the government."

There was silence for several minutes; then a different voice on the bullhorn said, "Say your name again, stranger."

"McLanahan. Patrick McLanahan."

There was another long pause; then the first voice said, "Is there anyone in the car with you?"

"Yes." Patrick turned toward the pickup. Brigadier-General

Kurt Givens emerged from the right-rear passenger seat . . . and Wayne Macomber, dressed in the Tin Man battle armor, got out of the front passenger side.

"Raise your hands, all of you!" the first man shouted. Patrick, Kurt, and Whack complied. "Is this your idea of talk, mister—sending in another robot after us?"

"Wayne insisted on coming along, as my bodyguard," Patrick said. "There is a Cybernetic Infantry Device, a manned robot, out there as well. Her job is to destroy the technicals and machine-gun emplacements if fighting breaks out. This is General Givens, the commander of Joint Air Base Battle Mountain."

"You want to start a war, mister, you've come to the right place! Now go away!"

"The general and I want to talk with Reverend Paulson," Patrick said. "Face-to-face. No one wants to start a war. I want to talk to Reverend Paulson about uniting our two communities."

There was another long pause; then the second voice said, "Bring out the robot and have it join you at the entrance." A few moments later they heard car horns beeping and floodlights illuminate all around the north side of the compound, and Charlie Turlock aboard the CID ran around the perimeter fence and joined Patrick and Whack.

"Is this how the government deals with fellow Americans?" the first voice blared angrily over the bullhorn. "Is this how—" And the voice abruptly cut off.

A few minutes later, Patrick saw a technical—a pickup truck with a heavy-gauge machine gun mounted in back, manned by a standing gunner—drive to the compound entrance, and a man emerged from the passenger side. He was tall and very thin, with long silver hair, wearing a black suit, white shirt, bolo tie—and, Patrick noticed, what appeared to be an Uzi slung on his shoulder. "Mr. McLanahan?" he asked.

Patrick stepped forward. Wayne moved forward with him. Patrick could feel dozens of gun muzzles swing in his direction, and he could see the technical on the pickup truck nervously switching aim between him, the CID, and the Tin Man. He held out a hand. "It's okay, Whack."

"That wasn't the deal, General," Wayne said, his electronically synthesized voice booming. "We agreed I was going to come with you at all times or we weren't going to do this."

"'General'?" the newcomer called out. "General Patrick McLanahan?"

"Yes."

The newcomer moved away from the compound entrance, stepped over to the Wrangler, and held out a hand. "I'm happy to meet you, General," the man said. "I am Reverend Jeremiah Paulson."

Patrick shook his hand. "Nice to meet you too, sir."

"Your reputation precedes you, sir." Paulson extended a hand to Givens. "We met many years ago, General, when you first took command of the base," he said. "You held many community forums every year to address issues between the local area and the base, and you've hosted many open-house and other events for the community."

"I think an important part of being base commander is open and frequent dialogue between the base and the community, Reverend," Givens said, shaking hands. "Unfortunately, those kinds of activities had to be curtailed as our funding was cut, our operations were reduced, and the people lost interest in the base. But I intend to reverse that."

"That is long overdue, General Givens." Paulson looked up at the CID and shook his head. "Such incredible technology," he said in a low voice. "Too bad it's being used against innocent American citizens."

"That was the FBI's idea, sir," Patrick said. "The White House authorized their use because of the radiological attacks in Reno. The FBI is gone now."

"But the robot and this man remain?"

"Yes, under my command."

"And what is your 'command,' General?" Paulson asked. "Why were you sent to Nevada to talk to me?"

"I wasn't sent, sir—I live here," Patrick said. "I've lived on the air base since January. I previously commanded the air wing here."

"Indeed? I was not aware of it. A man such as yourself, living out here in obscurity . . . interesting. What is it you do at the base?"

"I'm retired," Patrick said. "I fly volunteer missions for the Civil Air Patrol, mostly search-and-rescue missions; I fly volunteer charity medical missions for Angel Flight West; and I raise an eighteen-year-old son."

"Very good," Paulson said. "Being a responsible, God-fearing parent and serving your community are two of the most noble things a man can do. But why is a retired military officer given devices such as these? Under what authority do you use them?"

"At first I wasn't given any authority to use them, Reverend Paulson," Patrick replied. "They're here; my community and friends are in danger; I know how to employ them—so I acted. I've recently been given limited authority to use them by the president of the United States."

"Against the residents of this community?"

"Against threats to *our* community, sir," Patrick said. "The FBI believes you are a threat. I don't. I have to prove to the president that I'm right."

"Otherwise the war between us will continue."

"Reverend Paulson, I'm willing and ready to do whatever it takes to safeguard my home," Patrick said, "and I'm willing to battle anyone who wants to take away our freedom. So far, I haven't seen any evidence that you are an enemy. You have weapons, you have a stronghold, you have followers ready to take up arms and defend their home . . . well, so do we at Joint Air Base Battle Mountain, and we're not an enemy to the community either. We need to join together to find the common enemy and eliminate it."

"I am a minister, a spiritual leader only," Paulson said. "The people of this community came to this place and built their homes around my original church because they felt safer living together. We are all sovereign citizens, followers of the original U.S. Constitution and the laws of God. I don't give orders."

"I have no followers, Reverend," Patrick said. "As I said, I'm retired. I have no command or hold any office. But I am going to use the tools available to me to protect my family, my home, and my community. We share that goal. We should work together to accomplish that mission."

Paulson looked Patrick up and down, then nodded. "What do you propose, General McLanahan?"

Patrick turned to Givens. "Kurt?"

"Come live with us," Givens said to Paulson.

"Live with you? On the air base?"

"There's plenty of room for everyone," Givens said. "The base used to house almost six thousand, and we were in the process of expanding it to seven thousand—we have fewer than one thousand now. We have medical facilities, shopping, fitness, and recreation venues that are hardly used."

"I think that is a very generous offer, General Givens," Paulson said, "but most of the members of this community are distrustful of the government already—they won't want to move right into its lap by moving onto a military base."

"For those who don't want to move, they can stay out here," Buzz said. "But for those who are living in tents or those with young children, the base facilities might be better, at least temporarily. And even if you don't choose to move, the base's facilities will be open for everyone."

"But . . . how can this be possible?" Paulson said. "We have no money for any of this."

"President Kenneth Phoenix has issued a presidential order, directing the commanders of military installations all over the world to help struggling people in their local area however they can, consistent with the military mission and security, until the economic crisis is over," Patrick said. "Joint Air Base Battle Mountain will be one of the first to implement the policy."

"All persons who are able to work will be asked to work," Givens went on. "If paid jobs are available, they'll be paid, and some of the money used to defray expenses; otherwise, everyone able to work will be asked to contribute their skills and abilities to do jobs around the base that need to be done. The Department of Defense will provide subsidized food, shelter, utilities, education, job training, and health care."

"We have to start thinking about one community rather than separate civilian and military ones," Patrick said. "The separate communities only cause distrust and resentment."

"Won't some soldiers resent having outsiders on their base, eating their food and using their facilities without having to swear an oath, put on a uniform, or pick up a gun?" Paulson asked.

"Perhaps," Patrick said. "But I don't see the people in your community as malingerers—they seem ready to work if a task is needed. The military respects hard work and dedication. If everyone pulls together, this can work."

Paulson half turned toward the technical behind him. "I assume things such as that won't be allowed."

"You'll be treated like every other soldier and civilian employee on base," Givens said. "Legal firearms on base must be registered and stored in our armory, and will be fitted with an identification and tracking tag that assures they're not kept or carried on base; illegal or unregistered weapons won't be allowed. You will be allowed access to your firearms at any time as long as they are immediately taken off the base, and the ID tag will monitor that."

"What other limitations to personal freedoms will be imposed on us by the government?" Paulson asked.

"I don't know, Reverend—we're just starting this thing tonight," Givens said honestly. "We're starting from the standpoint that civilian residents on base will be given all the responsibilities and freedoms afforded to military residents. Our military members do give up a lot of their constitutional freedoms in the interest of base security and accomplishing the mission."

"This will be a work in progress, Reverend," Patrick said. "But the idea is not to limit your freedom, but to support you during tough economic times. You are free to leave at any time if you feel the loss of your rights outweighs the benefits extended to you by the government."

"I don't think this will be of much interest to the members of this community, General," Paulson said. "Living out here means freedom for these people, even if the conditions are sometimes harsh."

"We think they might be worse than harsh, Reverend," Patrick said. "We've noticed that two of your crop circles are dying."

"How would you know this, General?"

"I have been conducting aerial surveillance of about three thousand square miles around the air base, including this compound," Patrick replied. "My sensors detected the dying crops and the malfunctioning irrigation sprinklers."

"More of using whatever devices are at hand for your own purposes, General McLanahan?" Paulson asked suspiciously. He straightened his shoulders. "I do not approve of this, sir, and I do not approve of you," he said acidly. "General Givens, I thank you and the president for your offer, and I will present the idea to the people of this community tomorrow morning at community breakfast. If anyone wishes to move, they will be allowed to do so at any time. I will place them in contact with you and arrange a time for the transfer.

"But I will also advise them of General McLanahan's use of this combat technology and surveillance operations," Paulson went on, "and I will be candid with them: I believe General McLanahan to be as much an extremist as the others who roam this state and harm law-abiding citizens, and placing yourselves under his protection is the moral equivalent of endorsing his anticonstitutional actions. He is violating his oath to serve and defend the Constitution, and as such is a criminal in the eyes of the people and of God almighty.

"If anyone wants to leave this place, they are welcome, but I believe *you,* General McLanahan, to be an affront to the United States Constitution and the laws of God, and those who leave us and join you will be considered traitors to our community and faith. Never come back here, General McLanahan—you are hereby declared an enemy of the Knights of the True Republic. You have fifteen minutes to get off of our property or you will be considered criminal trespassers and dealt with accordingly." And he spun on a heel and walked back to the technical.

"Well, I think that went swimmingly," Charlie Turlock deadpanned in her electronically synthesized voice from inside the Cybernetic Infantry Device. After Paulson and the technical departed, the CID assumed the dismount position, and Charlie climbed out and ordered the CID to fold itself up for transport. "Think anyone will take us up on the offer?"

"And be excommunicated from Paulson's church? I don't think so," Whack said. He helped Charlie stow the CID in the back of the pickup. "Are you sure the FBI was wrong about these people, Patrick? Paulson's definitely got a one-track mind—and it's not a very peaceful track."

"I'm not a cop—I could be completely wrong about them," Patrick said. "Paulson may be a zealot and even an extremist, but a homicidal maniac using planes and radiological dirty bombs? I don't know."

"He could have an entire faction within his community doing the attacks, with Paulson's blessing," Whack said.

"I suggest we get out of here before we find out Paulson's watch is running fast," Buzz said. They climbed into the pickup and headed off back to Battle Mountain.

ELKO, NEVADA

LATER THAT NIGHT

Ron Spivey made liberal use of his employee discount to buy energy drinks to help stay awake during these graveyard shifts working at the convenience store outside of town. Well, he thought, only a couple more months of this, and then I'll concentrate on the new path. He was anxious to get started on it.

The night-shift manager, a woman named Matilda, was behind the counter. Ron took a broom and dustpan and headed out the door. "I'm going on parking-lot patrol, Matilda," he said.

"Bathrooms must be next, Ron," she said.

"Okay." Matilda insisted on spotless bathrooms, so he was sent back to do them after almost every customer used them. Another good reason to get the heck out and start a *real* career, he thought. He had a lot of newfound respect for persons who cleaned johns for a living.

It was a perfect summer evening—clear as a bell, not too hot, not too cold, no thunderstorms, and gentle breezes. The store was pretty quiet, but the truck stop about a quarter of a mile down the frontage road seemed busier than usual. Another sign that the economy was turning around? You wouldn't know it by business at the convenience store, but more truckers seemed to be on the road these days. The express shipping business was definitely hiring, so maybe things were starting to look up?

Ron laughed at himself. Sheesh, when did he ever think about stuff like the economy before? Maybe having a baby and a future wife changes a guy's perspective—even a brainless skirt-chasing jock's.

Finally, a customer. The car pulled up to the gas pump island farthest from the store, the one with the burned-out overhead fluorescents—he would have to get the big ladder out to change those. One guy got out, while the other guy stayed in the car. They were talking to each other through the windows, but Ron couldn't make out what they were saying. The parking lot was in pretty good shape, no broken beer bottles or the puddles of vomit that were more common on the weekends. The two guys' voices over on the far island were getting a bit louder. Uh-oh, he thought, boyfriends having a little late-night to-do? At last, some entertainment . . .

. . . and just then, out of the corner of his eye, he saw it—the gesture made by the guy pumping gas, his hand like a knife, jabbing at the guy in the car . . . exactly like the guy he saw in the car that hit Brad had been doing! Holy shit, he thought, could it be *them,* the same car . . . ?

Sweeping as he moved, Ron casually moved across the front of the store, trying to take his time but anxious to get a look before these guys drove off. It took him almost two minutes to move around, and it was a little hard to see because of the burned-out lights, but he finally saw it—the cracks in the windshield where he had hit it with his football helmet! Jesus Christ, they're *here!* He quickly headed back toward the store entrance, pulling his cell phone from his pocket.

"Hello?"

"Brad, it's me."

"Ron? It's almost three A.M., you dork. What's—"

"Shut up, dude. Those guys that hit you after practice? They're *here,* man."

Brad was now fully awake. "They are? Are you sure?"

"I saw the cracked windshield where I hit it with my helmet!"

"Holy crap! Did you call the cops?"

"No, not yet. I'll do it right . . . oh, shit, oh, shit, Brad, *they're coming into the store!*"

324   DALE BROWN

"What?"

"They're wearing hats and sunglasses, and they—" Now Ron was screaming, in a tone of voice Brad had never heard before: "Wait a minute, wait, no, no, *no* . . . !" And just then, Brad heard two gunshots, the clattering of the phone hitting the floor, a woman's scream, and two more gunshots. He then heard footsteps, murmured voices in an unintelligible language, and then a loud crunching sound, followed by chilling silence.

JOINT AIR BASE BATTLE MOUNTAIN

SEVERAL DAYS LATER

"Dozens of families a day from all over northern Nevada, California, Utah, and southern Oregon are making their way to Joint Air Base Battle Mountain here in the high desert of north-central Nevada to take part in a new government program to provide shelter, food, medical care, and jobs to the neediest among us," the television reporter was saying. Viewers could see three school buses approaching the base's main gate. "This is day three of President Phoenix's controversial new executive order that opens the gates, and the purses, of military bases around the world to civilians desperately in need of help."

Patrick was watching the television in his office, with Brad beside him. He didn't want his son out of sight for more than a couple minutes. The funeral for Ron Spivey, yet another Civil Air Patrol member gunned down by shadowy unknown assassins in just the past few weeks, was hard on everyone, but especially on Brad. His son rarely spoke and, as now, mostly sat staring off into space. His appetite was nonexistent, and he stayed mostly in his bedroom in their trailer, lying in bed but not sleeping.

There was a knock on the office door, and Timothy Dobson entered. He stood in front of Patrick's desk. "I'm so very sorry, Brad," he said in a quiet voice. "I wish I could've stopped them." Brad did not move a muscle.

"Were you able to identify them, Tim?" Patrick asked.

Dobson nodded. "Officially they are security officers assigned to the Russian consulate in Vancouver, British Columbia," he replied, "but Interpol says they are direct-action operatives of the *Glavnoye Razvedyvatel'noye Upravleniye,* or GRU, the Russian military foreign-intelligence service. The Russian foreign ministry denies all this. When asked of their current whereabouts, the ministry claims the men are on their way back to Russia as scheduled." Patrick nodded, his eyes filled with hate. "They are on all the no-fly and most-wanted lists. But they've been very successful so far in slipping away in plain sight." He looked at Brad. "You two are not safe outside the base, and with all these civilians coming in now, you may not even be safe here. The vice president is urging you—"

"I'm not leaving," Patrick said. "That's final. I'm not running. I'll find a way to locate these guys, and I'll hunt them down and eliminate them myself."

"They're professional killers, General," Dobson said. "They can move and blend in almost at will—"

"They may be professionals, but they made an amateurish mistake by being caught on a half-dozen security cameras that night," Patrick said. "They've got their faces on thousands of computer screens and wanted posters all over North America. They're under pressure to perform instead of missing their target, which will make them sloppy and vulnerable."

"Maybe so, sir," Dobson said, "but all the Russians have to do is bring in a different team. The chase starts all over again, with different faces."

"That would happen if we were in Washington too," Patrick said. "No, I'll find a way to stop them." He went back to watching the television; Dobson had nothing further to say, so he departed. A few minutes later, Patrick stood. "I'm going to meet the new group and help them get settled," he said to Brad. "Come along with me." After a moment's hesitation, Brad stood, his head still lowered. But just then, there was a knock on the door. "Come." Patrick was surprised to see Judah Andorsen come through the door, and he shot to his feet. "Mr. Andorsen! This is a surprise."

"Hope I'm not botherin' you, General," Andorsen said in his big, booming voice. He was wearing his usual outfit, the only one Patrick had ever seen him in: leather flying jacket, jeans, boots, cowboy hat, and leather work gloves. He shook hands with Patrick, then looked over at Brad. "This is your son, right? The one that found that crash survivor?"

"I don't believe you've met him, sir," Patrick said. "Mr. Andorsen, this is my son, Brad. Brad, this is Mr. Judah Andorsen." Brad raised his eyes just long enough to shake Andorsen's hand.

"Hey, I'm sorry about your friend, son," Andorsen said. "The news said it was an attempted robbery, and when your friend tried to call the cops, they went crazy." Dobson had somehow managed to get control of the security-camera tapes, so no one knew that it was really an assassination rather than a botched robbery. "You doin' okay, son?"

"Yes, sir," Brad said.

"We were just on our way out to meet the new arrivals, Mr. Andorsen," Patrick said.

"I don't want to keep you, General," Andorsen said. "I just wanted to stop in and say how proud I am to know you. Word has it that this whole program openin' up the base to folks from these camps was your idea."

"The base commander, Kurt Givens, and I came up with it," Patrick said. "The White House and Department of Defense signed on quickly."

"That's fine work, General, fine work," Andorsen said. "I want to help by hirin' some of the men who will be staying here. Miners, ranch hands, drivers, general laborers—I'm sure I can find at least temporary work for a good many of the men."

"That would be incredible, sir," Patrick said. "Thank you."

"It ain't nuthin', General," Andorsen said. "Now, I know a lot of these men lived in religious-like camps and communities, and— nothin' against God and religion and all—I don't have much use for the real hard-core holy rollers, if you get my meanin'. I don't want no illegals either. Nothin' against Mexicans or other hard-workin' folks from Guatemala or wherever, but if they sneaked across the border without botherin' to register like you're supposed to, they can starve, for all I care."

"You're the boss, Mr. Andorsen," Patrick said. "You hire anyone you wish. Any help you can extend would be great."

"If I could get a list with the names and work experience from you, General, I might be able to line up work for them within a week or two. No promises, mind you, but I think I can lend a hand. We'll provide transportation to and from and meals on the job site, of course, and we can probably kick in a little for some work clothing."

"I'll start compiling a list of those who want to work and get it to you as soon as I can, sir," Patrick said. He shook hands. "Thank you again."

"Don't mention it, General. Happy to help." Andorsen's attention was drawn to the TV screen. "Looks like someone called an ambulance." Patrick watched as an ambulance from Andorsen Memorial Hospital made its way on the wrong side of the highway toward the base, lights and siren running. It was followed by a Battle Mountain Fire Department fire chief's car, which stopped about thirty yards behind the ambulance. The ambulance stopped beside the middle of the three school buses. Curious passengers exiting the buses stopped to watch out the windows.

Patrick picked up his telephone and pressed a button. "Command post, this is Sierra Alpha Seven," he spoke. "Who called an ambulance? What happened?"

"Where in hell are those bozos runnin' off to?" Andorsen asked. The TV cameras showed two paramedics rush out of the ambulance and run back to the fire chief's car. "What, they gotta ask permission from the chief before they . . . hey, where's he goin'?" They saw the fire chief's car spin around and head away from the base. "What the hell is this? Why did they—"

And at that instant, a brilliant flash of light, a ball of fire, and a cloud of black smoke obscured the TV image. The middle school bus was blown apart almost instantly; the other two buses were tossed aside like toys and set ablaze.

KNIGHTS OF THE TRUE REPUBLIC'S COMPOUND

THAT NIGHT

Each gunner and driver manning the weaponized pickup trucks saw, heard, and felt the same thing before the lights went out: a hard *thump* beside the truck, a blur of motion, and a hard blow to the side of the head. "That's the last technical," Charlie Turlock radioed from within the Cybernetic Infantry Device after she neutralized both the gunner and the driver. She reached over and bent the barrel of the machine gun mounted on the technical in a right angle as easily as bending a straw.

"Machine-gun nests are neutralized as well," Wayne Macomber, wearing the Tin Man armor, radioed. "They were only half manned, mostly by older guys."

"We detected two less technicals than before," Rob Spara, manning the bank of laptops at the squadron, radioed. John de Carteret was orbiting the Knights of the True Republic's compound overhead at 9,500 feet, maintaining real-time surveillance and acting as a communications relay node for this operation. The sensor images were being beamed to Charlie and Whack as well as to Rob. "They must've lost more residents than we thought."

"I'm moving in," Patrick radioed. He was in the crew-cab pickup, with David Bellville driving, heading up the dirt road toward the compound. "Heads up, everyone."

But it was soon apparent that the layers of defenses set up around the compound were gone, replaced by residents with little more than walkie-talkies and flashlights. Patrick and David were not challenged—in fact, some of the residents left their post and followed Patrick's pickup toward the inner compound.

The gates to the inner compound were wide open, and David

drove right up to the church and outdoor meeting area. There was several sheriffs' patrol cars parked there as well. Patrick and David got out of the pickup and were met moments later by Whack. The meeting area was about half full. The residents seated there were silent, not moving—no one turned to look at them. "This is weird—kinda Jonestown-like," Whack radioed.

The three walked up the main aisle toward the dais. Again, no one made a motion to stop them or even looked up. Reverend Jeremiah Paulson was standing at the lectern, dressed all in black, his head bowed, a Bible in one hand, his Uzi still slung on his shoulder.

"Come on out in sight, Charlie," Patrick radioed. A few moments later, the CID approached the meeting area from the opposite side and walked right up to the last row of chairs, towering over the seated residents. Again, no one turned to look at it. They heard babies crying and a few sobs, but no one spoke or even moved.

Patrick stepped forward and stopped at the edge of the platform on which Paulson stood. "Reverend Paulson, what's going on here?" he asked.

"This is a memorial service for our murdered family members," Paulson said. "We are in deep mourning. We are observing a period of silent vigil that will last until daybreak."

"'Family members'?" Patrick asked. "They're not traitors to your community anymore?"

"They were never traitors, General," Paulson said. "They were always members of our family. They are now martyrs in the civil war that is tearing the Constitution and this nation apart."

"How many did you lose, Reverend?"

"Twenty-seven killed or wounded, including eleven children," Paulson said. "Whoever did such a thing is a monster and needs to be eliminated."

"Reverend, the FBI thought you engineered the attacks in Reno and Pahrump and the missile attacks against the drones doing surveillance over your compound." Paulson said nothing. "Many

believe you were responsible for today's bombing outside the base."
Still no response. "You weren't involved in any of them, were you?"

"We are a peaceful community, General," Paulson said. "Yes,
we have weapons, but they are weapons for self-defense only. We
would never attack innocents—only those who seek to do our
community harm. We care nothing about being spied upon, as
long as we are left alone to live our lives as God and the framers of
the Constitution intended."

"Then why didn't you speak out against any of it, Reverend?"
Patrick asked. "Why didn't you cooperate with the FBI, allow
them to search the compound? They could have refocused their
resources on the real extremists."

"I think you know exactly why I did not, General," Paulson
said, looking directly at Patrick for the first time. "The Fourth
Amendment to the Constitution of the United States of America.
The FBI had no warrants to search our homes—they wanted to
search simply because they wanted it, and that is not permitted in
the United States under the Constitution. Simply because a horrific
disaster or crime occurs is no reason to suspend the Constitution.
Do you agree, General?"

"I do, Reverend," Patrick said. "I refused to talk with the FBI
without my attorney present, even though a nationwide state of
emergency existed and almost every other member of my squadron
had already cooperated. They tried to blackmail my son to inform
on me for them."

"Then you understand completely," Paulson said. "We have a
right to be secure in our persons, houses, papers, and effects against
unreasonable searches and seizures. There is no caveat, no exceptions, no provision that says, 'Unless the FBI orders otherwise.'"
He sighed. "But there is too much distrust in our community, and
it is tearing us apart. We have decided to disband."

"You're breaking up the Knights of the True Republic?"

"I think the true believers will still push for true freedom, less government, and more personal responsibility," Paulson said, "but the idea that we can live apart from our neighbors in our own purist society is not realistic. Rather than ensuring our own happiness and security, it has turned our neighbors against us. That was not our goal."

"So what will happen?" Patrick asked.

"Most will go to your air base, look for work, and join with others to form a stronger, tighter community, with the help of the federal government and the military," Paulson said. "Some will probably join other independent communities; a few will try to form their own cells of like-minded idealists. Everyone is free to do whatever he or she chooses. As for this community: some will stay and try to keep it alive, but in the end, it's not separation and anonymity that guarantees success, but cooperation and community. We forgot that truth years ago, and it's hurt us. It's time to support the greater community once again."

Paulson reached down from the dais and extended a hand. "It was a great privilege to meet you, General McLanahan," he said. Patrick shook his hand. "You are indeed a patriot. I believed you wanted to use your technology to destroy our community. I see that I was mistaken. One word of advice, however: don't rely too much on the technology. You have some fine people here that want to help you rid our community of extremists—rely on *them* instead."

"I will, Reverend," Patrick said. He turned and started to leave . . .

. . . when suddenly Whack rushed forward between Patrick and the dais and shouted, *"General, get down!"* Paulson had dropped the Bible, swung the Uzi up into his hands, and aimed . . .

. . . but not at Patrick . . . he aimed upward from the bottom of his jaw. He closed his eyes, shouted, "God bless the True Republic!" and pulled the trigger. Except for a few children who cried out at the gunshot, no one in the audience moved or said a word as the lifeless body hit the dais.

JOINT AIR BASE BATTLE MOUNTAIN

A SHORT TIME LATER

Patrick led the others into the FBI hangar, with Whack carrying the folded-up CID unit himself. Patrick was surprised to see Michael Fitzgerald there, examining the bullet-ridden wreckage of the second Cybernetic Infantry Device, which had been hit by gunners in the Knights of the True Republic's compound. "Hey, Fid," Patrick said.

Fitzgerald looked at amazement at the Tin Man as Whack set the stowed CID unit in its charging cradle. "Who in hell are *you*?" he exclaimed. Whack didn't answer him, but took off his helmet, then removed the battery packs on his waist and put them into their chargers.

"It's kind of late to explain, Fid," Patrick said wearily. "What's going on?"

"I went over to the squadron to see if you needed any help with the surveillance," Fitzgerald said, "and Rob said you'd be over here. What happened? Where were you guys?"

"Out at the Knights' compound."

"Did you fight it out with them? I heard they have all sorts of weapons out there."

"No."

"Did you get to talk with Reverend Paulson? That guy is a real piece of work. He's definitely crazy enough to have loaded that ambulance up with explosives and killed all those people."

Patrick dropped into a chair, emotionally drained. "Paulson is dead," he said.

"Dead?" Fitzgerald immediately looked over at Whack. "Did you kill him?"

"Suicide," Whack said in a low voice.

"No shit," Fitzgerald said. "I'll bet the Knights will be on the warpath tomorrow."

"They're coming onto the base," Patrick said. "The Knights disbanded, and the compound is wide open, not guarded anymore."

"Wow—the Knights, disbanded," Fitzgerald breathed, shaking his head in disbelief. "Now I'll bet the cops can go in there and search for any more of that radioactive shit they've been using against government buildings."

"We searched," Patrick said, rubbing his eyes. "We didn't find anything. No explosives, no radioactive material, no shoulder-fired surface-to-air missiles. Just lots of guns and a few old light antitank launchers."

"No shit," Fitzgerald said. "So . . . so what does that mean?"

"It means we keep searching," Patrick said. "We start all over, first thing tomorrow morning."

"Well, you may be onto something with the Kellerman place," Fitzgerald said. "Somebody's definitely been out there—it looks like some supplies have been brought in, food and water, and the power's been turned back on. No sign of the place being broken into."

"Thanks, Fid," Patrick said. His brain was just too worn out to process this new information. "We'll meet tomorrow to plan our next moves."

"See you tomorrow, General." Fitzgerald took one last look at the Tin Man, the stowed CID, and the broken-up CID as he headed out the door.

"One of your Civil Air Patrol guys?" Whack asked, watching Fitzgerald depart.

"Michael Fitzgerald," Patrick said. "Lost his job with the Nevada Department of Wildlife just a few months from retirement, probably because of the FBI."

"He sure doesn't look ex-military."

"You don't need to be ex-military to join the Civil Air Patrol,"

Patrick said. "He specializes in cadet ground-strike teams. He's a good guy." He got to his feet. "I'm going home, guys. I don't want to leave Brad alone too long if I can help it. He's pretty busted up about his friend Ron."

"Why don't you just stay home for a couple days with Brad, maybe fly on out to see your mom in Scottsdale?" Charlie Turlock suggested. "General Givens has got the incoming community members taken care of—if we get any more, because of that ambush today—and we'll keep on helping with surveillance. If anything crops up, we'll give you a call and we can decide how to handle it."

Patrick said nothing for several long moments, then nodded. "That sounds really good, Charlie," he said. "I'd hate to lose a surveillance plane, but the Bonanza should be ready soon, so we'll be back to two planes. And it'd be good for Brad to see his grandma and aunts. I'll see how he feels. We can make it his dual cross-country, and if he feels up to it, he can fly his solo cross-countries from Scottsdale. That's all he needs for his check ride."

"Then he can take me flying, right?" Charlie asked. "He promised, as soon as he got his private pilot's license."

"Sure. He's a good stick, and the turbine Centurion is a nice ride."

"Cool. Hey, speaking of piloting—did Jason tell you about Brad piloting the CID?" Charlie asked.

"What?" The weariness in Patrick's face disappeared in a heartbeat, replaced by surprise and concern. "No! Brad was in the CID? When?"

"The afternoon before we first went to the Knights' compound." Charlie could see Patrick's face turning dark, and she added quickly, "He told me he got permission from you to ask Jason and me to check him out in the CID. You gave him permission, didn't you?"

"Yes, but . . . I don't want him training to pilot the CID anymore."

"Okay," Charlie said, a bit of confusion in her face. "But he's really good in it, a real natural. You should have seen him doing hacky sack with a—"

"No 'buts,' Charlie," Patrick said. "The CID was designed as a one-man killing machine, and the last thing Brad needs to be exposed to now is more killing." He remembered his close friend Hal Briggs, and how the normally cool, calm, collected Air Force security expert and Army Ranger literally went berserk when he entered combat aboard a Cybernetic Infantry Device—he eventually ran into a massed assault by Iranian Revolutionary Guards and was killed in battle while trying to destroy Iranian nuclear missiles. "No more CID training."

"Okay, Patrick."

Patrick spun on a heel without another word and departed.

"He looks totally stressed out," Charlie said to Whack.

"He's putting a lot of pressure on himself, and he's going to burn himself out if he's not careful," Whack said. "Good suggestion, Charlie, him getting out of town with his son. I hope he's smart enough to take it."

SCOTTSDALE, ARIZONA

A FEW DAYS LATER

It was an absolutely spectacular flight from Battle Mountain to Sacramento Executive Airport for Patrick, Gia, and Brad. Patrick planned the trip as a dual cross-country lesson: Brad had to make stops at three different airports spaced at least one hundred miles apart, at least one of which had to have a control tower, and he had to draw up a flight plan and annotate a sectional chart with the route of flight, visual checkpoints, and timing points. He also had to file a VFR flight plan, get a complete flight briefing by phone, talk to flight service to open and close his flight plan, and give and receive an in-flight weather observation to Flight Watch. Although Brad knew how to fly on instruments-only and was adept at using the advanced avionics in the P210 turbine Centurion, he had to demonstrate that he could navigate using "dead reckoning"—using time, the compass, and landmarks on the ground to determine where he was.

Patrick's two sisters, Nancy and Margaret, still lived in Sacramento and still ran the little Irish pub downtown that had been in the McLanahan family for three generations. After Patrick, Gia, and Brad arrived and were settled in, the five made a visit to the historic family memorial complex at the Old City Cemetery, just six blocks south of the state capitol. So many McLanahans had been buried in the cemetery over the past 150 years that many called it the "McLanahan Cemetery." For the past fifteen years, the cemetery no longer had room for any more burials, so Patrick's father, a retired veteran city police sergeant with thirty years wearing a badge, was the last of the McLanahans to be interred there— Patrick's wife Wendy's and his brother Paul's inurnment markers were in the historic family columbarium erected at the cemetery, as were vacant niches for the rest of the family.

Patrick and Brad spent a long time touching Wendy's marker, as did Margaret and Nancy with Paul's, with Gia respectfully looking on. Finally, Patrick kissed his wife's and brother's markers and patted them reassuringly. "I think it's so sweet that you decided to keep Wendy here, instead of bringing her to Arlington National Cemetery," Margaret said as they left the cemetery. "What an honor, for you and her to be laid to rest at such a historic place as Arlington, if you chose."

"It would be," Patrick said, "but I wouldn't be buried anywhere else but here, with the rest of the family. And this place is older and just as historic as Arlington."

The next morning, Patrick loaded Gia, Brad, and his sisters into the P210 Centurion, and they flew to Deer Valley Airport near Scottsdale, Arizona. Patrick's mother, Maureen, lived in an assisted-living facility nearby. Patrick's arrival became a major event, not only for his mother but also for every resident of the facility. They were invited for dinner with the residents, but Patrick hardly had a chance to eat because everyone wanted their picture taken with and an autograph from the famous aviator and general.

Patrick had registered them in the Scottsdale Princess Hotel using his middle name, Shane, instead of Patrick so they were able to enjoy a much greater level of anonymity as they sat out at the pool bar with drinks. Brad had gone upstairs to watch TV and chat with his friends back home, and Gia was on her way to a twelve-step meeting in Scottsdale. "This is very nice." Patrick sighed as he settled in with his second Balvenie single-malt Scotch. "The air and the temperature are the same, but Battle Mountain doesn't have anything as grand as this."

"Why in the world would you leave Las Vegas for someplace like Battle Mountain?" his sister Nancy asked. "I looked it up: it's a bump in the interstate, and always has been."

"I'm there not because of what Battle Mountain *is,* but because of what it *can be*," Patrick replied. "The base is an incredible facility. It's over seven thousand acres, with a hundred acres *underground*."

"Underground? How is that possible?"

"It's one of the most incredible engineering feats on the planet," Patrick said. "We can park B-52 bombers *sixty feet underground*. But that's not the best thing about Battle Mountain. It's centrally located between Salt Lake City, Portland, Reno, Sacramento, Phoenix, San Diego, Las Vegas, Seattle, and Denver, so it has a huge pool of well-educated talent it can draw from for advanced research and development. It has almost unlimited airspace for flying, it has pretty good weather most of the year, and easy access to Air Force and Navy restricted airspace for flight testing. Land and housing are cheap." He paused for a few moments, adopting his infamous "ten-thousand-yard stare" that even his sisters recognized. "It just needs someone to . . . to *commit* to it. It's ready to contribute, if someone would just commit."

"What the hell are you babbling about, big brother?" Margaret asked. She giggled. "Or is that just the second Balvenie talking?"

Patrick chuckled, then waved a hand. "I'm just babbling," he said, taking another sip of whiskey. "It's all moot anyway. The air base is closing down soon; they'll probably close down the airfield because the county can't afford the upkeep, and I've been asked to go back to Washington."

"Really? Doing what?"

"I can't talk about it yet," Patrick said. "It's not even a paid position. But we wanted to keep Brad in school in Battle Mountain to finish with his senior class. Once Brad is off to college, Gia and I will go to Washington."

"You and Gia," Nancy said. "Is there a 'you and Gia,' Patrick?"

He shrugged. "I hope so," he said. "Gia's working through some tough personal problems. By the time we get ready for the move, we should know." He set his drink down and leaned forward, looking directly at both his sisters. "But I really love her, guys," he said. "She strong, she's smart, and—"

"Great in the sack, right?" Margaret interjected.

"I was going to say 'caring,' Mugs," Patrick said. His subcutaneous transceiver beeped, and his intraocular monitor told him it was Brad. He picked up his drink and smiled slyly. "But yeah, she is," then held up a finger to tell his sisters he was going to take a call. "Hey, big guy."

"Are you watching TV, Dad?"

"No. I'm down here with—"

"The ex-president—Joseph Gardner—is on TV—and he's talking about your surveillance operation at Battle Mountain!"

"*What?* You're *kidding!*"

"He just mentioned *you,* Dad!" Brad exclaimed. "Hold on . . . now he's saying you were ordered by President Phoenix to spy on people around Battle Mountain so he could circumvent the law. That's nutso!"

"President Phoenix has nothing to do with what we're doing, Brad," Patrick said.

"Wait . . ." He could hear Brad take a sharp increase of air; then: "Dad, *he just mentioned those FBI agents!* He said you chased them out of Battle Mountain by threatening their lives!"

"Oh God," Patrick moaned. "It's begun . . ." His transceiver beeped again, and his intraocular monitor simply said "private." "I have to go, Brad. Talk to you in a few minutes." He took the second call. "McLanahan."

"Gardner couldn't even wait for the morning shows before dropping the next firebomb," Vice President Ann Page said. "I've got a call in to the Justice Department, and they'll tell us what's going to happen next. Based on what they've already said, you'll have to shut down your operation, and anyone who was flying those surveillance missions might get in trouble with the FAA. The FBI might confiscate your equipment to see if what you were looking at violated the law. The president will take some major political flak for this." She paused. "And you'll probably be indicted by a grand jury and asked to turn yourself in."

"Fine with me—I'll be happy to get in front of a judge and tell what happened," Patrick said. "I'm sorry the president will take some heat, but it's not his fault at all." That sentence got Nancy and Margaret's attention, and they stopped chatting with each other to listen.

"How did this get out, Patrick?" Ann asked.

"I've obviously got someone in my group who talked to the press or the FBI," Patrick said.

"Where are you now?"

"Scottsdale, Arizona."

"Get back to Battle Mountain right away," Ann said. "We don't want it to look like you're trying to flee."

"I'm with my sisters," Patrick said irritably. "We're visiting our mother. Why would anybody think I'm trying to flee?" Nancy and Margaret's eyes widened in surprise when they heard that.

"How soon can you get back?"

"I can't fly tonight," Patrick said.

"Why not?"

"I've had a drink," he said. "I can't fly after taking a drink."

"*Now* you're worried about breaking the law?" the vice president retorted.

"It's not just the law, Madam Vice President, it's safety of flight."

"*Madam Vice President?*" Margaret exclaimed in a whisper. "You're talking to *the vice president of the United States . . . ?*"

Patrick put a finger to his lips to shush his sisters. "Tomorrow I need to drop my sisters off in Sacramento, then—"

"Put them on a plane in the morning and come directly back to Battle Mountain first thing," the vice president said. "We've got to get out in front of this. Are you reading me, General?"

"Yes, ma'am," Patrick said. The connection was terminated.

"Were you just talking to the *vice*—"

Patrick held up a hand. "Not so loud, guys," he said. "I've got to go back to Battle Mountain first thing in the morning. I'll put you guys on a flight back to Sacramento."

"What's going on, Patrick?" Nancy asked in a whisper. "Why did the vice president think you were trying to flee?"

"She didn't, but other people might think I was." He stood up and kissed both his sisters on the top of their heads. "I'm sure you'll hear all about it on the news tomorrow morning."

Joint Air Base Battle Mountain

The next morning

They saw it the next morning from about thirty miles out: several columns of thick black smoke issuing from the base. Patrick was advised to stay away from the smoke but was still cleared to land.

"It's the housing area, Dad!" Brad said as they entered the traffic pattern. He looked carefully, and then his mouth dropped open. "I can't see our trailer through the smoke, Dad. Wow, it looks like dozens of trailers caught on fire!"

Patrick made the landing, taxied to his hangar, put the P210 Centurion away, then drove over to the Civil Air Patrol hangar. Several members of CAP were inside. "Hope you had a nice vacation, Patrick," Rob Spara said. "You heard the news?"

"About our surveillance operation? Yes," Patrick replied. "What about the fires?"

"They're saying it was rival survivalist or fundamentalist groups—whatever they are," David Bellville said. "No one really knows. It broke out early this morning. All of the civilians are being put up in shelters at the high school until they can be relocated." He put a hand on Patrick's shoulder. "I think your trailer was one of them, General."

"I had a feeling it might be," Patrick said. "That's how my luck has been running lately. Has anyone heard from the Justice Department or the FBI?" Everyone shook their heads. "I spoke with the vice president last night. She thinks everything is going to be shut down and the equipment confiscated by the FBI. I'd like to get copies of all the latest sensor scans, as many as we can save."

"Why don't we just erase everything?"

"We don't want to be accused of destroying evidence," Patrick said. "Besides, I think the images will prove that we're not violating anyone's privacy. And there's nothing illegal about making backups."

"I'll take care of it," David Bellville said, and hurried off.

"Should we get Dr. Masters to pull those sensors off the planes?" John de Carteret asked.

"Let's not panic," Patrick said. "The more stuff we do that looks like a cover-up, the worse it will go for us. The cover-up is always worse than the crime. I'd be more than happy to stand in front of a judge and jury and explain what we were doing."

Patrick put in a call to Jon Masters: "Where are you guys?" he asked over the secure voice connection.

"Ahhh . . . I think it might be better if you didn't know, Patrick," Jon said.

"Gotcha," Patrick said. "Probably so, since I'm sure I'll be questioned by the FBI soon. I'm surprised they're not here already. What's going on?"

"We were told early yesterday evening to gather our stuff and depart," Jon said. "Not the downlinks or surveillance equipment, but . . . you know, the *other* stuff."

"Gotcha. Who told you to take off?"

"Ahhh . . ."

"Gotcha. Talk to you soon."

Patrick, Gia, and Brad drove over to the housing area. Sure enough, their trailer was one of dozens caught in the blaze. They were prevented from going near it by base firefighters. "How did it start?" Patrick asked the deputy fire chief at the checkpoint.

"Too early to tell, General," the chief said. "The police were summoned out here last night because of some arguments between two or three groups, but everything broke up shortly after the police showed up. A few hours later, we got the call. It looks like the origin was very close to your trailer, sir."

"*My* trailer?"

"Good thing you weren't home—whatever was used as the primary, it was hot and powerful—more powerful than dynamite, maybe PETN or RDX," the fire chief said. "We'll start the investigation shortly, along with the Air Force Office of Special Investigations and the FBI. Sorry, sir. We'll let you know what happens."

They drove back to Patrick's office in silence. Patrick brought Gia and Brad something to drink and fixed himself coffee. "Everybody all right?" he said once they were settled.

"I'm cool," Brad said. "It's funny—all I have was the overnight stuff we brought on the trip, but I'm not bummed. I can't think of anything important I lost except maybe my laptop. I guess it's because I didn't have that much to begin with."

"Gia?" She had been completely silent since landing at Battle Mountain, and now she was staring blankly at some spot on Patrick's desk. "You haven't said much, sweetie." Patrick reached out and touched her arm. "Are you—"

"Don't touch me!" she cried out, jumping out of her seat so quickly that her drink and Patrick's coffee went flying. Gia wrapped her arms around her waist and began to sob. "I could have been *killed* last night if we were at that trailer!" She looked at Patrick and Brad in amazement. "You two are acting as if nothing's happened! First you say that we have to go back right away because you might have to talk with the FBI, and then your trailer is blown up—and neither of you seems to think it's anything out of the ordinary! What is *wrong* with you two?" And she stormed out, pushing the door open so hard that it rebounded off the wall.

"Gia! Wait!" Patrick shouted. He started for the door . . .

. . . and ran headlong into none other than Special Agent Philip Chastain, accompanied by another man he didn't recognize. "Just the man I want to see," Chastain said, showing his badge. "Going somewhere, General?"

"My girlfriend—"

"I think she wants to be alone right now," Chastain said. "I'm going to need a few things from you."

"I'm not answering any questions without my—"

"Oh, that broken record again," Chastain said. Patrick noticed that the agent was wearing a different kind of shirt, one with a much higher collar—obviously to hide the bruises on his neck caused by being manhandled by the Tin Man. "I wasn't going to ask any questions. I just need some things." Patrick glanced over Chastain's shoulder and saw David Bellville walking quickly away from the conference room. He gave Patrick a wink.

Chastain held up a document. "Warrant to seize computers, other electronic communications equipment, hard drives, and other documents stored here and in your aircraft hangar. Mind handing over the keys? I'd hate to punch the locks on your pretty little plane." Patrick nodded to Brad, who produced the hangar and aircraft keys. "Thank you, son. I have a warrant to search your trailer too, but I guess that'll have to wait until the fire inspector and OSI are done. Any other locked safes I need keys for?"

"No."

"Fine. Now, you're not under arrest, General—yet—but I'm telling you not to go anywhere unless you notify me first. It might not look so good for you at the grand jury if we find you've disappeared." He held up another document. "I have a warrant to search Jonathan Masters's aircraft and seize certain pieces of equipment, including the robot and the armor you terrorized myself and my agents with. The plane is not in its hangar. Where is it?"

"I want to speak with a lawyer before I answer any questions."

"You're not under arrest, General," Chastain said. He looked at Patrick carefully, studying every movement on his face. "Where did Masters go?" No answer. "When did he leave?" Still no reply. "I'll just check the control tower's records. But it's another example of how uncooperative you are. I'm sure the grand jury will want to hear that also. I still have my suspicions about you, General. You're not the Sir Lancelot in shining armor the rest of the world thinks you are."

He stepped closer to Patrick so they were almost nose to nose. "Do you know, Agent Brady will never be able to raise his left arm above his shoulder again, thanks to you and your buddy? He'll be driving a desk from now on, maybe get himself a medical retirement if they can't get the pain under control. And you know what else, you bastard? You know that pill you made me swallow? I'm told whenever it's interrogated and transmits a signal, it could cause cancer. I've got a wife and two young kids, you son of a bitch. Maybe you should have killed me, McLanahan . . . because I'm about to make your life a living hell." And he turned and stormed out of the office.

"What are we going to do now, Dad?" Brad asked. "Where are we going to go?"

Patrick spent several long minutes feeling a mixture of puzzlement and suspicion, then turned back to his son. "First, I want to look for Gia," he said. "She was pretty upset, and I didn't notice it. Next, we should get some lunch. After that, we should go to the store so we can pick up some supplies. If we find Gia, we'll go to transient billeting for the night; if we don't, I think we'll just camp out here in the office on cots, okay?"

"Sure. I can get some cots and sleeping bags out of the CAP storage locker."

"Good. And while we're at the store, I want to get a really good laptop. I've got some studying to do."

TEN

*A community is like a ship; everyone ought to be
prepared to take the helm.*

— HENRIK IBSEN

PATRICK'S OFFICE, JOINT AIR BASE
BATTLE MOUNTAIN

LATE THAT EVENING

Patrick was reviewing the hundreds of gigabytes of sensor data
that David Bellville had copied onto flash drives before their laptops were seized by the FBI. Brad was asleep in a sleeping bag on a
cot just a few feet away. Patrick had been staring at sensor images
for six hours and *nothing* was jumping out at him. He had the last
twelve hours of images in front of him from two different sensor
passes. The computer was flagging about a dozen points of interest, but when Patrick zoomed in on those particular spots, nothing
was apparent. The computer could tell him when *something* had
changed, but it couldn't tell him if that particular something was
relevant to anything. Besides, even if he wanted to take a look, he
couldn't—he had no planes.

Patrick activated his subcutaneous transceiver: "Jon?"

"Hey, dude," Jon Masters replied a few moments later. "How's it going?"

"Not bad. The FBI showed up and took all the laptops and downlinks."

"They've been calling every hour on the hour, the pricks. They'd like to speak to me, Charlie, and Wayne, and they say they have a warrant to seize my plane, the CID, and the Tin Man. I referred their butts to the legal department."

"That'll delay them a little bit, but not for long. Where are you?"

"Classified. Hush-hush."

"We're secure."

"You think so? I don't."

Patrick paused. "The comparative analysis that your sensor software does: it looks for *changes,* right?"

"I told you that already. It flags unusual changes in travel patterns over time. Where are you?"

"In my office. We're camping out here for the night. You heard about my trailer?"

"On the news," Jon said. "If you need anything, let me know. Gia is okay racking out in your office with Brad?"

"She's MIA."

"Again?"

"Again."

"Sorry, bro."

"All this was too much for her, I guess."

"If she wants to hang with the McLanahans, she's got to toughen up her act more than a few notches," Jon said. "I've worked with you for fifteen years and I'm *still* trying to upshift."

"Your middle name is 'upshift,'" Patrick said. "Thanks."

"For what?"

"For being there," Patrick said. "For standing beside me."

"I stand for nothing but the science and the profit, my friend,"

Jon said. "Everything else is . . . oh, hell, I don't know. If I'm standing anywhere, it's with my hand out, expecting renumeration. Ideas, gadgets, and juicy contracts, that's what I'm all about. You want anything else—well, pay me first, and then we'll talk."

"Sure," Patrick said.

"You see anything interesting in those sensor images?" Jon asked.

"No—I don't get it," Patrick said, frowning at the laptop. "I mean, I see the flags, but there's nothing there that I can see."

"What do you mean?"

"Well, the biggest cluster of flags is around one of the copper mines around here that belongs to Judah Andorsen," Patrick said. "It's called Freedom-7. But why the flags? It's a mine. They have trucks coming and going all the time. They take ore to a railroad spur that takes it to a main rail line and on to the smelters."

"But remember, Patrick, that the computer records and compares normal activity, and then flags unusual activity."

"I know. I get it."

"Then you've got unusual activity out there, my friend," Jon said. "Normal truck or rail movements wouldn't be flagged after a few passes. Stop trying to rationalize it. If the computer flagged it, especially over several days, something's going on down there, and you should go take a look."

"That's a problem too. They seized my plane and all the other planes with the sensors on them."

"Pricks. Can you send me some of those images and let me take a look?"

"Sure." It took just a couple mouse clicks to send a series of sensor images to Jon's secure e-mail address. "What are you going to do now?"

"I'm still talking with the legal beagles, but they're saying I have to go and turn myself in eventually—sooner, rather than later," Jon said. "I'll probably fly the Skytrain back to Battle Mountain with the other gadgets. What about you?"

"Not a hell of a lot else I can do except hang around here."

"Well, I'll probably see you out there soon, maybe even tomorrow if the legal department arranges the surrender that quickly," Jon said, "and then we can hang out together."

"See you soon, then." The connection was terminated.

Patrick stared at the sensor images for a few more minutes, then made another phone call. "Hello?"

"Hi, David. It's Patrick McLanahan. Hope I'm not calling too late."

"No, not at all, sir," David Bellville said. "I was just watching the latest blasts from your good friend Joseph Gardner on the evening news. Where does that guy get off saying all that nonsense?"

"Because the press likes controversy, and no one wants to take on an ex-president," Patrick said. "Listen, I've been looking over the sensor images, and I see a bunch of flags that I think we need to take a look at."

"Where?"

"One of the Andorsen mines down near Mount Callahan."

"Freedom-7," David said. "Me and Fid go hunting down near there every year. I've got work all day tomorrow, but I'll ask Leif if he wants to go—he knows that area better than I do. I'll have him take Fid along if he's available. The guy's been asking all over town about a job—maybe a ride will cheer him up."

"Thanks, David. I'll e-mail the images of the area the computer flagged to Leif. Let me know what he finds."

"Will do. Sorry about your trailer. If you need anything at all, just holler."

"Thank you. I will."

Patrick felt as if he had only gotten a couple minutes' sleep when he heard a loud pounding on his office door. When he opened the door, he found FBI special agent Chastain and two other agents with jackets emblazoned with FBI. "Executing the warrant to search your office, McLanahan," he said, pushing past Patrick into the room.

"You searched it yesterday."

"I'm searching it again." He stepped past Brad and went right over to the desk. "What's this?" he asked, pointing to the laptop computer.

"I want my attorney before I'll answer any questions," Patrick said.

"You'll need one, mister," Chastain said. He found the collection of flash drives and stared at Patrick angrily. "Withholding evidence? Putting you away will be a slam dunk, McLanahan." He and the other agents collected the laptop and flash drives, quickly searched the desk, then departed.

"What did he mean, 'withholding evidence,' Dad?" Brad asked.

"We didn't withhold anything, big guy," Patrick said. "The flash drives are just backups—they have the same data as the laptops they seized. And the laptop is new—we just bought it yesterday. He's trying to intimidate us, Brad—that's how he operates. He makes people feel afraid so they'll either talk when they're not supposed to, or start to lie, and then he's got you." Patrick had a troubled look on his face; he shook it off a few moments later, then clapped his hands. "Well, we're up, so we might as well get moving."

After breakfast at the nearly deserted base-exchange cafeteria, they went past the front gate back out to the housing area. J. Andorsen Construction crews were busy repairing the highway from the deadly bomb blast that seemed like an eternity ago but in fact was only two days. A security-forces cruiser was parked just in back of the entrance, and Patrick noticed an unmanned Avenger parked behind the former data-processing center about a quarter of a mile away.

At the taped-off investigation-scene boundary, which was a couple blocks away from where his trailer used to be, Patrick found the deputy fire chief. "Any information on the explosive, Chief?" he asked.

"Preliminarily, they're saying it was RDX, General," the fire chief said after checking around to see who might be in earshot—obviously he wasn't supposed to be sharing information with anyone. "Pretty common explosive in the military and industry, fairly easy to handle, easy to mix with plasticizing materials, easy to store—a favorite with terrorists. They say it was about three pounds, based on the blast radius. They haven't found the trigger device but it's a good bet it was a remote detonator, probably using a cell phone. It was probably tossed out of a vehicle—they're checking surveillance videos. It looks like they weren't sure which trailer was yours, because the trailers near yours were vacant where the blast occurred; since you were away also, they might've been confused." He looked at Patrick, concern evident on his face. "Looks like you have some pretty serious enemies, General."

"The list is pretty long, Chief," Patrick said. "By the way: you haven't seen that woman I was with yesterday around here, have you?"

"Sorry, General."

Patrick nodded his thanks and departed.

They drove the ten miles to town, checking the bus terminal, casinos, motels, and hospital, hoping to see Gia somewhere, but still no luck, so they headed back to the base. After they arrived at his office, he took a phone call: "Hi, Patrick, Darrow here," Darrow Horton said. "I'm on my way to Reno to talk with the U.S. attorney in person, and I should be in Battle Mountain by seven P.M. I'm bringing a couple of associates. Can you get us rooms somewhere?"

"Sure—I'll put you up right here on base at the transient lodging facility. It's just as nice as the casino hotels in town, and the all-ranks club has great food and is begging for business," Patrick said. "It'll be nice to see you. What's going on?"

"Based on my discussions with the U.S. attorney, I think he's re- luctant to indict you," Darrow said. "I'm pushing for probation and a fine in exchange for a misdemeanor plea, but he's getting pres- sure from guys like former president Gardner to push for a felony prosecution. So I'm going to apply a little pressure of my own:

"Jon Masters has arranged to fly in to Battle Mountain to sur- render his equipment to the FBI tomorrow morning," she went on. "I've called a news conference with you, me, Jon, Brad, the robot, and the Tin Man, and we're going to explain our side of the story and tell what crazy, irresponsible, and probably illegal foolishness the FBI has been doing out there. I want to tell the whole story, right from the very beginning—how the FBI was supposed to be going after extremists and ended up going after *you* instead, through Brad. I'm hoping the U.S. attorney will drop the case today after I tell him what I'm going to do, but if he doesn't, we'll smear Chastain and his goons all over the breaking-news segment on every TV channel in the country. All the networks and cable news channels will be there."

"Sounds good to me," Patrick said. "I'm ready and anxious to tell my side of the story to a judge, but I'm more than happy to tell it in front of news cameras too."

"You bet we will," Darrow said. "We'll be in their face every week polluting the jury pool until the trial starts. We'll make everyone in America thinks Gardner has a vendetta against you— which he probably does.

"Now, I probably can't protect you from what the Tin Man and CID did to those agents, and we might even be facing a felony plea, but I think we can avoid confinement," Darrow went on. "My plan is to have you admit that the Tin Man and CID were operating under your orders—I'm not even referring to the operators as per- sons. The U.S. attorney would rather focus on you than Macomber and Turlock, although they might get misdemeanor charges as well."

"I agree," Patrick said. "They were definitely following my orders."

"But you were protecting yourself and protecting your son from Chastain and Brady, the best way you knew how. Good. It'll be easy to make them the bad guys and the robot and Tin Man the defenders. So, how's Gia? Am I finally going to meet this woman?"

"She left sometime yesterday morning, after we got back from Scottsdale. I think seeing the trailer destroyed was too much for her."

"I'm sorry. Try not to let her distract you too much. Tomorrow will be a big day."

"Okay. Give me a call when you get close and I'll meet you at the front gate."

"Can't wait to see you again, Patrick," Darrow said, and she sounded *very* sincere about that.

TOIYABE RANGE NEAR MOUNT CALLAHAN, CENTRAL NEVADA

THAT SAME TIME

"Well, I can't see anything from here," Leif Delamar said. Leif was a retired mail carrier and avid hunter, and his rugged six-foot-five frame, creased face, and weathered hands were living portraits of his longtime love for the outdoors. He was looking through a pair of binoculars at the base of Judah Andorsen's Freedom-7 mine. He and Michael Fitzgerald were in Leif's Land Rover about a half mile from the mine at a barbed-wire fence that marked the edge of Andorsen's land. He handed the binoculars to Michael. "What do you see, Fid?"

Michael searched for a few minutes, then lowered the binoculars and gave them back. "Nothing. Looks like business as usual."

Leif studied the printout he made of the computer image, rotating the page so it was oriented the same way they were facing, then started tracing the different roads snaking up and down the face of the open-pit mine. "Okay, I see the two main truck roads going in," he said, "and the west terraces here."

"They're called 'benches,'" Michael said.

"Well, aren't we the mining expert today?" Leif quipped. "Anyway, I see the haul roads, and the benches, and . . ." He picked up the binoculars and looked again. "I see a couple tunnels built into the sides of the pit. Do you know what they're for?"

"Usually they're just relief bores to keep water from loosening the rock," Michael said. "They sometimes reinforce the walls with cables or shotcrete from inside the bores. If this mine ends up becoming a landfill in the future—most of them do—they also have to dig drainage tunnels to keep the pit from becoming a lake."

"You are just a veritable font of fascinating information this morning, Fid," Leif said. He focused in on one of the bores indicated as an activity spot on the printout. "Well, those bores look pretty big—almost like tunnels. I do see a lot of water coming out, and . . . hey, I think I see a couple cars lined up near one of those bores." He looked more carefully. "Why, I think one of those cars is a sheriff's cruiser."

"What?" Fid took the glasses and looked. "It sure does. What in heck is the sheriff doing down in an open-pit mine?"

"Doing his job, I hope," Leif said. "That's the first sheriff's car I've seen in days. Very weird." He took the glasses back. "I don't see anything else all that unusual. Maybe the sheriff is investigating something they found inside the bore, or they're . . . *holy shit!*"

"What?"

"There's a panel truck coming out of that bore!" Leif said. He studied the scene carefully for a few moments, tracking the newcomer, then exclaimed, "It's a blue Air Force maintenance truck!"

"A *what?*" Michael said.

"It's one of those big blue Air Force 'bread trucks' we see all the time on the flight line," Leif said. "The ones usually driven by the maintenance supervisor. Now what in heck would . . . ?" At that moment Leif was interrupted by the sound of a vehicle driving up the dirt road behind them. It was a two-door Jeep Wrangler, with two men aboard.

"Looks like a couple of Andorsen's guys," Michael said. "No sweat—we're not on Andorsen's property here."

Leif lowered the binoculars, folded up the image printout, stuffed it in a pocket, and watched the Jeep approach. It roared to a stop a few yards away, and the passenger got out while the driver started talking on the radio. "Hey, guys," Leif said. "We're just out here checking deer trails. What's going on?"

The passenger walked up to Leif and Michael, pulled a .45-caliber semiautomatic pistol from a hidden holster, and fired two shots.

JOINT AIR BASE BATTLE MOUNTAIN

THE NEXT MORNING

The cameras were rolling and the media crews were ready as the C-57 Skytrain II glided in for a landing and taxied over to where the podium was set up outside the Civil Air Patrol hangar. It shut down engines, the landing gear extended to make room underneath the plane to unload cargo, and the cargo-bay doors opened. Meanwhile Jon Masters walked out of the belly hatch and came over to the podium, followed by Wayne Macomber, wearing the Tin Man armor but carrying his helmet in the crook of an arm. Behind them, Jason Richter and Charlie Turlock retrieved the folded Cybernetic Infantry Device and carried it over to the podium.

"Ladies and gentlemen, this is Dr. Jonathan Masters of Sky Masters, Inc., a major American defense contractor and aerospace engineering firm," Darrow Horton said into the microphones. Beside her were Patrick and Brad McLanahan, already at the podium. "He is here complying with an order from a federal judge in Reno to surrender this aircraft, various electronic components, computers and storage media, and these two pieces of technology: the Tin Man armor system, being worn by Mr. Wayne Macomber of Sky Masters, Inc., and this: the Cybernetic Infantry Device manned robot, of which I think you're aware after one was attacked by extremists several days ago while on an FBI assignment."

Darrow nodded to Charlie, who then began to speak: "CID One, deploy." The large case began to move, and in seconds it had unfolded itself into the crouching robot. The reporters gasped in astonishment as Charlie spoke again: "CID One, pilot up," and it assumed the boarding position.

"This is Miss Charlie Turlock, an engineer who works at Sky Masters, Inc., who was piloting the robot when it came to General McLanahan's assistance against Agents Chastain, Brady, and Renaldo," Darrow went on. "They are all here to cooperate with the FBI investigations into the bombing outside this base, as well as the allegations made against General McLanahan that he was conducting illegal spying operations against local citizens, and the even further heinous allegation by former president Gardner that the president of the United States ordered General McLanahan to undertake these flight missions.

"But make no mistake, ladies and gentlemen: we are not here to be bullied into submitting to frivolous and intimidating activities by the FBI or by inflammatory accusations and outright lies by Mr. Gardner," Darrow went on. "First, we completely reject the idea that Special Agent Chastain return to Battle Mountain to conduct these investigations, in light of what happened here when General McLanahan defended himself and his son, Bradley, against the malicious actions of Agents Chastain, Brady, and Renaldo. He's here because he wants revenge on General McLanahan, and that is unacceptable. We call on the FBI to immediately assign another lead investigator."

While Darrow spoke, an Avenger security vehicle and a maintenance vehicle had arrived at the C-57, parking near the Skytrain's tail, keeping a distance while the press conference was going on but ready to service the Skytrain if necessary. The arrival of both vehicles got Jon Masters's attention—no one got near his planes unless he knew about it, especially ones with guns and missiles on it.

"Second, it is completely unclear why the FBI has ordered the seizure of Dr. Masters's aircraft and these two defensive systems, the Tin Man and the Cybernetic Infantry Device," Darrow went on. "They were not involved in either occurrence and are completely outside the purview of this investigation—Dr. Masters merely sold and installed the sensors that General McLanahan and his friends used on their *private* aircraft for *personal* reasons. Again, the FBI is using this opportunity to punish Dr. Masters, Mr. Macomber, and Miss Turlock for their previous actions, and that is completely unacceptable.

"I would like to invite General Patrick McLanahan to make a statement," Darrow continued. "As you all very well know, Lieutenant-General McLanahan is a retired veteran with twenty years of service in the United States Air Force, rising to the rank of three-star general. He has long proved himself the champion of the American people and of the cause of justice in every corner of the globe. Even when faced with tremendous odds and strong opponents, General McLanahan has consistently and unerringly taken the challenge upon himself, and he has taken the fight to the enemy, protecting our country, our people, and our allies from certain destruction.

"In retirement, General McLanahan's main job is raising his son, Bradley. But he also serves as a volunteer mission pilot for the Civil Air Patrol, the U.S. Air Force auxiliary, as does Bradley, and both were recently credited with a find and a rescue of an airplane crash victim. General McLanahan also performs charity medical flights for Angel Flight West, helping needy medical patients get lifesaving treatment free of charge. His is still serving his country and his community to this day. Ladies and gentlemen, I am proud to present my client and a genuine American hero, General Patrick McLanahan."

As Patrick took the dais, the Avenger air-defense vehicle suddenly moved its gun and missile turret from a stowed position to unstowed, and it began to move toward the C-57 Skytrain. Jon Masters turned and walked toward the aircraft.

"Jon, where are you going?" Charlie whispered.

"Why is that thing heading toward my plane?" Jon asked. "Whoever's driving that thing better be careful."

"It can wait, Jon."

"He should have a wing walker out there. I'll be right—" Suddenly the Avenger roared off at high speed toward the Skytrain. *"Hey!"* Jon shouted. *"Watch out!"*

Patrick turned and saw a blue Air Force maintenance van racing down a taxiway at very high speed, heading right for them! "What the . . . ?" At that instant, the Avenger's twenty-millimeter Gatling gun opened fire on the van. The audience screamed at the impossibly loud *BRRZZZZZZZ!* sound erupting from just a few yards away. Patrick waved at the audience. *"Get back!"* he shouted. *"Back toward the hangar! Run!"*

"Jon, get back here!" Charlie shouted, and she dashed off after him. Jon had run all the way to the Skytrain's left wingtip, waving at the Avenger. *"Jon!"*

"What's he trying to do—rip my airplane to shreds?" Jon shouted, pointing at the Avenger as heavy-caliber rounds continued to pour from the cannon. That's when he noticed the maintenance van heading toward him, faster and faster. "Hey, what's that van doing? Someone tell that jerk to steer away from—"

The heavy machine-gun rounds ripped into the van. Tires and glass exploded, and something inside the engine compartment detonated, blowing the hood completely off.

"Get down! Everybody get down!" Patrick shouted, and he grabbed Darrow and Brad and pulled them down to the tarmac . . .

. . . just as the van exploded in a gigantic fireball, less than a hundred yards away.

BASE MEDICAL CLINIC, JOINT AIR BASE
BATTLE MOUNTAIN

SEVERAL HOURS LATER

David Bellville walked into the waiting room of the small base clinic, dressed in scrubs and removing a surgical mask, cap, and latex gloves. The room was packed with people: some looked seriously hurt, with bandaged faces and limbs, while others had less serious wounds. He came over to where Patrick, Brad, Whack, and Darrow were standing, along with Rob Spara and John de Carteret, who had arrived at the clinic shortly after the blast. Three of them had some cuts and scrapes, and their clothing was burned in places; Whack was still in the Tin Man armor, but had suffered some burns on his face. "Hey, Patrick," David said.

"What's the latest, David?" Patrick asked.

"Your friend Charlie has some burns and a concussion," David said. "There were a number of severe burn injuries and injuries from the explosion, but luckily it was far enough away." He looked directly at Patrick. "There was just one fatality." Patrick closed his eyes, and he half leaned, half stumbled back against the wall for support. "I'm sorry, Patrick."

"What?" Brad asked, looking back and forth from Patrick to David in confusion. "Who?"

Patrick reached out and hugged his son tightly. "Your uncle Jon, son."

"Wha-*what*?" Brad gasped, and he started to sob into his father's shoulder. "Uncle Jon's *dead*?"

"I'm sorry, Brad," David said. He waited a few moments, then went on: "There's more, Patrick." He pinned a white plastic tag on their shirts. "They detected traces of radiation at the blast site— another dirty bomb. No lethal levels have been detected yet on the survivors—I think the bomb was so big that it cooked off most of whatever was in the van—but the blast site is pretty contaminated. The base is being evacuated and closed down. We're going to transfer the casualties to Andorsen Memorial any minute now—everyone else will be taken to the high school for more examinations."

"Jesus . . ." Patrick breathed, then hugged Darrow as well as his son. "I swear to God, I'm going to find these terrorist bastards and make them pay, I *swear* it."

"Let the authorities handle it, Patrick," Darrow said. "This . . . this is just too massive, too dangerous. It'll take the Army to stop those terrorists. Your son needs you right now. You've done all you can. Let the authorities take charge." Patrick could do nothing else but hug his son and Darrow—the energy just seemed to flow from his body like air escaping from a balloon.

"Dad?" Brad asked. "What's going to happen? What do we do?"

"We'll deal with it, son," Patrick said softly, hugging Brad tightly. "We'll be okay." He turned and looked toward the entrance to the clinic . . . and saw none other than Judah Andorsen talking with FBI special agent Chastain . . .

. . . and standing beside and behind Andorsen was Michael Fitzgerald! He looked at Patrick with a painful, horrified expression, then averted his eyes.

Andorsen noticed Patrick looking toward him and stepped forward. Fitzgerald did not move, and he kept his eyes averted. "Hello, General," Andorsen said. Both his voice and demeanor were completely changed—he no longer came across as the "aw, shucks" grandfatherly country rancher. "It's good to see you're okay. What a horrible thing, absolutely horrible. And I just heard they're evacuating and closing the base today. God, what a mess. I'll sure miss all of you, but I think it's the best thing for the community. Obviously the base has been targeted by extremists, and even the Air Force's best security can't seem to keep anyone safe."

He took a step toward Patrick, and sensing danger, Patrick pulled his son away from him and guided him into Darrow's arms, then took a step toward Andorsen. The rancher got face-to-face with Patrick, then said in a low voice: "As you know, General, I like aircraft, and I like airports. I like *this* airport—nice long runways, lots of hangar space, lots of land, and, of course, the cool underground hangars that my father and grandfather built. I think I'd like to have this airport, and I think the county will sell it to me for next to nothing right after the Air Force gives it to them—after it's been cleaned up and decontaminated, of course.

"I'm thinking I might get into the resort and hunting-lodge business—you know, fly wealthy folks in, have some golf and tennis and a spa for the ladies, take guys out hunting for bighorn and deer, then serve them a big meal in a five-star restaurant," he went on, happily smiling at Patrick's shocked expression. "We could turn the underground hangars into a big year-round shooting range. Or how about a big sex grotto, like Hugh Heffner's? The world's biggest brothel? That sound like fun to you? It's perfectly legal here in Lander County, of course."

He looked Patrick squarely in the eyes. "We don't need the Space Defense Force, the Civil Air Patrol, your high-tech gadgets, or any of you creaky retired ex-military jocks here after this base closes," he said, "and we certainly don't need hotshots like you who think the military is the be-all and the end-all. You've had your day, General, but as of right now, it's over. I have a suggestion for you: when you get out of federal prison, why don't you just go back to wherever you came from, go find a nice comfy rocking chair, and stay put? You're not welcome here. Take my advice, for the safety of your son and your friends: get the hell out of northern Nevada." And with that, he left, Fitzgerald following close behind him.

"Why was Mr. Fitzgerald going with Mr. Andorsen, Dad?" Brad asked.

"That's something we need to find out, Brad," Patrick said. He shook his head in confusion, then turned to David. "Didn't Fid go with Leif to the Freedom-7 mine?" he asked.

"Yes," David said. "I spoke with him while they were on their way out there. He didn't call you to tell what they found?"

"I never heard from either one of them," Patrick said. "I as-sumed they didn't get a chance to go." He wore a very worried ex-pression. "Now Fid is back—with Andorsen—and no one's heard from Leif. Not good." He thought for a moment. "We've got some work to do. Whack, I want the CID."

"I think it was blown over by the explosion, but it should still be operable," Whack said.

"It might have to be cleaned and decontaminated, but hope-fully it won't be damaged or unusable," Patrick said. "Check it out. We'll meet at the Space Defense Force building."

"I'll take care of it," Whack said, and he headed out the door.

Patrick turned to Brad. "You stay with Miss Horton, okay, Brad?"

"I want to go with you, Dad," Brad said.

"You can't. It's too dangerous."

"Hold on a second, Patrick," Rob Spara interjected. "We all want to go with you."

"These guys are dangerous—they're killers," Patrick said. "The Tin Man and CID are our best weapons to use against them."

"With all due respect, General—no, they're not," Rob said. "Those 'guys' are our neighbors—they may even be our friends. The best answer to this situation may not be the best weapon—maybe it's just one neighbor telling another neighbor to knock it off and join the real world again."

"We'll get the whole squadron," John de Carteret said. "I don't know how many guys we're up against, but we should be able to muster a bunch of guys to head on out there with you."

Patrick thought about it for a moment, then nodded. "We'll meet out at the Space Defense Force building," he said, "and we'll come up with a plan." He turned to Brad. He was about to tell him he couldn't go. But he looked into his son's face, and he didn't see his son—he saw the look of a determined, angry young man, ready to go to work, resolved not to stay behind.

He clasped Brad on the shoulder and nodded. "You're with me, Brad," he said.

ANDORSEN FREEDOM-7 MINE, NEAR MOUNT CALLAHAN, NEVADA

THAT EVENING

"The closing of the air base is only the beginning," Judah Andorsen proclaimed loudly to the three hundred men, women, and even children assembled before him in the massive hollowed-out cavern carved into the side of the open-pit mine. Standing beside and behind him was Michael Fitzgerald. "That base was a symbol of the waste, inefficiency, and incompetence of the American government. They failed to protect themselves, and they failed to protect the citizens that trusted the government to help them. Those people from the Knights of the True Republic lost their lives because the government promised to help them, and broke their promise. Government is incapable of protecting you. Only we the people can protect us. No one else but ourselves." The audience clapped and cheered their agreement.

"When the base reverts back to its rightful owners . . ."—and the audience chanted, *"We the people! We the people! We the people!"*—" . . . we will be able to solidify our control over how we are governed in this territory. We'll be able to see the enemy coming. They won't be able to fly in aircraft to watch us, or bring more weapons to kill us. We'll be able to better consolidate our influence over the various so-called established government entities, the corrupt county and state governments, and prove to the world that sovereign citizens can and must run our own lives, free of the influence of the broken and dysfunctional Washington bureaucratic elite. Remember this day, my friends and fellow patriots: today was the twenty-first century's 'shot heard 'round the world'—the opening shot of the renewed fight for true freedom."

At the mine entrance, two pickup trucks with four men, all armed with hunting rifles fitted with night-vision sniperscopes, stood guard just inside the closed steel gate and cattle guard. The pickup trucks were arranged nose to nose, blocking the road but making it easy for them to maneuver in case they were needed.

"Pretty good turnout tonight, eh?" one of the guards said. "I brought my brother-in-law and his teenage kids. They got to meet Mr. Andorsen personally."

"We might need a bigger cavern pretty soon," another said.

"Soon we'll move out to the air base," another guard said. "I heard that after it's cleaned up, we'll use—" He stopped, then started scanning the area outside the gate with his night-vision sniperscope. "Did you hear something?"

"What? Like a car?"

"No—sounded big, running, like an elk or something." He stopped, then reversed his scan. "Hold on . . . I see . . . *shit, what the hell is that?*"

Moments later, the Cybernetic Infantry Device ran up to the gate. "Evening, guys," Brad McLanahan said in an electronically synthesized voice from within the CID. "Nice night tonight, isn't it?" Brad shook the heavy steel gate experimentally a few times . . . then lifted it up, snapping chains, locks, and hinges, and tossed it aside as easily as tossing a shoveful of dirt.

"I'm going to need a little room here, guys," Brad said. He put both hands under the front bumper of one of the pickup truck and lifted, and the pickup flipped end over end through the air, finally coming to rest about twenty yards away. He reached over and grabbed the rifles out of the hands of two stupefied guards, then punted the second pickup truck away before disarming the other two guards.

Brad then grabbed the two guards he'd just disarmed and held them close to his head. "Would you mind dropping your radios on the ground?" They hesitated, numb with fear. "Drop them, *now!*"

Brad shouted. They did as they were told, and Brad crushed the devices under his armored feet before doing the same to the other two guards'. "Thanks, guys. My squadron mates will be coming through shortly. Don't get run over by accident in the dark. See ya." And he trotted away to the next guard post.

As Andorsen was speaking, a man came up onstage to him and whispered, "All of the guard posts missed a check-in, sir."

"Damn," Andorsen said. He turned to Fitzgerald. "We'll go out the north relief bore—that'll take us all the way to the north side of the ridge, about a mile walking. I've got two Harleys waiting outside the bore. We can ride to my airstrip near Austin and take the Turbo Commander to—"

Just then the entire assemblage heard the large, heavy steel doors at the back of the cavern rattle, as if it were being blown by a powerful gust of wind. Then they heard a metallic *knock knock knock*—followed by both doors being ripped off their hinges like banana peels, and the Cybernetic Infantry Device entered the chamber. "Is it too late for the door prize?" Brad asked in his electronic voice, holding both steel doors in his armored hands. He held up the doors and rattled them as easily as shaking two pieces of paper. "Get it? 'Door prize'?"

"Everybody take a good look—this is what the government has sent out against us!" Andorsen shouted over the terrified voices echoing through the cavern. "They sent the most destructive weapon in the Army's arsenal against unarmed innocent citizens. Don't be afraid of it! You want a perfect example of what the federal government is willing to do against sovereign citizens—there it is! The federal government will stop at nothing, and use every weapon it possesses, to squash your freedom!"

"This has nothing to do with the federal government, Andorsen," a voice said . . . and Patrick McLanahan stepped past

Brad into the chamber. "This is about your fellow citizens putting
a stop to your killing spree." Behind him came Rob Spara, David
Bellville, John de Carteret, and fifty more members of the Battle
Mountain Civil Air Patrol squadron.

"These are the criminals who have been spying on you!" Andorsen shouted. "These are the ones who tried to kill the Knights
of the True Republic, then lured them onto the air base and slaugh-
tered them! They are the ones using radioactive bombs. Don't listen to them!"

"My name is General Patrick McLanahan," Patrick shouted.
"You know who I am. I'm a retired lieutenant-general of the
United States Air Force and a member of the Civil Air Patrol—
and I'm also your neighbor. We are all your neighbors. I'm here
to tell you that Judah Andorsen has been lying to you. He doesn't
want to protect you. He doesn't want to create a peaceful self-
governing society. He's an anarchist. He wants to create an empire
in the heart of Nevada that operates by creating fear in the people,
our elected officials, and in law enforcement. He creates fear, then
proposes a solution: band together, join him, and he will protect
you. It's a lie."

"Who is creating fear now, McLanahan?" Andorsen asked.
"Who is ripping apart doors and killing our friends outside? You're
the real threat here, McLanahan, not I. You can't stop us. You can't
terrorize us." He waved his hands over the audience. "What are
you going to do to us now, General?" he asked. "You going to call
the police? Call the Army? Call the National Guard? You do that,
and you've proved that government only *takes* freedom, not pro-
vides it—and you're an instrument of the government, just as we
always thought you were."

"Why did you kill Leif Delamar, Andorsen?"

"You mean, the man spying on us yesterday morning?" Andorsen asked. "*Your* spy? He deserved to die."

"He was unarmed."

"He was a spy and a traitor, and spies and traitors are executed—that's the law of war."

"Why did you kill all those members of the Knights of the True Republic?" Patrick asked. "More innocents murdered, by *you*."

"They were cowardly sheep, betrayed by their leader into agreeing to come onto the air base for their so-called protection and assistance," Andorsen said. "They are better off dead than surrendering themselves to the government!"

"So who else do you intend on killing with radioactive dirty bombs, Andorsen?" Patrick shouted. "What other innocents will die?"

"I never used dirty bombs on anyone!" Andorsen shouted. Now the assemblage was looking suspiciously at *him* instead of Patrick or the CID. "That's a lie! *Prove* that I've ever used dirty bombs! Yes, I have explosives, and I've lashed out at enemies of this community! But I've never used dirty—"

"You're a liar, Andorsen," a voice shouted behind him. It was Michael Fitzgerald, pushing a cart carrying a large wooden crate with J. ANDORSEN CONSTRUCTION stenciled in black letters. "If you've never used dirty bombs, what's *this*?" And Fitzgerald kicked the crate open . . .

. . . revealing a large steel-and-concrete cask, marked with radioactive-material symbology.

"You planted that on me!" Andorsen shouted. "It's a plant! You're trying to set me up!"

"You murdered my friend right in front of my eyes, you lousy bastard," Fitzgerald shouted. "You had me spy on my friends and inform on them to the FBI. All I wanted was a job, Andorsen— you turned me into a traitor."

"No one's going to believe you about anything, you stupid loser," Andorsen said, "especially if you're *dead*!" And he reached into his jacket for his Smith & Wesson .357 Magnum revolver . . .

. . . but Fitzgerald was faster. He pulled out a Browning M1911 semiautomatic pistol and fired three times before Andorsen's revolver could clear the flying jacket.

"I may be a loser," Fitzgerald said, "but I can draw and shoot better than you any day." He stepped over the body, off the stage, and over to Patrick, Rob, David, and John. "I'm sorry, guys," he said. "I told Andorsen about your surveillance, the Tin Man, the robot, and the backups, and he told the FBI. I was just trying to get into his good graces so he'd give me a job. I set up Leif with Andorsen's guards, but I didn't think they'd kill him! Then I helped the van get on base. Jesus, I really screwed up."

"Let's get out of here," Patrick said. He turned to the crowd. "Go home, everyone," he said in a loud voice. "Go home, hug your family, and try to trust the government again. It may not be perfect, but it's ours. If you don't like it—fix it. Don't try to destroy it." He looked up at the CID. "Let's go, big guy."

"Okay, Dad," Brad said—and Patrick thought he could hear Brad's own voice, not the electronic one.

EPILOGUE

I find no hint throughout the Universe of good or ill,
of blessing or of curse; I find alone Necessity Supreme.

—James Thomson

Downtown Battle Mountain

Days later

Patrick emerged from the hotel hand in hand with Darrow Horton and walked to the hotel's parking lot. "Are you sure you can't stay one more night?" he asked. "I can fly you to Reno in the Centurion so you can catch your flight."

"When you get a *real* airplane, Patrick, then I'll fly with you," Darrow quipped. "Anyway, the U.S. attorney has dropped all the charges, and they said they'd talk with the FAA about those sensor things you put on the airplanes. It looks like Civil Air Patrol is interested in installing them on all their planes."

"Excellent," Patrick said. "That'd be a nice little piece of business for Sky Masters."

They were silent for a few moments; then: "Are you sure about all this, Patrick?" she asked. "You're giving up the appointment to be the vice president's space policy adviser?"

"Yes," Patrick said. "I've been to Washington and the White House already, and didn't really care for it."

"But . . . *I'm* in Washington," she said. "You and Brad could come and stay with me, and we could . . . take it from there?" He said nothing, which was all the answer she needed. "So what are you going to do?" she asked. "Go to Sacramento? Arizona? Las Vegas?"

"No—I'm going to stay right here," Patrick said.

"Here? And do what? The base is closed. With the base closed, Battle Mountain will practically be a ghost town!"

"I've accepted a job," Patrick said. "I'm going to be vice president of Sky Masters, Inc., taking over Jon's position. And my first order of business will be to move the company to Battle Mountain."

"What?"

"I've always said that this place has a lot going for it—wide-open space, good people, isolated but central to a lot of big-city talent, fresh air, and low costs," Patrick said. "All this place needed was a *commitment*. I tried it with the air base—now I'm going to try it with Sky Masters. I'm going to hire the best young minds in the country and build the next generation of bombers, space systems, weapons, satellites, or whatever the newest technology will be, right here in the 'Armpit of the World.' In ten years, this will be the space and technology capital of the world."

"Unbelievable," Darrow said. She gave him a kiss on the cheek. "Well, if anyone can pull it off, you can. Good-bye, Patrick. Call if you need me." And she drove off without looking back.

Patrick drove the Wrangler to his rented trailer about a mile away, down a long dirt road and up a short rise. In the fading light of sunset, he looked at the excavation for the foundation of his new home. It would have a great view of the growing city and the soon-to-be bustling airport, and plenty of room for visiting sisters and their families, dogs, maybe horses—and grandkids, of course. He couldn't wait to get started.

Patrick went inside and poured himself a Balvenie on the rocks. It was when he sat down and activated his intraocular monitor that he noticed he had an e-mail message . . . from Gia. It read: *I heard you were going to Washington and would be in the White House. I can't go to that place. I'll get better and try to build a life here out west, and when you are ready to settle down, please call me. Love, Gia.*

Patrick immediately hit reply and began to compose a message, telling her that he wasn't going to Washington, that he loved her and wanted her back with him and was going to stay right here . . . but he erased the message. Gia needs to get better, and I'm not quite ready to help her do that, he thought. When we're both ready, maybe. He answered e-mails—including irate ones from President Phoenix and Vice President Page—finished the drink, and went to bed early.

Later that night, a four-door crossover SUV drove up the dirt road toward the trailer, then backed up the rise so the car was pointed back down the road. All of its lights were extinguished. Two men silently got out of the vehicle and dashed for the trailer, guns drawn, wearing night-vision goggles and bulletproof vests; two more men stayed in the car, on guard. With expert ease the two assassins broke into Patrick's trailer, made their way to the bedrooms, and began firing at the beds. They turned and dashed back out the front door, getting ready to arm an incendiary grenade to burn down the trailer . . .

. . . and ran headlong into a lone, dark figure standing at the base of the stairs.

"Hello, kiddies," Wayne Macomber said, dressed in the Tin Man armor. "Fancy meeting you here." When the assassins raised their weapons to fire, Whack reached out, grabbed their gun hands, and squeezed. The assassins screamed and dropped to the ground, clutching masses of bone, blood, and tissue mixed with crushed metal.

When they heard the screams, the two assassins in the car shoved the vehicle in gear and hit the gas . . .

. . . and ran headlong into a twelve-foot-high robot that had appeared out of nowhere right in front of them!

"Hello, kiddies," Brad McLanahan said. "Fancy meeting you here." On the robot's radio, he asked, "How was that, Uncle Wayne?"

"Come up with your own taglines, kid," Whack said.

"Okay. How about . . . I've got a crush on you guys." Brad reached across the width of the SUV, putting a hand on the doors on either side, then brought his hands together. The SUV's sides crushed together like a paper cup, pinning the screaming assassins inside.

"C'mon, you guys—now the cops have to clean all his stuff up," CIA operative Timothy Dobson complained. "You guys were just showing off."

"No, I like it," Patrick said, emerging from his hiding place with another glass of Balvenie on the rocks in his hand. "Good job, boys—good job."

ACKNOWLEDGMENTS

Thank you to Jan and David Bellville, Rob and Shari Spara, and Janet and John de Carteret for your generosity.

Thanks to my fellow members of the Douglas County Composite Squadron of the Civil Air Patrol, Minden, Nevada, for their help and encouragement, especially to former squadron commander and my instructor pilot Arden Heffernan; instructor pilot and deputy commander of cadets Russ Smith; Mike Allgaier, a tireless and dedicated CAP member who taught me a lot about mission-scanner and mission-observer procedures; and Brad Spires, squadron commander and my mentor in guiding me through the process of getting mission-pilot qualified.

AUTHOR'S NOTE

Your comments are welcome at readermail@AirBattleForce.com! I read all e-mails and reply to as many as I can.

Although I am a member of and mission pilot in the Civil Air Patrol, this novel has not been endorsed or approved by the U.S. Department of Defense, the Air Force, or the Civil Air Patrol.

The C-182 Skylane, C-172 Skyhawk, and P210 Centurion are products of the Cessna Aircraft Company, Wichita, Kansas. The G36 Bonanza is a product of the Hawker Beechcraft Corp., Wichita, Kansas. The MQ-1 Predator and MQ-9 Reaper are products of General Atomics Aeronautical Systems, San Diego, California.